THE LEFT-HAND WAY

TOR BOOKS BY TOM DOYLE

American Craftsmen

THE LEFT-HAND WAY

TOM DOYLE

TOR®

A TOM DOHERTY ASSOCIATES BOOK

NEW YORK

This is a work of fiction. All of the characters, organizations, and events portrayed in this novel are either products of the author's imagination or are used fictitiously.

THE LEFT-HAND WAY

Copyright © 2015 by Tom Doyle

A Tor Book
Published by Tom Doherty Associates, LLC
175 Fifth Avenue
New York, NY 10010

www.tor-forge.com

Tor® is a registered trademark of Tom Doherty Associates, LLC.

The Library of Congress Cataloging-in-Publication Data is available upon request.

ISBN 978-0-7653-3752-8 (hardcover)
ISBN 978-1-4668-3458-3 (e-book)

Tor books may be purchased for educational, business, or promotional use. For information on bulk purchases, please contact the Macmillan Corporate and Premium Sales Department at 1-800-221-7945, extension 5442, or write to specialmarkets@macmillan.com.

First Edition: August 2015

Printed in the United States of America

0 9 8 7 6 5 4 3 2 1

To Beth, the heroine of my life

ACKNOWLEDGMENTS

For their help with this book and their support of *American Craftsmen*, I'm very grateful to numerous individuals, blogs, and groups, some of whom are listed below:

Editor Claire Eddy, for making it even more fun to write this second book knowing that she would be the first reader of the finished manuscript. Thanks also to editorial assistant Bess Cozby.

Agent Robert Thixton, for his perseverance on my behalf.

Publicists Ardi Alspach and Wiley Saichek, for all their efforts to get the word out, and Stephanie Dray, who was generous with her own experience.

Dominick Saponaro and Irene Gallo, for their work on the wonderful covers for the American Craftsmen series.

The members of the Writers Group from Hell, who labored with me for a year on *The Left-Hand Way* in serial draft form.

The awesome folks at the Washington Science Fiction Association and the Baltimore Science Fiction Society.

Jim Freund, Fast Forward TV, the Libation Liberation Front, Jean Marie Ward, and Dungeon Crawlers Radio for their enthusiastic and knowledgeable interviews.

My friends and family, whose support has been especially vital this past year, particularly Eric Robinson, Karen Chamberlain, Serena Viswanathan, my aunt Jane, my mom, and my brothers John and Bill.

My sources. Like its predecessor, this book has too many fictional allusions to list all their sources here, but for some of its contemporary material, I'm especially grateful to the following nonfictional sources (and any errors remain my own):

Top Gear, for sensory details regarding the Chunnel's service tunnel; http://www.topgear.com/uk/photos/TG-drives-the-Channel-Tunnel-2012-11-09.

Joseph Menn's *Fatal System Error* (Public Affairs, 2010), for inspiration regarding Roman's employment in Kiev.

Moira Fitzgibbons, for a crucial bit of Latin.

Note: I've chosen to spell Babi Yar in its better known variant rather than the transliteration from the Ukrainian, Babyn Yar.

CONCERNING CRAFTSMEN
AND AMERICA'S SECRET HISTORY

A craftsman or craftswoman is a magician soldier or psychic spy. Throughout American history, such practitioners have been serving their colonies or country and feuding with each other.

The American craft leadership is divided between two clandestine locations: H-ring and the so-called Peepshow. H-ring commands the craft military service from far below the center of the Pentagon, while the Peepshow at CIA headquarters in Langley, Virginia, engages in psychic farsight of events distant in space and time.

Craftspeople may possess one or more of a wide variety of preternatural skills. The most common powers are associated with enhanced combat, but this may reflect the bias of covert use. A relatively common power not directly related to combat is the panglossic: the ability to speak in one language and yet be understood in multiple other languages. One group of craftspeople, the Gideons, specializes in tracking. Oddly, they've taken on some hound-like behaviors with their craft practice.

Two mutually antagonistic families have played an unusually significant role in their country's history: the Endicotts and the Mortons. Both families have been crucial to American military success since the Revolution. Endicott family members often have a strong power of command. Their heirloom is the sword of John Endicott of Salem, their first American ancestor.

Since the founding of the first English settlements in Massachusetts, the Puritan Endicotts have opposed the nonbelieving Morton family, who descended from Thomas Morton of Merry Mount, but who later took up residence in Providence, Rhode Island, in their notorious, sentient House. The typical Morton family member can change the local weather and can see the sins of others as glowing letters radiating from their bodies. Like most of the Endicotts, the Right-Hand Mortons are dedicated to the service of their country and the moral use of their power. However, the Left-Hand Mortons (and the Left Hand generally) were obsessed with life extension by any means and power without compunction. Under the leadership of the twins Roderick and Madeline, the Left Hand worshipped otherworldly gods and engaged in psychic parasitism, possession, and mass killings of mundanes and other craftspeople. For his experiments on spiritual transmigration, Roderick would bury people alive, but only Madeline survived this test.

Prior to the Civil War, an alliance of other families with the orthodox Mortons defeated the Left Hand. Abram Endicott dismembered Roderick with his family sword and took Roderick's head as a trophy. But Roderick's head did not die, causing Abram to experience a crisis of faith, and Madeline corrupted the vulnerable Abram to the Left-Hand way.

Madeline and Abram used the Left-Hand way to live on in other bodies. By World War II, they had penetrated the craft military command and the Pentagon's new H-ring, and they succeeded in placing Roderick's undying head at the center of the Chimera machine, a fusion of digital and alchemical technology. In this synergistic combination, Roderick became the most powerful oracle in the world, but he remained Madeline and Abram's imprisoned slave.

With the assistance of Roderick's craft and predictions, Abram and Madeline gained power and killed off potential rivals. Then Roderick made predictions about the threat that the remaining Morton family posed to Abram and Madeline, setting off the events told in *American Craftsmen*.

In that history, Captain Dale Morton is the last craft-practicing scion of the Morton family. His father has died under mysterious circumstances, apparently insane, though his ghost appears rational. A dispute between the top oracle at Langley, code name Sphinx, and the Chimera machine leads to Dale's assignment to kill a Persian sorcerer. This mission goes horribly wrong, and Dale is left cursed and weakened. Dale resigns from the service with the secret intention of finding the traitor within the craft who set him up. He suspects that the traitor is Sphinx.

Thwarted in his attempt to stake out Sphinx, Dale meets an apparently mundane civilian, Scherezade "Scherie" Rezvani. The Mortons have the gift of often foreseeing their own deaths, and Dale dreams that he and Scherie are in mortal peril. He also learns that his enemies have apparently killed his mentor, Colonel Hutchinson. He plans a party in which he will attempt to trap his enemies, particularly Sphinx, and to aid Scherie to escape, even at the cost of his own life.

Meanwhile, General Oliver C. Endicott assigns his son, Major Michael Endicott, to watch Dale for signs that he is turning toward his Left-Hand heritage. Shortly after hearing of Hutchinson's supposed death, Major Endicott crashes Morton's party, seeking to arrest him.

At the party, Sphinx sacrifices herself to save Dale from his true enemies. Endicott and Dale encounter an intruder dressed in the same guise that Roderick used to wear: the shroud and masque of Poe's Red Death. Endicott retreats, and Dale brings down the House of Morton on this supposed Red Death (later revealed to be a possessed Colonel Hutchinson).

Scherie saves Dale from the wreckage of the House, and they escape to the Sanctuary, a hidden land for America's lost things and the spirits of craft veterans. There, Dale summons Sphinx's ghost and learns part of the truth about the Chimera machine: that it has some human spiritual component. Then, Dale and Scherie face off against a squad led by Sakakawea, who is really Madeline in her latest body. During this fight, Scherie discovers that she is a craftsperson too, with a strong ability to dispel any ghost or possessing spirit. She first used this power unconsciously in her childhood against the ghost of a deceased family friend who was psychically violating her. Rather than face Scherie's power, Madeline flees her current body for another awaiting her in H-ring.

Dale and Scherie decide to go to the Pentagon, where Scherie will attempt to exorcise Chimera. They are joined by Roman, a Ukrainian craftsperson who has been operating undercover as the Morton family fixer. With Roman's stealth skills (and the hidden help of Roderick), Dale and Scherie are able to penetrate all the way to H-ring.

Within H-ring, Roman disappears, but Scherie and Dale are joined by Major Endicott, who has discovered the true nature of Chimera and the presence of Madeline and Abram. A series of combats ensues, during which Abram kills Major Endicott's father and Scherie dispels the spirits of the physically defeated Madeline and Abram. Madeline's ghost is absorbed into the collective Left-Hand Morton spirits. Roderick pleads for release of his spirit as well, and Scherie appears to dispel it.

Major Endicott's father is buried in Arlington. He's replaced at the head of countercraft ops (C-CRT) by General Calvin Attucks. Weakened by her possession, Colonel Hutchinson allows herself to die. Dale and Scherie marry, while Endicott still faces the difficulties of Christian craft dating. Scherie joins the craft service and hopes for a mission to Tehran. The Endicott-Morton feud comes to an end.

Unknown to all of them, Roman has smuggled Roderick's consciousness out of the United States to Ukraine, where Roman has arranged a new body to hold Roderick's spirit.

THE
LEFT-HAND
WAY

PROLOGUE

THE COURT OF THE RED DEATH

And Darkness and Decay and the Red Death
held illimitable dominion over all.
—Edgar Allan Poe

In Pripyat, the first snow of the year fell early on the deserted city and on the steel arch that hung over the Sarcophagus covering the ruined Chernobyl power plant. The windless cold was appropriate for this urban tomb, but unseasonable for early autumn, and the below-freezing temperature and snow were confined to this small, desolate pocket of Ukraine.

Seven Russian soldiers, five men and two women, arrived singly at the exclusion zone that enclosed the town, having entered the country in civilian dress by car, train, plane, bus, and boat. They were *spetsnaz magi*—special forces mages. One of them had been in Kiev for over a year; the Kremlin had kept him in place and ready for such occasions. Two had crossed through Belarus, whose Moscow-dominated craft authority had raised no fuss.

Over and under their body armor, the seven wore the latest hiking gear, which was as well suited to their task as most uniforms. All of them claimed to be tourists visiting the ghost town, though the exclusion zone was closed for the day. The guardians of the exclusion zone were bribed to allow entry, or in one overzealous instance, temporarily subdued.

The seven weren't surprised that they had been allowed to get so close to their target. Moscow precog had been able to see high-probability paths for them that ran as far as Pripyat without interference from the Ukie Baba Yagas. Beyond that, their target stood across their timelines, and nothing was certain.

Their weapons were necessarily a compromise, portability and concealment being greater priorities than for most operations, though two had brought rocket launchers, as bullets might not suffice. While they assembled the launchers for use, another mage waved a Geiger counter. They all wore radiation badges. The area was supposed to be safe for short stays, but it was also supposed to be free of hostile magi, and how their Left-Hand target might use the local low-level radiation was unclear. Was it just to provide cover, or did he actually derive some energy from it?

They rendezvoused in the northwest corner of town. Pripyat's great housing blocks still stood, ugly, for 1970s Soviet wasn't much prettier than Stalinesque. Snowmelt dripped through the now skylit ceilings; first floors bore the brown high-water marks of flood damage. In the distance, the Sarcophagus surrounding the plant prophesied a self-inflicted apocalypse.

With a quick look-over, the soldiers assessed one another with professional scrutiny and mutual respect. Seven of the best combat magi of the Russian Federation, all here for one man. They could scarcely believe the overkill. Though perhaps one of them was not truly elite: of the two women, the tall one code-named Vasilisa was unusually thin for a craft combat soldier. She was here for a psychological reason that none of them cared to dwell on: she resembled the American's dead sister, Madeline.

None of the *spetsnaz* had doubts about their leader, a highly decorated major with the cryptonym Ogin, whose great-grandfather had died holding the line outside of Moscow during the Great Patriotic War after months of delaying the enemy at every turn until nature could bring winter down on their heads. Ogin had fought against Chechen shamans, Chinese border crossers, and mystic Bond-wannabes from the West, and he was long overdue for a promotion. Ogin's presence alone would have sent a clear message: the Russian craft authority had decided that the new power in Kiev was not tolerable.

Ogin held a monocular to his eye and scanned from right to left, then down the road that provided a long, clear line of sight in the direction of the melted reactor's tomb. He let out a disappointed breath. Though it was perhaps too much to expect that their target would come out into the open to engage them, it would not have been inconsistent with his profile or previous behavior.

Would Roderick hide in the operational buildings of the plant? Ogin hoped not. Though they had chosen a minimally staffed day for this operation, innocent civilians still worked at the plant, maintaining and containing the reactors, and craft collateral damage did not play well in the Kremlin.

On to the necessary thoroughness of professional soldiering. "You'll commence the search pattern," said Ogin. He reiterated their assignments and pointed out directions, but even as he did so, his orders were moot.

From the direction of the ruined plant came a false sunrise of craft power, glowing radioactive red. Ogin raised his monocular again and saw a single man moving toward them along the *prospekt* between the ugly housing, not trying to hide or seek cover. He was as tall and straight as any tsar in procession. About him, motes winked brightly in the night vision, as if isotopes were losing their half-lives on cue. A gray shroud covered his body and legs, making his movement look like hovering. A mask gave him the gaunt face of a stiffened corpse with a rictal smile. His shroud and face were spotted with blood.

It was the American they called the Red Death. For the first time in mortal memory, Roderick Morton was coming forth for battle.

They would not attempt capture or negotiation. Ogin signaled, and the seven moved with incredible speed, with himself and four others taking positions that would attack the American from the west and drive him toward the river, and two flanking farther out to deflect an escape run. A full circle would have looked pretty, but avoiding a circular firing squad was more important. They found cover behind the carcasses of abandoned trucks and the brush gone wild. They had spells ready and, like a sports squad, some were more magically armed for defense, others for attack. They saved their spells; they would need them. First, though, they would employ their clear advantages in number and armament—simple physics always had its place.

The cold eyes behind the Red Death's mask followed their movements and gave no sign of concern. Then, as if giving permission, Roderick nodded at Ogin.

"Fire rifles," ordered Ogin. The seven shot their automatic weapons at Roderick to soften up the target and test his abilities. This man, powerful as he was known to be, had never been known for field combat in the flesh.

Some of the bullets curved away from the American, some ripped through his shroud, and some seemed to pass harmlessly through his body. But some shots must have been hitting the American with real force, because the impacts shook his frame, vibrating him like a drum. These hits were insufficient, for the American remained standing, always bringing himself back to attention. The explosive tips weren't exploding inside him, and the armor piercers weren't carving him up.

So Ogin gave the next order, and his soldiers lobbed some hand grenades and fired the rocket grenades. Use of explosives was regarded as more dangerous in craft ops, because it was hard to have a good friendly fire protection chip when a near miss would still be close enough. But Ogin preferred that risk to the risks of direct contact with this target, or even physical proximity to him.

Explosion after explosion shook the ground. Pieces of the pavement and clods of earth flew up and out in all directions. The smoke and dust obscured the view. "Hold fire."

Bits of the remaining glass in the broken windows of the buildings tinkled as they fell with the snow to the ground. The view cleared; the American was down. Ogin's lieutenant stepped forward from the left flank. "Moving in on target."

Some instinct gripped Ogin's heart. "Hold." This gave him a moment to justify his snap judgment. First, the unseasonable snow was still falling, which indicated that the American's craft might remain hard at work. Though the American was down, he appeared to be in one piece. And, like many of his Hollywood countrymen, this man was known for theatrical treachery.

Ogin knew some theatrics himself. He yelled in English: "Sister fucker!"

Like a practice-range target, the American sprang to his feet, then ran, not at Ogin, but right for one of the women, impossibly fast, with a gale wind blowing before him. Ogin thought he could see rage in the Red Death's terrible mask.

Why couldn't they just let Madeline rest in peace? thought Roderick. Yes, he had been waiting for them to come closer, not for any tactical reason, but for simple pleasure—he would have enjoyed their terror when he sprang up and punched his hands through their armored chests. But their rude, clever major had made him change his plan.

So be it: seven opposing craftsmen, six to kill, one to hurt. Seven probably seemed an extravagant number to them, but they would learn how insultingly poor it truly was. He forgave them their ignorance; in their brief lives, none of them had seen someone of his power. Despite the additional pain and difficulty, he would kill each of them with individual means and attention, lest any observers think he wasn't a fully rounded threat.

As he ran toward his first target, bullets again hit him like incredibly fast sledgehammers, and bits of his own gore flew away from him. The probability of not being killed was vanishingly small, but craft was about probability, and he stretched that chance to hold his own precious life. The shots still hurt like hell. In the design of his new body, Roderick had demanded heightened sensitivity, even to pain. Everything had to have its cost, and even he wasn't beyond those red equations. Though the agony tempted him to stop their guns from firing, that spell would spoil his surprise.

To replenish his power, he sucked at their energies, as he had once tapped the whole city of Washington, but this focused drink had more noticeable effects. As their thoughts and movements became slightly more sluggish, he saw the seven's sins. The tall woman in the center, of course, was a relative innocent—the better to bait him to charge into their middle.

He wouldn't be so easily profiled. The other, shorter woman, to his left of their center, was his first target. She had stepped out from her cover and was moving her hands and speaking a steady stream of Russian invective against him, trying to work a subtle knife of craft between his spirit and his body. *Oh no, dear, that trick has been tried, and by better than you.* Besides, no mind-body crack to work here. This corpus was his alone, created especially for him. The world's most powerful exorcist, Scherezade Rezvani, might still pose a threat against his soul, but no one else.

But this pretender was giving him a headache. Even as she, terror stricken, screamed at him to "*get the fuck out of that body!*" he replied with, "*Please be silent*," and with a quick hip-chambered karate punch bashed in her skull. Silence.

One of the flankers and two of the main line had rushed to fold in their formation to defend their comrade, hitting him with their full arsenal of magic. He let their force fall upon him. He felt the air depart from his lungs in a local vacuum, but it would be minutes before his new body would notice. He felt epileptic shocks shoot across his synapses, and for a moment the world took on strange electric hues, but this was nothing to a mind that had been integrated with a machine. He felt his bones question whether they should remain unbroken, but they stayed whole, for no part of this body would obey another magus.

With improvisational speed that no other craftsman could have managed, he hit them back with their own spells. *"Air, please move."* *"A short, sharp shock, please."* *"Bones, please break."* For a few seconds, they fought with their pathetic defenses, then collapsed—strangled, convulsed, and broken.

Down to three, the major, his lieutenant, and the tall woman they were calling Vasilisa, who stood behind them, like an arrowhead pointing away from him in the direction they'd like to flee. The major had maintained his calm throughout, giving orders even as the recipients perished. Such admirable nerve could not be suffered to live. As his partner in the demonstration, his lieutenant would be perfect. Time to show them what he'd learned in the machine.

"Please shoot each other once in the stomach."

He had left them with complete awareness of what they were doing, yet they didn't fight it hard. They thought they were safe. Their rifles would have safety chips (what his former countrymen called Stonewalls).

They didn't understand. His time as a living dismembered head connected to the Pentagon's Chimera machine had given him abilities that made their digital safeguards useless. He had them fire single shots just to allow the savor and frisson of their failure.

One shot quickly followed the other. Oh, the sweet anguish, the horror and betrayal on their faces, as they doubled over and sank to their knees. But now he had to finish it, before it became too difficult and tedious. *"Please finish killing each other."*

The shots exploded simultaneously. Lovely. He had killed them all, except for the tall woman. Lovely.

He advanced on her, ardent with blood thirst and more. Stunned, she stumbled as she stepped away, then rolled and scrambled backward to get farther from him, legs pushing wildly. But she was beaten and slow and cornered against some brush. Standing up again to her full height, she ceased trying to escape, but her face didn't yet reward him with the stigmata of terror. She was fiercely professional, steely eyed in the face of his Red Death. What lay beneath her mask?

He bent forward, close to her lips, and spoke huskily in Russian. "You remind me of someone."

Had she been briefed on his background? Did she understand him? Oh, yes, he could see she did. Her hard eyes went wide with charming sexual horror, her mouth gaped with inviting terror.

"Would you like to come home with me? I could show you many things. Wonderful things."

Even though he was waiting for it, the force of her response was surprising. Both her hands gripped his throat, and as she pulled him closer, her teeth snapped at him, and some curse against his life slammed like the bullets against his chest. Refreshing. Madeline had been like this.

He backhanded her face as he had so often slapped Madeline's. The counter blow flattened her. *"Please pass out."*

With admirable restraint, he had merely rendered her unconscious. Still, as she lay powerless on the ground, he had to remind himself— it wasn't Madeline. *You are to carry my message. But not the message you think.*

Sensing a farsight audience, he took a step northeast toward Moscow and that place below Lubyanka that he and the combined force of the West had never seen. Then he turned his face west toward Langley and Vauxhall Cross. His left hand was open at his side, displaying its deeds laying about the ground, while he shook his right fist at the gray sky. "Insult me again, and I will bury you all!" *Look at this work, fuckers, and despair.*

Very good, enough theater, drop the curtain. With a bow and a sweep of his hands, he said, *"Screen up, please."* This old dog had learned some Ukrainian stealth tricks.

He removed his mask and admired the art he had created here. The white snow was splattered with red, like his mask and cloak. It was as pretty as he had planned, but if it snowed much more, the effect would be ruined. He asked the snow he had summoned to *please stop,* and it began to taper off. The Russians had brought some lovely guns, but he would leave those for his Ukrainian friends.

That just left Vasilisa. His desire hadn't all been pretense. To play with her a little while would be divine. No use thinking about it—if that was what he'd really wanted, he should have kept another one of them alive. He forced himself to turn away from the girl (no, "woman"—he had to keep up with the times) and plodded back through the town toward the nuclear plant.

Oh, his poor body. He hadn't let it show, but he was wounded all over. He would need some help with its healing and repair. To fit in, his face had Slavic features, which he resented, and his light golden hair seemed inappropriate to his disposition, but otherwise, his body was a wonder. Roderick had been an intellectual during a time when the benefits of physical exercise weren't fully appreciated. His current Classic-sculpted form was a narcissist's dream, but Roderick more appreciated its combat efficiency than its aesthetics.

He found his black-and-red Bugatti Veyron where he'd left it near the plant. Inside the plant, the workers were waiting for Roman's signal that it was safe to venture out again. Roderick pointed his electric key and pushed its button, unlocking the car doors and starting the motor. He smiled; simple technology could still make him feel young.

He let the car warm up while he changed his outerwear. His shroud wasn't designed for warmth, and neither was his full-body armor (he wasn't so foolish as to rely completely on his own power to stop every little projectile). He picked up his parka from the passenger seat, put on his boots, spat up a bullet, and pulled out his smart phone (a term that, due to his recent unpleasant employment in the Pentagon, gave him flashback chills). Roman Roszkewycz answered. Out of habit, they spoke in English.

"Good day, O great and powerful colleague," said Roman. "Did you have fun?" An implication there? Roderick sometimes had too much fun.

"I've left one alive," said Roderick. "But some paramedics had better hurry, or she'll freeze out here." Or if she didn't show up soon in mundane hands, her handlers would kill her remotely—any party of this significance must have that sort of implant.

"You're the one who dropped the temperature," noted Roman with his usual ill-timed humor. But perhaps sensing Roderick's mood, he changed the subject. "She'll tell discouraging story?"

"It should buy us a few more months." And next time, maybe they'd think twice about sending a Madeline doppelgänger, unless they meant business.

"Excellent. Come home to Kiev. We do lunch, yes?"

Roderick hung up. Home to Kiev. He wondered if the Russians thought he lived up here, in this poisoned ghost town that would have made Poe's head spin. He had broadcast his intention for months to be here by regular visits and the blood rite on the ground. But, new flesh or no, only an idiot would actually live here. Yes, the Babas had Chernobyl projects, but Kiev was more his speed. Roderick had a nice modern home, craft-hidden of course, that looked out on a park in Kiev. He loved that park.

He put the car in gear. Now he could relax and let himself bleed a little. They could clean the car, or replace it. Better watch that he didn't bleed out, though. The concentration of armor-piercing rounds in his chest meant a lot of metal was hanging close to this heart. But this flesh improved considerably on nature. Even now, snakes of tissue reached across wounds to knit together, perhaps too quickly—he wanted to avoid healing too much, as it would make bullet removal that much more difficult. Ah, the agony remained acute, but after all those years of decay without clear sensations of any kind, he wanted them all, and besides its ops value, lean physical pain had some charm. Pain was how he knew things were interesting.

As he drove along the largely deserted two-lane route through mostly empty countryside, he reviewed the results of the skirmish. The important question was whether his enemies understood his primary message. It wasn't the obvious one that the Ukrainians wanted and that would be confirmed through back channels: "live and let live." Hah. His enemies wouldn't believe it, but perhaps they'd give him time.

No, the unspoken real message was that the dangerous secret of Left-Hand craft immortality was out of the bag and on the plate. It had been easy for the Right-Hand craft world to be good when they had no way to be so bad. When those previously dutiful servants of their various governments heard of what he had done today, deathless in this wonderful body, many more would join his cause for that secret alone.

He already had many friends in place within the craft forces around the globe. Soon, he'd have an army, which he'd need. Not only would those who wished to continue to repress the Left-Hand way, the way of unshackled power and life extension, be gunning for him, but those who desired to take his secret without sharing wouldn't want him alive after they'd extracted it. He wished they'd speed up their killing of each other over him. Then the dynamics of Family vendetta would take over, which had undermined national duty from the beginning, and he could get on with his real work.

Feh, mere physical immortality. They could all have it, and may it bring them much joy. Eating, shitting, screwing, the animal functions—it was all so mundane. Better than life as the talking head in the Chimera machine, but far from divine. That would all change for him, and soon. He just needed a little more time before the world and the Ukrainians figured out what he was really up to.

Time. Out of paranoid habit, he glanced at the rearview mirror. Instead of the road or his reflection, he saw his old, oozing face. Embarrassing—he'd had this vision before. It spoke to either a trite psychology or dubious craft, and he wanted nothing to do with either. He pressed harder on the accelerator. He imagined he was a terrifying driver. He had no regard for life, and no fear for his own. Having this body made him feel more like Madeline: reckless, carnal.

He turned on the car stereo, and Adams's *Doctor Atomic* played. Technological magic. He steeled himself for another look in the mirror, and saw his Slavic face. Good. Part of how he was going to win this time involved seeing himself with greater clarity, and not taking himself too seriously—at least, not until he won.

In the meantime, he had a few scores to settle. As he drove into greater Kiev on the now four-lane highway, it disturbed him more and more that the craftswoman in Pripyat had attempted Rezvani's expulsion trick. The Russians might have gained intel of Rezvani's power, so all the more reason to remove her and her colleagues from the playing board. And Madeline—even dead, he needed to do something up close and personal to her.

Like the *spetsnaz* with their safety chips, when his American targets relied on technology, he would enjoy their horror at its betrayal. With Ukrainian support, he could hack their craft-encrypted phones and fake any of their communications to each other. Scattered by duty across the globe, they wouldn't be able to warn each other of their danger as he played with them.

The low sun glared down on the unseasonably warm city—the least he could do. When the Babas were done repairing him downtown, he'd return to his new house and the tall, thin woman who waited for him, upon him. He had lost count of the number of her predecessors. He no longer learned their real names. He called them all Madeline. Eventually, they reminded him of Madeline in a bad way and had to go. So many of these Ukrainian women disappeared into the maw of the sex-trafficking trade every year that his personal demands went unnoticed. At least his women had the consolation of meeting their ends closer to home.

Madeline, have you been watching? Have you seen what I have done?

He had worried about being an expat. In his nineteenth-century life in the House of Morton in Providence, his magic had been tied to the American land and recharging had been difficult overseas. But this country's power flowed freely into him, confirming his hope that he had passed the usual limits and boding well for his plans. A would-be god had to think bigger than nation-states.

He looked forward to relaxing and appreciating anew the view of the park from his house. The name of the park was Babi Yar. Here, the Germans had executed more than one hundred thousand mortals. Roderick disliked Germans, but he liked the feeling this place gave him. Until his imminent apotheosis, it would have to do.

PART I

THE INNOCENT KILLERS ABROAD

Because I could not stop for Death,
He kindly stopped for me.
—Emily Dickinson

Led with delight, they thus beguile the way,
Untill the blustring storme is overblowne;
When weening to returne, whence they did stray,
They cannot finde that path, which first was
   showne,
But wander too and fro in wayes unknowne,
Furthest from end then, when they neerest weene,
That makes them doubt, their wits be not their
   owne:
So many pathes, so many turnings seene,
That which of them to take, in diverse doubt
   they been.
—Edmund Spenser

CHAPTER

ONE

For the record, I, Major Michael Endicott, veteran spiritual soldier, didn't take the news about Roderick's survival well.

"Major, please, *calm down.*" My father's replacement at countercraft ops command, General Calvin Attucks, used a touch of reassuring craft with his raspy Harry Belafonte voice, but that magic hadn't ever worked on me, even from Colonel Hutchinson.

"I'm plenty calm, sir," I answered, shaking the pain out of the fist that I had just slammed on my father's former desk. "But we've got to go to Ukraine right now and kill him." Here I was, an Endicott advocating the assassination of a Left-Hand Morton because no one else here in the Pentagon's secret H-ring had the sense to see the immediate threat. I sounded just like my father. Like much else in the army, this wasn't fair. Neither was Hutch's death. As Attucks's cousin-in-law, her picture was on his desk along with his wife's. Hutch had died to get rid of Roderick forever.

"You understand, sir," I continued, "this isn't just a Family thing. Dale agrees with me. He said that if farsight spotted Roderick, we should go after him ASAP. He said his ancestor is like a cancer—he'll only grow."

The general shook his bald head, probably still a little surprised that, after centuries of interfamily feuding, an Endicott was quoting a Morton as authority. Still surprised me a little too. "Major Morton is hardly an objective voice," he said.

"Meaning what, sir?"

"Meaning Roderick will want to kill Scherie as much as he wants to kill Dale, you, the Endicott family, or anyone else."

"OK," I said, "what are the Ukrainians going to do about it?"

"The Ukrainians have made it distinctly clear that they'll fight to keep him, and the Russians have been even clearer that they consider this to be within their sphere of influence, so they get to handle it and no one else."

The Ukrainians. If I ever got my hands on that bastard Roman Roszkewycz, he wouldn't slip away again without some serious damage. "We should nuke him from orbit. He's World War III waiting to happen."

"Michael, we're working on it. For now, that's all I can tell you."

Lord, give me the patience to accept this BS. Amen. My little prayer seemed to help, but only for a moment. "Sir, while I appreciate the news, why are you telling me this?"

"Besides you being a target?"

"Yes, sir. Besides that." I was always a target.

"I have other news. You're going to London. Tomorrow."

"London?" Ah, shoot. Attucks was smiling at me the same way Hutch used to when she'd given me a particularly unpleasant assignment. Some people, like her and the general, had the wrong impression about me and travel. I enjoyed travel, when it was for fun or combat. But my work didn't mix with pleasure, and some places were just plain hostile to what I did. Though it wasn't as bad as Prague, London was definitely on that list. American Endicotts running around there using the power of command probably reminded the English of some ugly arguments during the World Wars, or maybe they still remembered the thumping we'd given them during the Revolution and at New Orleans.

"The Brits have been losing craftsmen lately," said Attucks.

"They've been in some high-risk fights," I ventured, but I knew that wasn't where he was going.

"They're concerned about a traitor at a high level. Until we get it straightened out, we can't cooperate on anything important. We need their Magic Circus cleaned up before any joint ops against Roderick."

I asked the obvious: "Isn't that something for Langley to worry about?"

"The Peepshow wants you," he said. I never cared for those words; when Langley's center for precognition and farsight had last selected the individual for an assignment, it had meant serious trouble for me and Dale.

"And Roderick is connected to this?"

"That isn't established," he said, "but he may try to take advantage of the situation."

Another high-level mole hunt at MI13? H-ring still talked about the disaster of the Philby years, which was even worse in the spiritual sphere than in conventional intelligence.

"They won't be happy," I noted, "to have an American minder."

"They don't have much choice."

When Endicott left Attucks's office, Eddy Edwards came into the room through a hidden door. He looked more like muscle than the typical man in his post: acting director of the Peepshow at Langley. General Attucks gave him a narrow gaze tinged with a little anger and much doubt. "Edgar, are you certain you know what you're doing?"

"No," said Eddy. "If we were certain, they would be too, and it wouldn't work."

"My honored ancestor didn't take a bullet for this republic's fate to rest on a bad quantum bet."

Eddy raised his eyebrows, and Attucks didn't need him to say his thoughts. For the Attucks Family founder, Crispus, taking that bullet had been a bet too. Crispus had wagered his life on very long odds for American freedom, though it would be a long time before his own descendants would see it.

But the odds seemed longer on this current wager, with perhaps even more riding on it. Even if the good guys won, three good craftspeople would probably be lost because of Attucks's orders.

"If there was another way that even came close . . ." Eddy's dark eyes lost the farseeing conviction of his preacher ancestor Jonathan, and held the sorrow of that other Edgar, the storyteller who had come too close to the craft for his own health.

"If there was another way," said Attucks, "you'd tell me, and I'd order it. But there isn't, so God help us all."

R oyal Navy Commander Grace Marlow, MI13, reviewed the American's file with growing unease. This evening, she was working in a small office set aside for her service within "Lubyanka-sur-Thames," MI6's glass-and-permastone headquarters at Vauxhall Cross. Her service had been planning to move into new offices in the City at Fenchurch Street, but when that building began melting parts of parked cars, other arrangements had to be made.

The American major, who would arrive tomorrow morning, bore the code name Sword, as if that in any way hid the identity of a man who carried his heirloom weapon everywhere he went. The surveillance photos and video showed a face that wore the distinctive Endicott features, like a young and beardless version of mad John Endicott. He also closely resembled his great-grandfather, who had been in England during the Second World War.

Grace Marlow's own appearance was distinctive: tall and athletically slim, a narrow face with a mouth that, though sensually full, enemies would still describe as cruel, and black hair with a curl that hung like a comma over her right eye. The one flaw on her face was a short vertical scar on her right cheek, though it was so thin as to be more of a beauty mark than a deficit. As with Endicott, older members of the service said that she resembled her great-grandfather.

Grace Marlow could neither forget nor forgive what the Endicott Family had done to her African ancestors. Enslavement and torture were not things to be taken lightly even when they happened to strangers, and the Marlow ancestral memory was longer than the history of the United States. But Grace Marlow had gained her position as one of MI13's best operatives through a cold professionalism even in the face of personal outrage. She certainly hadn't gained it through moral inflexibility. She could deal with an Endicott or any other fascist Puritan of the American service.

The reason for her unease was a growing sense of attraction for this particular Endicott. Usually, this was an instinctual preparation for a certain type of assignment, where seduction of the opposition or even an ally was thought desirable by the higher-ups. Albion had given her and many in her family this spiritual gift—an enthusiasm for what others might consider the unpleasant necessities of duty.

But this wasn't that sort of assignment. She was not to get too close to this man, who was to be tested, sweated, and generally discomfited in very unerotic ways. If, despite his ancestral history, the land itself was telling her otherwise, she didn't appreciate the information. This man was associated with the Mortons and the release of Roderick into the world, so at best he was a fool, and at worst he was the enemy. The Endicotts were the opposite of stealthy, so the major's file held a great deal of early information from farsight reports and physical surveillance. This material dried up around the time of his encounters with the Mortons. His tie to the Mortons and Roderick was the particular problem for which MI13 had summoned him, though he was, she hoped, still duped by the cover story of a mole within the service. Certainly MI13 had had some recent setbacks of concern, but the probable source was the very Roderick that Endicott had assisted to freedom.

She flipped through his file's photos again, though her eidetic memory made this an unnecessary exercise. She was particularly troubled by the source of her attraction. With his blond hair and stormy gray eyes, Endicott was an acceptable physical specimen, but she was rather democratic in that regard, and race, nationality, and gender weren't excluding factors for her. Despite his apparent lack of poetic imagination, he was sufficiently intelligent not to embarrass his date in company—again, a low bar. None of this explained her focused feeling of heat when she studied his image.

No, it was the barest hint of something she'd seen in the video surveillance. There, almost buried behind the digital technology and beneath the humility of his serious pride, she thought she'd caught a glimpse of his soul, and it was like sunlight seen through semiprecious stones. It was one of the secrets of her practice that when she focused on a soul, its beauty or ugliness was no mere metaphysical abstraction. She saw a person's psyche as a component of their carnal selves, and she responded carnally to it.

From his file, Endicott did not seem morally or spiritually complex enough to be stimulating such a reaction, though she'd never been able to fully correlate psychic beauty with specific traits. She might be imagining what she'd seen; she'd only know for certain when she saw him in person.

But that wasn't one of the necessary exams. The first test would begin immediately on his arrival. For that charade, she had hired two of the usual unpleasant muscle from London's craft underground, after screening them for any Renfield connections—the Renfield Family loved subverting Her Majesty's Government more than life or payment in advance. Grace Marlow would know more about Endicott's true powers after they'd tried him by surprise; then, the Walsinghams would get their hands in for the next round. C had signed off on anything within twenty-four hours of arrival that didn't damage the guest.

It was late, and tomorrow would be a long and probably unpleasant day. She drove her Aston Martin back to Marlow House (her lineage had dropped the final "e"), then sat by her unlit fireplace with a sip of brandy before bed. Above her mantelpiece, paintings of the masks of comedy and tragedy stared back at her, but her family's ghosts left her in peace. She considered ringing the Don, her former mentor within the service, but he now lived in semiretirement in Oxford (of course), and this was far too trivial an operation with which to bother him at this hour. In any event, she could practically hear what his advice would be in his own professorial voice: "Dear, if you smell trouble, move towards it. Mind your op, bring a gun, and dress to kill."

Only selecting the gun would cost her any further rest—that, and saying her nightly prayers as she removed her cross necklace.

B efore I packed, I sent craft-scrambled text messages to Dale and Scherie with the signal of Roderick's survival that I had insisted on before they had departed for PRECOG-knew-where: "Evite to a Masqued Ball. RSVP immediately." This was a breach of security and just a bad idea with agents in the field, but the news was urgent, and as I had told Dale, the regs that made us fail to communicate had nearly gotten us all killed. Sure, if I asked, Attucks and Langley would say they'd informed the Mortons, but I was disinclined to trust anyone regarding Roderick, and if something happened to either Scherie or Dale, I wouldn't want to answer to the other for my silence.

Within the hour I had their replies, both "Yes" with a "thank you" added from Scherie. Nice of her. Between themselves, they could deal with finding a safe place or retreating to their charming and psychotic House of Morton.

It still felt strange that the centuries-old Endicott-Morton feud was over. But it occurred to me that the other Families would soon find out about Roderick's survival, and some of those wouldn't be as disciplined as myself in response. Roderick, Madeline, and my ancestor Abram had killed many of our loved ones, and as I well knew, Family vengeance had a longer history than Family service. But their future actions had nothing to do with my orders.

On my flight to London the next night, I fell asleep almost immediately. I woke up with an electric jolt. I found the flight path animation on my seat's video screen. We had just passed into UK airspace, and for some reason that border was more touchy than Canadian or Irish airspace.

During the Second World War, the American Families had come here in force. The expedition had been effective, but sometimes tense with the locals, so H-ring had reminded me that, despite the special relationship with the United Kingdom, I wasn't allowed to practice craft, which was the H-ring word for spiritual power, and that I was not to fraternize with the locals, which was the H-ring phrase for no sex. That second rule bothered me, because I wasn't going to have a problem following it.

Sure, since my father's death, I'd been searching Christian singles ads with new urgency, but I couldn't find a category of women willing to commit to a soldier whose gear included supernatural powers of (admittedly) dubious provenance and walking and talking bits of bad theology (aka ghosts), and whose idea of minimum commitment ran unto death and beyond. By definition, those conditions meant women already in the spiritual services, but my family wasn't even popular among the Christian practitioners. Foreign practitioners, even British ones, were out-of-bounds.

At Gatwick passport control, the ghosts were thick on the ground. I saw ghosts more now after having accepted my family spirits. A World War Two ATS woman in trench coat and helmet, an old man in naval dress uniform, and a more faded First World War teenager with rifle and bayonet eyed me and all others with supernatural suspicion.

The suspicion of ghosts didn't trouble me, but something else did. My visit was unknown here to anyone outside of a few people at the Magic Circus, and I was dressed as an American businessman, like every other businessman on my flight. Yet the uniformed woman who took my passport paused a few seconds too long with it, the tweedy old man in the next line over kept looking over at me and smiling, and too many English others either seemed to notice me or avoid my gaze unduly. People were paying too much attention to my supposedly commonplace cover. It could be mundanes getting unconsciously caught up in someone's intense spiritual focus, but that was the level of attention a secret agent might expect in China, and not what a spiritual soldier should feel here in the UK.

God, what's going on? No answer. I didn't have the Morton gift of viewing sins to see if anyone here wasn't what they seemed. What I could do, without breaking the rules, was get a few prayers ready, so I began meditating on a countercraft prayer, something to silence any opposition.

After clearing customs, I was greeted by two bulky men in cheap suits, craft or craft muscle. They were as H-ring had described them, though in person they appeared more gentlemanly than American muscle, and instead of the flat affect of our thugs, they smiled with their teeth as their eyes tried to drill holes through me. *Judge not, lest I report you*, I thought. The shorter of the two gave me the call: "Here to see the marbles?"

"I seem to have lost mine," was my response.

One would think that this sort of spy stuff wouldn't be necessary on friendly ground, except no ground is truly friendly for spiritual ops, and a problem with working for one or another of the world's most secret organizations was the frequent uncertainty about whom one was dealing with.

The two men took my luggage, and then the taller one reached to take my sword case. "We'll put this in the boot."

"Thank you, but no."

The shorter one's smile broadened. "My friend means . . ."

"I know what he means, and this stays with me."

A shrug, and then we got in the black limo sedan, the tall man driving and the shorter man in the back with me. I was already thinking about a prayer to make a sharper point when, at the last minute, a third man got in front on the passenger side, lean and pale, middle-aged and too old to be muscle in the strict sense, but with a raptor's eyes.

"Hold on," I said. "This wasn't in the plan."

"Extra security," said Shorty. "There's been some trouble."

Even though I was in-country because of that trouble, three escorts seemed excessive for any threat between here and London. I would have been more suspicious, but this was typical of the games that a host country played with visiting spiritual ops, so I focused on my prayers and let it go.

We drove up the M23 as I tried to adjust to the usual vertigo of jet lag and being driven on the wrong side of the road. Trees, thick or thin, seemed to line the whole highway, with pleasant autumn colors starting to show. I might have enjoyed the view if we weren't going so fast. In this, the middle of nowhere-in-particular England, we were passing all other cars, clearly exceeding the speed limit, which was unusual for spiritual ops, as we tried to blend in as much as possible.

"What's the hurry?" I asked, expecting some more blather about security that would make me feel less secure. Abduction from a friendly airport by men who recognized me and knew the passphrase seemed like paranoid fantasy, even by service standards. But things seemed to be going in that direction at the same excessive speed as the limo.

The taller man at the wheel smiled and said, "Excuse me, sir. I'm going to put up the divider so you can speak with my colleague in private."

In any version of reality, this was nonsense; I had nothing to say to anonymous muscle, and I wasn't interested in what he had to say to me. But that wasn't the serious problem. Shorty, feral eyes and smile and all, was pretending he wasn't frightened to be stuck with me back here, and his acting was terrible.

The glass divider was already going up, and a staticky screech had started up from the stereo. Despite the risk to the blade, I stuck my sword case between the glass and the roof to stop it, and prayed at the driver. *"In God's name, stop the divider."* But that hadn't been one of the prayers I'd prepared, and the stereo sonics were distorting and dampening my voice. The power of command didn't always require the target to hear or understand my orders, but it helped, and the driver seemed impervious to anything less. The third man knocked my sword case back, then pulled a gun and pointed it at me for the second it took for the divider to finish closing. He was sneering at me with ill will and bad teeth. At least the sonics stopped.

Shorty had recovered, not enough to take a swing, but to bark some craft at me, *"Die—no, I mean pass out, pass out quicker."*

Lord, please smite him. But I needed to be the Lord's tool, so I used one of my prepared prayers. *"For Christ's sake, shut up."*

His mouth flapped silently, then he cowered against the limo door on his side. *He was trying to get me to pass out.* Sure enough, the men in front had put on breathers that resembled expanded diving masks. Gas might already be flooding the limo. *Lord, fill me with your spirit.* My lungs relaxed into stillness. For the next minute, I'd have to fight at full exertion without breathing.

I had always expected this sort of death overseas. I had fulfilled God's plan by scourging the Pentagon, and I was destined to perish, absurdly and badly.

But not this fine morning. I fumbled my sword out of its case and sheath. Not a lot of room to work with the blade here, but Shorty wasn't resisting. I thumped the pommel against the glass, directing my captors' attention to the point aimed at Shorty's heart. *See, I'm going to kill your friend.*

Their eyes and cheeks crinkled with amusement, and I saw no deception. They didn't care. I turned to threaten Shorty to some helpful action, but he was already unconscious. Still breathing, though. That was something—they were trying to capture, not kill me.

Then, the already speeding car accelerated. The third man brought up his gun again, and lowered his window. Behind us, a silver sports car of some British make was racing in pursuit. The third man waited, calmly assessing his shot.

Good, they'd be distracted. The open window would let air in the front, but I suspected that wouldn't help me enough in the back when I had to start breathing again, and that was seconds away. I thought about punching some airholes, but then another idea came to me.

The divider glass looked thick enough to be bulletproof. But the seats—were they armored all the way through? I thought not. Leather and vinyl tended to respond better to me than glass and metal. I brought my sword back at a slight angle. *In Christ's name, I stab at thee.* I jammed the blade with Spirit-aided force through the lower part of the seat. The blade sang where it touched some metal components, but went clean through, only to get stuck at the last. The limo swerved, as the driver arched his back away from the seat. Of course— the driver wore body armor, so I had pricked him, but not run him through. Good—I'd want a chat later.

A minicar and a minitruck squealed and ran onto the shoulder. The pursuing silver car weaved through the chaos with professional style. Friend, or another foe?

My driver had moved away from the sword point; then, focused on avoiding traffic, he relaxed his back. I shoved the blade again toward him, then twisted. Mouth gaping in pain in the rearview mirror, the driver pressed down hard on the accelerator, the motor revved up an octave, and he swerved again, running us through the guardrail and right off the road. We leapt over a ditch and through a fence. Bump after bump, each like a small crash. None of us were wearing our seat belts, and sleeping Shorty and I collided against each other and the divider glass. Then, ahead, a white form turned to face its oncoming doom, dark eyes stupidly accepting its fate.

Baa. Bang! Sisss. The limo had finally stopped, but not before hitting a sheep. Correction: killing a sheep. Bits of bloody wool everywhere. That would look just great on my report to Attucks. I missed my father's open mocking of these misadventures. *Mutton to do about it now.*

Ouch. I thought I must have banged my head. My door was still locked. The driver was lowering the divider, probably for the benefit of the thin man and his gun. The sonics screeched again. I pulled to get my sword out of the seat, but the thin man's gun wasn't up, and his attention was behind me.

I could have just punched them both, but from the thin man's re-action, I sensed a weapon was pointed at the back of my head. I risked a glance. Behind us, the pursuer got out of the car, an Aston Martin, and shouted at us. "Police! *Nobody move!*" A woman. Being in Eng-land, I guessed she was of West Indian origin. She held a massive long-barreled gun out toward us in one hand, while the other was making some crafty gestures that seemed to be encouraging us to stay put. "*Everybody freeze.*" She wore an office suit for people too rich to actually work in offices.

With my sword freed of the seat, I kept it low, and turned my at-tention again to the men in front, just as all the door locks clicked. Quicker than nature, the passenger door had been opened, and the third man was gone, nowhere to be seen. The woman was running toward us; the one combat-ready feature of her attire was her flat rubber-soled shoes. Despite his wounds, my driver already had his hands up against the roof. Shorty was snoring.

Desperate for breath, I reached for the now unlocked back door. "Hands in the air, Major!" yelled the woman, stopping just feet away from the limo. In a lower voice, she added, "And not one bloody word from you, Endicott."

As if charmed by her Received Pronunciation, I took a deep inhale of the drugged air, slowly raised my empty hands, and smiled. I couldn't fight the whole country, and at least she knew who I was. The mission had started as well as expected.

CHAPTER

TWO

On the other side of the world, Major Dale Morton waited for his contact in an anonymous bottle-keep club above the expat bar Geronimo's in the Roppongi district of Tokyo. Mundane foreigners congregated in Roppongi, and magical foreigners joined them there because it wasn't as supercharged as the rest of Japan, which was riddled with small shrines like craft fuel stations marked for convenience. All that native craft could mess up the foreign practitioner.

Dale sat wearing one of those dreadful soldier-on-vacation outfits (a white sports coat with a loud floral shirt, completely inappropriate for Tokyo autumn) that his old buddy Chuck had favored and that Dale normally despised. But the style fit Dale's cover, and he had to live his cover, particularly when he was also hiding his purpose from some of his own side.

His cover was that this trip was part of some extended R&R, processed in H-ring as a well-deserved reward for last year's country-saving exertions. Dale wasn't much for this sort of R&R or skullduggery. He should be in uniform and in combat, where he was competent, but that was a soldier's self-pity, so he stowed it. Better, he should be with Scherie. He missed her with a ferocity that surprised him.

Because it would appear natural to do so, Dale checked his phone. No messages, texts, whatever. That was good. The only messages for this phone would be emergencies, and the only true emergency would be Roderick returned. In Roderick's former life, he had cut a bloody swath across the American craft that hadn't been equaled before or since. Dale suspected that a resurrected Roderick would be an even more powerful threat.

For months, the House had been creaking with unease and the Left-Hand revenants had been moaning, and within that spiritual mass, Madeline's still distinctive voice sounded shrill with anger. Hearing these omens of Roderick's survival, Dale had delayed this mission. Then, realizing such a resurrection might make this mission vital, he rushed it forward. Perhaps he hadn't prepared well enough.

Autumn's chill was in the air outside, but inside held the usual cramped excess warmth of Tokyo. Dale ordered a gin and tonic because the club's bartenders got most everything else wrong. Intellectually, Dale knew he was drinking too much. Any good bar subconsciously charmed its patrons, and the Mortons had to be very careful of their substances at the best of times. But, like a fly trap for alcoholics, this club had some more overt craft to encourage him to drink. For him to stay too long, night after night, would be slow death. Some here were on their way to the afterlife, and some had passed over. Ghosts who resided in Japan were particularly ghoulish, with Day-Glo worms wriggling inside them, so even Dale could tell the dead from the merely dying.

This club would soften him up quickly. Was that why Kaguya-san wanted to meet here?

Downstairs at Geronimo's, young Australians sang, snogged, and drank in ascending order of proficiency. Up here in the club, the older and creepier denizens of the British Commonwealth and the expat demimonde sweated overpriced booze in light-fabric suits and tried to buy class. "Class" apparently included the black velvet Olivia prints of nude or mostly nude women that hung on the walls.

Mixed in with the usual vipers were an international assortment of craftsmen and mundane agents who came and went and passed each other cigarettes and lighters with displays of affection, covert information, or both. It was harder than usual to pick out the spies, as even the investment bankers seemed to think they were in a Bogart movie. But one of these snakes was not like the others. At the opposite end of the bar, a Chinese man wearing an incongruous yet tasteful Armani knockoff was sipping a Coke and displaying the usual situational awareness tics: taking frequent advantage of his clear view of the entire club and entrance while sitting with his back to a wall and near the only other exit. The Chinese hood's excess situational awareness had blown his cover; his tradecraft was worse than useless.

Up until this moment, the only noticeable absence from this gathering of mystery men was Dale's Japanese countercraft colleagues/competition, who mostly kept their distance from this and other Roppongi free ports. They figured that if the *gaijin* magi were here, they weren't somewhere else below radar and causing serious mischief. If serious mischief occurred, well, the Japanese craft black-ops group had a well-known name, so colorful as to seldom be spoken by the wise guys. Most Japanese secrets and conspiracies were like that—hidden defiantly in plain sight.

Dale looked up from his empty glass and glanced toward the entrance, and there was his contact, Kaguya-san. Years before, Dale had staged from Yokosuka in support of a Japanese op in North Korea, where Kim Jong-il's craftsmen had been trying some desperate magics, and Kaguya-san had gone in with him. Afterward, Dale and she had broken (shattered, really) certain craft fraternization regulations, and he hadn't regretted it for a second. In Japan, the issue of craft contact felt different, and Dale assumed he wasn't alone.

Kaguya-san's appearance reminded him of all the reasons for his misbehavior. Her red dress was in the snug-fitting style they called bodycon, short for body conscious. The style went with the place, so it was good cover in that sense, but not in any other. The few Western women in the club gave her the once-over, trying to assess if she was one of the giggling, mouth-covering office ladies whom they vociferously resented beyond what feminism called for. The Western men's admiration was checked only by their prior exposure: they had seen such before. As for Dale, he loved his wife, but he wasn't dead and dispelled. Kaguya-san was as stunning as ever, with everything from eye to calf still better than nature could have rightfully intended.

Dale stood and motioned toward the neighboring seat that he had kept empty with great effort, and Kaguya-san greeted him. "Morton-san. *Konbanwa*. So good to see you again, eh." She didn't need the panglossic language craft for him to understand; she spoke a form-perfect English that still had something Japanese about it, and which sometimes fell into Canadian vowels. "Eh" and "ne" might end alternate sentences.

"Kaguya-san. It's been too long. You are well?"

"Yes, thank you. And you have married, ne? *Omedeto gozaimasu*."

"Thank you," said Dale. She wasn't putting him off sexually; rather, she was letting him know as a favor that her superiors were aware of Scherie.

"It is very nice that you asked to see me," said Kaguya-san.

"You were kind to agree," he replied. She waited, silent, looking at him expectantly. Right to business then, which was unlike her. Had Japanese farsight guessed why he was here?

"I'm here about my father," he continued. "Before his breakdown, he came here, to Tokyo." Perhaps to this very club.

"Very strange, Morton-san." But no surprise showed in her eyes. "You never mentioned this before."

"I didn't discover it until recently. I want to know what he was doing here. Did he ask your agency any questions? Did he meet with any other practitioners here?"

She sucked the air through her teeth, and he knew what was coming. "Further queries would be . . . difficult, ne?"

She was playing this more Japanese than necessary. "Kaguya-san . . ."

She dropped the formalities. "I'm very sorry, Dale, but I can't tell you anything."

"Miki, why can't you speak?" She remained silent. He had been in conversations like this with her before. She wanted to tell him something, but had been ordered not to discuss certain things directly. "Perhaps we could talk about something else. What's been on your mind?"

A barely perceptible nod. "I've been thinking about craft morality and culture."

"That's very interesting," he said, encouraging. "I've often wondered if craft morality differs among nations."

"Yes. In particular, it seems that your American craft distinctions don't suit us anymore."

A chill went down his spine. "Evil is evil, everywhere."

"What is evil about wanting to prolong life?" she asked, a Socratic irony in her tone. "We've had centuries in the East where life extension was thought to be the right of a powerful man." That was a more Chinese perspective, but he took her point, and maybe China was her point. Unlike everyone else in the club, the Chinese man at the end of the bar was very deliberately not looking at Kaguya-san.

Dale tried another gambit. "My Family had a great interest in the Taoist alchemies."

"Then you've had useful experience." Lips parted, she showed a hint of small teeth as with her fingernail she drew a lazy circle on the bar top. She implied many things: that he had turned Left Hand, that he knew their secrets, or that he knew how to fight them.

In Japan, honest feeling was often the best reply, and his feelings about the Left Hand were clear. "Theoretically, life extension is harmless, but practically, well, it's always different than that. When my Family sought immortality, it involved psychic vampirism, possession, and killing lots of people. And it never stops at just life extension. The goals become grander, and the killing goes on and on." Or in Roderick's case, the killing seemed to become the main point.

Kaguya-san nodded once with emphasis. "I've told my friends that you would not be interested in helping anyone pursue this."

Again, a great deal of ambiguity—helping whom do what?—but it was clear she was looking out for him with her people. "Thank you."

She closed her eyes, as if seeking calm amidst discomfort. "Others are going to want to discuss this with you."

This was very bad news, and raised a swarm of new questions, but one seemed particularly urgent. "Why now?"

"You've never told me, Dale, whether eternal silence is one of your family gifts."

She was asking if Dale could kill himself with craft rather than break under interrogation. The answer was no, not readily enough, but he carried a mundane means: a saxitoxin-impregnated needle. "I have a remedy," he said. Then he repeated: "Why now?"

She gave him a closed-lip smile. "You should ask at home. In person. And soon."

With unaccustomed abruptness, she stood up and walked for the door. She must have hit her information limit, perhaps passed it. He half thought of following her. Yes, she'd told him to scram back to the States, but she couldn't mean this minute, and now that their business was done, they could get a few drinks, rent a karaoke box, sing badly together. Maybe she would let something else slip. All very innocent.

"I had a friend like that." In a snap, his father was sitting where Kaguya-san had been, cooling the air and making the *I'm watching you* gesture at Dale. "So don't try to pull one over on me." Despite Scherie's dispelling power, the Family ghosts loved her and were perhaps overly protective. Infidelity in the craft was perilous to all concerned—contact had consequences. Though mundane generals seemed to regard mistresses as a privilege of rank, Dale wouldn't dare translate fornication into adultery—at least, not now that he was thinking more clearly.

"Hi, Dad. You're a long way from House." Ghosts often found overseas travel difficult.

"It's easy for me to be here. I've been here before. But you already knew that." He was dressed civilian, like he had been when he had gone East on some never disclosed quest that had driven him insane, leaving an alienated Grandpa and young son Dale behind. "You're tracing my last known whereabouts before I went nuts. How did you find my trail?"

"Your expenses. Abram and Madeline had purged your official accounts, but you went off H-ring and used a Morton offshore account and credit."

"Followed the money? Well, that should do it then. You won't get farther than this."

Great, so he wasn't going to make this any easier. "Let's take a walk."

"Why?"

"Because if I'm going to look like I'm talking to myself, I want to do it out of doors."

They stepped out onto the packed sidewalk at Roppongi Crossing. Fog and mist blurred any view much beyond the brightly lit intersection. It would be a long walk back to the Hotel Okura, but this might be a long conversation. Dale put on his Bluetooth earpiece so he could speak to his father aloud and have it look natural, and they headed toward a less crowded back way to the hotel. Dale still kept his voice down in case more discerning listeners were nearby.

"Where's Grandpa?"

"Home. He doesn't know what you're doing here. Don't make me tell him." A problem of the reconciliation between his dad and grandfather—the old ghosts could and did gang up on him.

"What were you up to here, Dad?" This topic was going to be risky. It had made his father nervous before, and when a question agitated a ghost, he tended to dissipate before he could answer.

"They took my statements in the rest house."

"The place they kept me in after that Persian magus cursed me?" His father nodded. "All the statements you gave there were cut out from the record—sometimes literally with a razor blade." That was what had started Dale on this quest. The mole triumvirate of Madeline, Abram, and Roderick had left a wide trail of unreasonably suppressed information. Their response to his father's last mission had been particularly thorough, meaning that mission may have contained a possible threat to their plans, perhaps a threat to the Left Hand generally. It was good tradecraft to follow up on such suppressions, and Dale finally had a long enough leash to investigate on the spot. His mission only felt personal; this was spy business of the best sort.

"What were you looking for?" Dale asked.

"I can't remember what I found. It blew out most of my mind, then the treatments took out the rest." A ghost had a distant way of speaking of life's tragedies. "I do know that it was a mistake."

"Dad, please. That wasn't what I asked. What were you looking for? I think you remember that much."

"Natural for sons to want to surpass their fathers." Dale's father sometimes had an emotionally careful way of putting things, but Dale still heard his statement as *So, you think you're better than me?*

They were walking past the Roppongi Cemetery, a spiritual maw of darkness in its center into which the local energy spun in a slow, twisting vortex.

Dale stopped walking and heard the distant telltale of trailing feet stopping too late. Not much more time for chat. "OK, Dad," he whispered quickly, "I'm going to try this hypothesis out on you. When our revered ancestor Joshua called the other Families in for the siege of Roderick and Madeline, it wasn't just because his grandpa Elijah had disappeared. The Left Hand was too close to finding something."

"They looked, they failed. Leave it be. This path is the one I was afraid of, the one I tried to keep you away from." Agitated, he was fading into the fog. "Leave it be."

Knowing better than to try to summon his father back, Dale pivoted and started walking briskly. The tailing steps kept pace, but didn't try to approach, so nothing acutely unpleasant seemed in the offing, except Dale's having to think of his next move. He had no further leads. Maybe Kaguya-san and his father were right, and he should go home. His father was definitely correct about the money trail: it ended here with his father's return flight. When Dad had next turned up in the record, it'd been in the woods near Mount Weather, Virginia, and he'd been raving.

Only in between here and Virginia, his dad had found something, and he seemed worried that Dale would too, which meant the quest wasn't impossible.

Sensing a change in the tailing rhythm, Dale looked back in the direction of Roppongi Cemetery. Nobody, not even a ghost. Roppongi Cemetery had few spirits, and few of those had the substance of craft veterans. All those war ghosts were somewhere else.

Then it hit him—one place he could go. Where his father, a Morton, would have gone for information if the living weren't talking: the Yasukuni Shrine to the Japanese War Dead. Dale would wait until it opened tomorrow, and not risk a nighttime break-in. Shit, here he was again, going to the Underworld, only this wouldn't be the mine theater or Elysian field of the Appalachian's Sanctuary, but a true Hell, human-made and terrible beyond myth.

The trailing footsteps left off just before Dale reached his hotel. Dale was following footsteps too, and for his father, this way had led to madness.

When the sun rose, Dale itched again to talk with Scherie. But he kept to contact discipline and told himself that she must be fine.

No shadow trailed him by daylight as he taxied to Yasukuni, passing near Budokan. *I don't want you to want me*, he sang to himself, thinking of what he would find at the shrine.

As Dale approached the shrine's main hall, he ignored the museum to his right, with its suicide machines of war, and couldn't see the smaller shrine for foreign war dead, as it, unlike the main shrine, attempted no permanent binding of souls. He hoped the main hall, with its traditional broad and curved tiled roof, would be close enough, as the spirit house behind it was barred to the public.

A gray-haired, white-robed priest stood at the line of the large posts and double lintel of the last *torii* gate as if to block Dale's path, but when Dale came close, the priest smiled, bowed, and backed out of the way. This was the first thing that scared Dale: they might want him here.

As Dale passed through the *torii*, he felt a low rumble of sentience. The craft glowed in a way familiar to him from his own House—a grave light display like a horror-show Christmas. Yasukuni might seem to the unaided eye like many other Shinto shrines across Japan, but a craftsman could see its true distinction: this place was a magnificent and heinous spiritual trap.

The mechanism was quite simple; its success inexplicable. The craft priests listed the names of those who died during a war and then ritually "enshrined" them—that is, bound them to this spot for eternity. Most of the enshrined dead were from the Second World War. The ritual didn't catch everyone that it named, but even a 10 percent success rate would mean two hundred thousand souls, and the Shinto priests were much better at their craft than 10 percent. So many souls made the spiritual force of the House of Morton seem puny.

Dale called these trapped spirits "souls" because, once enshrined, no other spiritual echo of these soldiers could ever be found. If something like a true soul survived after death, Yasukuni appeared to bind it.

Dale understood the political protests against "honoring" war criminals at Yasukuni, but the poor mundanes had it all wrong. This sort of binding was the worst type of punishment, and the protests should be for all those craftless and relatively innocent souls trapped here, away from family and friends, identity slowly crushed and fused with an angry, suffering mass.

Why did those priests do this horrible thing? Because it made Ya-sukuni a spiritual engine of tremendous power. The official story was that the craft priests had hoped that, properly used, Yasukuni could have turned the tide of the war with a literal spirit wind, or kami-kaze, and right up until the bitter end, some political leaders believed them. But wiser heads prevailed, as any Imperial craftsman could see that Yasukuni had become too powerful and raging to tap without risking all Japan. By the time Japan surrendered, it was too late for the Allied or Japanese magi to do anything about this spiritual reac-tor, as an attempt to defuse it might set it off.

For Dale, caring greatly about these soldiers' souls could have been considered hypocrisy. He had some of his own family's spirits bound forever at the House, and that those spirits were all Left-Hand might seem too fine a distinction here. But he allowed himself to care any-way; it was good moral hygiene against the ever-present Left-Hand voice in his brain.

In the constitutionally enforced peace, the shrine had grown qui-eter from decade to decade, like a radioactive site as the waste decays in the cold mathematical progression of half-lives. The ambient en-ergy had helped power the miraculous postwar recovery and rise to economic greatness, but such material concerns would have seemed trivial to those who had designed Yasukuni. Some old craft priests still prayed for the day that they'd find a greater use for this power.

To Dale's ears, the noise of the shrine was like the cacophony of Yoyogi Park, where dozens of rock bands played at once, each sepa-rated from the next by only fifty feet or so. The shrine mixed screams of horror and ecstasy with a polyrhythmic drumming, like the beat-ing of many giant hearts driven to synchronize and resisting beyond their last breaths.

What had Dad been up to? Dale hadn't slept well while trying to figure out what his father's questions to the shrine might have been. Then, Dale decided that he'd simply ask the shrine: *What did my father want to know?*

Dale didn't attempt to go into the main hall proper, but stood before it in the middle of the courtyard, as if waiting outside the barred window of a jail the size of a world. With a penknife, he cut his hand under his jacket and let the blood drip onto the concrete courtyard. No one tried to help or stop the stupid *gaijin*; apparently, no priest cared if he wanted to stick his head in this monster's cage.

He hoped he wouldn't require the death trance to speak with these spirits, but only one way to find out. "Good day, honorable spirits. My name is Dale Morton of the House of Morton. Would discussion of my father be convenient?"

The chaotic screams and flashing grave lights stopped. Various Japanese voices broke the silence from all sides, sounding like the schizo debates of the Morton Left Hand.

Then, a single, panglossic voice, terrible, like the god of hydrogen bombs and hurricanes, spoke Dale's damnation. "*You shall not leave this place.*"

Dale immediately tried to flee, but he was paralyzed below his neck. He could move his head and eyes, meaning he could see a one-eighty-degree sweep of his new home in hell. Every person and thing in view was frozen in their tracks like a game of statues. Physical time outside of his head had stopped, or slowed so much that Dale couldn't tell the difference. But spiritually, the shrine was more alive than before. Its screams deafened not his ears, but the part of his brain that heard. Its spirit lights grew garish with glowing appetite and moved closer to his face and inside his very eyes. Dale saw his future: a subjective eternity with these rapacious revenants howling around, and within, his skull.

Frozen mute, and abject in horror, perhaps he had found what had destroyed his father's mind.

CHAPTER

THREE

Lieutenant Scherie Rezvani was limping in the dark, soaking wet and seeking cover, and, despite her best craft efforts, bleeding badly. *Blood—if they're like Gideons, they can track that.* Light-headed, caught between the fears of panic and passing out, she moved across the old city, trying to dodge the next bullet. Some fucker had shot her, here, right in the middle of Istanbul. A gun of her own would have been nice, or any weapon at all would do. Her throwing knives were used up. Death seemed very near; Janissaries and the other city ghosts were growing clearer around her. Oh, and another spirit was also here in 3-D Technicolor clarity, a person she had thought she had finished with forever, and might just dispel again for spite.

She imagined explaining to Dale her failure to survive. *Not my fault.* But how the hell had it come to this?

Just over an hour before, she had watched the sun going down over the heights of old Istanbul from the Galata Bridge. Domed mosques and the water of the Golden Horn, lovely and romantic, so of course she was viewing it all with another couple, while Dale was thousands of miles away. Bastard husband hadn't even called—sure, no calls except in emergencies, but since when had Dale started following the rules?

She didn't even have the soldier's consolation that this was what she had signed up for. Her primary mission, the one for which she was best suited, was Iran. But mundane and craft confusions there had put a hold on her vocation of revolt, and the U.S. had no immediate need for her extraordinary ability against possessing spirits and ghosts. So first they'd sent her on the usual training runs paired with another craftsperson. Among those watching her performance had been the shrinks. Prior to killing that Gideon in the Poconos to save Dale, she had been virginal, with no combat experience. A new killer usually had some reaction, if only because he felt he should. But she felt nothing for her first kill, and as for Madeline, Abram, and Roderick, she had merely delivered the bad news: they were already dead.

They'd called her reaction atypical, but she had always known she was special. The shrinks had seen this reaction before in some of their best soldiers, so they gave her a pass and General Attucks ordered her first solo op: glorified guard duty with an acceptable risk level. Among the Iranian dissidents in Istanbul were a craftsperson couple, the Safavians, and like their fellow exiles, they needed protection from the assassins that Iran would send to kill them. Experience had unfortunately shown that the locals couldn't be trusted for that protection on their own.

Dale and Michael had made a scene about her value, which might have been sweet of them, but most of it was about Roderick's possible return, which diminished her previous performance against him. Their protest also made it seem like they weren't treating her as a full comrade in craft.

So here she was, out on the bridge with the Safavians. In preparation for a future mission, Scherie had been debriefing the couple on Iranian craft and improving her contemporary Farsi idioms. The Safavians were frankly minor practitioners. Come the revolution, Iran would want a new craft order, but the Safavians were more likely future liaisons than leaders. They were older than Dale and herself, and their ideas of fun seemed so sedate that Scherie found it hard to understand why they wanted to risk leaving the safe house rather than staying locked up tight and secure. But confinement had nasty long-term psych effects, so Scherie had to meet their demands for a twilight walk and a fish sandwich fresh from the boat. As the safe house was up in the İstiklal neighborhood, that meant crossing the bridge over the Golden Horn.

Superficially, Scherie's walking gear would have suited any fashionable İstiklal woman who needed good cover for her little surprises: long boots, the better to hide one's long knife, dearie, with a blade in the toe besides, and a skirt with pocket-like slits for grabbing the other blades strapped to her thighs. H-ring considered it "bad form to arm agents with more than their craft" in allied states, so knives were the best she could do.

Istanbul wasn't a feminist paradise, but Ms. Safavian was clearly enjoying walking bareheaded and bold. Mr. Safavian, displaying his own graying head and precisely groomed short beard, smiled at everyone. Despite their situation, an outing in a city still new to them had a romantic quality, as if they were promenading tourists. The little sparks of the craft of many nations were like candles on date night. It would be nice to promenade with Dale here—later. So early, and already so many laters.

The Safavians passed a postcard seller, mostly images from the old city, the Sultanahmet district. Scherie wouldn't take her party farther than the fish boats in that area, a morass of residual magics and freelance craftsmen, feral and amoral. But seeing Hagia Sophia on a postcard made Scherie resent this restriction.

As if in response to her card viewing, Scherie heard a familiar yet strange voice over her left shoulder: "Here is wisdom. Let her with understanding speak the name of the Beast."

Startling the postcard seller, Scherie swung around, ready for combat. The Safavians were smiling at a food vendor, blissfully unaware. But Scherie saw the black-lit halo of the terribly thin and tall Left-Hand spirit in their midst, now wearing the face of her original body. Scherie whispered the riddle's answer: "Madeline."

"You got it in one. Hello, sister."

Great, Madeline is haunting me. Yes, when Scherie had exorcized her into the afterlife, Madeline had been absorbed into the Left-Hand Morton collective spiritual entity, but it was still Her, acting as the evil revenants' creepy, dominate voice.

Scherie found it easy to ready her anger for dispelling this nightmare. "Enjoy your trip home."

Madeline raised a hand, palm out. "Wait."

Scherie paused, troubled by something like human concern in the monstrous specter's thin face.

"We have many things we could teach you." Oh, that royal "we" sent a shiver down Scherie's back. "Craft unknown to your consort."

"Right. Your price?" Not that Scherie cared. She was no folktale fool, and if the *Thousand and One Nights* and *Children of Dune* were clear on one thing, it was never to seek the help of malevolent spirits.

Madeline smiled with the indulgent sadness of one who can see through lead. "We can haggle later. For now, just take a good look around you, craftswoman."

Huh. Other than not wanting to let Madeline out of her sight, the advice was sound. Scherie looked, and spotted the problems immediately, just like in training. Stealth cover or repression craft had its own signal, and that signal was moving toward them from both ends of the bridge. She stifled her pleasure at success. The Safavians were in deadly danger.

Scherie guessed the hunters were the local equivalent of the Gideon hounds: the Dogs of Istanbul. Despite their name, they were a multinational assortment with no local loyalty. Two of the good ones would be a serious challenge. Scherie needed to get the Safavians back to the safe house and call in support. Fortunately, they were far from trapped. The bridge had two levels and restaurant after restaurant on the lower one, which made for a maze of escape routes, and she couldn't have asked for a more public, crowded venue to limit enemy action.

Madeline could wait. "Sir, ma'am, we have to go now. Back to the safe house. Follow me." She started on a path that would put them on the west side of the upper level with no pursuer between them and Galata.

"They aren't after *them*." Madeline flared her nostrils in disgust as she effortlessly kept pace with Scherie. "They're probably double or triple agents anyway. No, sister. These Dogs are hunting you."

"Bullshit," said Scherie. She didn't believe she was on anyone's kill list for her father's sins against the Islamic Republic. A list that included every relative of every exile was too big to take seriously. Scherie herself hadn't had time to make craft enemies. "I'm going to protect these people."

"You'll just get them killed too. They couldn't pull a rabbit from a hat, but if you're with them, the Dogs will kill them to cover their real target. You."

This was nothing but distraction. Scherie needed to save her breath and ready her mind for combat. She needed . . .

Before Scherie's party turned a corner to cross through a seafood restaurant, one of Scherie's pursuers came close enough on the upper level for her to blink-assess him. He was dressed as local police. Hell, he might be local police as his cover job. He had a gun, and was close cut and clean shaven in Turkish police or military fashion. She couldn't see his eyes, so maybe he spared a glance for the Safavians, but she felt his tracking craft on her like a hare senses a hound.

He was tracking Scherie.

Still, maybe he saw her as the key to the Safavians. How would Madeline know differently? "You have one shot," said Scherie. "How do you know they want me?"

"The Morton way," said Madeline. "We see their sins, even of intention, and murder has intensity and degrees. They intend your killing in a very first-degree sort of way. The two other intended sins are weak afterthoughts, almost manslaughter."

"That level of detail is beyond Dale. It's certainly beyond you ghosts."

"Did you think *I'd* be an ordinary spirit?"

The fierce pride in this first-person statement convinced Scherie. She stopped the Safavians. "I have new intel. I'm the target. You'll continue this way, take the stairs back to the upper level, and get back to the safe house. If support hasn't already arrived, call it in. Go."

The Safavians looked at each other with a love and understanding that might have been beautiful if it didn't threaten FUBAR. "We will stay and fight with you," said Ms. Safavian.

Only one thing to say to that. "*Fuck off. Now.*" Scherie's strong language always worked with ghosts, and sometimes with the living. The Safavians strode hurriedly away, glancing back at Scherie with more fear than they had shown at their pursuit.

Great—with the Safavians heading to the Galata side, Scherie would have to go the other way, into the old city. She needed immediate extraction. As she chose a different path through the restaurant, she got out her cell phone and texted on the trot: "XTRACT."

Scherie ducked into a different restaurant, and Madeline was again at her elbow, passing through the people Scherie had to bump aside, chilling all. "He knows what you'll probably do."

"Who knows?" asked Scherie.

Madeline shook her head. "Going solo was a good start, but still a high percentage prediction, so he'll have a response to it. Whatever you'd normally do now, do something different."

Something different? With the Safavians going toward Galata, there wasn't another way to go except toward the old city. A bridge only had two ends. A bridge . . .

And then the penny dropped. "You want me to—"

But Madeline was shushing and shaking her head more emphatically. "Don't even say it. Just do it."

Scherie turned and ran out an exit. She gave a quick look over the rail. All clear, but she needed another reason besides the word of the treacherous Madeline. She didn't need to wait more than a second before she had a good one: a new Dog on the old city shore near where pedestrians exited the bridge, head tilted back as if sniffing for her.

She assumed a symmetrical Dog on the other old city side exit. Too many by land.

So one by sea. Without further thought, Scherie took a big breath, and leapt into a crouch atop the rail. She let her breath out and pushed off in a long dive, filling her lungs again as she fell toward the Golden Horn.

She plunged through the oily surface into the cold water; her concerns with toxins were focused on the lead from guns. Her clothes weighed her down, which for the moment was good, but might be a problem later.

Keeping her eyes open and willing them to *see*, she swam underwater in what she hoped was the direction of the Eminönü ferry docks. She had the preternatural endurance of a combat craftswoman; she could swim 250 meters without a breath, so she would have to come up for air at least once before she reached the docks. There, she would have options. If the real city police didn't delay her, she could hop the ferry across the Bosphorus or toward the airport, or get on the train toward the airport, or even double back toward Galata and the U.S. Consulate (not the safe house, though). The fake police would have difficulty covering all her possibilities.

Angry angled lines slashed down in front of her eyes. Holy shit, they were shooting at her. She almost let out her breath in shock. They were creating a public scene, risking a craft disclosure that would bring the wrath of all mundane authority, foreign and domestic, down on their heads. She skewed the paths of the shots away from her, but they continued to fall around her, slowed in water to a visible, eerie beauty.

She swam deeper, changing direction slightly. She didn't like how close they had come to her position. They must have an idea of where she was going. Not good, but the docks were still her best bet, even if she had to swim farther on. If anyone was foolish enough to dive in after her, she still had her knives.

A blur, just ahead and to her right. She focused—*see, dammit*—and beneath the old city shoreline found a round, blue-green glow, like a craft-hidden entrance. She remembered something from her stateside briefing on the secret sewers and cisterns of the old city. She ignored the glow and swam harder for the docks. Her clothes were slowing her down. Her head and heart began to pound, and her lungs hungered for air. Her combat instructor had been emphatic on the dangers of underwater swimming. If Scherie pushed too far, she could pass out and drown, but with bullets flying she didn't want to come up until absolutely necessary.

Then Madeline reappeared, also glowing, though with the distinctive black light of the Left Hand, long finger pointed at the underwater entrance. *God, I still don't trust that revenant.* But the entrance was so much closer than the docks and hidden from surface view. So long as there was air near behind it, and not a blind alley of dark water for her to drown in. It would be like Madeline to point the way to death.

For magic assistance, Scherie readied an image of an opening door, but when she reached the entrance, she found only an open stone maw, craft camouflaged from mundane view, and crumbling underwater steps angling up the hole into darkness.

Hands up to keep from hitting her head, she pushed up off a stone step and, after a second of heart-pounding need and panic, broke into dark air. She gasped. The air stank of rot and re-rot, and she gulped it down like perfume. She felt for the stairway and pulled herself up it and out of the water.

The echoes of her dripping mixed with other drips in the darkness. *Heat,* she thought, with an image of warmth flowing from the air into her skin, and she felt warmer. She emptied her boots. Whatever happened, this outfit was never returning to her closet.

Every tool or weapon she carried was rated for extreme environments, so she squeezed her still-functioning cell phone out of her clothes and turned it on to use as a lamp. The stairway ended where a tunnel began, running more level, but still inclined, with a trickle of water down its center. The tunnel stones were time-polished and slippery, and her feet smacked against their surface with the wide, tentative stride of someone jogging on ice. Rats scattered at her light, bats squeaked and fluttered their leathery wings, and she smelled their shit amidst the general damp and decay.

After a minute, the tunnel opened into a chamber. If this was a cistern, it made the Basilica Cistern look like a village well. This vast, cavernous structure, filled with columns, was like something made by Tolkien's dwarves, and from the glows of camouflage craft Scherie could tell that it went on farther than conventional sight showed.

Directly ahead of her were the backs of two tall statues that also served as karyatid-like supports. She moved between them, then turned to view them. A man and a woman, crowned, sat on high thrones as if guarding the way Scherie had come. They were Byzantine, but instead of calm, affectless nobility, they wore the faces of deranged, fanged demons. Greek letters marked them as "*basileus*" and Latin letters indicated they were "*imperator.*" Scherie guessed this must be the Byzantine co-emperors Theodora and Justinian in their dark aspects, as hinted at in the *Secret History* of Procopius.

As if drawn to distant kindred, Madeline manifested, her outline more distinct but still monochromatic. Was she wearing a pants suit? "You can summon aid here. The local Left Hand will make a deal."

"I've got other ways of calling for help." Scherie turned on her cell phone again and started dialing.

"You stupid bitch!" said Madeline, swiping at the phone, chilling Scherie's already cold hands.

"I'm still breathing, ghost bitch," said Scherie.

"He can listen to any call you make."

"Is this a trivia game? Who the fuck are you talking about?" But Scherie now noticed a series of texts that had been sent to her since her SOS, all from THE_INLAW:

I apologize, but I will not let your message
go through.

Again, my deepest thanks for liberating me.

In gratitude, I have not ordered any particular
suffering to accompany your death.

(I didn't want you to have to hear this from
my sister.)

Good-bye. Roderick.

Oh God, no. She had failed. Roderick lived. She had to get to Dale, to warn him, and Endicott, and the whole frigging free world.

She should have kept her mind on local concerns. The scrape of stone and metal echoed from the east to her left. From the north, the slap of feet in the tunnel she had come from. They had found her. In this forest of columns, she could see nowhere to hide from multiple pursuers.

Through the dark, phone light held out in front of her, Scherie ran south, slaloming between the columns.

The guns' thunder echoed; shots ricocheted off stone that was too close, throwing up bits of gray shrapnel. She didn't try to turn off her phone to lose them; the Dogs could track by all senses, and she needed her sight. She skewed their shots aggressively, but they'd be putting their own spins on the bullets.

Then, a shot meant for her chest bent south, and she felt some giant kick her in the rear. She fell. Her phone skittered away from her across the stone. She crawled back away from it, and leaned up against a column

Aw, fuck. She'd been shot in the thigh. Not in that whole Morton Pentagon fuck-up had someone gotten a piece of her. She was going to die like a stupid raw recruit, and all she could think of was how she had let everyone down.

Scherie focused her mind on containing some of the damage to her leg, but she also had at least two Dogs to kill. She readied her knives—two for throwing, and the third for close quarters. She readied her craft to guide her knives like missiles, to make them drive home.

Madeline appeared. Was she here to gloat? No. She was looking more substantial. In the dark, she could pass for the living. She limped about like . . . like a killdeer faking a broken wing.

The shooting started again. Madeline cried out like the banshee she was, then folded to the ground. The Dogs moved in. The glow of their craft played off Madeline's black light like a laser show. The Dogs didn't seem to notice Scherie; they only had eyes for Madeline. Like a snake with its prey, she fascinated them. They did not acknowledge each other; these two weren't working together. The Dogs, despite their name, seldom did.

Scherie picked out her targets. She did not aim for the chest—though big in area, too often body armored. Arm or leg would not be enough damage. She steadied her breathing, and aimed for their throats.

Her first throw was a clean hit with the messy arterial aftermath. The second curved away from the other Dog's throat and just nicked his arm.

This delayed his bringing his gun to bear on her for a second, and in that second, forgetting all pain, she was already on him. With a martial "*Kiya!*" she slammed her remaining knife at the base of his throat, but at the last the point slid and merely scratched him, driven back by craft. She restrained his gun hand, but his free hand came up and with a crunch connected with her face. A dizzy darkness called. His gun moved up to finish her, then jerked away toward some other target. *Madeline.* With all her anger at this debt and an underhand thrust, Scherie drove her knife forward again, this time craft-impelled for his heart, through Kevlar, meat, and bone.

His body dropped back away from her, taking her knife with it. In a near faint, she folded to her knees. First things. Triage. She wrapped her hands around her leg. *Heal, fucker.* Her hands came away bloodier. The bullet was still in her leg, its damage contained, but not for long if she had to move. And she had to move.

She retrieved her phone. In its light, she could now see the pillar that had sheltered her. It had a gorgon's face carved into its base. Appropriate. She crawled to her second victim, and pulled at the knife. It wouldn't budge. Some combination of craft and Kevlar had frozen it in place. In the distance, more noises. No time to retrieve her other knives either.

She stood, spasming, and with her right leg swinging stiff as wood, she made her way farther south until she stumbled out of the vast cavern onto a wooden walkway. The emergency lights revealed one of the known, tourist cisterns—by its location, she guessed the Basilica Cistern. It was like the cavern she'd been in, only smaller and with the floor covered with a pool of water. Scherie was on the walkway for sightseers. She followed the exit signs. The "*open*" spell had lost a little of its zap, but was still at ready to help force the locked doors.

Madeline was out on the street before her, waving her on like dead Captain Ahab inviting his crew to follow. Scherie wanted a better choice, but she didn't have one. The evening tourist foot traffic avoided her, assuming she was some local unpleasantness that the guidebooks hadn't warned them of. Smells of the nargile's tobacco and diesel exhaust mixed unpleasantly.

It was harder than she thought, walking through the pain. Wasn't she supposed to be some great healer? Her skirt was sopping wet with water and blood, and red ran down her leg. The trackers would find her trail with ease.

She crossed the street and tram tracks and moved across the plaza that had been inside the racetrack of the Hippodrome. A crowd roared like ocean surf in her head, "*Nike!*" Victory. But that had to be a hallucination, or the ghost of the place rather than the people—for those days were fifteen hundred years ago, and no mortal's spirit could sustain itself so long.

Indignant gulls and crows flew around her, and the mangy mutts of the plaza trotted toward her, menacing beyond their size. Ghost scenes obscured her view of the present, and the faded spirits of Janissary soldiers, killed by their own emperor, seemed to bar her way with oversized muskets and swords.

At the far end of the Hippodrome, Madeline stopped waving and stood to the left of an ancient column. As Scherie approached, she recognized it: three coils of scarred and twisted deep green bronze, a triple-helix that had once ended in snake heads. A low fence and a shallow ditch encircled it to block the public, but without guards on hand, these were mere discouragement for a determined vandal. Few knew what an astounding piece of history these sad remains were: the Serpent Column, taken from Delphi by Constantine the Great for his new city.

This history didn't exactly warm Scherie's failing heart. This column symbolized the Greek victory over ancient Persia, and its entwined craft-conductive design was likely cursed to kill practitioners of Persian descent. *I should have known.* Here at last, the trap. "What now?"

"Touch the pillar." Madeline made it sound obscene.

Scherie could see Madeline all too clearly now. The tall and thin black-lit halo had filled in with her pale face and her male clothes—a Victorian man's bright riding gear, complete with a crop for enforcing discipline on the collective Left-Hand spiritual herd. "Madeline, before I die, I'm going to dispel you for good."

"Please. I won't allow my brother to succeed."

Scherie looked back the way she had come, and the world wobbled like a shaky camera threatening to fall. Two new Dogs in military uniforms, bearing assault rifles, were moving in for the kill. No choice, then. The column would probably incinerate her, but better it than these Dogs.

Too exhausted, Scherie couldn't imagine climbing down. She leaned forward over the fence and awkwardly tumbled over with a smack of wet clothing, though she automatically rolled as she fell—drills were good for something. Pain and darkness competed for her mind, and darkness was winning. She stretched her hand toward the column. A low green glow moved up its snakes like an electrical Jacob's ladder.

Around the fence, people pulled themselves up and close, then bent down to stare at her. A few would-be nighttime guides were shouting in their numerous languages for her to get up and out. The two soldier Dogs would be here soon, no doubt as ready as their dead fellows to shoot her, even in public.

This can't be right, touching this. But her blood-smeared palm made contact.

Nothing. She readied some last spiteful energy to dispel Madeline. But, standing above her at the fence, the ghost wasn't gloating. "Keep your hand on it!"

Fine—to the absurd end. Scherie couldn't have moved much even if she had wanted to. She was about a ten count from passing out. Nine. Never mind . . .

Then, like the static of a winter's day, a brief shock of craft energy made her fingers jump; it might have hurt if her leg wasn't demanding all her capacity for pain. The energy seemed to push her a few steps back from unconsciousness.

Cutting through the multilingual chaos around Scherie, a woman's voice came out of the column, vibrating her hand like a restaurant's buzzer. In what sounded like Greek, the voice posed what might have been a question.

Scherie responded in panglossic. "I . . . I don't speak Greek. Please repeat."

"*Do you wish to claim sanctuary?*" asked the voice, in English or panglossic.

Scherie knew of one Sanctuary, but that was distinctly American craft. Didn't matter.

"Yes. I claim . . ."

The force hit her like water from a fire hose, knocking her soul out of her skin for a second, then passing through her. The guides stopped shouting. People shook their heads, confused, and turned away. All the city ignored her; all except the Dogs, who had reached the fence, but for some reason weren't shooting.

"What is your house?"

Always on about the ancestors. The House of Morton was loaded with evil baggage, but that House Rezvani even existed was a secret, one probably unknown to this pillar voice.

"I'm a Morton by marriage."

Silence. Dale had warned her that there'd be moments like these, when someone would stand in judgment of her connection to his line, and her life might hang between their greed and fear. But the voice left her dangling. *"Wait."*

Scherie couldn't say how long she waited. Longer than an hour, less than a night. More Dogs gathered, men and women, standing over her at the fence, quietly staring at her. They waited for her hand to slip like a pet anticipating a scrap tumbling from the table. No, they were more jackal than dog. Even in her hallucinating desperation, she was awed—what power in the world could remotely hold back these hunters from finishing her?

The night tourists and drinkers veered away from the Dogs, but no one seemed to notice Madeline's presence, and its chill, as anything but the weather. Scherie could no longer distinguish Madeline from the living. That communal Left-Hand ghost stood silent vigil, as if waiting for Scherie to die. Wounded and wet, Scherie could delay shock and hypothermia, but they would keep their appointment eventually.

Things went black. Then, a man's voice. "Madame?"

A hand on her arm. She shuddered, revolted, trying to shake it off. But she couldn't move.

"Madame, you can let go now."

"I can't," she whispered. She had lost control of her muscles, gone rigid, cramped beyond pain. "Who are you?" She had no craft to put into the question.

"The oracle sent us."

Scherie ceased to question. With the gentle firmness of medical professionals, men pulled her hand off the pillar and placed her on a stretcher. Scherie felt the stretcher rise, though her vision was a narrow tunnel in front of her, so she didn't see how they were hoisting her. She heard the Dogs; could they be actually snarling? Her head lolled, and she saw one of them, near enough to smell his meaty breath, who seemed to be straining on a leash that was about to give way.

A man, close to her ear, spoke loudly. "Back, Dog, unless you wish to violate Oikumene law and meet our kindly hounds."

Still snarling, the Dog backed away.

Scherie saw the world move above her, then stop. A Red Crescent ambulance had parked on the quiet night road, and with easy efficiency she was placed inside. The last thing she remembered was the warmth as the needles went in.

PART II

ON HER MAJESTY'S SPIRITUAL SERVICE

Have a care: I will work at your destruction,
nor finish until I desolate your heart, so that
you curse the hour of your birth.
—Mary Shelley

CHAPTER

FOUR

When the drug haze lifted enough to think, I found myself strapped upright in a metal chair. Not the first time I'd been in this position, but that didn't make it more comfortable. My head was full of pain and endless interrogative snippets, as if in my twilight mental state I'd already been answering questions for a while. They were asking one now.

"Why did you release Roderick Morton?"

Release? As if we'd done it on purpose. Not good. Worse, I felt like I'd replied to this question before, maybe half a dozen times or so, which meant they weren't buying my answer. That was bad because, drugged or not, I only lied when it was my duty, and I wouldn't have lied about that.

My eyes focused, and through the intimidating lighting, I beheld my audience. Five people: two men and a woman in business suits that radiated craft, a man in a lab coat, and their muscle of the compact English thug type.

"Who are you?" I rasped. The answer might determine whether I'd have to inflict serious harm to others and self.

The three suits spoke with Received Pronunciation in flat unison. *"Answer us."*

God help me, I almost did. Ouch. Seemed they'd been hitting me with craft compulsions with their many questions, as I already felt spiritually bruised. I itched to slam them back with words of command, but right now I'd waste them on anatomical impossibilities.

I'd wait to give them a very specific and effective order, because I'd probably only get one shot.

"I've already answered you." *We tried to kill him, you idiots.*

A pause, and in the silence the room felt like a true oubliette, a place to forget the unwanted. The space had a regulation polish, so it wasn't likely to be an improvised location chosen by non-governmental others. No doorway or observation mirror that I could see.

"*Why did you release Roderick Morton?*"

My headache became a more active pain, but I continued to assess my situation. I didn't know fashion, but I knew uniforms, even the unofficial ones. My three inquisitors wore expensive Carnaby Street suits, decades past glam, like Austin Powers had finally grown up and gotten a real job but still liked a touch of color. This was the style of the Magic Circus, the very organization I was supposedly here to help. But I had been sent here on a mole hunt, so they might not be friendly at all.

If they were Magic Circus, their unusual ability to coordinate would mark these three as the legendary Walsinghams. "You're trying to sweat me?" My voice had gone cold. *This sort of thing wasn't done, old chaps, even by legends.*

"*Tell us,*" they chorused again. God help me but it hurt.

"I think I've told you everything a few times already. I think you'd better give me a phone line to my superiors."

The woman inquisitor nodded at the lab coat man. He held out a syringe that glowed with insidious comfort to relax the mind. They were going to give a psychoactive drug to a spiritual operative. "*In God's name, stop.*"

Lab Coat froze. But I had played the Lord's trump card early. What next? The service's muscle was usually the weakest mental link. "*For Christ's sake, undo these straps.*"

My inquisitors were already up out of their chairs. The two men were trying to restrain the muscle. That was good. But the more tactically aware woman grabbed the syringe from Lab Coat and walked up to me with a model's poise and sneer. "What would you like me to do, Major?"

Daring me to try the power of command on her, which meant I better think of something else. One thing still didn't make sense— they hadn't called for help. But I could.

"The Endicotts believe in ghosts now."

She hesitated, maybe because she didn't see the relevance, maybe because she did.

"A change in doctrine," I continued. "You may have missed it; Roderick can be very distracting. But yes, we know our family ghosts aren't demons, and we talk to them."

She smiled. "Best of luck with that here." We both knew no foreign ghost could get into this place.

"You're mistaken," I said. "I'm not going to *summon* a ghost." My opponent's smile vanished as I continued. "You think Left-Hand Mortons are scary. You're right, of course. They terrify me and every decent human being. But you've forgotten who I am. I'm an Endicott. And though the Mortons changed the weather, and saved Washington's rear end, my ancestors were at Saratoga and New Orleans, and we hammered your best to a red-coated pulp. So let me be clear. You inject me with that, and I will command my own death. My ghost will return home, and the remaining Endicotts and all our relations in the other Families will come for you and yours." With a turn of my head, I took in the room. "All of you and yours."

And the spiritual services of our two nations will be at war. Yes, it was a bit extreme, embarrassing even, but she was threatening to screw up my spiritual power for no good reason at all. If I had more time, a slower escalation would have been more prudent.

But she wasn't giving me time. "You're bluffing," she said. "It's suicide. The unforgivable sin."

I wasn't going to argue the moral distinction between the duty of self-sacrifice and the sin of suicide; I already knew it well enough. "You'll sit down, now, or in five seconds, I pray for death. Five . . ."

The woman wasn't moving. Oh, well. See you soon, Father, in "Four . . ."

"That will be enough." A door had appeared in what had seemed to be a blank wall, and the woman who had found me on the freeway stood there in a Royal Navy uniform, as tall as anyone in the room. Syringe Woman took a step back, looking as nervous and relieved as I felt. The muscle took advantage of the moment to shrug off his restrainers and then shambled forward to unbind me. Lab Coat folded to the floor.

I flexed my stiff hands and stood up as steadily as I could. The freeway woman looked at me with frank distaste and anticipated my next question. "Does anyone have a phone for our guest? No? Then use mine, Major." She handed me a government Blackberry-style phone that glowed with craft.

I realized that I didn't know enough to make a good report. "Who are you, and where am I?"

"I'm Commander Grace Marlow, MI13. We're in a borrowed room at MI6."

No sign of deception, but that wasn't my strong suit. I dialed Attucks. Whatever the hour was, he sounded fully awake. I told him my story in undiplomatic language, but my London audience didn't react. "Sir," I finished, "it's obvious I can be of more use elsewhere." *So please get me out of here.*

"Your situation isn't exactly what we agreed to," said Attucks.

"Agreed to, sir?"

"Don't let them inject you with anything, but otherwise, please cooperate."

"What did you agree to, sir?"

"We'll discuss on your return."

"You could have warned me."

"That's all, Major." He ended the call. I didn't wait to hand the phone back to Commander Marlow, because holding a disconnected phone next to my ear would just confirm that I was a loser. As Marlow pocketed the mobile, her cool demeanor couldn't hide a trace of smugness. She had known what Attucks would say. Some kind of deal had been made, and no one had told me. Why had my own fed me to these British lions?

The room was silent. Very well, might as well get this over with. "You have questions."

"Yes," said the Suits, who were seated again as if nothing had happened.

With an open palm, Marlow signaled an interruption. "New questions?"

Without hesitation, the Suits again chorused, "*Why did you release Roderick Morton?*"

Before I could protest, Marlow shook her head and said, "I've been listening. Do you have any new ground to cover? If not, the Major is leaving."

"We were promised access."

"You've had your access and more."

"Please, Commander, just a few more minutes," said one of the men. "His conscious resistance and meta-responses are intriguing."

"You were told you could talk to him, not stress test him for idle curiosity."

Syringe Woman was pissed. "You don't have the authority . . ."

"C says no," said Marlow, dry and cool as any martini. "Good day, sirs, ma'am."

We left the room through the door that Marlow had used and entered a conference space set up for observation. "Your response to the interview was excessive."

"Those interviewers were assaulting an American spiritual officer here as a guest of your government."

"And you respond with the power of command and a threat of war. You seem oblivious to any concerns but your own. This morning on the road, how many cars were you prepared to smash, how many people were you prepared to kill, merely to save yourself?"

Was this that British humor I'd heard so much about? "I'm not used to rogue craftsmen running about and attacking servicemen in a supposedly friendly country."

"They were our rogues."

"What?"

"They are denizens of the London craft underground with long police records and a history of activity on behalf of foreign powers. We were going to bring them in, but we decided to hire them first to bring you in."

The London craft underground didn't have a true American equivalent. It was a legacy of British class structure and the government's belated covenant with non-aristocratic practitioners. "But using rogues makes no sense," I said, "unless . . ." *Long police records.* "You wanted to know if I could see their sins. You thought I was part Morton." And all Left Hand.

"Given what we know about Abram, is it so unlikely? They may have exceeded their instructions, but they were under a suspended death sentence anyway, and you were in no real danger."

All very easy for her to say. "If I had been a Morton, I also could have manipulated the air and avoided the gas." And some of this headache.

"Right again," said Marlow. "I have only one more question. If you truly could not see their sins, what tipped you off that something was different?"

So they could fool the next guy better? I had been ordered to cooperate, so I cooperated. "Several things. But it moved from probable to definite when they picked up the third man."

"Third man?" A pause, then, "Ah, yes. That's what did it?"

"Yes. If he had been there for the pickup, it might not have been as odd, though three minders would always seem excessive. After that, everything looked like enemy action."

"So, next time we should only use two."

"That's SOP most everywhere."

"Thank you." She seemed distracted. "You've been most helpful."

"I have?"

"I must be going."

"I thought . . ."

"Oh, yes, your hotel." She retrieved a soft leather briefcase from a chair, opened it, and with the usual practitioner's avoidance of contact handed me an envelope. "Your things are already in your room. Enjoy your stay."

Oh, this was too much. I spoke as low as I could. "I was told I was here to assist in a mole hunt."

This seemed to bring back her focus. I'd never imagined dark eyes shooting lasers, but I felt torched by her gaze. "In typical fashion, you didn't ask yourself if you were qualified. You're not in your jurisdiction, and know nothing of the ground."

"I've come a long way."

"I doubt that you're new to disappointment. The Crown has appreciated your cooperation." Translation: *We're done with you.* "Good day, Major."

She was turning to the exit in dismissal. I insisted: "Do you or do you not have a mole problem?"

"We do have a mole problem, but it's on your side of the Atlantic."

Oh, to be gone in an instant and escape this infuriating woman forever. But I felt the nakedness at my side and suspected that one item wasn't in my hotel room. "Where is my sword?"

Marlow tilted her head with a frown, and her eyes flicked down, but, relenting, she spared me the Freudian joke. "On your departure, I'll deliver it to you personally at the airport. My word as an officer."

So she knew its importance. That would have to be enough, as I had fought and threatened too much today, and I wasn't about to beg.

Anonymous security escorted me through the exit, and I stepped out into twilight, alone, into the cold drizzle in which Londoners took such perverse pride. Looking about, it was indeed MI6's headquarters at Vauxhall Cross, so at least she had been telling the truth about that much. In contrast to suburban Langley, the MI6 Building was deep within London. Its rounded, clean, turret-like structures gave it a modern castle fortress aspect. Langley dismissively called it "Legoland," but I thought it was another Tower of London. That association chilled me—in spiritual sight, the Tower and Tyburn still glowed with the residue of practitioner blood from the days when the nobility had ruled spiritual practice with a mailed fist, and clerical celibacy to keep new Families from forming had been the only refuge for a new practitioner. Even for a praying Christian, all else had been Ex-22: "Thou shalt not suffer a witch to live."

The envelope from Marlow held my government passport, some pound notes, and the address of my hotel with a message that Her Majesty's Government had already covered the charges. In other words, I had the exact minimum to reach my hotel and check in, and nothing more. I would have enjoyed defying my hosts' constraints, but a change of clothes was too tempting, so I hailed a cab.

During the ride, I weighed my situation and found it wanting. My hosts didn't trust me. MI13 had brought me here on a pretense and didn't seem much concerned with my well-being. Their mole story was probably more right than most of them knew, which added to my risk.

The risk didn't bother me as much as Commander Marlow. She had been right: on the freeway, I hadn't considered the other lives at stake. I was guilty of selfish pride and, as she implied, not for the first time.

But why did I care what she thought of me? She was nice looking, but that didn't explain why my mind looped back to her every other minute. She had that RP British accent, those aristocratic cheekbones crossed by the trace of a scar, and eyes like cold dark pools until they burned their heat into you, but I had met and worked with women from all over the world, so I wasn't swayed by what other Americans might find exotic.

Even if I were attracted to her, and even if I could've altered her opinion of me, she was a foreign craftsperson, and that I couldn't change. She was forever barred to me by long custom and very present government threats. The special relationship between the UK and the U.S. wasn't that special. I supported this policy completely, and it was my duty.

But, God help me, I was thoroughly sick of my duty. I was twenty-nine, and duty had kept me a virgin. Christian novels made this sound easy and natural, but it had been neither. I figured from my reading of the Bible that the so-called sin of Onan was the deliberate failure to reproduce, and my virginity was that sin. I'd been on dates, and they hadn't always been physically innocent, but I'd always stopped short of the deed. My job had always provided the excuse, though virginity seemed particularly ridiculous in the carpe diem military.

Dating could wait. I had to think of my next steps, though my head resisted, still hurting like my one tequila hangover on the morning of repentance. I arrived at the upscale chain hotel where MI13 had booked me, in the middle of Belgravia. The neighborhood was wealthy, but also notoriously underoccupied by the rich transients from many lands who held foothold residences here. Sinister, like an anti-Rapture had taken all the non-believers and left behind just the many cameras of the British Argus to witness whatever the bad guys might have in store for me.

Making such paranoid connections on the fly may have been an Endicott gift, but that same paranoia made my family reluctant to talk about it. For me, it felt excessive, just a short bunt away from schizophrenia. Unlike the gifts of the Spirit, it didn't feel good to use.

At reception, I gave them my operational name and they gave me a room. MI13 had booked it, so I assumed they knew its number. Were real killers with inside knowledge coming for me? They usually were. "Please change my room to a lower floor." They did, and they sent a bellhop up to move my luggage. I didn't add any forbidden spiritual fanciness to further obscure my location. If the bad guys had the info from inside MI13, maybe they wouldn't check again at the desk.

In the luggage delivered to my new room, I found my mobile. First things first. Yeah, it would be great to show up the locals and get the bad guys like a Western gunslinger or a Japanese ronin, but I wasn't staying in this country a minute longer than necessary. With Roderick back, I had friends in trouble. Evening had arrived here, so back home it was midday. I called the Pentagon's travel office, but they said they couldn't get me anything at an authorizable price for an earlier day. Rather than waste time going up the chain, I called the airline myself and found an unreasonable price for a 9:50 a.m. flight tomorrow morning.

I had the money. Few of the old Families were poor, and those poor ones largely by choice. But both my Puritan and practitioner pasts usually combined to insist on restraint. Wealth was a legacy to be grown and held in trust for future generations; earthly indulgence was the sin that led to others.

Indulgence or no, I would have spent twice as much for a flight an hour earlier. Sure, I'd been humiliated, but I'd gotten used to God and the Devil's amusement at my expense. I wasn't running away from that; I was running toward my friends.

I made another pair of calls direct to Dale and Scherie. No answer. She had told me she'd be in Istanbul for babysitting; he had said Tokyo, but wouldn't tell me why, "for your own sake, Mike." I tried Attucks, but he wasn't taking my call.

As I hung up, the schizo wave washed over me. Everything I had sensed today went into what the Peepshow called semiotic overload, and the entire world consisted of nothing but tactical clues. I hated this feeling almost as much as I hated farsight oracles. The similarity of my antipathies itself became a clue. Langley and H-ring's farsight games played out like statistical 4-D chess, with moves and countermoves calculated along many timelines. What would I call this ugly opening? I'd been made vulnerable, and I didn't think my superiors had consented to it to satisfy the inquisitive in MI13. I'd name this stripping of my usual protections an "Ishtar gambit" (I knew the classic pagan stories too). I was being dangled like naked bait in one of H-ring's stinking probability games to draw out the enemy.

I changed clothes as if rushing to battle, though the style was international casual. I knew of too many practitioners killed in their rooms. Hotel rooms, with their one exit, were terrible tactical places. Most times, this sort of thinking was PTSD or the public posing of a young vet, but I was in a combat situation. I wouldn't be sleeping tonight; sleep was for idiots. My drug-induced nap hadn't been the healthy kind of rest, but it would do. I abandoned the rest of my luggage. Except for my sword, I never packed anything that I couldn't afford to lose. *I'd better get that sword back, or the family ghosts will be pissed.*

Now I had to choose where to hole up instead. I could go to the airport earlier and wait on standby, but for practitioners international airports were like hotel rooms on a large scale, a sort of cul-de-sac with many bad ways to exit. A quick abduction and I would be off to a far nastier place than England. I could try the American Embassy, but as they knew nothing about my mission here, they might not be helpful. A metropolis like London offered the easiest solution: plenty of very public places kept the lights on and the people hopping all night. *Nessun* fricken *dorma*. And it was Friday. (Thank you, Lord.) Of course, if my enemies didn't care about craft secrecy, all bets were off, but that would mean graver threats than to my single life.

I left the hotel and wandered across some of the Z (as in Zevon) coordinates. Trader Vic's, Mayfair, Soho, Chinatown, Lee Ho Fook's. These non-historical spots were all places of power, but not for me. The streets were jammed with nightlife seekers. I couldn't find an Indian restaurant with less than a two-hour wait, so I ate some McDonald's like the tourist I was. After a few hours of me walking, the town started slowing down. What some practitioners called the History Channel kept leaking into my view: Dickensian slums filled with Dickensian ghosts, old pubs and music halls pervaded by prostitutes of both sexes—always very young. Odd that I was seeing dead people who weren't my family; in a few months I'd gone from seeing little to seeing too much. I was strung out from the day.

I checked my phone. No messages, and no signs of tracking or tapping. Spiritually enhanced devices were something like quantum-entangled communications: I could tell when someone was trying to listen in. I checked the local news feed. It reported a fire in my hotel, but no details. Another bit of collateral damage from my travel. I prayed no one was hurt.

I searched for the nearby twenty-four-hour places, and naturally found the dance clubs. A rave would be the perfect bolt-hole, with the usual bonus of it being an extremely ridiculous place for me to be. My grandmother had told me that being a Christian practitioner was to be in a perpetual state of irony with one's life. I saw this all the time.

I chose the New Gargoyle because the club's name added to my sense of absurdity, and that was unfortunately a good sign. My clothes were anti-hip, but they let me in anyway ahead of the younger and restless. Right after the door, the kids started in with "Hey Yank, want a trip?" The military haircut only seemed to encourage them. They knew the "Yank" without a word from me; they always knew. Besides any sin, designer drugs were a bad idea for a practitioner.

I found an elevated part of the floor with a good view and multiple points of departure. A low-level craft glowed throughout the club and pulsed along to the demon-hammer beat. The DJ seemed to add a little power to the mix, probably unconsciously. The young, alive, and beautiful danced, and no sign of a kindred soul in the lot. But in a moment I was dancing too, and the workout did me some good. Form didn't seem to matter, except for the few who were putting on a show. Sometimes it was just a lot of hopping up and down. Pretty women with flying-saucer-sized pupils smiled at me and rubbed my scalp. I just smiled back and they danced away.

The more I got into the rhythm, the more the ghost space of the old Gargoyle Club asserted itself. Again, I saw ghosts of strangers:

American servicepeople stranded in London because, for some reason, they couldn't go home.

Other than those lonely spirits, the hallucinogenic music, the mind-
less groping of the other dancers, and my freewheeling paranoia as I
anticipated an attack, this dancing was kind of fun. As personal oracles went, fun was not a good sign.

Someone was moving their extended thin white arm in time to the
music. The arm left a craft afterimage on my retina like the glow sticks
some of the dancers held. There he was: the third man from the car.
Car Man was waving at me, his killer's eyes flashing ultraviolet in the
club lights.

OK, you have my attention. I took a photo of the asshole with my
phone, and with a touch sent it to everyone at H-ring. Car Man smiled,
and seemed unconcerned. He made gestures toward the rear of the
dance floor. Two men and a red-haired woman emerged from the
darkened bar alcoves, glowing with the true power that made the background craft of the club seem like nothing. They moved through the
crowd, caught in the jumping frames of a strobe light, wearing the
nerdy glasses of the young Elvis Costello or Buddy Holly—an odd
choice for prospective combat. With their female accomplice trailing,
the two men grabbed two women who were dancing together, no doubt
in a very suggestive state for trance, and in some combination of craft
and mundane action compelled them toward the emergency exit sign,
with no protest or sign of alarm from anyone.

Car Man had slid into a clear spot on the floor just below me. He
held up two fingers, made a slash across his throat, pointed at me,
pointed at the exit, then followed his three colleagues. No sign of deception in his threat gesture.

So there it was. Two random people were being held hostage. Should
I call the police? If I didn't show, would Car Man stop with just two?

Didn't matter. These rogues had my name and number. I would
fight for the druggie damsels in distress. Oh, I briefly wondered if
Marlow's harangue earlier had been part of a long-game set up, but

that didn't matter either. A straight-up choice of life for life (two lives!) felt vastly different from my reckless endangerment on the road. Not logical, but typical. My father's ghost would chew me out when my spirit showed up in Arlington, if I didn't get stuck here with the WWII crowd. H-ring would have ordered me not to fight, as any Peepshow game would require a few more moves and a bigger payoff for my sacrifice. But I really, really didn't give a Mach 5 fuck what H-ring and Langley thought just now.

I did care what happened to Dale and Scherie, but they weren't here. *Sorry guys—I hope you're OK.*

I followed the kidnappers. That was when it got weird. I started to feel good—too good. A little high. Had someone slipped me something? But no, my coordination seemed fine, other than bumping into endless dancers.

As I walked to the exit marked by a green sign, I tried to think of a plan that would get the two club women out of this alive. Car Man had packed a gun earlier, so they'd be armed now. I could dodge a couple of rounds at a distance, but I was pretty sure they'd just shoot me up close the moment I left the building.

So, I'd pray for four people to drop their weapons through a closed fire door. *Sure, why not.* I stood to the side of the door to avoid the inevitable bullets. I heard some confused high-pitched syllables and low voices on the other side, so they could hear me. "*In Jehovah's name, drop your guns!*"

The low voices stopped, but still some fearful squeaks from the hostages. Neither silence nor squeaks suggested that anyone had been disarmed against their will.

I was at bottom. *Lord, I'm listening.*

Nothing. If I was at bottom, why the heck was I feeling so good? *Eli, Eli, feet don't fail me now.* Shame to die just when I was enjoying the party.

"Supper's ready, Major. Come out, or we will kill them in five, four . . ."

The countdown was like an echo of my stunt with MI13. *Enjoying the party.* What was that thing Morton had pulled at his going-away party? He had disarmed everyone with a prepared bit of craft that had made our guns too hot to handle. But he could only do that with the power of the House of Morton. I was overseas with no such spiritual fountainhead. But what the heck.

"Jesus, Lord and Savior, please disable their guns!"

For most of my life, I'd taken God and his miracles for granted. Mission after mission I was his instrument; I said the words, and he made them so. What had been a sacred duty had become a job.

Then from outside came the yells and screams of the disarmed and the clacks of metal on pavement, and I was again in awe. *Thank you, Lord. Even if you've only given me seconds, I will not waste them.*

For I was already moving through the door and into an alleyway. Time dilated to an eternity in the blink of an eye as my tactical senses went into a spiritually accelerated sharpness. The glow of a weak bulb a couple of backdoors down lit the scene. The one private security camera dangled, lens pointing at the ground. No risk of violating the craft secret, though I had been hoping to attract some attention. The alleyway smelled of puke and urine, of damp and motorcycle exhaust.

The abductors had dropped their red-hot guns and backed away from the door. The two men held their hostages as shields in front of them, bringing my charge to an abrupt halt. Their free hands sought knives, and the red-headed woman already had some sort of Bowie blade at a tense ready. I took a step back toward the wall, limiting my foes to one-eighty degrees of opportunities. From the way they lifted and flared their noses to catch my scent, they were Gabble Ratchets, the British equivalent of the Gideons, though I couldn't tell whether these were government or underground. Only Car Man on my far left seemed relaxed—angry as he flexed his burnt hand, but relaxed. "Underground" didn't fit him; "veteran, elite, and professional" did.

"Don't move, or we kill them," said the Ratchet woman in some non-standard Brit Isles accent, speaking loudly as if she didn't care who heard, or maybe she was still deafened from the club's loud music. Car Man grimaced, but nodded in approval of the threat. The club women's eyes darted, confused and finding only terror. One of them had north Indian or Pakistani features; the other looked to have south China somewhere in her lineage. *Not clipping the more numerous Anglo-Saxon roses.* I wondered if that meant something.

"I'm here," I said, dropping into normal time. "*For Christ's sake, let them go.*"

Perhaps this prayer moved the Ratchets a twinge, but they didn't comply. I looked closer, and saw why my commands hadn't worked, though my prayer to disable their guns had. The Ratchets had monitor plugs in their ears like some musicians and soldiers wore, so they could block out my words. Their eye gear was capable of head-mounted display, which I was betting could obscure the motion of my lips. For them, any loss of vision and hearing would be worth the trade-off; I could still try command, but I wouldn't get the strong and immediate results I needed for combat. Dead certain now—they had come prepared specifically for me, and maybe the airport limo had been about capture, but this was a kill squad.

Car Man, with naked cold eyes and exposed ears, seemed not to care about my commands. But two others were still vulnerable, and I'd remove them from the equation. "God loves you," I told the club women. "*Sleep.*"

In an instant, the women were inert weight in their captors' hands. Car Man grimaced again with something like embarrassment, then made a little shooing gesture with his hand. Ratchet woman ordered, "Just drop the feckin' girls and get the bloody major."

The men did as they were told, and the dancing queens splashed down into cold, dirty puddles. I tried another prayer: "*Lord, disable their knives,*" but whatever spiritual power had worked the gun miracle was gone now, so the Ratchets advanced on me with their long knives. Car Man struck a match and lit a cigarette in his cupped hands. I was aware again of the empty space at my side. I had always thought

I'd go down with the Family sword in my hand. Now both that and my primary spiritual power had been stripped.

Against the long odds, I again stepped into the accelerated frame of spiritual combat. I dodged the knife blow and deflected the arm of the man nearest me. Then I went in close and forced the knife from his hand and used him in an orbital swing into his colleague before elbowing his face hard enough to hear the satisfactory crack of his heads-up glass wear and his nose. I was now within the reach of the second man, and I forced his knife as well, trying to steal it for myself, but it flew out of his hand, so I boxed his earplugs with my fists. Two down for a four count.

But even as the second man reeled away, the woman said "*slow*" and "*heavy*," and as I too slowly turned to face her, I had to stumble back to avoid her first slash. She caught me with the back swing, nicking my raised forearms, ruining my nice jacket. Then, I was crouched back against the wall, and the other two men were up again and on her flanks. This was it. *Into your hands I commend my spirit.*

FIVE

Y ou retrieved the major. Good." A new voice, the click of her shoes echoing down the alleyway. Commander Marlow had arrived, perhaps to finish me off. I found this oddly comforting. She wore a long, white fur coat, with seemingly no concern for PETA, the muddy streets, or her effect on me. Car Man twitched with conflicting silent signals, but Ratchet Woman just said, "Yes, ma'am."

Retrieved the Major. Marlow did not sound like one of my executioners. I gave her the benefit of the doubt. "Commander, they're dangerous . . ."

"That's enough from you, Endicott. All right, then, let's get him into my car."

Marlow moved toward us. The expressions on the Ratchets' faces were all wrong. This was not part of their plan.

Marlow kept talking. "You weren't going to do him here, were you? Just because there aren't any cams doesn't make this a good place. You were seen."

Car Man had thrown his cigarette to the ground in disgust and was reaching under his coat, probably for his own knife. They would kill Marlow.

I brought up my bloody arms. "Don't you dare touch her!"

Marlow's shoulders sank; she glared at me in exasperation. "Major, how many times do I have to tell you . . ." But as her right hand reached up to slap me, her left hand tucked under her coat and retrieved something longer and thinner than what Car Man would find.

Sometimes spiritual power is just enhanced sleight of hand. As her right hand threatened me, her left threw the object to me. In a flash, I snagged it out of the air. My sheathed sword.

The combat was short and intense. I had seen my family and comrades fight. I'd seen the ineffable dance of the Morton school of Native American–inspired martial arts. But I'd never seen anything like Marlow. She was like some warrior angel out of *Jesus Christ, Superstar*. The flow—not anticipatable, visible only in retrospect, like a river wild, with limbs that, as if acting on their own initiative, found human bodies to be target-rich environments, full of collateral damage. As she fought, she spoke what sounded like Latin—the charm of British public schools mixed with craft. I stuck to plain English prayer.

We hurt all of the Ratchets pretty badly, but they'd probably live. Car Man had again disappeared. The club girls remained asleep. I stared at Marlow. She was winded, but even as her chest worked, her face remained focused, as if still seeking targets. "Never seen combat, Major?"

I wanted to say, *no, not like this, never so beautiful.* Instead, I resheathed my blade and quipped, "Thank you for the sword, but I really would have preferred a gun just now."

"Right, so you could bless the bloody bullets? Did you really have to bring God into this? Isn't that somewhat blasphemous?"

I ignored her and pulled a plug from the ear of one of the men. It could be some nasty craft, but I needed to hear, as I expected this to be used against me again. Holding it close, I heard noise cancellation plus "*Stay on mission*" in a continuous loop, delivered by a steady, craft-inflected voice. *Stay on mission.* Good advice, if I knew what the mission was. It was nice being saved, but not my usual position, and Marlow's reappearance had that schemes-within-schemes sort of timing.

I turned back to her. Down the alleyway, she had retrieved an old khaki duffel bag. "What brought you here?" I asked.

"Your third man," she said. She was pulling stuff out of the bag—motorcycle helmets and leathers.

"What about him?"

"I didn't hire a bloody third man. He didn't show on any of our cameras, and I didn't see him at the crash."

"He ran off just now," I said.

"A bloody Renfield," she said, practically spitting the words. "Running our Ratchets. Here, put this on." She handed me one of helmets. It was matte black with a tinted visor.

"No, nothing suspicious looking about this at all," I said, but I put on the helmet, keeping the visor raised for the moment. "So he has serious stealth."

She took off her fur coat and stuffed it in the duffle. She revealed a shoulder holster with a sidearm, perhaps a Walther PPK, that she had never drawn during the fight. My eye also caught the yellow of a golden cross necklace as she dryly said, "Yes, serious stealth, unless you're lying about the third man in your car."

In answer, I gestured at the scene around us.

"Right, then. Wear this." She handed me an aviator jacket. On the back was stitched a Venus/female symbol with the cross pointed to the right side and a partial Union Jack within its circle.

"Um . . ." This seemed more embarrassment than even I should have to face in twenty-four hours.

She pointed at her own version. "I'm wearing the same," as if that answered any objection. After an inadequate wipe at the blood on my arms, I put on my jacket, and it fit better than I would have thought.

"This for the security cameras?"

"It's not for the summer collection in Paris," she said. She tossed me an empty messenger bag and threw another one over her shoulder. "Let's move." She put down her visor and ran down the alleyway, and I followed her. We turned, and turned again. She opened a doorway—it was a twenty-four-hour sex shop. We cut through, and I was happy that everything was a bit dim through my visor.

Parked outside the sex shop was a touring motorcycle, a serious bike that would seat two people, but with excess chrome and a laughable number of mirrors on it. "What happened to your car?"

"It's too well known," she said. "This will be harder to recognize."

Under the long seat ran a tube that may have been designed for the bike's tools or rolled-up plans and posters or an umbrella, for all I knew. I secured my sword there, then gestured at the bike in the vain hope that Marlow might let me drive it. Marlow shook her head as she threw her leg over the machine and started the motor. I climbed on behind her. Marlow gave a single trial rev of the motor, and we were off.

"What is the farsight game that you're playing, Major?" Marlow's clear voice in my ear surprised me. Our helmets were rigged with wireless, so we could talk during the ride. Marlow sounded unhappy with finding herself on my side.

"You think H-ring told me?" I said. "Look, I'm on a flight out of Gatwick tomorrow. Just get me on it. We can deal with the fallout long distance."

"You're not getting on any flight tomorrow."

What would they do, stop me at security? "I appreciate your concern, but . . ."

"Any passengers onboard with you would be at risk."

"They'd blow up the plane?"

"They burned out your hotel room. Unless you did that yourself." She paused, as if thinking something through. "How did you get those Ratchets to drop their guns?"

"Blasphemous prayer," I said. Then, realizing that was actually a very good question, I said, "Sorry. Let me get back to you on that." Other than an unexpected miracle, I had no idea where the power for that disarming prayer might have come from.

We were moving fast, west and north and away from the heart of London. The cold drizzle sprayed and accumulated across me; the wind stole heat even through my helmet. I was underdressed for conditions, and I had put the aviator jacket on over damp clothes. On the other hand, the chill was helping me to keep calm and carry on as I sat snugly behind Marlow and tried to hold my hands at my sides, whatever the difficulty in balance. I kept reminding myself that she was another spiritual soldier, just uncomfortably close. I tried my spiritual exercises as a preventative against pneumonia, attempting to control my breath and body heat. A weatherperson would have been nice right now.

We kept going at speed. Our destination was definitely outside of London. "Where are we going?" I asked.

"It won't take too long." Not an answer, but it fit with my guess, so I let it pass.

"Who are we going to see?"

"He's the former C, the former chief of MI13."

"What's his name?"

"We call him the Don. You should address him as sir."

The Don, as in the Professor? That almost confirmed our destination, but as a term of address, "Don" sounded more like a crime boss. He probably had touches of both. "What's his family?"

"You don't need to know."

No surprise. But she could tell me one thing. "You trust him?"

"With the safety of the realm and my life, in that order."

The tactical paranoia hit. It never did any good to try to play the farsight game when you were a piece in it, but since Marlow seemed to care about this man, I let some of my thinking slip out. "Maybe we shouldn't bring him into this. Isn't this exactly where farsight would see you heading? This could go badly." Though whether for him or us, I didn't say.

No matter. Marlow ignored me.

It was no surprise when we rode into Oxford. In the early hours' dark, I could only appreciate snippets of gothic structures as we passed through what seemed to be the middle of town. After traveling mostly along back roads, this path seemed odd.

"Why this route?" I asked.

"It might confuse the trail."

Through spiritual sight, I could see her point. The ghost map of the city differed surprisingly little from the current buildings, and the whole area glowed like Time Square instead of a college town. London was vast with history and power; Oxford was concentrated.

We turned right—north, I thought. Marlow made a warding gesture. The only spiritually significant building I saw was a pub, with a sign featuring some raptor carrying a baby. Oh, that place: The Eagle and Child. C. S. Lewis, J. R. R. Tolkien, and the other Inklings had met there regularly, as had some of the Oxford elite of British spiritual power. Far too much practitioner talk and too many code phrases had spilled out here along with the English beer, and the writers had been listening. As the Endicotts and Mortons knew, the writers were always listening.

We left the college area behind and came to a residential suburb. A couple of turns, and we pulled up in front of a quiet home with two gables facing front. A wooden slat fence was topped with a crosshatched wood screen that might serve as a trellis of some kind, but was cleared now.

"What should I do with my sword?" I said. Bringing a sword into a stranger's house was a touchy business.

"I wouldn't leave it with the bike," said Marlow.

"Thieves?" I asked.

"Owners," she said. "On behalf of HMG, I borrowed the bike from the English people."

"You stole a motorcycle?"

"One of my many gifts," she said. "But we may need to leave by different means, and in a hurry. He has a place by the door for such things."

As I removed my sword, Marlow added a warning: "Take care. The Don will detect any deception, no matter how covered with craft. It's the gift he used to crush the penetration of MI13. You'd better be honest."

"That won't be a problem," I said.

For a moment, her face betrayed the pressed lips and tilted glance of a mother disappointed at her prevaricating child. Then, all was smooth and cool again.

At the fence gate, I felt a ward. "*Bhili*," said Marlow. The ward vanished, and she opened the gate.

"What did you say?" I whispered.

"It was proto-Indo-European," she said. Why didn't the English use their own language?

An archway of trees made a path from the gate to the door. The shape was as symmetrical and even as a cathedral's nave, the perfect expression of constant and patient gardening. To the side of the door was a box that looked like something for old-fashioned milk delivery. Marlow took the sidearm from her holster and put it in the box, keeping me in view for all but an instant.

I gestured at the milk box. "Do you trust this man this much?"

"When the service was riddled with craft moles who maneuvered him into professional exile, he remained true. Then he came back and destroyed them all."

That sounded familiar, so I just nodded my head. Despite my misgivings, I left my sword in the elongated milk box. Marlow had already demonstrated that she understood its value to me, and if I didn't trust her at all, I should just hop back on the bike and go.

Marlow knocked at the door, seemingly unconcerned with the hour or whether the Don was at home. The house wards felt fresh and strong even if the stone was ancient.

A minute passed, then the door opened and revealed an old man wearing the incongruous combination of bed slippers and a tweed jacket. He had silver hair and defiantly good teeth for his generation. His face wasn't so much wrinkled as economically etched with a few deep lines. He had a Roman nose long enough to detect malodorous schemes against the realm, and eyes that sparked with the good and evil that they must have seen. He was the perfect English image of a modern wizard.

"Grace, how good to see you." He took her hand in both of his. His voice had a slight quaver. "We've been worried about you. Is this the American?"

Grace said, "Yes." We came in from the cold.

CHAPTER

SIX

Attucks met the three civvies at a craft-service safe house in Georgetown on Dumbarton Street near Rock Creek Park. A narrow nineteenth-century row house surrounded by covert-friendly neighbors, including his own place, it was ideal for a meeting that had to be off the records of even H-ring and Langley, and more pleasant than his office below the Pentagon. He would have held the gathering at his own house (he hosted a regular Sunday brunch for practitioners), but he didn't want to involve his wife, Katrina Hutchinson, cousin of the late colonel. Kat was a PRECOG captain, and probably would twig to something going on, but after what had happened to the Russians, he wasn't going to read her into this op, much less bring her along.

He had arranged this meeting after Endicott's call, when Langley confirmed that Endicott's near-term return was even more unlikely than his survival. The four magi sat with their late-afternoon decaf coffees around a domestic, round dining table, assessing one another with skill both mundane and preternatural.

Attucks's plan involved using the best that H-ring had to offer, but Eddy had told him that, without the Mortons and Endicott, no number of current military practitioners would ensure success, and that he'd have to find other world-class firepower whose loyalty could be trusted. His three guests weren't currently in the service, but these others had cause to hate Roderick Morton and the Left Hand, as each of them had lost someone in the craft assassinations he had inspired through Madeline and Abram. They'd been content with quiet mourning only because they had thought that the perpetrators had died in the destruction of H-ring, but they'd all come to Washington when they'd learned of Roderick's survival, and they all wanted to know the same thing.

"When and where do we get to kill him?" asked the woman called Queen. She came from Louisiana, land of so many magi, and dominated the craft world of New Orleans, mixing a blend of the African, Celtic, and Cajun lore of her ancestors with her American magic. The government had allowed her continued practice, as she'd served for a brief time and had sent her tribute of children to fight the craft wars, "to die for the magical descendants of dead white folks." She hadn't known the Left-Hand art of animating the dead, so she'd been as shocked as anyone when one of her sons returned home as a zombie, and even more surprised that the zombie had tried to kill her.

"Soon," said Attucks. "And you'll be there."

"You don't trust us with the details." said the man called Longhouse. A descendant of Hiawatha, he had traveled from the Upper Peninsula of Michigan, where he had lived with the tall, pale Lumberman. The family of Lumberman's father had cleared forests from Finland to the Midwest, but Lumberman had chosen to follow his mother's peripatetic lineage and plant trees. One had to follow the times. Lumberman and Longhouse used their craft to protect and nurture their saplings. Lumberman's surprise had come when his family's ancient axe, now a weapon of defense, had seemed to turn on its master. But it had been Lumberman's own hands betraying him. Longhouse had thanked the trees for their dead branches as he had burned his dismembered lover's limbs, which had still twitched with the evil animus that had possessed them.

"Trust," said Attucks, "has nothing to do with it. Our opponent is the greatest farseer in the world today. If too many people are even thinking about the details, the timeline will grow in farsight prominence, and our chance will be lost."

"Is the chance real?" asked the man called Alchemist from San

Francisco. He and his father had played with chemistries that conventional science and their unconventional Chinese ancestors had never combined. One day, a healing balm they'd developed had eaten away the father's hands and then had rapidly consumed the rest of his body. Alchemist had tried to douse his father with possible antidotes, but while his father still had lungs and a mouth he screamed in terror the names of the transdimensional gods of the Left-Hand Mortons.

A real chance? Attucks decided he could throw these vengeful allies that much of a bone. "Langley sees no timeline for Roderick beyond this operation. When we act, he's gone."

Attucks wanted to add that he was probably sacrificing three of his finest officers overseas to bring about that outcome, but he didn't, and not just from secrecy. His mother had warned him that "revenge was never grateful," and he wouldn't take the lack of gratitude of those present kindly just now.

S cherie slept. She had no idea if she flew by plane, sailed by high-speed vessel, or rode by ambulance. By the time she came to, cotton mouthed and confused but with her pain thoroughly managed, she was in something about the size of an airport shuttle van. She raised her head, and through the strongly tinted windows she saw a dry, hilly countryside that looked nothing like greater Istanbul. They were on a highway, and the snatches of signs had Greek letters. She was in Greece.

Though she was surrounded by medical supplies and devices, she also saw boxes marked in Greek and English with "Ministry of Culture." So the van was not an ambulance, and she was being smuggled to her destination. But where was that?

Weak, and not sure of the craft of all present, she tried speaking English. "Where are we going?"

"Shhh." A woman seated to the right of Scherie's gurney smiled at her. "Rest. We're nearly there."

Scherie remained quiet, but she continued to assess her surroundings in case she needed to act. To her left, Madeline appeared, though she had faded back to black-and-white outlines.

"You didn't kill me," whispered Scherie.

"You are useless to us dead," said Madeline.

"What use?"

But Madeline ignored her question. "We won't be following you to your destination. That place is inimical to us. But we'll be waiting for you. Time is short, so don't be lazy."

"Lazy?" Scherie's anger had returned, but Madeline was already gone.

Scherie slept more, until their winding turns woke her again, feeling nausea along with everything else. They were driving up a roadway along a decent-sized mountain, great gray rocky outcroppings to one side and a long drop to the other.

They pulled to a halt. A Greek and English sign said that they were near the Delphi Archaeological Museum.

"Sorry, but we have to sneak you in." They unfolded a "Ministry of Tourism" tarp and covered her with it. She felt herself being carried into the building, then into an elevator that went down farther than a small museum's basement should go. From the elevator, they bore her for another minute, then removed the tarp and placed her on a bed. Though underground with no windows, the illumination was like sunlight and seemed to carry warmth with it. She drifted off again.

Scherie dreamed. Dale was surrounded by darkness, and the darkness was going to consume him, eat him like acid until he was part of it.

"Fuck, no!" She was up with her hand at the man's throat and a spell of death ready to speak.

"*Easy, daughter.*" A woman's voice, as the man was having difficulty breathing, much less speaking. Aghast at herself, Scherie let go. "He's a healer from the Asclepion. He came all the way up from Epidauros just to see you."

The man cleared his throat and frowned. He was elderly and thin. He could have been ninety, though he radiated so much health that he might have been a thirty-year-old with wrinkled skin. "I was finished anyway."

"I'm so sorry." Scherie was feeling much more alive. "Thank you."

The man, still frowning, nodded his head and left. Scherie turned her attention to the woman. She was heavy and round in the Greek fashion, but stood straight, like royalty, more regal than the craft aristos of America.

Scherie decided to introduce herself. "I'm Scherie." She didn't get into the complexities of last names. Then she said hello in Greek, which was about the limit of her knowledge, and added, "Thank you for saving me." That she was saved, and not just in another trap, was a big assumption, but in this case it didn't hurt to assume the best.

"You're of Persia, aren't you? A Persian at Delphi. The gods were always great ones for irony." The woman laughed gently and smiled like sunlight on a wine-dark sea. "I'm the Pythia. You are here as a suppliant, but I have much to ask you, to ask of you. You have heard the bad news about Roderick Morton?"

"Yes."

"Then you know we do not have much time. We have a lot to tell each other. I do not know yet whether we can trust each other, but perhaps we must. The Left Hand is rising again, and whether we wish it or not, we will go to war."

In his agony at the shrine, Dale had only one comfort: the revenants were not killing him outright. Their binding must block that, or they'd do it all the time.

The spirits whirled around him as if driven by cyclones, though every physical object was motionless. They were forcing their thoughts into him. For all their intensity, images of the emperor and empire didn't find much purchase. But their love for the land, the nation, the people, were so akin to his own that it took all he had not to sink into confusion, and from there into a new, alien certainty.

Mind buckling, Dale counted his few resources. He had his craft, but in a contest of sheer power, he was a fly against a windshield. He had words, but nothing with which to bargain, perhaps not even a recognized status.

He tried bargaining anyway. He yelled above the howling: "I am a guest here!"

The shrine quieted long enough to reply. "You are mortal, and not of our kind. Be silent, and submit."

"Why are you doing this?" But the shrine wouldn't speak again to him, and the howling rose.

So much for the rights of guests. Dale's thoughts blew away in the spiritual wind, or shattered like glass in the shrine's whining keen. He needed help, but the only aid that could reach him quickly enough through space and time would be his Morton dead.

Dale's blood lay pooled on the ground, frozen immobile like everything else, but available to help his call to the departed. He wouldn't summon the Left Hand here to contact this awesome power; Dale would rather die. So, he went down his orthodox list in chronological order. "Dad, a little help?" "Grandpa, can you hear me?" Then, with desperation, "Captain Richard Morton, please report for duty."

No response but the continuing keen of the shrine. Dick Morton was Dale's great-grandfather. Great-Grandpa had been a good man, a great man, but he was not one of the friendly ancestors. Bumping heads against the old British mages, he'd had the audacity to challenge their weather ability on the eve of D-day, and won. Then, he had joined up with Third Army as Patton's own wise guy, and he'd nearly died during the winter of '44–45 in the final takedown of the Teutonic

Knights. He had visited Japan during the occupation before he'd been killed in Korea defending the retreat to Pusan. His son, Grandpa, still shuddered to think of him. When Dale was a kid, he'd thought Grandpa, in the flesh or spirit, seemed fearsome. Great-Grandpa still seemed that way.

It had been too much to hope he'd come. Dale tried to think of another ancestor who was sufficiently recent and powerful enough to act for him. But he couldn't think another thought, could not speak another word. Dale's head felt like it would both split open and implode as the shrine's spirits whirled faster.

Then complete stillness.

The stillness was a harbinger. In an instant, Dale was face-to-face with Richard Morton's ghost, ready for service in World War II fatigues; the man who in life had calmed any storm.

The old revenant glared hard at Dale. "You," he spat, not hiding his contempt, though Dale wasn't sure what he'd ever done to deserve it. "Can't handle anything by yourself, can you?"

"Not this, sir."

As if finally deigning to give the shrine some of his attention, Great-Grandpa nodded over his shoulder. "What is this, some kind of doomsday machine?"

"Yes, sir." Only then did Dale realize the strangeness of being able to think and speak again. A small miracle—the force of the shrine spirits had lightened up on him and played over Great-Grandpa's outline like dark flame.

"By what right do you come here?" said the shrine.

"I'm here under the authority granted by the Showa Emperor himself." He cited the relevant treaties, known and secret, chapter and verse, dating back to the surrender and occupation. Dale had forgotten this aspect of his ancestor. "And I am one of your kind." The dead.

"You may speak."

Great-Grandpa turned again to Dale. "Well, soldier, what do you have to ask that was important enough to risk the Morton line and perhaps the entire world for?"

The words slapped Dale down, but it was far too late to undo the risks he had taken. The only way out was forward. "Ask them what my father was looking for."

Great-Grandpa seemed all the more disgusted that this madness was genetic. But he asked.

The spirits whirled clockwise, then counterclockwise. "When your father asked his questions, we did not see the danger. We see it now."

More dangerous than you? thought Dale. "Tell them that the truly dangerous didn't want anyone to know about my father's quest."

"We take the long view," said the shrine. A very creepy echo of his father's words.

"You're getting nowhere," said Great-Grandpa.

"Suggestions?"

"You've put nothing on the table. Treat this as a negotiation. What do you have that they'd want?"

It was true. The shrine seemed hungry, craving something besides more souls. Had his father failed because he didn't have what they wanted? What did he have that his father hadn't? Then he knew—not what, but who.

"I know someone who can free any who want to leave here," said Dale. "My wife. Tell them."

The howl of the shrine went quiet. Then, what had been a unified voice broke into schizophrenic civil war. "We are bound forever." "No *gaijin* could free us." "Strike now, venture all."

Dale asked, "Do you sense any deceit?"

The spirits grew still and quite. "If she can do so, send for her. Have her do it now."

No good to lie to them. "It'll be a few days, maybe weeks."

"Then you'll stay until she comes for you!"

Dale's mind would be long gone in another objective minute. He struggled with what to say, what he could offer. But the howling was rising, rising . . .

A voice in the storm. Dale wasn't sure he understood. "What did you say?" asked the shrine.

"I'll be your hostage," said Great-Grandpa.

"No," said Dale.

"No what, soldier?" said Great-Grandpa, bringing all his intimidation to bear on Dale.

Not this time. "No, Captain. I don't enjoy pulling rank, but as a major, I'm ordering you not to stay here."

Great-Grandpa smiled and laughed. It was a terrifying thing. "Try to stop me, Major." Then he winked at Dale. "Though you've got brass cojones, I'll give you that."

"They'll crush you."

"They'll try."

"Wait. At least make them answer me first."

So Great-Grandpa posed Dale's question again. In the voice of a million tombs, the shrine replied, "Your father asked where magic comes from."

"What?" If it wasn't so tragic, Dale would've laughed. *Like a little craft baby, wondering why the sky was blue.* "What did you tell him?"

"Most of it comes from the land or people's need. He knew that. But a very small portion of power leaks in from elsewhere."

Oh oh. Dale had an idea of what that might mean. "Where?"

"There are worlds where things like us are all that remain."

The old terrible gods of the Left Hand? Perhaps. "And how does the power get here?"

"Like calls to like."

"You're in touch with these worlds?"

"That is all we told your father. Our deal is complete. Go."

"No, one other thing. Where did he go next?"

But this time, Great-Grandpa didn't echo him. "They aren't listening anymore. Some of them are getting very impatient with you. And some don't want you to keep your promise. You need to leave."

"But where do I go?"

"Anywhere but here. Go." Great-Grandpa smiled ironically. "Don't be too long."

Dale tried to turn away, and nearly tumbled to the ground as his body moved again in ordinary time. A crowd of visiting school kids were filing toward the museum. He couldn't see his great-grandfather anymore.

Think. Dale's father had gone on from here. Where? Like his father, Dale had only the thinnest of trails to follow. But Dad would have also seen the possible connection to the Left-Hand gods. Dale knew a trail that might lead to them. It would be an evil road, so despite his sense of urgency, he was glad that he had to call Scherie first, and bring her here to free these spirits and his great-grandfather's ghost. Even though Great-Grandpa was dead, Dale wouldn't leave Family here for anything.

Screw protocol. Back home and in Europe, it was yesterday evening. As he walked away from the shrine, he dialed Scherie's number. No answer. He dialed Endicott's number. No answer. Then, with growing unease and despite wishing to remain off their radar, he dialed H-ring.

They told him the news and the last known locations. He didn't ask for more details or question the delay. He ran. *Hold on, Scherie, my love. Hold on, Endicott, you asshole. Wait for me, Roderick. I'm coming.*

PART III

TINKER, TAILOR, SOLDIER, MAGE

I believed thou wert greater than Merlin;
and truly in magic thou art. But prophecy is
greater than magic.
—Mark Twain

If a man were porter of hell-gate, he should
have old turning the key.
—William Shakespeare

I will not cease from Mental Fight,
Nor shall my Sword sleep in my hand:
Till we have built Jerusalem,
In England's green & pleasant Land.
—William Blake

O Lord our God arise,
Scatter her enemies,
And make them fall:
Confound their politics,
Frustrate their knavish tricks,
On Thee our hopes we fix:
God save us all.
—"God Save the Queen"

The Don's house felt like the House of Morton when I first entered it: sentient, hostile, and upset. In the hall was another Morton touch: an antique clock ticked, and ticked. It was unclear whether we had woken the Don up. Either he didn't have much farsight or forewarning, or he didn't want to show that he had them.

Farsight, and a sentient house. Maybe that was why Grace hadn't worried about bringing us here. Farsight had trouble peeking into these old Family houses.

Grace. He was calling her Grace, so I'd started thinking of her that way. Not very professional, but probably inevitable.

We sat in his den, Grace and I in chairs facing his. The remnants of a real wood fire were still red in the fireplace. Without the contemporary courtesy of asking, the Don lit his pipe and began to smoke. The pipe triggered my memory of him from his file in H-ring. This was the last scion of House Dee, Christopher. His file photo was out-of-date (he was naturally publicity shy), but he seemed to have reached old age early in trade for being unchanged for years. His true age was subject to dispute. Some said he'd fought in the Second World War, but he didn't seem that old to me.

On the mantel was a photo of his dead wife. Odd that they let him, the last practicing descendant of John Dee, get through life without begetting children.

As I sat, the old man made a lazy gesture with his hand, and I noticed a tea service laid out on the table to Grace's left. Perhaps he had expected us. "Please, you've had a long evening in the weather. Have something warm to drink. I would offer you both some brandy, but . . ."

"Tea will do nicely, sir, thank you," said Grace.

I agreed. "Thank you, sir." As I watched Grace pour, I wondered again about her cross necklace. Did she avoid strong drink on moral principle, or was she merely concerned with remaining alert?

Now that I was looking for it, the evidence that the old man was of the Dee Family was everywhere. The Dee coat of arms was painted above the mantel, which I recognized from its motto, "Hic Labor"— "This is the hard task."

In the 1580s, the other court mages of Queen Elizabeth pressured the first well-known practitioner in the line, John Dee, into exile. But when Dee heard of the gathering of the Spanish Armada, he covertly left Bohemia for the coast of France, eluding the agents of France's House of Guise. There, Dee participated in a great working with the weathermen of England against the Spanish fleet, summoning the winds that first delayed the Armada, then disadvantaged its ships in the sea fights, and finally destroyed it.

Like any good Puritan descendant, I thought Dee and his colleagues were heroes. Even if the Dee Family's beliefs differed from ours, John Dee had helped to create the great "Protestant Wind" that had changed history, and had allowed United States history to happen.

With a calm, benevolent aspect, Dee waited for us to begin. "Sir," said Grace, "we have another mole problem."

"I hope you don't expect me to root out this viper. The last case nearly finished me, and I would hate to expire with an investigation still open."

"No, sir, this won't be your operation. But some of our own have been attempting to kill the major, and for a short while I need help protecting him. I would also appreciate your insights as to who might be behind this."

"You are safe from any pursuit here," said the Don, turning his head to address me. "When the Magic Circus was compromised, they still could not see within here, and no small number can enter against the will of the House." His words reminded me too much of the House of Morton to be completely reassuring.

After Grace outlined the events of the day, she and the Don began to speculate on the treason within MI13, but they used internal crypt-onyms and jargon, so I couldn't follow, and it was clear they didn't want me to. The Don's voice had the lullaby quality of lecturing pro-fessors everywhere.

Instead of listening, I exercised my broader curiosity and situational awareness. The polished wooden bookcases against the walls held the works I might have expected to see. A couple of shelves held the local Oxford eavesdroppers and spiritual veterans: Roger Bacon, Lewis Car-roll, Charles Williams, Tolkien, Lewis. A hand-bound version of Spen-cer's *Faerie Queen* was next to a DVD box set of *The Prisoner*. Other than an annotated *Macbeth*, the Don had no Shakespeare in this room—the Bard's views of the craft were, at best, theatrical. Pride of prominent place went to the great cautionary tales on the perils of the pursuit of the Left-Hand way: Shelley, Stoker, Wilde, Tolkien again. *Dracula*, *Frankenstein*, *Dorian Gray*, and the "Akallabêth" section of *The Silmarillion* were not meant so literally as Poe's tale of Roderick and Madeline, but they were sharper on the critical moral points. Left-Hand craft would destroy your soul, your loved ones, and eventually, like a viral plague, your whole nation. These shelves constituted a road map of the English spiritual world, for those with the eyes to see.

Only a few non-literary objects were on display, the most impor-tant being a bust of Richard III, the tragic hero of English practi-tioners. On a side table, a chessboard had a few pieces moved in an opening of a game.

My eyes blurred. I was very, very tired. To doze by the fire would be marvelous. We could all doze together.

But even as my thoughts began to dissolve into dream-like non se-quiturs, a noise, light as a draft through a keyhole, whispered into my ear. *No. No. No.* Each "o" lasted a whole breath, a low moan of hate and perhaps fear. The House of Dee's focus was now upon me, and it would not let me rest.

Typical. Sentient houses seemed to take a while to warm up to me. I sat up, paying greater attention. Only a few minutes had passed, but time felt precious.

The Don noticed my renewed focus. "Would you like to report home, Major? My phone or computer is at your service." He pointed at a black landline phone. His timing was (unsurprisingly) uncanny. I very much wanted to report home, but all indications were that the local spiritual service was compromised, and therefore national signal intelligence could be directed against me. If I used my phone, I didn't think they would be able to decrypt what I was saying in a timely way, but they might find me. I could use the Don's phone or computer, but that involved a level of trust I didn't yet feel, even though the Don's manner was easy and charming, and he was the first person in this country who seemed happy to see me.

"Thank you, sir," I replied, "but no. I think we should discuss my next move." *Away from here.*

"Agreed. Grace, dear, we've forgotten our guest. We can speculate about our housecleaning later." He chuckled, as if suddenly thinking of something. "Your willingness to help him is noble, a true beau geste given his family background."

"My duty, sir," she said, not amused at all. Dear Lord, what had my ancestors done now?

"Oh, I'm certain you've exceeded your duty here," said the Don.

"Excuse me," I asked, "are you talking about Abram?" If so, they had taken his sins rather personally. But the House was flaring in anger—did it dislike my ancestors too?

"No, not Abram," said the Don. "Stephen Endicott."

"Oh, him," I said. The Mortons used to bring Stephen up as a reminder that not all evil was explicitly Left-Hand.

"So," said Dee, rubbing his hands together like an eager grandfather, "here we have one of those historical ironies so common in our

vocation. One of you is the descendant of men who made their for-
tunes trading other men as chattel. The other, a descendant of the enslaved, and more—a descendant of Tory craftspeople who left your
unfree Republic. When given the choice, those craftspeople fought
for their British liberators and followed us home after our defeat at
your hands."

Huh. This was a different, less friendly tack by the Don. Yes, it was
true: Endicott money had been in the slave trade, and if there was one
great sinner in my lineage before the revelation about Abram, it was
Stephen, who had conducted the trade personally. But did he have to
highlight this for Grace?

I glanced at Grace, wondering how seriously she took this family
history. She was nodding in grim agreement. *Great, another family
with a long-standing vendetta against the Endicotts.* I wanted to argue, to talk about my family's penance, but then I realized we still
hadn't gotten around to discussing my departure, and we had more
serious problems than whether Grace liked me as a person. Or at least
my brain was insisting on those priorities.

All the while, the House's murmurs of anger continued. I was anxious, on edge, and I didn't know why. But before we discussed my escape, I could deal with one source of tension. "Is there someplace I
could wash up?" What I really needed to do was piss like a weatherman, but that didn't seem like the right thing to say.

"The kitchen is out and to the left," said the Don. His obtuseness
had to be deliberate, but I said nothing—I could find the bathroom,
or the WC, or the loo, or whatever they called it here.

The one I found was next to a master bedroom that had been set
up on the first floor, allowing the Don to use the stairs less frequently.
When I flicked on the light, everything seemed ungodly bright.

In order to be somewhat truthful, after I relieved myself I rolled
up my slashed sleeves to wash my face and hands and forearms, bloody
from the fight—they might need something more. Once when I had
visited the Mortons, Dale had told me, "Don't talk like House isn't

there." So with the cover of the running water, I had some direct words with the House of Dee. "You know, I realize I come on a bit strong, but other Houses have grown to like me. So just give me a break, and I'll be out of your hair, or halls, or whatever."

A breeze like a sigh of exasperation chilled me. Oh, well, that would have to do. The sink's water turned a dirty red as it ran over my arms and hands and down the drain. *Guess I did need to wash up.* The red thinned, and the draining pink seemed to form squiggly lines pointing down and up. *I must be tired.* I splashed and rubbed my face, then looked up into the mirror to see if I had missed any grime or blood.

Lord help me—something was wrong with my face. I had a hint of a black-light glow. I shut off the bathroom light and saw the craft glow clearly. Oh no. I'd been touched by the Left Hand. Cursed. I couldn't trust myself. I needed to warn Grace and the Don. I . . .

Needed to get a fricken grip. The Left-Hand glow wasn't coming from me. I scanned around the bathroom, but always came back to the mirror. The mirror had some random fuzziness about its edges, as if some stealth craft had been applied, then broken.

"Major." From the other room, Grace's voice calling for me.

"Just a minute," I said.

I wasn't proud of prying into someone else's medicine cabinet, but the necessity was obvious. What evil could this old guy have in there?

A white cardboard box with a prescription label stood out from the common toiletries. Glycerin trinitrate—nitroglycerin for the old guy's heart? No, the box was the source of the glow. With no time for precautions, I opened it. Inside, I found a metal syringe, brass colored like the alchemical alloys I'd seen in Prague and H-ring, with a plastic cap over the needle. Most practitioners wouldn't have recognized it. I don't think I would have, except ever since Prague I'd been expecting it.

The waves of anger from the House were rising. No time for internal debate—I stashed the syringe in my jacket pocket. But the chessboard had reminded me to think a move ahead. I wouldn't run out there fighting like I had in Prague, but I needed to leave, preferably with Grace. That meant I would have to distract Dee for a moment once I returned. For that purpose, I looked, really looked, for some antiseptic. I didn't see any. Good.

I returned to the den, even as Grace was again calling for me. I thought I saw a momentary flicker of annoyance from the Don when I re-entered the room, like I was some buzzing insect. Then, with some of his previous charm, he asked, "Were you looking for something, Major?"

To play out my honest distraction, I showed him the cuts on my forearms. "I was looking for some antiseptic."

"You Americans are so fragile. Let me get you a first-aid kit."

Grace rose from her seat. "I'll get it, sir."

"No, Grace, I will," he said, sounding preemptive and a little snappish. He stood slowly and left the room.

Time to persuade Grace to leave. I whispered toward her ear. "We have to go. I found something Left-Hand in his bathroom."

"Left-Hand? I cannot stand that American euphemism for evil."

"Neither can I, but let's leave now and discuss it later."

Grace shook her head once in casual disgust. "Of course he has objects once used for evil here. They are the harmless trophies of a righteous life."

"I'm getting out of here," I insisted.

Grace's lips parted as if about to reply, but then her eyes widened, and her face lost its usual cool veneer. From the direction of Grace's gaze, I wasn't the immediate problem; the person who had just re-entered the room was.

"*Stay seated.*" The Don was casually pointing a gun at me. My mistake for letting an untrustworthy Dee out of my sight. The weapon looked like Grace's own Walther PPK, which the Don could have retrieved through inside access to the milk box. "*Major Endicott, do not move.*"

He was trying to command me. God help me, it felt like he was succeeding. Endicotts weren't used to being commanded—not a pleasant sensation. For now, I didn't attempt to resist and sat at perfect attention. His own power meant that I couldn't command him in turn, not here on his home ground—no more than I could have commanded Dale Morton in his House.

The Don sat, seeming at perfect ease as he addressed Grace. *"I'm sorry, dear, but he is with the other side."* He was using a subtle suasion with her. *"You can't see it as clearly, but he's glowing with his treason. He's choreographed this entire scenario. He suborned our own people. From what the House tells me, I suspect he was about to plant evidence against me."* In response to this last, Grace's face set back into its usual professional coolness. "Oh," continued the Don, "did he already say he'd found something?"

The House was now wailing in my ear: *Fool! Fool!* And I was— despite what the Don had just said, the House had been trying to help me all along. It had woken me from the attempt to lull me to sleep and guided me to his Left-Hand syringe. These old Houses didn't like it when their owners went bad.

Now that I was looking for it, I saw the glow coming from him. His pipe had provided a literal smoke screen, masking his unhealthy preservation in spiritual formaldehyde. His smile was ghastly, like a Red Death in training. I had a sense that dying here would be like all those who had died in the House of Morton—no one even saw their ghosts afterward.

"We'll have that information now, Major. How did you release Roderick? What did Abram teach you? Can you leave your body? Are you Abram, or are you Oliver Cromwell Endicott?"

Yes, I bet he wanted the answers to some of those questions, desperately. If he could figure out the Left-Hand secrets, he wouldn't need the supplier of his syringe. I saw ahead a couple of moves: this alchemical drug wasn't likely to provide immortality; instead, it was probably a life-extending mix that would keep him going long enough for the next step, a step that Roderick could provide.

The bit the Don had said about me being my dead father was to piss me off, so I channeled my anger in a different direction. "I have a question. If I'm so dangerous, why haven't you shot me yet? Afraid that might seem excessive to Grace?" And was that gun he was holding, like its U.S. service equivalent, chipped against shooting her, so that her opinion still mattered? I was betting it was.

"I'm sure my friend Grace can see that you're with the so-called Left Hand," he said. "If she's not yet certain, she will be when she sees what you've been carrying. *Hand it over.*"

Oh, he had been playing so well until then. He'd made two mistakes: trying the power of command twice on an Endicott, and showing his need. As if in response to his display of weakness, I felt again an external power that shouldn't be available to me here flow up through my feet. This time, though, I had an idea where it was coming from. *Thank you, House,* I thought. *I'll do what I can with it.*

As if obeying the Don's command, I brought out the syringe and offered it for a moment in my open hand, then grasped it tight and close. I smiled at him. "You want this? I'm guessing this stuff is pretty valuable, and pretty dangerous. I think to be safe, I should dispose of it right now. Detecting any deceit, Professor Dee?"

Could Grace see what I saw—a junkie's cold-sweat need? I couldn't tell. Her mentor, a perfect detector of deceit, could also lie pretty well.

So I kept talking. "Grace, how old is Chris here? Remarkably well preserved, isn't he? Do you think this is the usual reward for a righteous life of spiritual practice?"

"Dear," said the Don. "I hope he's not deceiving you. I need to know that you're with me on this if I'm going to be able to continue my questioning."

Grace gave him an irked look. "Sir, you know I hate his Family. I will never trust them."

"I don't mean to nitpick, but you've said a small untruth somewhere in there."

Grace's eyes went to the ceiling, and she replied like a corrected student. "Hate is against my Christian duty, so I do not truly hate them all."

"Very good," said the Don.

No, not very good at all. My dilemma was elegantly simple. If I went for the Don, Grace would assume I was the bad guy, and probably kill me. If I gave the Don even a flimsy excuse, he'd shoot me.

As if seeing the scenarios on my face, Grace said, "Give it up, Endicott."

I thought of one last way to complicate the situation and perhaps give me some maneuvering room. "Here, you take it," I said, offering my open palm toward her.

"No," she said emphatically, "to him."

Was there just a flash of something in her eyes, or was that just the most misleading of my Christian virtues, hope?

It didn't matter. I prepared my prayers and one request. With as much disregard for its safety as I could risk, I tossed the syringe to the Don, as I prayed like I had as a little boy: *Let's go fast, Jesus.*

The speed of the world slowed. The Don snagged the syringe. Still a blur at this speed, Grace was up and moving toward her former mentor. "*Still,*" he said. Grace froze, caught by the Don's word. She had tried to intervene.

With Grace on my side, I could act against the Don. I sprang for him and his gun. With the fluid grace of a young man, he stepped aside. His hand lashed out, and a dark spiritual force pushed me hard to the floor. "*Die,*" he said, bringing the pistol into line with my head.

But I had remembered how Abram and Joshua had taken the House of Morton with the help of the House itself, and even as he wished for my death, I made my request. "*Hit him, House.*"

The bust of Richard III flew at the Don, and though he dodged a direct hit, it jostled him, and he fired a round that splintered his wooden floor. He'd get me next time. "*Grace, in God's name, act!*"

In a heartbeat Grace was on the Don, though this time all the artistry of the alley fight was gone. She stripped him of the gun with her left hand, and with blow after blow, she pummeled him to the ground with her right fist. "Why?" she said. "Why? Why? Why?"

She was going to kill him.

I was up on my feet again. "Commander," I said. "We can't."

"I fucking well can," she replied.

"It fits the rogue narrative."

She stopped. "Right. Let's tie him up, then."

We bound him with the phone and computer cords. As we worked, the Don, animated by his hideous alchemical strength, regained consciousness. *"In Jehovah's name, not a word of craft,"* I commanded, and again I felt the power of the House add to my authority.

"Not a word," the Don agreed, and he leered through blood and pain at Grace. "A shame. Immortality would have suited you, though some of my colleagues want only Anglo-Saxon stock preserved. You saw me as a grandfather figure, I dare say. Sit on my lap, and we'll see what kind of grandfather I can be."

Grace slapped him once, hard. "Traitor." I saw the tears threaten in her eyes and knew in an instant that I hated this man more than I'd hated anyone in the spiritual world, present or past, for bringing this woman such sorrow. God forgive me, but it was true.

A noise put me back into combat awareness. It was a knock at the door. The Don chuckled quietly and whispered theatrically, "Here's a knocking indeed! If a man were porter of hell-gate, he should have old turning the key."

From the door came a voice. "Professor, sir, are you all right? Let us in."

The House had locked the door. "Excellent work, House," I said. "Please continue to keep them out." Then, realizing that I didn't know whether the would-be assistants to the Don were his own creatures or misinformed MI13 agents, I added, "Use any means short of killing them."

I heard a chuckle echoing in the water pipes. How did the Mortons live in such a place?

Grace frowned with mild concern. "You're talking to the House?"

"Can't you hear it?"

She finished a last knot on Dee's bonds and picked up the gun from the floor. "Let me know if it says anything important."

I would've advised her on House conversational etiquette, but the knocks at the door had changed to serious battering, followed by small-arms fire against the door. This was answered by windowpanes exploding, not inward, but outward against the intruders, who yelped in distress. Another voice from the door. "Don't shoot, you might hit the Don."

"Dear Grace," said the Don, "you should have been true to your ancestry and left this American to rot." What the hell did that mean? "You're on the wrong side of history, dear, and I've seen enough history to know. Genies do not go back into bottles. Why shouldn't we have through craft what technology will bring within a few generations to everyone? We don't have to persuade all of the mundanes to accept it. Only a few of the important ones."

I had ceased to listen closely, as this seemed designed to keep us from doing the obvious: getting the hell out of Dodge. Still, having thought through our options, I wanted the local expert's opinion. "Word of two against one?" I suggested.

Grace shook her head. "Even if they aren't suborned, they won't believe us."

I grabbed the syringe from where the Don had dropped it on the floor. "I'll be taking this with us."

The Don convulsed in an effort against his bonds. "No!"

I made a last prayer. "*In the name of the Lord, sleep and repent.*" The Don's head slumped in its bonds. There, now he wouldn't discuss us until we'd had a head start. I hoped he enjoyed being commanded as little as I had.

The wind was building up in the House, as if a storm were breaking inside. I knew a few things about sentient houses with paranoid occupants, and one fact seemed particularly relevant now. "House, where's the secret way out?"

The door to the den slammed impatiently again and again as the gale roared. *This way, this way and hurry.*

We left the den, and a door off the kitchen swung open. We peered into the darkness. Stairs, leading down.

"Wait, I need my sword . . ." But even as I was speaking, a blast of air was carrying my sheathed sword end over end to me. I reached out and grasped it. "Thanks, House. You're the best."

As we descended the stairs, we used our phones as lamps. That reminded me of an important duty. "House, please let me place a call."

"What . . . ?" But Grace must have realized the necessity. The time to signal home was now, when the only place they could trace us to was already blown.

I called the UK safe number for American spiritual agents. A woman's voice answered: "Car service."

"Yes, for Mr. Sword," I replied. "He's leaving soon. There is more evil in the village than he can say."

A pause, while the poor rookie must have processed what that coded signal of local practitioner hostility might mean for her own future. "Understood," she said. "Any instructions for the driver?"

"Tell him we'll have words when we meet." Yes, Attucks, serious words indeed. "And be sure my friends know that I don't intend to remain in the village, so stay away." I ended the call.

We hurried through the narrow passage with as much speed as our limited light allowed. Our escape route was more like a medieval tunnel than the terrible grandeur of the Morton subbasement, but some recent widenings and ornamentation with occult symbols indicated Dee's future ambitions. Emerging from the walls, two centuries of Dee ancestors tipped their hats to us, though one or two spirits snarled. Left-Hand objects were arranged in niches, but not as the trophies of which Grace had spoken. Rather, saving things that God wanted utterly destroyed was the biblical sin of Achan, and all of these objects retained their evil power.

We exited through a craft-hidden gap in a stone fence, which must have been at least two blocks distant from Dee's house. Grace pointed at a car parked on a driveway. She said some words to the car as she worked a small bit of metal into the door lock and then into the ignition, and within seconds, we were driving off in our stolen Vauxhall Vectra, whatever that was. Its lack of style must've been killing Grace.

As Grace drove us toward the center of town again to break the craft trail, she spoke rapidly. "I can try to get you to the Irish Republic on a fishing boat. The Provisionals did it all the time, so it can't be too difficult."

"No," I said, "I have to go to Ukraine. This is going to get worse." Then, the tricky bit. "Will you come with me?"

"Your orders, the reason you're here . . ."

"I don't care. It's the usual farsight bull crap, and I'm not playing for them anymore. There's only one direction for me to go." I was going for my friends, who must also be in peril. What would convince Grace to join me? "When you first heard about Roderick being back, what did you think?"

Grace sighed. "Kill him. Kill him now."

"That's what I'm going to do," I said.

"You know what happened to those Russians—seven of them—who went after Roderick? It's suicide." Even in service, a sin too far for her. Good.

"I prefer to think of it as long odds that invite divine intervention."

That got the briefest of smiles from her, which I also thought was against all odds and a divine intervention. Then, with her usual coolness, she said, "I know a way." She retrieved her phone and said, "British Airways."

"What are you doing?" I asked.

"I'm booking us a flight from Gatwick under one of my covers."

"I thought you said flying was too risky for all concerned."

"Right. We won't be on the plane."

"Boat, then?"

"No, still too great a risk."

"Train?" The Chunnel seemed equally risky to me, but perhaps she knew otherwise.

"You've caught the scent, but you're still not there."

"OK. We can't drive off the island, I'm not a great swimmer, and trying to walk on water would be, as you put it, a bit blasphemous, so what do you have in mind?"

She waved me quiet as she booked a flight to the United States. Then, she ended the call and said, "Bicycle."

"Bicycle what?"

"We're going to bicycle to France."

CHAPTER

EIGHT

I might have protested about biking conditions on the English Channel, but Grace explained about the Chunnel service tube, which doubled as an emergency exit from the UK for spiritual practitioners if things ever regressed to the bad old days. The quickest way for us to cross the Channel undetected would be to bicycle through the service tube. So Grace drove us toward Folkestone and the British entrance to the Chunnel.

I should have rested in the car, but I had too much on my mind, and too much to say. "Thank you for saving me again. That was nice work, by the way. You were pretty economical with the truth with the human lie detector."

"Another of my many gifts," she said. Stealing and lying. I was sensing a pattern here, and it seemed to involve the Ten Commandments. But she couldn't have deceived Dee much. She must really hate my family.

"Do you think Roderick could have possessed him, or brainwashed him?" said Grace. Despite being fully justified, she must have been rethinking her rage at his profound betrayal. She wouldn't bounce back any time soon from that treachery.

"He was old," I said with some care. "The Left Hand can offer one thing that many old men can't resist when death stares them in the face."

"Death stares me in the face all the time," she said. "Why would it be different for him now?"

"Maybe because now his decline and death seem unnecessary—a waste."

"He was incorruptible," she insisted.

"Even for someone so old, the practice makes life feel too sweet to give up." I refrained from adding another motivation. Dale had hinted that sex had been involved in my ancestor Abram's corruption. The Don seemed to have lust on his mind as well.

"I suppose an OBE and a pat on the back no longer suffice," said Grace. "I hope we didn't kill him."

I didn't reply to this. Without the syringe, he might die soon anyway. Instead, I said, "His family's motto is too appropriate."

"You know Virgil?" she said, sounding more surprised than when she had seen the Don with a gun.

"That much," I said. Dee's motto, "Hic Labor," was from the *Aeneid*, and referred to the difficulty of escaping Death, which for the last scion of the family had apparently become the overruling obsession. How many more like him were out there?

We reached Folkestone and the Chunnel entrance in the early morning of a dark, gray, monochrome day. Nearby, the large hillside chalk drawing of the White Horse glowed with warding craft. Kent was another Zevon location. Was I finding an oracle in a pop song? I supposed the Gabble Ratchets were something like werewolves. If so, that meant they'd still be on our trail.

When we parked the car, Grace handed me a pill. "Amphetamine, half dose. You'll need to be at your most wakeful for just a little while longer."

At the end of the drive, I had been drifting mentally, so I popped the pill. "What about you?"

"I'll be fine for another few hours. Let's go."

"To simply walk to the service tunnel entrance?"

Grace gave the cross around her neck a kiss. "Yes," she said.

My view of the world changed into the fish-eyed lens of the stealth screened. Of course, that was why we had gotten so far: Grace was skilled at stealth. I should have realized. Stealthers like that bastard Roman tended to be particularly colorful when they weren't invisible, and Grace's choices of vehicles and clothes were as colorful as any I'd seen.

We jogged unseen past the check-in booths, then followed a side road that led down to a rectangular opening between the tracks. A light drizzle descended, but the pill was kicking in, and the weather couldn't get me down.

Within the rectangular entrance was a chamber with enormous yellow airlock doors closing the far end. Grace opened the first of several hidden storage compartments within the floor on each side, revealing the mountain bicycles, each with a large reflective number on it. They were twenty-one speeders but otherwise generic, not fancy, like the commuter bike rentals in some major cities, and they looked old and thoroughly used.

"Most are leftovers from the construction," said Grace. "They're only intended for one more ride."

We pulled up two of the bikes. At the airlock, Grace found a craft-hidden panel, which she opened to reveal an alphanumeric keypad. She entered the password, and the characters appeared in the display: "Platform_9.75."

"Cute," I said, as one of airlock doors hissed open.

"Whistling in the dark. This is a backdoor escape route for the spirituals of an entire nation, if the realm turns against us again."

The door open just enough to let us through, and we walked our bikes inside. Grace hit a hidden pad on the other side, and the door began to close behind us.

"By the way," said Grace, "when we entered here, we triggered a warning alarm in MI13. We have to reach the halfway point to escape England's spiritual power. The maths on their response time should just work out, so I suggest we get moving."

We opened the next airlock door, closed it behind us, and rode into the service tunnel proper. "From here," said Grace, "we need to go about twenty-eight kilometers to cross the spiritual border." Initially, we biked on a slight decline, which was good, because whatever the amphetamine was doing for my head, my muscles were still at their limit.

After some miles, the overhead lights were no longer lit, but the bikes had headlamps powered by our pedaling. Grace used some stealth to conceal us from an oncoming service vehicle, and like bike racers we had to ride up on the curve of the tunnel to get by.

We rode together side by side. Almost nice, this biking holiday with an MI13 agent. Almost, until I started thinking again. My family background could really hinder me sometimes, because I didn't realize what we were heading into, until it was too late.

"This tunnel, for spiritual purposes, it's a wound in the earth, right?"

"Yes," agreed Grace.

"This is an Underworld place," I continued.

"Yes," said Grace, a bit impatiently.

"And a borderland," I continued. "So, how many ghosts are we going to have to pass through?"

Sure enough, first in ones or twos, the national ghosts became visible. Some were relatively recent, like World War II's Old Home Guard. But some looked Napoleonic era—a long stretch of time for spirits, if I trusted more experienced viewers.

Great, I thought, *now I'm in that hippie-dippy Joseph Campbell's pan-religionist gobbledygook. Sorry, Joe, but despite this Underworld detour, I don't believe in heroes and heroes' journeys.* I wasn't called to adventure; I was ordered on missions. I didn't return with boons; I ran back as fast as I could, sometimes on fire.

The UK national ghosts didn't trouble or even regard us; they kept their dead eyes focused ahead against any threat from the continent. But then I saw my first personal ghosts. Maybe it was my exhaustion plus the pill that allowed this deeper trip into the Underworld. Amphetamines weren't the usual Left-Hand concoction for entering the realm of death, but here they were a sufficient gateway drug.

Whatever death magic was happening, I saw not just my own ancestors, but what I took to be Grace's as well. Abram was not among them, praise the Lord, so he must have been truly gone. My father's spirit was driving his favorite red Corvette along the side of the tunnel. I saw plenty of him back home—but sitting next to him was Mom! She had died when I was a kid while on some mission saving missionaries. She smiled and waved at me, scarf blowing in the spectral breeze. Someday, could I call her back to the house? I'd been missing her my whole life.

Our other ancestors rode horses or bicycles, or just ran along with us at unnatural speed. Other than my mom, my ancestors didn't acknowledge me, but instead engaged in a ghost game of chicken with Grace's ancestors, each riding or running in intertwining paths, staring at each other with angry grimaces. Their dead eyes were only alive with their hostility to each other.

My ancestors were pissing me off. "Show respect, or by God, I'll . . ." What, kill them again? Short of expulsion, I didn't have enough experience with ghost discipline. It didn't matter. My ancestors didn't embarrass me by actually attacking. Grace just gave her ghosts a warning glance, and they kept themselves in check as well.

"They really don't like each other," I said.

"Yes," she said.

"What's going on?" I pointed at a young man in a British redcoat uniform from the Revolution, the darkness of his skin still seeming incongruous with his clothing despite what I'd already learned. The redcoat was staring bayonets at a man dressed as a merchant sea captain whose face was all too familiar. "Who's that soldier glaring at Stephen?"

"Let's keep riding," Grace said.

After a short while, she continued. "In 1764, your Stephen transported a cargo of African slaves to the New World. One of them was that man, my ancestor Toby Howe. As the Don said, during the Revolution he joined the British cause, and my family has served the Crown ever since. But for generations afterwards, Toby's spirit described the horrors of the Middle Passage to his descendants. He only faded into our House when I was a child; I'm surprised to see him again, even in this place."

"Stephen was directly involved," I said, just to acknowledge that I understood her import.

"Yes," she said, "but the Endicott craft lineage's involvement with slavery didn't begin or end with Stephen. Even after clear evidence of the dangerous relationship between slave ownership and evil craft, your ancestors continued to profit from the trade."

This was enough, far more than enough, to justify her contempt for my family. Yet the way she had said it sounded more like something on the surface, rather than fundamental. As evil as it was, the slave trade was a broad and pervasive sin (more so than most want to remember), and the anger of Grace and her family felt extremely focused. "That's not all of it, is it?"

"No, it isn't." Grace stared at the way ahead as she spoke. "I have another, earlier, practitioner ancestor—too long dead to appear even here. Her name was Tituba of Salem."

"Oh," I said. Tituba, an enslaved woman, was one of the first people accused of witchcraft during the madness that afflicted Salem in 1692. The involvement of mundane Endicotts in the trials wasn't particularly significant, but behind the scenes the Endicott spiritual lineage had some hand in the witch hunts. The exact extent of that involvement was still disputed—the Mortons claimed that we had directed the whole macabre circus to eliminate a few rival practitioners, while my Family's historians argued that we only contributed to, at most, "one or two" of the executions.

"Tituba survived," I blurted out, not having anything better to say.

"Yes, she survived. Your Puritan family was very fastidious about honoring its word, and they had promised Tituba that if she used her gifts as instructed and accused everyone that they told her to, she would be spared. So she accused, and accused, and accused, and she survived. But tell me, Major, as a recent convert to the reality of ghosts, what sort of spirits do you think haunted and hounded Tituba until the hour of her death and beyond?"

We pedaled on in silence until I could think of anything that might be worth saying. I spoke with quiet uncertainty. "We've repented. I've repented."

"Whatever it is you've done in recompense, do you think it's enough?"

I didn't hesitate. "No."

Grace turned her face from the path ahead and stared into my eyes. I didn't dare blink or look away. Was she reading my sins like a Morton? Looking for deceit like the Don? Her own eyes remained beautiful, but again I saw sorrow, both recent and older than her life, and I hated myself for my part in it.

As if from far away outside herself, she finally spoke. "In you, I see hope. I'd rather not. But my duty is first to keep us alive and moving. So ride on, Endicott."

The air grew muggy, and concrete dust motes fell in our headlight beams. With a deep rumble, a train passed in one of the rail tunnels. Eventually, the service path curved and curved back. "That's where the crossover chamber is," said Grace. "Maybe another eleven kilometers to the true border." The bicycles lacked odometers, but I knew we must have been approaching the edge of Britain, because in the twilight ahead of us hovered the spirit of that damned crazy oracle Sphinx. Dressed in her same aging hippie best that she was wearing when she died, Sphinx moved toward me like a silent film image, and then she was past me, and I heard her voice just over my left shoulder. "You're going the wrong way."

I turned my head right and left to check behind me, but Sphinx wasn't there, which meant she was in my head as a possessing spirit. Before, that would have been an intolerable evil to be met with the Lord's full artillery of prayer and imprecation. Now, it was a minor annoyance in one of my longest days. Under my straining breath, I told her, "You're a little late."

"Probably doesn't matter. Mate in four moves." Then she cackled.

"Is that a warning or a how-to book?"

"Oo, you're better at this now. Both, neither—you've got more timelines springing from this moment than Lee at Gettysburg, though most of them don't end well."

"Meaning I'm free?"

Inside my mind, an eye winked at me. "Right, like oracles and neo-Calvinists believe in that crap. But yeah, as free as we get. Good luck, or Godspeed, or whatever—all the same to me now." With that, her spirit fluttered out of my head.

Even as Sphinx was departing, Grace said, "Stop," and signaled for silence. Far behind us, I distinguished a sound that had grown unconsciously familiar in the background.

From a sleeve of the fur coat she had strapped behind her on her bike, Grace pulled out and extended what looked like a small antique nautical telescope. After looking down the service tunnel, she wordlessly handed it to me.

I looked. It was actually a night vision monocular with range-finding capability.

"I may have erred slightly," Grace said.

At the limits of my vision, a vehicle was moving toward us, rapidly. I heard no echo of motor noise, so it must have been electric. The vehicle filled the lower part of the tunnel. Even if they failed to shoot us, they could run us down and crush us.

Grace pointed ahead of us—a wall of spiritual energy. "There's the true border. I believe they'll be stopped there, though it'll be closer than I would have liked. Let's go."

Even as she spoke, a craft-concealed door at least as massive as the airlocks we'd passed through became visible and began to swing close.

We pedaled furiously the last couple of hundred yards. Grace was shouting. "Hold that door!" But long before we reached it, the door completely shut against us.

We skidded to a stop at the midway point. Here, screened from mundane view, a half-dozen skeletons were chained to the walls as warding warnings to would-be trespassers and invaders. One of the skeletons was in tattered SS garb, which seemed anachronistic for a tunnel from the '90s and yet utterly appropriate.

A line of French soldier ghosts stood shoulder to shoulder guarding the door. One of these soldiers was a faded veteran of Napoleon, while a more sharply defined spirit wore the uniform of the modern Foreign Legion. An apparent civilian was also with them—a woman in a red cap who sat on a spectral stool in front of the line, completely focused on her knitting. Something about her presence didn't bode well.

Grace had murder redux in her eyes as she spoke to the French ghosts. "I invoke the compact. Let me open this door." The ghosts shook their heads. Grace was incredulous. "The French are deliberately barring our way."

"I thought . . ."

"Yes, it's in the compact that this is an open escape route in both directions. There's only one possible justification for barring us. They must think the UK has been corrupted, and that we carry the contagion."

The vehicle was approaching; they'd probably start shooting soon. Without much hope, I pleaded with the French spirits. "I'm an American. An ally."

Some of the French ghosts gave a Gallic shrug. I should've known, but still—so many American craftsmen had died on their soil, and that was the best they could do?

No use trying to open the door anymore—our pursuers were too close. I drew my sword from its sheath. "I assume they've sent enough to beat us," I said.

"That would be the usual protocol," noted Grace.

"You could shoot me," I said, "maybe even without killing me. Then they'll give you time to explain. You could end the rot."

"You're not one of your service's intellectuals, are you?"

"A simple 'no' would do," I said.

The hostile vehicle slowed, and the passengers started firing at us. At this distance, their shots were easily skewed, though the bounces were so chaotic as to be dangerous.

Time to use all the spiritual gifts I had. How had I gotten that extra power outside the club? I had been desperate—check. Submitting to God's will, I had prayed. *God, you'd know best, but I think this one is important. Please help us.* Check.

I felt something. It bubbled up through my feet the way the spirit entered me in my own home. I felt like singing. *Oh God, no, anything but that.*

The force of it wouldn't be denied. I raised my sword, opened my mouth, and burst into tuneless song:

> *And did those feet in ancient time*
> *Walk upon England's mountains green?*
> *And was the Holy Lamb of God*
> *On England's pleasant pastures seen?*
> *And did the Countenance Divine*
> *Shine forth upon our clouded hills?*
> *And was Jerusalem builded here*
> *Among these dark Satanic mills?*

In my atonal ecstasy, I was dimly aware that Grace was singing too—something different. Her mellifluous voice was everything mine wasn't. She was singing "God save the Queen." So I kept going with my own song.

> *Bring me my bow of burning gold!*
> *Bring me my arrows of desire!*
> *Bring me my spear! O clouds unfold!*
> *Bring me my Chariot of Fire!*
> *I will not cease from mental fight,*
> *Nor shall my sword sleep in my hand,*
> *Till we have built Jerusalem*
> *In England's green and pleasant land.*

I felt a rumble that was no train, more like a giant tossing in its slumber. The car was nearly on us, bullets everywhere. I was scared for Grace, and afraid of what I might do next.

But it was my sword that acted. My Family's totem was very important to me, but it never had been a separate object of power. Magical objects were rare, and usually Left-Hand. So I was shocked when my sword glowed like a new sun, and flashed lightning at the oncoming car.

The car made a sound like an electric transformer exploding, and the smell of ozone filled the air. Its six passengers scrambled out and advanced on us, guns firing with deliberation. Car Man, the one Grace had called a Renfield, was with them, this time conspicuously in the lead.

Grace returned a few shots; then as one, we rushed them. "Try not to kill them," I yelled as I sliced at the gun-wielding hand of one of our pursuers. Grace grunted skeptically in acknowledgment as she blew out a woman's kneecap. Having gotten this far, I wanted to exit the UK without killing anyone and improve the odds of patching things up later.

I was a holy terror. I said my prayers of breaking and wounding, and each prayer hit home. Grace was again her artistic martial self. Car Man was the last to go down. He was good—despite my commands, he got off a shot at me at close range. I stabbed him in both legs to keep him from again leaving the scene. This time, I wanted him to have to deal with the consequences of others fighting. If we had a minute, I also wanted him to answer some questions.

Only after all of our opponents lay strewn about the tunnel did I see that Grace had taken grazing shots to her shoulder and leg. "Are you OK?" I asked.

She gazed at me in unabashed horror. I looked down. Blood was soaking into my shirt. My blood. I'd been gut shot, right into the scar of my old sword wound from the Pentagon fiasco. I had felt nothing. *This power has some serious safety issues*, I thought, as I slumped to the ground.

The line of French ghost soldiers moved into a file and the knitting woman spirit got out of the way as the midway door began to open. Grace dragged me to the other side of the door, and punched the button. She yelled, "Keep that bloody thing closed!" as the door slowly shut.

On the French side, a line of British soldier ghosts extended from the border. They stood at an attention that would have put the old Buckingham Palace guards to shame. Grace applied pressure to my bleeding gut with one hand as she spoke in French to her phone with the other, saying something like "Mayday."

I was fading out, perhaps dying. I might have accepted this death if Grace had looked down upon me like an angel and given me her blessing. Instead, to the confusion and distress of my weakening mind, she hissed at me in continued horror.

"You drew the power of Albion," she said. "Who the hell are you?"

CHAPTER

NINE

In the Baba Yagas' headquarters in Kiev sat the haunted man. He was not haunted by a ghost, but by a voice. The voice said, "I am Ukrainian, like you. Don't do this to me!"

Contrary to the folklore about the residence of their namesake, the building on Independence Square that held the Baba Yagas' headquarters did not move. It merely appeared to do so, to the extent it appeared at all—a natural security precaution by a craft service known for its stealth skill. To a sensitive enough mundane observer, it most often looked like an old stony wing of a neighboring structure instead of its stand-alone modern glass and metal reality. Only an authorized employee could find it without craft. One aspect of the shape of their ancestral namesake's hut survived in the '90s structure. The walls of the first-floor lobby of the building were all glass, and the two thin, naked elevator shafts with adjacent low-angled escalators might give a predisposed mind the impression of feet.

The ten-floor building was also used by Ukrainian intelligence and hackers. From this one location, an astounding portion of the world's cyberattacks and extortions originated. These concentrated hackers were only the tip of the Ukrainian spear. From all over the country and the world, independent hackers each day offered the services of thousands of their zombie machines. The Chinese might still dominate in cyberwarfare, but they had incredible numbers. Ukraine tried harder.

The haunted man, Roman Roszkewycz, sat in a top floor sunlit corner office decorated with memorabilia from American Westerns. His graying goatee and mustache complemented his saturnine mien. Roman coordinated all of the craft (and some of the non-craft) hacking in the country, and many other dubious enterprises besides.

Despite his coup in obtaining Roderick Morton, Roman was not in charge of the entire Baba Yaga service—he had been away too long, and anyway he was too busy to be in charge. Roderick was a powerful yet expensive weapon for Ukraine. He'd made many of Roman's questionable enterprises possible, but the American also required their constant profitability to maintain his immortal frame and his peculiar pleasures. The Left-Hand biotechs conducted Roderick's body work in a secret bunker below the basement—the Left Hand consistently craved burrowing into the earth and the land's power. Too much of Kiev was burrowed like that, from medieval catacombs to underground shopping malls.

As for Roderick's pleasures, those had kept the American at home today; he was resting after his most recent affair.

As long as Roman kept the hacker extortion and other rackets running smoothly, Roderick more than paid for himself. *At least I'm not robbing the innocent*, Roman thought, *as the innocent don't have much cash.* The typical targets for Roman's hackers were online gambling outfits operating offshore of the United States, several front operations for organized crime syndicates, and even other denial-of-service extortion operations. Roderick's cyber-craft gave them that much of an edge.

With his cowboy boots up on his desk, Roman followed a stream of text reports on his tablet. He seldom heard his hackers speak, as many of the men and woman who worked on this part of the Baba Yaga operation were uncomfortable with direct verbal interaction. They were practitioners too far along the autistic spectrum for army service or covert field operations, but well suited to DoS attacks.

For Roman, thinking about the text reports acted as a cover for his plans. Roderick almost certainly couldn't read minds, at least not directly. But from what Roderick had done to others, Roman assumed that Roderick could see him through tech-craft or farsight at any time he wished. Thoughts caused involuntary facial expressions and tells, and intentions brought certain timelines into prominence, so Roman didn't consider Roderick often, and when he did, he didn't focus on the American to the exclusion of other thoughts and activities. When Roman spoke with Roderick, he used the affable cadences that had taken in the younger Morton.

The list of things not to think about Roderick was growing. The Baba Yagas had wanted a Morton primarily for defensive purposes, but Roderick had been suborning key figures in the craft services of other nations, and usually not in the interest of Ukraine. When the craft services or, gods forbid, their mundane masters responded, they might do so collectively, and the Baba Yagas would again have to go into deep hiding, as they had when Stalin had killed Roman's great-great-grandfather, a blind *kobzar* minstrel and craft leader.

A few months ago, Roman's colleagues had asked him to deal with the situation. Roman preferred renegotiation to treachery. He had indicated to Roderick (very politely—Roderick was obsessive on manners) that perhaps his ol' pardner might lay off the international intrigues for a month or two, and perhaps slow down with his unique style of speed dating.

Roderick had just smiled at him. "Thank you for your advice."

Perhaps Roderick had appeared to slow down, or perhaps some suasion had been used, because Roman's colleagues now seemed to think everything was fine.

Roman read his e-mail. Everything was not fine. It grew more difficult to avoid thinking about the women he gave to Roderick. His mind kept coming back to them. Irrational. They would have been destroyed anyway; most were halfway gone when he found them. Sacrifices of war. But Roman hadn't known there'd be so many, so quickly.

Roman always watched them, in part to establish the pattern of watching, so Roderick wouldn't suspect if he ever had a reason for particular attention. He also watched to honor their unwilling sacrifice. But mostly, he watched because, if he couldn't, it meant that he had to stop sending them to Roderick. Each woman was like a mouse introduced into a sentient snake's cage. For a while, the predator might make a pet of the prey, but whatever Roderick's variations on the theme, it always ended the same way.

The last (no, most recent) woman they had given to (fed to) Roderick, had been different. It had been a rush job; she had known something was wrong. "I am not a whore," she had said, as two large men had frog-marched her into the waiting van. "I am Ukrainian, like you. Don't do this to me!"

But Roman had done that to her. It had ended this morning, in the darkness before the dawn. By tomorrow, Roderick would be expecting another delivery.

Poker-faced as his Western heroes, Roman read some more texts; the money kept rolling in. Gods, he wanted a drink now. He kept a full bottle in his desk, untouched, the way some depressives kept a loaded revolver. No vodka for him. One shot, and he'd start laughing about Roderick, because that man of many women and long nights might fear only one person, and she was named Scherezade. Then, Roman wouldn't stop laughing and sobbing until Roderick came for him and solved all his problems forever.

Roman did not want such an untimely death, so instead, he read some more messages and tried to forget the last straw. No, not the women—after a few decades of troubled dreams, he probably could have taken their murders with him to his grave. The final insult: perhaps sensing some disaffection, Roderick had visited Roman the other week in his office to offer him a gift. "You have not asked for the ichor serum," he'd said.

Roman had given a one-armed shrug. "I've got time."

Roderick had smiled thinly. "You have realized that with the others, it is a tease: life extension with an implicit promise of my patented-brand of immortality, a promise which we may or may not choose to fulfill. But you have done everything I have asked, and more. I haven't had that sort of aid in two centuries, and the universe does not respond well to karmic debtors. When you are ready, just say the word, and it is done."

Roman had allowed an ambiguous but intense emotion to reach his face. "Thank ya, pardner. I'll let you know."

"Thank you, my friend," Roderick had said, and left, seeming pleased with himself.

It had been then that Roman had realized that, though he could've born the weight of his sins for a lifetime, he couldn't bear them forever. How dare this American offer what no one should have, in return for what no one could forgive? *I'm not a whore. I am Ukrainian.*

Roman had also realized that his Baba Yaga colleagues must have been as compromised by Roderick's promises as any foreign practitioner. Whatever he would do next, he'd have to do it without them.

After five more minutes of his reading messages, a new report came in. Roman read it, then stopped, frozen with fighting the horror and hope that were welling up to express themselves in his face, in his blush response and pupil dilation. Through indirection and careful charting of its blind spots, Ukraine's indie farsight now predicted that the timelines of his American former friends were converging toward Kiev. They couldn't see whether any of those lines actually made it to Ukraine. But the Americans were coming, and Roman doubted their business was with him.

Roderick would see this future too. Probably he had already seen it, or even planned it. Roman hoped he'd focus on it to the exclusion of much else. In any case, Roman didn't have much time. He picked up the desk phone for internal communication, and punched the number for the hacker-floor minder. "Send Lara up. I'm tired of her marking up my memos."

He hung up. What he had said was true—Lara kept sending him corrections to the Slavic cowboy grammar in his department instructions with a persistence that was extreme even among her peers. That was how she had attracted his attention among all his other autistic-spectrum programmers.

In a few minutes, Lara entered his office without knocking and sat in a chair opposite him. She hadn't been skimmed at the border from human trafficking or from the streets of Kiev, but her fate would be the same. One way or another, she would be the last woman he gave to Roderick.

Roman had interviewed Lara the day after Roderick's offer. Physically, she met Roderick's preferred profile—tall, pale, and unpleasantly thin—which was a small and even suspicious miracle. Her long and wispy fair hair was virgin to stylist and rarely combed. She had some farsight ability and was difficult for others to farsee. Where she fell on the autistic spectrum was hard to say, as craft might reverse or amplify some symptoms such as sensory sensitivity. Her resting face was frozen in affect, like the mask of a stern queen, with no facial or other tells, though Roman had seen her fake some social reactions from necessity or choice.

"I respect your right to privacy," said Roman for the all-seeing Roderick's benefit. As he had in the Pentagon an emotional lifetime ago, Roman created his strongest stealth bubble. In an instant, the view outside the bubble went fish-eyed. Within the bubble with him, Lara didn't even blink.

"As we discussed, you're to report to Mr. Morton," said Roman. "But first, for my own conscience, I need to confirm that you understand what this assignment means."

She stared at him—no, through him, and he felt like he'd been talking to a cat, with even less chance of a reaction. But, without breaking her gaze, she spoke. "It means pain and death. It is endurable for our land. You mean to rid Ukraine of him. You will succeed."

Like any craft veteran, Roman could hear the resonance of oracle in a statement, and he could sense horrible possibilities hidden within this positive augury. But he didn't question her. If what she said was true, the benefit far outweighed the likely horrors to himself, and to interrogate her on the cusp of her sacrifice would be the sort of ingratitude that could lead to further disaster.

As for Lara's hard-to-read feelings, Roman believed she had less regard for her fate than he did for his. All that mattered to her was Ukraine and a plan to save it. Anyone who interfered with those things wasn't a person, but an object for disposal.

"I'll have someone drive you over."

"No," she said. "Everyday I get myself to work. This is no different. Do you have the injection?"

Roman opened his office mini-fridge and, moving aside a couple of cans of Coke, retrieved a brass-colored metal syringe very similar to those manufactured in the basement of this building and sent to Roderick's international allies. But it contained a different alchemical stew. Roman held the syringe out to her. "Shall I . . . ?" he started to ask.

"No," she said. "I'll do it myself."

She took the syringe that would make her one half of a suicide bomb. Even if she succeeded, Lara would not survive. First her skin, then her entire body, would melt into its target, nano-craft suffusing nano-craft, and their conjoined flesh would dissolve together into a protoplasmic puddle on the floor. Lara knew all this. He had explained it quite clearly to her at their previous meeting. As far as he could see from her face, she had no concerns as she injected herself. But this wasn't the painful part.

"Anything else?" she asked.

Roman thought there should be something else, something to say. "No. Thank you, Lara."

"I haven't done it yet. But I will. Good-bye."

"Good-bye," said Roman. Lara had already risen and was on her way out the door. In every word she had said, he had detected no deception. What a rare person to lose.

In the face of such unquestioning loyalty, Roman had still kept one secret. Even if Lara failed to touch Roderick, her death would trigger a nano-craft swarm that would burst through her corpse and home in on the nearest Left-Hand power source. He hadn't dared tell her; he barely dared think it. It was his true best hope of destroying Roderick's body.

But the poisoned woman was just the first step of Roman's plan. In another drawer of his warded desk, Roman kept a small needle-like tube of alchemical plastic. The needle contained the merest sliver of the craft-infused neurotissue that had held Roderick's consciousness when Roman had brought it to Kiev. Roderick had politely demanded that it all be destroyed, but he seemed unaware that Roman had saved this sliver. An unsurprising but very fortunate blind spot. The alchemical needle reminded Roman of the hidden needle that had, according to the tales, held the soul of Koshchiy until its destruction killed the so-called "Deathless" one. Roderick would require something more multilateral and multistep.

So Lara, embedded with a Left-Hand craft antithetical to that sustaining Roderick, would destroy the American's body. Then Roman could use the sliver of neurons to bind Roderick's spirit and prevent him from finding another host. Roman knew from experience that Roderick would be quite vulnerable bound to such insignificant flesh—he was not as adept at jumping or hijacking bodies as his sister had been. Roman would then hide that sliver away from the world, and Roderick would be imprisoned and helpless for as long as the Left-Hand craft sustaining the neurotissue lasted.

Or perhaps Roman would die like all those women, if not immediately, then in whatever Left-Hand wrath pursued him after this attack on their leader. But he had risked death before for a far worse cause: to bring this monster to his homeland. Today's risk felt good, and he would not shame himself with cowardice with Lara's sacrifice imminent. Roman watched his monitors, readied the needle, and waited.

PART IV

KICKING EDGAR ALLAN POE AND MURDERING THE ORIENT EXPRESS

Give me no light, great Heaven, but such as turns
To energy of human fellowship;
No powers beyond the growing heritage
That makes completer manhood.
　　　　　—George Eliot

The French are polite, but it is often mere
ceremonious politeness. A Russian imbues his
polite things with a heartiness, both of phrase
and expression, that compels belief in
their sincerity.
　　　　　—Mark Twain

Yes, poisonous thing! Thou hast done it!
Thou hast blasted me! Thou hast filled my veins
with poison!
　　　　　—Nathaniel Hawthorne

In the British Museum after nightfall, a compact, thuggish-looking man in a security uniform entered one of the gallery rooms of the ancient Greece and Rome collection. The day before, this same man had served as the muscle during Michael Endicott's interrogation. Despite broader recruitment, the agents of MI13 hadn't completely escaped the class weaknesses of their forebears and, in the way of aristocrats with their servants, they tended to discuss matters in front of him that he didn't officially need to know. But for the *Oikumene*, he needed to know a great deal.

The man looked about to be make sure no other guard was in the vicinity. Standing in the room's one blind spot, he took out a small remote and clicked it at the cameras so that they'd continue to show an empty room. He brought his mind to an intense focus and touched a bronze statuette, a half meter in height, purportedly of Alexander and originally dedicated at Delphi. Quietly, almost subvocally, he gave his call sign. "Herakles calling Pythia. Come in, Pythia." He paused, repeated the message, paused, and repeated again.

Finally, a response. *"Pythia here. Herakles, dear, are you well?"*

"I'm fine, ma'am. I thought you should know this at the first opportunity. The American, Endicott, has disappeared, along with his minder, Grace Marlow. There's been some trouble with Dee in Oxford, but either the higher-ups don't know the details or they don't dare discuss them. And early this morning, there was an incident in the service tunnel involving some Gabble Ratchets, the border ghosts, the French, and a large summoning of the national power to unknown hands."

"*You were quite right to report, Herakles.*" Good intelligence was 90 percent timing, and belated news wasn't news at all. She asked a few questions to check his sources, but she never kept him on the line longer than he could plausibly be on a round and off camera.

But before she signed off, she said, "*Herakles, be ready. We will be at war soon, and it sounds as if the Left Hand may again be active in MI13.*"

"Will do, ma'am. Herakles, over and out."

As he resumed his round, Herakles reflected that he might soon die for the *Oikumene* and the Pythia, and he smiled. That he loved his leader from afar did not surprise or distress him, or give him a single sleepless night, for he knew his history. Englishmen liked their heroes, but worshipped their heroines.

"Paris, this is Pythia. Come in, Paris."

Merde, merde, merde! thought the old man with "Légion Étrangère" tattooed on his arm and a smell of Gauloises about him, though he'd quit smoking years ago. The call had been coming in every hour on the hour. Well, only one way to make her shut up. Stealing the museum security uniform, forging the identity, and getting into the Louvre after closing was almost too easy—the temptation would probably haunt him the rest of his life, as so many temptations already did. With the focus that only extreme annoyance could bring, he touched the bronze statuette of Athena the Warrior. "What is it? Are you trying to wake every sensitive in the city?"

The Pythia sighed. "Who is this?"

"Hermès Cubed." Then he gave the code phrase. "The Empire never ended. Plutonian Shore died last week—no funny business, just his age and kidneys, and his replacement won't be back from Indochina until next month. You're calling about the American and the *Anglaise noire?*"

"Yes," she said. So Hermès Cubed told her why the foreign couple wasn't his problem anymore.

I n Delphi above the *Oikumene*'s bunker, the tourists came and went. Scherie could watch them on the HD screen in her room. For some ineffable reason it was comforting, lessening her disorientation, which must be why they had this view.

But now, Scherie had turned her attention to her host, the Pythia, who had come to her artificially sunlit room. With her apocalyptic words of craft war, the Pythia had left Scherie hanging for a day, claiming that Scherie should rest and that she needed to "make some calls." Now Scherie had to make some calls too.

Scherie held her phone up to illustrate. "I need to report in. Also, I need to call my husband."

The Pythia smiled with kindness but no joy. "Roderick is monitoring all conventional communications, and when he chooses, he can control them."

In a flash, her memories of the trauma-packed hours in Istanbul came together to support this new information. "He controlled my phone."

"Yes," agreed the Pythia. "We could pass word unconventionally, but you said Major Morton is in the Far East, and our network doesn't extend there. Besides, we need to talk first."

"Yes, let's talk." Without prelude, Scherie sat down on the edge of her bed. Talking to this Greek woman might violate Scherie's oath of secrecy, but the Pythia seemed to know a great deal already, and Scherie was desperate for help. "Who are you?"

The Pythia took the room's only chair, sitting next to a potted laurel tree. "I'm the current head of the craft *Oikumene*. The position used to be called 'priestess,' but now it more resembles the secretary general of the craft UN. Over the centuries, we've had many roles, but one role has remained constant. We fight the evil known as the Left-Hand way."

"Centuries?" asked Scherie.

The Pythia nodded. "We don't know who first recognized that the Left-Hand way is evil; that discovery, like the discovery of craft itself, predates history. We began as one group of practitioners in mainland Greece. We watched for the monsters who demanded young men and women to feed their energy-draining labyrinths, or who chopped the living limbs from sleeping guests to create ichor-filled new bodies, or who made stews of their own rendered children to extend the lives of themselves or others. When we found them, we destroyed them."

"Then all the old stories . . ."

The Pythia waved a hand. "Far from all are true. Many are true only in some small detail. But it's not just our actual work that was preserved in myth. Some of those ancient stories are propaganda we created against Left-Hand ideas. You would recognize those stories as well—cautionary tales about attempts at immortality gone wrong, spread throughout the Greek, then Roman world. Then, the Christians, as little as we thought of them at first, proved very effective against attempts at earthly immortality." The Pythia nodded at Scherie. "Islam followed the same course, and all was well in the Western world, at least in the narrow terms of battling the Left Hand with the support of the mundane religions."

"Forgive me," Scherie said, "I'm very grateful for your help when I had nowhere else to turn. But that was an exceptional circumstance. What do you do in today's world that the craft services can't?"

"As you must know in your very bones," said the Pythia, "craft is tied to Mother Earth. But even before the fracturing of the Mediterranean world, the craft has also been subject to human territorial boundaries, and those divisions have only sharpened with time. Still, a few powerful practitioners are not subject to such limits, and others manage from their homelands to threaten many nations. The *Oi-kumene* strives to maintain the old union of practitioners in order to respond to such global threats. Roderick Morton is such a threat."

"Then you'll help me kill him," said Scherie.

The Pythia looked bemused. "How do you intend to do that?"

"I drove his spirit from his head."

"Yes, I know. But we've seen the result of that."

Scherie felt a little angry and embarrassed at this summary of her action in H-ring. "If I can summon the Left-Hand revenants of the House of Morton, they could consume him as they did Madeline."

"Madeline?" The Pythia shook her head. "She, or they, have been manifesting about the shrine's outskirts, waiting for you. Even if I trusted their intent, I'm not certain of their ability. Roderick's immortality has been different than Madeline's was. We'll need to carefully consider this." The Pythia stood and stretched, for once moving more like a Greek peasant than a queen. "Hmm, I need to get some exercise. The perils of sitting still for so much of the day for my oracle work."

Scherie stood up as well. "One other thing. There's someone else you should contact. He promised to aid Dale and me against Roderick."

The Pythia's eyes narrowed with intensity, and the smile left her face. "Who?"

"Major Michael Endicott."

The Pythia closed her eyes and nodded. "Then I have news for you. Please, sit down again."

By the time his train pulled in to Narita airport, Dale had fully and firmly realized that, though the news had come through H-ring, it was Roderick who was calling him out like a schoolboy, and that Dale was responding in almost the rashest way possible.

Roderick was a probable explanation for the interference and delay in communications and for Scherie's disappearance. The surface response to Roderick's survival was to search for Scherie, help her, then go to Endicott (*Sorry, Mike*, he thought, *those are my priorities*). But anyone like Dale would go quickly to the next level of response; the best defense was a good offense, and the only sure way to protect his wife and friend was to kill Roderick as swiftly as possible.

So far, so good. Killing sorcerers was what Dale did best. But Roderick would expect Dale to come charging as soon as he got word, and Dale couldn't even know where the trap was: in the journey, at the goal, or both. To have a good chance of success, Dale needed to see another level of response, a further move ahead.

He couldn't do it. If H-ring was right, Roderick or his minions had attacked Scherie and Endicott, and Dale's mind couldn't get past that outrage. Maybe Dale could figure out some better moves as he traveled, but he had to get within striking distance of Roderick as soon as possible.

From his farsight or his deep schemes, Roderick would know Dale was coming, but would Dale's old semi-treacherous friend Roman know too? Dale imagined that, by now, Roderick and Roman might feel some tension in their working relationship. Before Dale boarded his flight, he sent a message to the handle Roman had used during the years he had worked for Dale. "We need to talk," he said. This message worked for Dale whether Roderick intercepted it or not and whether Roman read it or not.

From Tokyo, Dale flew to Seoul. He would stick to short hops. If he went east back to the U.S., someone in authority might try to stop him. Going west, only bad guys would try to interfere. His route had some obstacles. Landing in China was out of the question, but overflight was a risk he was willing to take.

At Seoul's Incheon International Airport, Dale made it through the floating security ghosts—long-haired, legless, and faceless—and found a flight to Ulan Bator. A nonbeliever, he still had a weatherman's fondness for the old Mongolian god of the open sky. A plainclothes Korean practitioner, his sins arranged with Confucian orderliness about his person, stopped Dale at the gate. "This way please." He must have seen the flight-or-fight decision on Dale's face, because the man added, "No worries, Morton. We just want to give you a message."

"Couldn't it wait?"

The man's eyes flicked toward the plane. "Maybe not."

They entered a small security station. The man's face regarded Dale with placidity and inappropriate amusement. "The message is simple. We've made no decision regarding your ancestor's technology, but if we decide to use it, we'd prefer to work with you instead of him. You have certain advantages."

"Which are?"

"You are mostly sane."

"Some would dispute that."

The man nodded in a bow-like motion. "Yet our offer stands."

"I'll consider it," Dale said, which he knew could be a polite way of saying "no" in the region, and therefore wasn't a lie.

"You could stay here while you *consider it*," the Korean said. "No strings attached. We have reason to believe our neighbors will not be as reasonable, and it would be such a waste if you did not make it home."

"Thank you, but I have to leave, immediately. My wife . . ."

"She's in danger?" The man's amused face fell. "My apologies. We had no intention of interfering with your family. Your plane is waiting, I assure you. Go." Dale got up and left the room. The man called after him, "But if you have things you'd like to share, please remember us."

Dale trotted back to the gate. Upon boarding the plane and commencing his preflight sin examination of his fellow passengers, he saw a familiar figure standing in the aisle just behind his row, dressed in a World War II WAC uniform.

Madeline, the voice of his ancestral dark spirits, smiled like death by sex. "There's room for one more," she said, pointing at his seat.

"Hi, Auntie. I hope you haven't come to gloat. It ill becomes you." Dale took a last look around at the passengers' sins and saw no would-be terrorists. Then he stowed his small bag and sat down. "Why are you here?"

"Your wife says 'hi.'"

Despite his opinion of Madeline's honesty, Dale felt relief. Scherie was alive, maybe. Unless Madeline was claiming to have met Scherie's ghost?

As if responding to Dale's thoughts, Madeline said, "She's in a place we can't go. We're waiting for her to come out and play again." Madeline's idea of play wasn't reassuring, but her tone was lighter than any time since her ghost had entered the Left-Hand collective. "Don't you want to know where Scherie is?"

Ah, so that was the game. Dale lowered his voice to a whisper. "Auntie, don't you want to kill me?"

"Yes. But what has that to do with anything? *I* have my priorities straight. I want to destroy most of the living and the dead, but I've learned how to exist amidst alternative and chaotic tensions, and *we* have adapted. My brother seeks only absolutes."

"So, hypothetically, if I want to kill Roderick . . ."

"Take your best shot, nephew. But we think you'd do better to retrieve your wife first. She's the one who can really hurt him, and I do so want to hurt him. After she's with you, we might have other advice. But we have nothing for your current trajectory."

They were interrupted by the noises and crew movements of departure, and Dale by his own thoughts. As the plane taxied and turned onto the main runway, Dale asked, "Where is she, Auntie? Please?"

"Great dark gods!" said Madeline. "What ever happened to the Morton sense of fun? You could challenge me to a duel of wits, impress me with your repartee, threaten me with your power, and instead you beg? You realize, we were the fun Family. That was why none of the others liked us."

"Yeah, that and a few too many corpses."

"True. Ah, well. She's at Delphi."

"Delphi? The *Oikumene*?"

"Still painfully very much in business," she said. "We don't expect that she'll stay put, but we won't be telling her where you're going."

"I'm not sure I'd want you to, but why not?"

"She's too important to throw away like this."

On *this*, Dale felt strong weather craft like a fist punching out from the west toward the rising plane.

"Ah, you feel that," said Madeline, bending to look at Dale, her smile gone as feral as during the fight in the Sanctuary. "We'll leave you to play with your Chinese friends. One way or another, we'll be seeing you soon."

Korean security had kept the flight free of explosives and assassins, but that was the only good news. The minute Dale's flight passed into international air, the Chinese weathermen repeatedly aimed microburst-type phenomena at the plane. Then, when they were over China proper, they sent his old friend sandstorm for him, whipped up into the stratosphere. Dale had the image of the fine yellow sand of Inner Mongolia mixed with Beijing smog spiraling up in a helix, led by a fist of wind. He had to do more than calm the local winds; he had to redirect the sand, which, like volcanic ash, could destroy his plane's engines.

While Chinese weathermen were unrelenting in their attempts to kill him during the remainder of the flight over PRC territory, Dale had an interesting conversation with them through texts. Like everyone else, they said they were pursuing Dale because they thought he knew the Left-Hand secrets, and since he wasn't selling them to the Chinese, he must be giving them to others. "But I don't know anything about it." *Then you're useless*, they said, and kept attacking his flight.

But, although he didn't know the Left-Hand craft of life extension, Dale was a Morton, and therefore the best weatherman in the world. Though he was far from home and the work was demanding, it was the work he did best, and the air itself seemed to feed some power back into him. Yet by the middle of the flight, Dale's usual meditative approach to craft had failed him. Sweat poured down his face and soaked his clothes, and he was gripping his armrests like a panicked flight-phobe. When they finally got to Mongolia, Dale saw that one of the pilots had to be assisted off the plane, looking as bad as Dale felt.

Dale found an Aeroflot flight to Moscow. The Mongolians and Aeroflot weren't as good at finding the assassins and the explosives. Dale had some craft words and actions with the killers and bombs, and they remained unconscious or inactive for the duration. He had the energy for such, as he didn't have to deal with more weather assaults or other spooky action at a distance. Much of his flight was over regions that, though nominally Russian, were still dominated by the shaman craft families, and nobody wanted to wake that hot mess up again, particularly in the area of weather.

With belated regret, Dale considered that he had been too visible on these flights, and that the passengers on the planes may have noticed inexplicable things during his efforts: the abrupt changes in weather when he said "*be calm*" aloud, the men and women passing out in their seats when he spoke to them, and, for the more sensitive, the shadowy image of a woman who seemed to float next to him, whispering. The passengers who were paying particular attention to Dale got what suasion he could muster. But he was tired with still a long ways to go to reach Roderick, and at his best he couldn't have swayed so many. Nor did he get a chance to sway the pilots who must have seen the directed sandstorm over China and its strange dispersal better than any passenger.

In Moscow, Dale's run of luck ended. Two Russians halted him, plainclothed except for the severed dog's head and broom handle pins of the Oprichniki, the ancient secret police branch of the Russian craft service. Their sins were unpleasant to look at. "Major Morton, you're to wait here as a guest of the Russian service."

"I'm in a hurry. My wife . . ."

But the Oprichniki were not so easily moved as the Korean had been. "As far as we know, your wife is not in Kiev. Something is about to happen there, and though it has a low fate index, we will not let you fuck it up."

While Roman waited for Lara to arrive at Roderick's, he allowed himself the small dream that he might have a future. Ukraine had been disappointing in its efforts to establish itself on the world stage. He could push events here, or he could deal with Russians (who might be more open to discussion with Roderick gone), or . . .

His reverie was interrupted when Lara appeared in the video from the camera outside of Roderick's home. Roderick had designed the house with more of the retro-future look of the American 1960s than any contemporary style. To any normal person with craft or historical awareness, the house's location was chilling. Though most of the ghosts had departed or had been (more or less gently) dispelled from the Babi Yar Park area, the dark residue of what had happened there remained. The park hummed in anticipation.

The door of the house swung open, but no one was there. That such an effect might be mere technology didn't lessen its frisson for a new entrant unless she knew very little of normal anticipatory fear. Lara probably appreciated that she hadn't had to touch anything new to her.

She entered the house's public part, public to the extent that Roderick had visitors who were allowed to exit. She walked left with regular, precise steps into the living room, which had two adjoining bookcases filled with books of modern art. She turned and continued toward the house's rear, which opened up to a view of the park. From the kitchen on the right (sparkling clean), across the dining area in the center, and to the observation nook on the left, it was nearly continuous window—not energy efficient, but aesthetically charming.

Roman zoomed in on Lara's face. Her eyes took in the view and the objects about the room with autistic fairness, giving little priority to the human.

Behind Lara, one of the bookcases slid aside, revealing an entrance to another room. This was not the usual burrowing of the Left Hand. "I'm trying to live more sensibly," Roderick had said, as if everyone had secret chambers somewhere in their home.

Lara entered the chamber. It was split in two by a translucent red curtain, now partially opened. The divided space resembled a parlor and a bedroom of a wealthy antebellum New Englander, if that Yankee was something out of Poe's nightmares. The windowless chamber was lit only by candles and whale-oil lamps. A nicely upholstered sofa was set behind an ornate rectangular box, decorated in the chinoiserie style popular with the wealthy merchants of nineteenth-century Rhode Island. The box might serve as a table, but whether it was also a coffin was an empirical matter. Roderick placed some of his "friends" in the box to see if they could make the leap that his sister had. But he didn't pursue this seriously, often neglecting to have a new body available for them to jump to.

Re-creations of portraits of Roderick and Madeline hung on the wall. The originals had turned into blackened reminders of the Family shame in the House of Morton. Below and between the portraits was an oversized jewelry armoire that held Roderick's tools. The enormous four-poster bed dominated the other partition of the chamber. Its size seemed more suited to a sporting event than sleep or amour. Neatly arranged about it were restraints that ranged from gentle to maiming.

From behind the red curtain, Roderick emerged into the parlor. He wore a smoking jacket, and carried a white dress draped over his arm. "You're late. Please put this on." He threw the dress at her. She caught it, then reached a hand toward him. He waggled a finger at her. "The dress first."

Lara stripped down to her inelegant bulky underthings that contrasted with a graceful though excessively thin body. Then, she slipped into the dress, a garment appropriate for a bride or a corpse, or both. It fit her well enough; either Roderick foresaw his victims' sizes or they were close enough in type.

Roderick studied Lara, head to toe, then turned to address the portrait of his sister. "Madeline, I know you can see me. Please watch this. Please watch what we do."

Lara stood in the dress. "What do we do?" she asked, flat voice matching flat affect.

Roderick nodded and smiled. "Once upon a time, I loved a woman very much. She hurt me for centuries. I never got to hurt her back." He gestured with his hand toward the sofa. "Please sit down. I'm afraid this is going to take a while, though not nearly as long as I would like."

Lara sat down. "You appear to have a psychological problem," she said. "Perhaps you should get help."

Roderick turned to the armoire and, one by one, brought out and displayed his tools. The first few were the standard sensual aids, but they quickly descended into devices of pain, mutilation, and death. "Sometimes I like to be friends first. I pretend it's like me and Maddie in the early days, before we cheated death. We have a little romance, but then something goes wrong—something always goes wrong—and I have to start over again. But now I have other guests coming, and hardly any time to prepare. So, no long walks and dining al fresco for us, dear."

Roderick flourished each of the items of his kit for unsuccessful surgery, waiting for her reaction. Her face looked progressively more distressed as she made little sobbing noises and said, "Please. Don't."

Roderick put down a Japanese flensing knife and took up his last tool, which appeared to be a simple tube of alchemical alloy. He flicked it forward, and a line of metal sprang out. "The sharpest edge in the world. I was saving it for . . ."

Roderick stopped speaking and stared at Lara, puzzled. "You're just sitting there. Why haven't you tried to run or fight yet?" He sniffed the air. "You smell all wrong. No fear sweat. And your sins are confused." He moved closer and stared into her eyes, then down at her throat. "Hmm. Your face shows distress, but your pulse is calm. You're not really afraid of me at all, are you? Why would he send someone like you?"

She was quick, hands like cobras seeking to touch him. He was quicker, leaping back, but he drew back his knife slower, thinking it some protection. Her index finger just grazed the nail of his right thumb. It bubbled, and the bubbles spread.

Without hesitation, Roderick sliced off the end his thumb. "Oh, no you don't!"

Lara advanced on him as he scrambled back toward the bed. "Let's make love," she said. But some instinctive aversion to touch seemed to be reasserting itself within her.

"*Please sit down*," he commanded.

Straining, Lara took another step toward him, reaching out with her right hand. A centimeter had melted from her index finger, leaving a black wound and an unsupported fingernail.

"*Down!*"

She crumbled to the floor. Roderick found a pair of black rubber gloves more suited to a butcher than a surgeon and with a wince snapped them on, covering his hands and wounded thumb. "Now see what you've done, you forced me to be rude, you goddamned . . ."

Then, slowly, like the painful start of a two-stroke engine, Roderick started to laugh. Tears came to his eyes. "Oh, that's the other trigger, isn't it? I'm supposed to kill you. This has been delightful, but I've no time for riddles. You're too precious to destroy—like destroying a fine gun instead of the assassin behind it." He waved his hand at the hidden camera mote.

W ith the wave of Roderick's hand, the images from his house disappeared on Roman's computer. As the Americans would say, the jig was up.

Roman was prepared for this possibility. Sprinting and driving all out, Roderick would take at least ten minutes to get to Roman's office. In a second, Roman grabbed his case with all the money and IDs he'd need to flee with one hand, and clutching the needle with his other, he was out from behind his desk and running, stealth full on.

Flinging open his office door, Roman stumbled backward, true terror gripping him for the first time. There, on his office threshold, stood a man dressed in a lab coat and nothing else, dark hair still slick from immersion in an alchemical tank. "You forgot that I keep my bodies downstairs," said Roderick Morton.

One last play for the great fixer, thought Roman. Using his remaining stealth and glamour, he retched and bent over. He covered his mouth with his hand, gulping hard as if trying not to throw up, but swallowing something small and plastic instead. He was still trying to get it down when Roderick gave him a barefooted kick in the head, sending him tumbling backward. "I completed transfer just before your poisoned package arrived, and I ran my former body as a meat puppet. I was preparing to depart at a comfortable pace, but you had to try this. So now I have to devote special attention and materials to you."

Roman tried to scramble farther away. Maybe he could break the window glass and fall to his death.

But no deity was listening to Roman's prayers today. Roderick grabbed Roman and threw him into one of his office chairs. *"Please be seated,"* said Roderick. "We haven't got much time, and we must make the most of it."

ELEVEN

I awoke, seated again. Would I never get to lie down?

A window to my left showed me snatches of a misty, flat, rural countryside going by beyond a broken line of leafless trees and side slopes. Not in the Chunnel, but I was on a train. *Lord, I'm usually not serious in my complaints about your will, but if this is the afterlife . . .*

I looked to my right. Grace sat there, dressed ordinary Parisian instead of English craft-glam, as if for a weekend holiday in the French countryside. *Maybe I spoke too soon, Lord.*

"Major?" she said, some concern in her voice.

"Call me Michael."

"Mike?"

"Uh, Michael, please. Though people who save my life can call me what they like." I looked at my watch, which said a day had passed. Under the French business-travel clothes that I was now wearing, I felt my gut. Smooth, not even a bandage, and no pain at all. "Are you a healer as well?" That ability didn't fit her pattern of powers for sin in the name of the service.

Uncharacteristically, Grace averted her eyes downward. "No. Not like that."

"I didn't know the French were such good healers."

"Not the French," she said.

"Are you going to tell me?" But then, I realized her eyes already had. Only one way remained that I could have been healed so quickly and completely. I patted my pockets for Dee's syringe. I was in different clothes, but that wasn't why it was gone. Grace had injected the Left-Hand alchemy into me.

It felt like jumping out of a plane and both chutes failing. Then every bad emotion competed for my heart: the two worst were anger at Grace, and despair, that sin of sins.

To calm myself, I spoke calmly. "How much did you give me?"

"You were going into shock, dying. I had to save you."

I closed my eyes. "How much?" But again, I knew the answer already. "All of it."

The Endicotts weren't like the other Families, where it was no big deal if someone went into black ops or drank some vile potion to talk to the dead. We never used the Left-Hand craft, even to save someone else's life, much less our own. I looked at my gut in spiritsight and saw the radiating glow of a black hole sun chakra.

"Do you know what you've done?" A stupid question.

"Yes," she said, in a small, hopeless voice. Then she regained herself. "Or I thought I did. I thought I was defiling an Endicott to save his sorry life. But I was wrong. You can't be just any bloody Yank. You summoned the old power of Albion. Who are you?"

Oh, this was too much. I started to laugh, bitterly, veering toward hysterically, then reined it in when I saw Grace's eyes checking the exits and her hand touching her sidearm. "You think I *know* how I summoned that power? Well, commander, it's worse than you think. Even in wartime, we Endicotts are more territory bound than most. I've always felt more disconnected overseas than the Mortons, or Hutchinsons, or any other family. Now, I'm feeling everywhere at home, if only for spiritual power."

As if in answer, that power was rising up into me, through the seat, the train, the tracks, the land. "I can feel it now," I said, "and I have no bloody idea which country we're in." That could be a problem. "Where are we?"

She sat, looking at me, silent for a long moment. Finally, she said, "You shouldn't say that."

"Say what?"

"Bloody. It's a bad, probably sacrilegious, word, and I know you don't like to say such things."

"You say it."

"I say lots of things. To answer your question, we're crossing Belgium, on a train, in a sleeper car, first class double cabin, ticketed through Prague."

Oh, sweet Jesus. "Not Prague again." Absurd trouble always found me in Prague.

"No, we'll get off at Berlin, and take a chance on a flight from there."

"To Ukraine?"

"Right. Kiev."

Kiev wasn't where the Russians had fought Roderick, but it would do as a base to look for him. I tried not to think about being in a sleeper cabin with Grace, so I thought about ticketing. I stood up—though I was healed, that still hurt. "We should move to an empty cabin."

Grace rose and gently pushed me back into my seat. "I know protocol. We're not in the cabin that I booked. We're not even on the same train. But they'll figure all that out eventually. We can only hope it's after we're gone."

"Who knows where we are?"

"That's uncertain," she said. "Too many people know where we've been. The local French helped us, but they didn't care for my use of Left-Hand craft on you. They seemed to have their own internal troubles brewing, so I didn't discuss our plans with them and went stealth for our departure. I also sent a message to the Confessional. It's a break in the chain of command, because the chain of command can go wrong. A story vital to the defense of the realm that needs to be told goes to everyone, including the very top craft authority." That wasn't the prime minister she was talking about, but her majesty herself.

"So they know we're alive."

"They know I'm alive. They'll figure out you're alive soon enough."

The accent was still killing me. No, not the accent. Her voice, because it was hers. Time to swallow my pride and get back into Grace's good graces. "Thank you for saving my life," I said. "I owe you."

She nodded, with just the hint of a Mona Lisa smile on her lips. "Yes, and I intend to collect. But first things first. Sandwich?" At Grace's feet lay a picnic basket with a baguette sticking out through one of the flaps, which had to be a bit of staging on her part. She opened the basket, and inside were the sandwiches. I was as hungry as I've ever been, and not just for food. Despite everything we'd been through, despite what she had done to save me, Grace seemed radiant. But food didn't require discussion, so I ate.

After much silent chewing, Grace said, "This trip, going eastward towards a great evil. It reminds me of something one of my ancestors did."

"Frodo Baggins was your ancestor?" Her eyes flashed at me. "Sorry. Please, continue." Honoring the ancestors was something all spiritual practitioners seemed to share, whatever the culture of those around them.

"It was Charles Marlow's journey up the Congo," she said. "The Crown sent Charles to investigate, and eventually destroy, an evil practitioner who was hiding in the midst of a greater evil, King Leopold's genocidal disaster. The target magus was using the millions of deaths to cover his own killings, experiments, and abominations. The farther Charles went up the river in pursuit of this vile man, the more powerful the magics arrayed against him. I expect it will be like that now."

"Wait," I said, "that's like *Apocalypse Now*, which was based . . ."

Grace gave me a look, lips pursed and head tilted, as she waited for all the pennies to drop.

"Oh, he was *that* Marlow." Somehow Conrad had gotten away with including the name of a real practitioner in his stories, including *Heart of Darkness*. "I should have put that together myself."

She smiled. "Yes, that's one thing. Here's another." With sureness and ease, she kissed me.

Even non-religious craftspeople weren't big on casual touching. Grace's kiss was like the lightning I'd called down in the tunnel. "Wait, I . . ."

"We have a few hours. If you have a better way to pass the time, I'm all ears, and lips, and *mmm.*"

She was warmth and closeness, and her closeness felt as natural and good as a prayer and its answer. But too many things felt natural now. I balked. I was all for women expressing their desires boldly and straightforwardly, but as a practitioner, this intimacy was threatening in too many ways, and I was a practitioner dosed up with Left-Hand alchemy. If she was using suasion, I'd never know. "I can't trust myself," I said, moving my lips away from hers. "I need to know. Am I just another duty for you?"

Anger flashed from her eyes; then she closed them, and her face went calm. "You're right. I know your background, and I still came on like this was just a bit of fun. A nice ride, because tomorrow we die. If we don't die today."

"So, it isn't? I mean, it's not just a bit of fun? Don't get me wrong, it's not a bad idea. Not the worst sin I could think of." I took a deep breath. "You are the most exciting woman I've ever known. But I don't know how it is for you. You wear that cross, but all your gifts, well, they seem to have a pattern."

She said it for me. "All my gifts allow me to sin effectively. But all my sins are in the name of defending the realm. Never for myself. Nothing for myself."

"Nothing?"

"You mean, did I enjoy them? Of course, as with anything, to achieve excellence, I had to enjoy them, at least a little, even if it's just the enjoyment of being good at them. You should know right now: I have slept with several men and a couple of women for the Crown, and they were convinced by my passion, and shocked by my betrayal." She held a hand to my lips. "Before you say anything, just think a moment. You also sin. Like me, you kill."

"But that's different," I said, "that was . . ." And then the logic kicked in. "For Queen and Country?"

"For Queen and Country."

That reminded me of the big long-term problem. "I'm an American."

"Do you always talk so much?" She seemed more teasing than upset.

I grimaced and shook my head. I usually didn't get the opportunity.

"We're on the run," she said, again with teasing emphasis. "We'll be lucky if we survive long enough to worry about national issues."

I nodded, trying to keep my stupidities to a minimum.

"Look," she said, "I have you at an advantage." All too true. "I've studied your file thoroughly. I watched our surveillance footage of you, again and again." She had that embarrassed look again. "You're a good man, good in ways that I would find difficult to credit in a mundane, much less in our line of work. I think you'd be good for me. I would like to get to know you better."

"Even though I'm an Endicott?"

"Your name doesn't seem so very important, now I've seen you, and been with you. I am a Marlow, and we don't worship the Bard of Avon, but 'a rose by any other name' might apply here."

"So, I'm not just a challenge?"

She smiled, very wickedly. "True, part of the attraction is the challenge. But far from all of it."

I felt the crossing of a border; we must have been entering Germany. "Thank you for talking about this." I took her hand in mine. "Anything physical is a serious thing for me."

"So let's get serious."

Lord, it's not by the Numbers (or any other book in the Bible except the Song of Songs), but I think this might be the right move. Please forgive me if I get it wrong. I kissed her.

The kiss, the touch, was even more electric than the first. I had complete focus in the moment, as if this were some particularly difficult bit of prayer that I had to get right to save some fellow soldiers. But then, from somewhere, a distraction, a buzzing noise. Not a pleasant buzz in my head, more like a mechanical mosquito. It sounded like my phone. I had turned it off, but maybe while I'd been unconscious someone had turned it on (just like its owner). The universe seemed intent on preventing me from lying with a woman. I broke our kiss. "Just a moment," I whispered.

Pulling against a playful tug from Grace, I fumbled for the phone. The off button wasn't working, and there was a message on the screen.

Dear Major Endicott:

My regrets to you and yours, I know you've had a hard day's night. I had thought that my scenario in which I destroyed your ancestor and my tormentor Abram would suffice, and that I would not have to pay personal attention to your demise. I was mistaken. I find that I need to keep killing Endicotts, or I lose some of my new-found joie de vivre. Please forgive my imposition.

As for the device you hold in your hands, you may be an expert texter, but the jester on the hill laughs at you. Cry for "Help!" all you want; the only one who will hear you is me.

Here, there, and everywhere yours,

Roderick.

P.S. I loathe you. ;)

"What's so distracting?" asked Grace.

According to Family lore, Roderick always got a little punchy before doing something particularly horrible. "We need to run," I said. "Now."

Then the train blew up.

"Do you intend to keep me here as a prisoner?" asked Scherie. She could only hope she was being rhetorical.

"There's no need for dramatics," said the Pythia. She set down a tray with lunch for both of them on the table in Scherie's room. The grilled lamb and the inevitable Greek salad looked and smelled delicious, but Scherie wasn't going to let hunger delay her another minute.

"Then I'm leaving," said Scherie, as she continued shoving her few effects into a Delphi museum souvenir bag. She wore a souvenir T-shirt, head scarf, and sunglasses, all without having seen the shrine or the museum except through the video streams. She hoped no one asked her what she thought of Delphi on her way to Athens.

"But how will you reach Endicott? We've only just found him. After Calais, he could have gone back to your country. He could be anywhere."

"No, not anywhere." Bag over her shoulder, Scherie stepped into the corridor and walked toward the elevator, and the Pythia kept pace with her, waving away the staffers who approached them. "The *Oikumene* hasn't been in a real shooting war in a long time, have they?"

"I do not see what that has to do . . ."

"It's basic military training," said Scherie. "Soldiers don't run away from enemy fire, and they don't hunker down. They do what every bit of common sense says they shouldn't. They move into the fire, into the fight."

"That is disturbing. You're too important to risk."

"I'm a weapon, and I'm too important not to deploy." That was the lesson she'd taken away from the fight in the Pentagon. Perhaps Scherie was fighting the last war, but she had shit little else to go on.

The elevator opened immediately, and the two women took it up together. Scherie tried for a better good-bye. "Thank you for everything you have done for me. I am grateful, but before I can help you, I have to help those close to me. But we will return."

Pythia shook her head and said, "I wish I could be as certain. We can see very little on this path. *Adio*, Lieutenant Rezvani."

"*Adio.*"

The elevator opened. Scherie exited it alone into the museum, as if she had just taken it up from the other exhibit level. She ignored the entering tourists and strode out into the bright cool day.

She walked away from the shrine area toward the town. She would hop on the first bus to Athens, if she couldn't hitch a ride. She hadn't been able to appreciate the beauty of the area before leaving the *Oikumene* bunker. The shrine and town were on the side of a spur of Parnassus, and below to her left Scherie could see a wooded valley. The far-off Gulf of Corinth sparkled. Tall cypresses guarded her way.

As Scherie crossed the boundary of the shrine's power, Madeline appeared, strolling on her left, using a long spear as a walking stick. Her long hair was pinned up in the ancient style, with just a strand provocatively out of place. She was wearing a chiton, the basic woman's garment of classical Greece, and it had Greek letters and a right-pointing arrow stitched into it.

"What's your shirt say?" asked Scherie.

"I'm with stupid."

"Very funny."

"No, the simple truth. You're leaving this place, which is safe, and going somewhere else, which isn't."

"I'm not discussing my plans with you."

"You don't have to. But wherever you're going, wouldn't you like some nice weapons as souvenirs?" Madeline shook her spear at her. "Just a little knife, even? I know I would."

Scherie stopped her rapid clip along the walkway. She had been planning to improvise arms purchases, but the *Oikumene* could help with that. "I wasn't very nice to my hosts just now."

"They'll forgive you; you're important. Yes, we know that the ancient office of Pythia and her *Oikumene* seem very mysterious and mighty, but who the hell do you think *we* are? Now go back down there and tell that stingy bitch to open up her armory and to drive you back to Athens, ASAP. They can also see to your other travel arrangements. You're a Morton now, and we do not suffer fools or anything less than first class gladly."

As she spun on her heels, Scherie thought, *Madeline Morton, empowerment coach.*

Rezvani's return wasn't a great surprise to the Pythia; the Left-Hand revenant had been circling the shrine area like a shark, and those dark spirits had a way of making people more demanding. The Pythia and her staff were annoyed at the tone of Rezvani's demands, but not the demands themselves, as they improved Rezvani's chance of survival. Her physical examination had been negative, so it was essential that she live long enough to meet her husband again.

After the American left for the second time, the Pythia made her calls. She hadn't discussed her other concern with Rezvani; it was something that took time to understand. In repelling Roderick's attacks, Endicott had displayed the transnational power.

This had happened many times before. Often in response to some inchoate need, a hero of the *Oikumene* would arise, a great magus who could summon the power across many lands. With that strength, a practitioner could break down the old craft boundaries and do battle with his or her generation's incarnation of the Left-Hand way.

In a sense, the *Oikumene* wielded something like that power through its multinational members, and in such an institution, diluted and dispersed, the power was relatively safe from corruption. But in an individual, even a well-intentioned one, that power had an inevitable consequence. Such a magus could build an empire for himself.

Alexander and Caesar had vividly displayed the problems with those who had started with good intentions and way too much craft. Unfortunately, the solution to those problems hadn't changed. The *Oikumene* would not let things get as bad as they had in earlier times. They would watch Endicott, and if he showed any taint of imperial aspirations or the Left-Hand way, they would kill him.

Almost to his disappointment, Dale wasn't being taken to one of those legendary craft subbasement dungeons of Lubyanka. He had become an expert on evil fortresses below the earth's surface, and he would have liked to view the structure and its craft. But Dale was also an expert at taphephobia, the fear of being buried alive, so he was relieved when the Russians told him that he was bound for one of their rooms for foreign guests in the Mercury City Tower. "On an upper floor," his escort emphasized. He must have read Dale's file.

Despite this escort's courtesy, Dale did not like or trust him. His suit and shirts were indistinguishable from a successful Russian mobster's.

Dale had once enjoyed the green Gorky Park of midsummer here, but this was the grim Moscow of late autumn. That did not disturb him so much as the view of the Mercury City Tower's copper-colored cladding, which reminded him of the alchemical brass-colored alloys often used for Left-Hand craft. The post-Soviet Russians had a way of flirting with the Left Hand that made Dale uneasy.

The Russians hustled Dale through the Tower's lobby and took him up in an elevator to an unnumbered floor. Dale counted the seconds and listened for any telltale noises. It wasn't the second floor, but it probably wasn't one of the top floors of the seventy-five-story building either. When they left the elevator and walked toward their room for him, it seemed to Dale from the openness of the floor plan that the Russian craft service had at least all of this floor of the Tower; they probably enjoyed having some space to themselves and away from the Federal Security Service over in Lubyanka.

At the door to his room, Dale said, "I wish to speak with the American Embassy," and made the other standard protests for the record.

His escort heard him out and replied, "We are just delaying your travel for national security and your own safety. The usual protocols do not apply."

"Whatever is happening with Roderick, I could help."

The Russian seemed grimly amused by that. "Americans. Always wanting to help." Then he shut the door on Dale.

Compared to the many cheap hotel rooms Dale had known, this "guest suite" was nice enough, though it locked from the outside. The room had no windows, but the lighting design helped one forget that. The bed was simple, but a damned samovar occupied the space where a coffeepot might have been. They had even given him hotel-style sample-sized toiletries.

For food, he was greeted with some dark bread and caviar (not an extravagant amount, just a taste to be welcoming) and bar nuts and pretzels. Within the hour they offered him a full meal, but Dale ate little—his current concern for Scherie wasn't helping his old PTSD stomach. As the jailers would prefer it if their guest found a way to occupy the time instead of attempting to escape, they also provided bottles of Stoli and Laphroaig, and satellite TV with enough international channels to assure the guest that he wasn't missing the end of the world, so calm down.

They'd probably want Dale to give the place a favorable review at CraftPrisons.com.

Other than dealing with his food, no one came to talk with him.

The geomancy of the structure and its location oozed power, and Dale sensed plenty of human energy keeping an eye on him. He was anxious about Scherie, and even gave Endicott a thought just to relieve the monotony, but for all he knew the Russians were right, and Roderick was in the karmic crosshairs. For now, Dale had nowhere to go, so it wasn't time to break out. Yet.

Exhausted, he took off his clothes and lay down on the bed, and after a few flips through the TV channels, gave up. Perhaps the Russians had inadvertently done him a favor: after his travel, he wasn't ready for Roderick. Though the Moscow ground wasn't friendly to him, the Tower harnessed the local energy so effectively that it had some energy to spare, even for a foreigner. Letting the power seep back into him, Dale fell asleep.

"Major Morton." Dale awoke into darkness and stone-cold fear. Someone was in the room and had spoken his name.

Show me their sins. A glow of letters illuminated a tall woman's form, sitting very still in a chair facing the bed. For a moment, Dale was worried that Madeline had, despite all, found a way to incarnate again, for this body was surely her type. But Dale looked at her sins, and saw only a few of the usual acts committed in the line of duty.

"You could have knocked," he said. This stranger had a dangerous disregard for her own safety.

She answered in heavily accented English. "I wish to have advantage. You are Morton, like him."

A sudden rush of guesses about this woman and Roderick hit Dale, and all of them were bad news. "What is your name?"

"No need to know," she said. "You can call me Vasilisa."

"Vasilisa." A Russian fairytale name. "Can we use panglossic? Language craft?"

"No," she said. "No craft. English."

"OK, no craft. You've met my ancestor." Dale spared her the name.

"Yes," she said. "He killed my friends. All of them."

"Just now?" If so, Dale needed to leave immediately, as this meant the Russians' hoped-for solution was gone.

"No. Weeks before. He did not kill me. But he gives nothing free."

Oh, this was bad. No wonder everyone was after Dale. He had not realized that Roderick had been so active in the craft world. "He let you live?" asked Dale. "To do what?"

"To tell story," she said. "To scare everyone. To scare me. To show all how big Left Hand is. When I wake up, my boss ask about devil body, devil power. Your devil makes them want Left Hand."

Yes, Roderick would have known the effect of his appearance. "What did he look like?"

"He wore mask," she said. "Red Death. But we know what he look like. Russian. Like model Soviet worker—big jaw, blond hair."

Dale got out of bed and turned on the light, not caring that he was in underwear. He began to put on his clothes. "I have to leave here, to kill him."

"Yes," said Vasilisa, insistently. "Leave here. I cannot sleep. They will hold you here." Her voice cracked, and she shook her head in desperate negation. "He will come here for you. He will find me."

"How can I leave?"

"Come." She stood and walked toward the wall.

Vasilisa raised a fist, and Dale jerked aside as she gave the wall of his suite a solid smack. This action revealed a glowing keypad. She pressed some numbers, and a section of the wall slid aside to uncover an office building window above a narrow interior shelf, an appropriate arrangement for when the guest wasn't being held incommunicado. Dale could see the lights of Moscow at night, and all those lights were far, far below him.

Vasilisa pointed emphatically at the window. "You go."

"You want me to kill myself," said Dale, "so Roderick doesn't come here."

"What is problem?" asked the Russian, brow furrowed. "Break window, step out, problem gone." She gave a forced little smile.

"I'm missing something here. Do you think I can fly?"

"Yes, yes, you fly."

"I don't know what you've heard, but Mortons can't fly. Maybe glide a little, but not down this."

"Is stupid!" She looked at her watch. "Time is up. You hurry."

"We need to use panglossic."

"Fine. Very stupid, but no difference now."

Dale said, "*Panglossic,*" Vasilisa said something else, and a small flash of craft came from both of them. Vasilisa continued speaking, but now she sounded like a particularly erudite and exasperated professor. "You idiot! Look. Some of my *spetsnaz* colleagues and I have had a disagreement with the Oprichniki on detaining you, a very strong disagreement. We want you on the scene, yesterday, and we'll deal with any fallout."

Dale heard the noise of an approaching copter. Against the night sky, a patch of greater darkness moved toward the window.

"Despite our measures against your captors' monitoring, they will have detected this use of craft and be on their way. Fortunately, we have only seconds to leave here anyway. We have already weakened this area of the wall. Break the fucking window!"

Dale focused on the copper-colored window, and visualized a strong pressure differential between the immediate inside and outside of the building. He put his hands to the ice-cold glass, gave a strong push of body and mind, and said, "*Break!*"

With a crack and a whoosh, the window and the whole section of capping material fell down toward the ground. Dale hoped no one was hurt; Vasilisa seemed not to care as she pushed Dale aside just in time to avoid two weighted fast ropes that shot through the window from the copter's open side door. Dale stood on the narrow shelf and wrapped a rope through his feet and held firm to it, while Vasilisa first removed the weights, then prepared her own rope.

Behind them, the door to the suite was opening. They had timed this a little too precisely for Dale's taste. No room for error, and there was always error.

"Now go!" shouted Vasilisa, giving him a shove forward.

With a hop, Dale and Vasilisa sailed into the cold Moscow night. The helicopter dropped slightly with the sudden weight. They swung down, under, and then behind the moving copter on their his-and-her lines, as if the building itself were trying to pull them back.

They dangled in the open frozen air, but they didn't remain still. Even before they had stopped swinging, Dale went into combat craft mode to speed his climb up the fast rope. A caving ladder or a basket would have been nice, but they were relying on his skills, and he wouldn't disappoint.

A snap of air, and a tug against his jacket, flapping in the wind. Damn, he'd liked that jacket, and now it had a bullet hole through it. Above the wind and the rotors, the explosive retort of rifles echoed through the airways of the night, and a couple of shots pinged off the copter's armor. His former captors were shooting at him, and shooting at their own too. This gave Dale a bad feeling beyond the usual concern for his own safety or that of his rescuer. Was this division part of what Roderick wanted? The bad guys' fire was craft-impelled, but in combat mode Dale had instinctively skewed the ballistic probabilities, and the bullets snapped the air in curves around him. But he hadn't had enough craft to save the jacket. Damn.

Behind him, a louder explosion than the guns. Dale wondered about those line weights that Vasilisa had left. The copter slowed, allowing the ropes to swing closer to plumb, and Dale felt his line being drawn up even as he continued his climb. After some more long seconds, hands reached down to help Dale and then Vasilisa into the copter, which accelerated again, away from the skyscraper and Moscow.

Instead of a greeting, a *spetsnaz* man said, "Her English is shit, yes?" in his own rough accent. The *spetsnaz* probably had money on the answer, which from the narrowness of the timing was self-evident.

Dale had had enough of internecine conflict. As he sat down, he asked, "We're not going all the way to Kiev in this, right?"

"Go to base, near Kubinka. From base, jet to Kiev."

"Aren't you worried about pursuit?" asked Dale, pointing behind them, and repeating for emphasis. "Pursuit?"

The *spetsnaz* chuckled grimly. "Who chases Morton in air?"

He had a point, but he was still wrong. The pilot reported that a couple of other copters were already in pursuit, and a jet would be on them in seconds.

It was nighttime, so the public wouldn't see. Dale focused. "*Storm shield,*" he said, and a cyclonic spherical shell of wind formed around them, moving with deadly swiftness at its interior peak, but giving a fair warning of turbulence at its edges. *Here comes the twister.* A favorite spell, but one he used rarely because of its demands.

Despite Dale having done what no other weatherman in the world (save perhaps Roderick) could do, the *spetsnaz* seemed disappointed. "Why not lightning? Why not crash them?"

"I don't want to kill them if I can help it."

The *spetsnaz* waggled his open hand. "A few is no problem."

I bet, thought Dale. "Already a few, back there," he noted.

"That was flash bang. No big deal. But I understand."

Vasilisa, silent until now, grabbed Dale's arm for attention. "I'm a little busy here," he said.

"You will kill him?" Even in panglossed Russian, she still wasn't speaking Roderick's name.

Already feeling the fatigue of his work against their pursuers, Dale said, "Yes." Because the longer Roderick lived, the worse things would get.

PART V

UKRAINE GHOSTS REALLY KNOCK ME OUT

Here, you may look in whatsoever direction you please, and your eye encounters scarcely any thing but ruin, ruin, ruin!
—Mark Twain

Camilla: You, sir, should unmask.
Stranger: Indeed?
Cassilda: Indeed it's time. We have all laid aside disguise but you.
—Robert W. Chambers

THIRTEEN

A few believers might have interpreted a train blowing up and interrupting our carnal pleasure as a sign from God. Such believers were assholes. Yes, God wanted me pure. No, he didn't kill innocents for that.

First we heard the blast and felt the rumble. The train car bounced once, hard. Then the world started to tilt sidewise to the right as we ran off the rails. Our limited baggage, the picnic basket, and the remaining food toppled onto us. The cabin shook horribly as the car skidded along on its side; it seemed to slide forever.

The train stopped. I smelled smoke and other fumes. Our window appeared to be our best exit. We were together against the cabin door and wall. Grace pulled her hand away from her head and it was a little bloody, but she didn't seem to be otherwise hurt. "Let's get out of here," she said.

We stood up. We'd have to climb out. "Wait," I said. I bashed my phone against the floor, which was now a wall. Then I opened the door a crack and slipped the phone out, shutting the door behind it. Some smoke slipped in, further encouraging a quick departure. The train's injured and scared were yelling and screaming.

Grace checked her phone. "My GPS says we've just crossed into Germany. We're near Aachen."

"Great. Now drop that phone too."

"Why?"

"Roderick. He's got some kind of cyber-craft from his time in H-ring. He was able to turn my phone on remotely."

She repeated my moves as if her phone were some scalding hot vermin. More smoke and screams came through the door. Time to go.

I lifted Grace to the window. I'm not sure the window was actually an emergency exit. Grace placed her hands on it, and like the window or lock to any vehicle she encountered, the glass gave for her, popping out like a bad contact lens.

She peered out through the open space and, apparently satisfied that there was no immediate threat, was up and out. Cold mist drifted down on me. With her still bloody and now wet hand, Grace helped me up, and when I stood next to her on the side of the wrecked car, the world went fish-eyed with a stealth bubble. The bubble had irregular curves to it and didn't seem stable.

"How are you doing?" I asked.

"Still a little wibbly wobbly from the crash," she said, sounding unprofessionally tipsy. Was she concussed? "I'll cover both of us for as long as I can. Where are we going?"

My first instinct was to help the other passengers; I shared some blame for their situation. But before that, I had to make sure that I wouldn't again be making them a target.

German border ghosts were keeping their watch on the Rhineland and on us, but they weren't approaching. In the background of the screams and shouting, I heard a whirring noise and looked up. Multirotor drones circled above the wreck, one high up, the other close in, hovering over survivors. These weren't little toys for the hobbyist; they looked military grade. But unlike the big fixed-wing Predators, these rotor jobs weren't very fast. Only one way they could already be here—they were sent in advance. That meant the trainwreck was just our enemies' opening move, perhaps just to soften us up.

The drones didn't appear to be large enough for serious armament, though just one clean shot at close range would be a problem. The armed threat was on the ground. Two boxy-shaped unmanned ground vehicles were crawling rapidly toward the wreck on hybrid wheel/caterpillar treads. These camo-colored robots could have been for bomb disposal, but once again, they were far too early on the scene. Also, they were bulkier than usual for disposal work, and they each appeared to have a Gatling-style Minigun for one of their "arms."

From somewhere—the drones, the robots?—an amplified voice was giving orders in a succession of languages. In English, it said, "Please remain calm and still. Help is on the way. Do not move from the crash site."

Clutching his injured arm, a passenger ran for it. A robot fired ahead of him. The man hit the dirt. "Please remain calm and still . . ."

Once again, I was appalled at the effort Roderick and his allies had made to get me. Perhaps they had sent drones to avoid capture of their agents, but I think it was also to avoid my power of command. Sure, some humans on the other end were watching and listening, but my power of command was limited to the range of a natural voice. Otherwise, all sorts of craft would be transmitted wirelessly around the world. Perhaps Roderick had mastered that trick, but no one else.

The stealth bubble flickered, and Grace leaned against me. Trouble— her concentration and craft were failing. The lower hovering drone turned and whirred toward us for a closer look. One of the ground robots also used its treads to make a two-point turn and moved in our direction. "Help is on the way . . ." The robot raised its gun arm into a sighted alignment on us. Somewhere, many miles away, a human waited for the order to take the shot.

I knew from Roderick's message who the real target was. So, I let Grace drop onto the smooth surface of the train. "What . . . ?" she said, as I jumped away from her to the ground.

As I leapt forward and down, the robot's rotor-gun spun, and shots filled all the places I'd been moments before. I rolled with my landing, and came up into a sprinter's stance, ready to run as long as I could to give Grace time.

My hands and feet touched the ground.

This old, old ground. It was like kissing Grace all over again, only twice as powerful and no fun at all. I had lain exhausted in my Family's house after giving everything and more in combat, recovering from wounds physical, mental, and spiritual. I'd felt the spiritual power of our ancestral place enter me and the Spirit heal me.

But here, I felt such a tremendous power that I thought I'd explode with it.

The robot had re-sighted on me, and the other robot was closing. "Do not move . . ."

Miles away, but I could feel them, the men and women who worked these machines. They were somewhere in this land; they were its natural subjects. As if I were some kind of herald of the Kingdom, I cried out in a loud voice. *"In the name of the Lord of Hosts, you will stand down!"*

Like shot birds, the flying drones fell out of the sky. The robots made some noises as they locked into a standby position. "Please . . ." they said. Then silence.

I scanned three-sixty for any backup threat. Nothing, but I wanted to keep giving orders. First, clean up this mess. Then, mobilize all NATO forces. Then, bring order back to the West. It would be so simple, like dominoes falling. Then I could bring God's word back to the whole world.

A hand touched my trembling arm. Unheard, with her preternatural skill, Grace had left the train and stood next to me. "Are you OK? What do you want me to do?"

Like the whole world was asking that question. I was shaking with it. The rocks and stones themselves awaited my commands. It hurt so much I started laughing through the tears. To give my mouth something to do that wasn't an order, I spoke to my enemy, my only true enemy, through clenched teeth. "Just because I wanted a little nooky, Lucifer, doesn't mean the old 'world for my soul' deal is going to fly. *Get the fuck to the rear, Satan!"*

Like a flame sucked up by a tornado, the power left me. Grace and I leaned into each other. She whispered in my ear, "I do hope you weren't speaking to me, dear."

"No," I said. "You're an angel, but not fallen." I knew my German geography as well as most experienced officers. From here, the closest international airport would be Frankfurt. Locals were starting to arrive on the scene—EMTs, firemen, press, and the curious. "We need a car," I said. "Are you up to it? A very fast car."

"That, I can arrange," said Grace.

Grace stole a gull-wing Mercedes, and I drove it down the autobahn toward Frankfurt. Normally, she would have driven, as sports car racing matched her skill set, but she was probably concussed, so she let me take the wheel. I'd driven and flown all sorts of vehicles in all sorts of conditions, and if I hadn't been in combat mode and worried about the traffic, driving at close to two hundred miles an hour would have been the most mechanical fun I'd ever had.

I repeated to Grace what I could remember of Roderick's message. "Are there some pop culture references that I'm not getting?"

"Roderick appears to like the Beatles," she said with desert dryness.

"He also blew up a train!" It had been like something I'd seen in battle. Then the realization hit me: this was now a war. Roderick had used conventional means, which could be blamed on conventional terrorists, so he wouldn't immediately draw down the united wrath of the great powers for outing the craft, but this sort of display would have repercussions. Roderick didn't seem to care.

I wasn't sure how we'd get a flight in Frankfurt that he couldn't find and attack; I'd leave that to Grace, when she'd recovered enough. I had another problem. "I'm a little concerned about this international power thing that I've been tapping into," I said.

"Oh?" she said.

"I'm thinking that I'll have to draw on it to fight Roderick."

"That is a problem?"

"Yeah. The power, this last time, it wasn't neutral. It made me want to do things. To make others do things."

"Oh," she said. "I like to do new things. And if you expect me to kill you to save the world, that isn't going to happen."

"Maybe just a little nudge back to reality?"

"I'll find a way to distract you," she said, closing her eyes.

Despite her head injury, I let Grace sleep—I'd wake her soon enough to check on her. Trying not to be distracted, I passed another two cars. Ahead was Frankfurt, and Kiev, and Roderick. He had killed so many innocents; had he already killed my friends? I had to stop him. But who then would stop me?

G race and I boarded a plane to Kiev. She had regained her con-centration and her stealth, and our seats slid in and out of the flight attendants's counts—whichever caused the least trouble. With this stealth and a short enough flight, Grace thought the odds were good we'd make it. I prayed she was right or that Roderick would be otherwise occupied; I didn't want these passengers on my conscience if they died with me.

During the flight, we didn't display much affection. Perhaps things were too new between us. Perhaps it was just me. Like Dale and Sche-rie, many other practitioners moved quickly into romance and mar-riage with the confidence of a spiritually fated love. My Family had always avoided this; we believed the risks of spiritual manipulation were too great to trust such sudden delusions of destiny. In the ab-stract, this made perfect sense, but it was hard to keep that cool per-spective now that I was caught up in a spirit-driven *something* for the first time. I couldn't deny it anymore; my heart was full of far more than a carnal desire not to die a virgin. My upright, logical center was lost in a sea of feeling for Grace, but the very strength of that feeling made me want to step back from our closeness. Did Grace feel this way too? As with anything important, I prayed on it, but that only seemed to make the emotions stronger, and that couldn't be right, could it?

Grace looked at me, eyes filled with uncanny understanding and amused pity. "Poor boy," she said, giving my hand a friendly squeeze. "You'll figure it out."

So instead of exchanging more affectionate words and caresses, we slept in the way that only soldiers who've learned desperation for rack time could. We could do nothing else, not even if someone decided to hit the plane.

My sword was above in the overhead rack. I'd used some strong suasion to get it through security, though the blade wouldn't be very helpful.

When we awoke for landing, I asked Grace where Roderick would be. "Do we go to Chernobyl?"

"I don't think so. We're not sure how he convinced the Russians he was living there, but we think he's in Kiev. Maybe he's in the city's catacombs. He could be anywhere down there. The Ukrainians are known for their stealth."

Remembering Roman, I agreed.

We arrived at the Kiev Boryspil Airport at an off hour. At passport control, the lines weren't long, and the mundane world seemed quiet and normal. But the spiritual world was an ectoplasmic mess.

Only two ghosts manned this border, which even for a relatively new state seemed strange. From the cover of unoccupied passport control booths, the two spirits were shooting at each other. A babushka with the rifle and look of a Second World War partisan shot at a man dressed in Cossack garb. "Surrender!" she bellowed. "You're serving a foreign devil."

The Cossack shot back across the room. "He can bring us back!" he yelled. "In new bodies!"

"Can't, and won't!" yelled the babushka.

Grace said something in Latin about *omnilingua*, and only then did I realize the ghosts were speaking Ukrainian. I understood them, and I hadn't consciously used panglossic.

No other spirits and no craftspeople that I could see, though if they were like Roman, that might not mean much. I spoke toward Grace, but my question was addressed to the ghosts. "Where are the other spiritual guards?"

"No foreign powers in this time of crisis," chorused the ghosts. It seemed to be the only thing they could agree on.

I thought the babushka might share our interest. "We're here to remove Roderick," I said.

Another exchange of ectoplasmic rifle fire flashed. "They've gone to headquarters," yelled the babushka. "Some summoned." She spat. "Some not. But good luck finding that place before you're old. This is Ukraine."

The Cossack also had words for us. "I have alerted craft security. You will wait for their arrival."

No, we wouldn't. Two combat-fatigued ghosts couldn't even give us a burn, and the babushka now seemed to be delivering covering fire for us. Our passport person seemed nervous—a mundane can generally sense a spiritual disturbance without actually seeing it. I suggested she let us through, and she did, as did customs.

"The Baba Yagas' headquarters will be difficult to find," said Grace.

"Unless some of them want to be found," I said. If the ghosts were fighting, the living would be too. I pulled out a tourist map, and I saw—no, I felt—how the city lines converged on the rounded end of Independence Square. That would be like them: hiding in what should be the plainest sight in town.

With more money than time, we took an unofficial airport limo. The car smelled like old incontinent dog and sausage. The young driver seemed anxious to practice English with us and to point out the numerous horse-chestnut trees, though they were autumnally bare. As a capital city, Kiev had defensive, rainbow-hued beams that shot from Orthodox domes, Stalinist concrete blocks, and modern glass and steel. The beams were distracting, but they weren't very many or very strong.

As we approached the city center, the traffic slowed, then halted, though it was the middle of the day and nowhere near rush hour. The driver got on his phone and relayed the news to us. "Is big bullshit. Maybe government shoot government. Good, but you not go there."

"It's OK," I said. "We'll get out here."

Despite the driver's protests, we exited the car with our limited belongings and walked in the direction of worsening gridlock and some ineffable wrongness. I felt the wrong before we saw it, tugging me like a river current flowing toward an abyss of darkness. Craft alarums rang like the many church bells, probably not heard since the Germans took the city. Ghosts were moving with us in the direction of the wrong; a group of three tried to interfere, shouting, "Two very powerful foreign mages are moving toward headquarters with bad intent." But these ghosts were soon shouting at other spirits.

At the rounded far end of the open square was a modern, narrow, glass-box building, distinct from its stony and older neighbors. That, and the riot of ectoplasmic and craft forces shooting out from it, told us that we were at the right place.

Whatever power had kept the Baba Yagas' headquarters hidden had now flagged or was otherwise occupied in the conflict, allowing mundanes to pin the building down in their view. From the streets and the square, curious people stared at the structure, seeing it clearly for the first time. After a minute or so of looking, most gawkers shuddered and made for distant ground. Security forces began forming a perimeter, but they were unhurried and for the moment more concerned with the people outside the building.

Ghosts from all over the country seemed to have gathered in the square. Some were fighting each other within the perimeter, others just stared up at the building in ghastly silence. No practitioners were working outside to contain this situation and reassure the crowd. Conventional gunshots from the building reverberated into the square.

The physical aspects of the drama were all playing out in the open, in public view. As for the spiritual, anyone with any sensitivity would know that something strange was going on. If the global media took this seriously, it might have very bad implications for practitioners everywhere.

Dark clouds were gathering above the disorder, but they only complemented the mood. If Roderick was summoning weather against us, he'd need a bigger storm.

Perhaps noting that we were steadily studying the headquarters, two of the uniformed men in the perimeter were looking in our direction. Grace indicated a Ukrainian fast-food restaurant, so we ducked into it. Inside, it smelled like McDonald's fries with a side of borscht. Customers were muttering about terrorists or cursing with the odd triple epithet of "Jewish Communist Masons."

We stood at the restaurant window with a view of the Baba Yagas' building across the hemicircle. Eyes forward, Grace said, "I can get us through the mundanes, but what then?"

First things first: would we go up, or down to some damned Left-Hand basement? Another look answered that question. A corner of the top story facing the square was glowing with the blood-red heartbeat craft that was Roderick's signature. He wasn't hiding his work.

Assaulting the wizard's tower was a sport for gamers. "I don't want to call on that much power." I had the now familiar feeling that a foreign place was still good ground for me, and I could again lose myself all too easily in the power that I could summon.

"We can't stay in here forever," said Grace. "It'll make me a vegetarian."

As if in answer, the ectoplasmic fire dwindled, stopped, and the ghosts in the square all turned toward us. Then, a wail like the truly damned went up, echoing around the square.

The ghosts outside the building fled, their faces the full spectrum of fear and terror. No, they hadn't been looking toward us, just in our direction.

Grace stood poised for imminent combat. "Something's coming," she said. "Something terrible. Is it Roderick?"

"I don't think so." I knew of only one power in the world that could cause so many dead so much fear. Not daring to hope or drop my guard, I said, "I think it's my friend." We stepped out of the restaurant.

A woman dressed like an American tourist from Hades was striding down one of the streets that curved like comet orbits into the square. She looked a little leaner, a little meaner, than even a few weeks ago. She stopped near the police line, chanting with Buddhist steadiness that stream of angry sailor's profanity that powered her craft, adding a touch of panglossic so any spirits would be clear on what she wanted them to do with their ghostly parts. Some of the locals laughed nervously at the apparently insane Yankee, others were answering with epithets of their own.

I hadn't been this glad to see a Morton since the Pentagon. But the police didn't look happy about this foul-mouthed observer, probably taking her remarks personally. "Come on, we have to get her away from there."

Then, the news got even better. Another familiar, dark-featured figure was running around the pond in the square toward the building. "Scherie!" he called.

Her mouth stopped, hanging open mid-invective as she turned. My two friends embraced with the fierceness of those who cross battlefields to meet. The security folks seemed to relax; some of the crowd applauded and hooted. "Yankee, get a room!"

Grace was watching with me. "Your friends?"

"Yeah."

"Those are the Mortons?"

"Yeah. I'll introduce you."

CHAPTER

FOURTEEN

I strode out to them ahead of Grace, hands and arms open. But they only had eyes for each other. As the ranking officer, I'd have to chew them out about that lack of situational awareness. Later.

"Sorry I'm late," Dale was saying, "tough commute." He looked Scherie over top to bottom, and he must've seen something in his craft-sight that he didn't like at all. "You've been wounded!"

"So?" she said. "Don't I get a special party, or club membership, or something?"

"Um, attention," I said, from not more than five feet away.

Their heads whipped around together. Oh, yeah, I wouldn't ever let them live down this moment of tactical surprise. "Did you miss me?"

My family was never big on emotional display, romantic or otherwise, so I was a little taken aback at their full double-armed hugs. "Mike," said Dale, "you magnificent bastard, you're alive."

Scherie tried to look displeased. "What is it with you two and suicide missions?"

"And what are *you* doing here?" I asked.

"I'm here because I knew you'd be, and I mean you in particular," she said, jabbing at me with her finger.

A small sound of polite throat clearing behind me, so I made introductions. "Scherie, Dale, this is Grace, one of our friends from the UK."

Dale's eyes went a little wider with appreciation and dangerous mirth. "Friends, eh?"

But Scherie cut him off. "Greetings from the American Families," she said, in echo of my welcome to her in H-ring on that bad day. Sometimes karma worked out OK.

In the language of her people, Grace still seemed a little gobsmacked. "You're the Mortons?"

"Yes," said Scherie, putting a little New England drawl into it. "You seem surprised."

"It's nothing," Grace said. "I was just expecting something more gothic."

Scherie smiled. "That's the House. We're more American contemporary."

"That was a truly impressive exorcism," Grace noted. Scherie's smile broadened with justified pride.

"In her spiritual area, she's a nuke," I agreed.

"You were going after Roderick without her?"

Shrugging had been drubbed out of me early, so I said, "Maybe."

More gunfire echoed from the building. Somebody with a bullhorn was suggesting that the building's occupants come out with their hands up so that they could be killed more conveniently.

"Anyone else feeling underdressed for this chilly environment?" asked Dale, cocking his finger toward the building like a gun.

"I could obtain some small arms quickly," said Grace. "But whatever is happening in there will be long over before I could find heavy armament."

Scherie had the thin smile of a cat trying to keep a large canary in her mouth. "I may be able to help."

Minutes later, we were peering into the back of an SUV that Scherie had parked just down a narrow street from the square, in front of a house museum for a Ukrainian poet. We were staring at all the weapons: big honking cases of firearms and ammunition.

"I love you," said Dale.

"Me too," I said to Scherie.

"Special relationship forever," said Grace.

"It's all courtesy of the *Oikumene*," said Scherie.

"The *Oikumene*?" I asked, neutrally. "They're active again?"

Scherie nodded. "They want to help bring Roderick down."

Dale and I gave each other a glance. Whatever our differences in perspective, we both apparently had reasons to be suspicious of these Pan-Hellenes bearing gifts. The *Oikumene* cared for nothing except their narrow vision of the global order, and their help against Roderick would have a price.

But Scherie said, "It's a little scary that we all came here. We're a bloody-minded bunch."

"Moving toward the fire," said Dale. "Though I wasn't sure you paid attention during training," he added, with a duck to avoid an anticipated smack. Then he nodded at me. "And I guess I should start expecting you to show up whenever needed too. So, how do we go in?"

"I can get us in," said Grace.

Dale looked at me for confirmation. "She got us across Europe," I said.

Grace, Dale, and I ditched our bags in Scherie's car. Scherie was the only one of us who still had her phone, and I asked her to leave it in the glove compartment. Without the phone and with Grace's stealth, perhaps a busy Roderick wouldn't be able to track us so precisely. Grace spoke her Latin, and the world went fish-eyed. I had my sword and a .45. Dale and Scherie had a matching set of MP5 submachine guns and 9mm pistols—very domestic, those two. Grace had . . . well, Grace had somehow found an experimental needle handgun and a flechette rifle in Scherie's stash. Not weapons that I would ever be caught dead with, but she looked good with them. Heck, she'd look good wielding a two-by-four with a nail in one end.

Scherie said the *Oikumene* weapons were all Stonewall safety chipped with the latest patch against Roderick, but I personally thought if Roderick could command that much against ourselves, we'd be lost whether the weapons fired or not.

For maneuvering in stealth mode, the street was narrow, and the crowded square was worse. We would have had a tight squeeze through the perimeter to get inside the Baba Yaga's headquarters, but just then, a file of people emerged from a doorway in one of the pair of stairwell shafts running up the sides of the glass-enclosed ground floor, and, hands held high, walked out of the building.

They were as pale as a sunless dawn, and they stumbled repeatedly as they moved toward the perimeter, as if even the cloud-dimmed light of day was more than they were used to. They avoided the solicitous touches of EMTs and flinched at the less friendly hands of the police. One of them tried to protect her laptop, which caused much shouting and rough handling. But no one made good on the bullhorn's earlier ironic threats.

As they were escorted through the perimeter, we slipped in the other way. At a safe distance, I whispered, "Those guys have some craft."

"Their sins are all computer-related," said Dale. "I had trouble reading them. Online fraud, hacking, denial-of-service attacks, that sort of thing."

"They were helping Roderick with his Internet stunts," I said.

The first floor was empty except for the bodies of the killed and the too wounded to move. The escalators trembled, and rust-red rivulets of something craft-infused that wasn't quite blood ran down them. We wouldn't take the escalators.

The elevators had a death-trap vibe too, so we found an emergency stairway that the computer staff had used, and we went up. Dale took point, and I didn't argue, as he was better at finding traps. Rather than exhaust herself, Grace let her stealth screen slip. Too many here would be as good at hide-and-seek as she was.

We passed the doors for the second and third floors. At the fourth-floor door, Dale held up his hand for us to halt. "There's a craft trip-wire on the next flight of stairs."

A message with an enter arrow was tacked to the door. I read the Ukrainian: "This way please for the competition." *So it is a game,* I thought.

"You can read that?" asked Scherie.

"I'll report later," I said. Dale pushed the door, but there was no handle on this side. He aimed his rifle at the bolt area. "Get ready," he said, then started uttering some craft to help bullets penetrate without ricocheting.

"Wait," said Grace. Dale lowered his weapon, and Grace touched the lock and whispered something. A soft click of the bolt. The door would push inward. "I'll go point here. I'll be able to obscure us as targets in the first rush."

I felt the door. Nothing more wrong behind it than the rest of this place. Grace called for her stealth again, and held her flechette rifle at ready as we lined up on either side of the door. We all dropped into the slowed-down world of combat time sense. Grace kicked open the door.

Entry itself was the standard, deadly drill. The door area was clear, but the rest of the room was a forest of cubicles, with a central corridor that ran to the elevator shafts. Getting through would be like an urban street fight in miniature. Though we were obscured, that didn't stop some Ukrainian practitioner from taking a couple of blind shots at the stairway when he saw the fire door move.

We all scrambled for dubious cover behind cubicle walls. More shooting followed, but not directed our way. Living people in the same spiritual service were shooting each other. It was one thing for ghosts to fight (they didn't have much to lose), but this was craft civil war. It also meant the practitioners had guns with no Stonewall devices. Given

Ukrainian history, that wasn't a big surprise—who was on what side could change pretty quickly.

The shots seemed to be moving away from us, so we went after them. We worked in quick relays down the cubicle corridor. At the end of the corridor, a freshly and mortally wounded man lay propped up against the elevator bank. With no time for chitchat, I went right to compulsion. *"In God's name, what's happening here?"*

"The phone." With weak, faltering hands, he clawed up at me. "Get me to the phone."

"What phone?"

"First one to the phone wins."

"Wins what?"

"Life," he said. And with a long, rattling breath, he was dead. *Lord, please have mercy on his soul.*

We made our way to the other wing of the building and found a similar picture of cubicled desolation. The gunfire was muted; the shooters had gone up the stairway. We followed. For five floors, the gun blasts punctuated the echoes of running feet. We were stopped again on the ninth floor.

Someone had tripped the trap, and the way up was clogged with rubble. The door was swinging wide open, and the sounds of the firefight within were unmuffled. We stayed out of any line of fire, backs up against the wall. "Wait," said Grace.

"What is it?" I asked.

"I'm concerned that he's allowed us to get so close."

"We still have another floor to go," I said.

"Not just in the building," she said. "Did he want us to come to Kiev?"

Like the Russians at Chernobyl, I thought. He would get people to the ground of his choosing.

"Allowed us to get so close?" said Dale. "I was practically carrying the planes on my back."

I responded to Grace. "You're wondering if it's a trap. It almost certainly is. But it does no good to try to dodge his traps. He's had a century to look at the future. We just have to beat the probabilities he's seen. We have to be better than he expects."

As we entered the ninth floor, I saw the message on the door. "Welcome to the ninth circle. No stairway to heaven for you. Please take the elevator."

Well, if the writer was Roderick, nice of him to make his snare somewhat obvious. Once in that metal box he could do almost anything to us, though each option had problems. Dropping the elevator ten floors might seem the most straightforward path, but that wouldn't necessarily do much damage to alert craftspeople. Remote-operated firepower waiting for the door to open on the tenth floor would be simple enough, but he'd have to cover the near corners or risk someone getting through. Keeping us locked in for killing at leisure might be his best bet.

We reached the ninth floor elevator bank just in time to see a woman's body slump to the ground and the doors closing behind someone else. "Rude of them not to hold it for us," I said.

"Shh," said Grace. "Listen."

We stood close to the doors and heard the hum of the elevator moving the short way up the shaft. A muffled chime sounded, and the doors quietly rumbled as they rolled open. Automatic gunfire exploded in a ten-second burst. The doors rumbled shut.

A voice said something, and then we heard the visceral male screams of someone not in terror, but in such pain that they can do nothing else. The screams were muffled, but they continued for five of the longest minutes in my life.

When the horror finally ceased, we stepped away from the doors. "Gunfire, a pause, and then screaming," said Grace. "Explanation?"

Scherie closed her eyes as if in pain and responded to its cause. "Not this time, motherfucker."

"What is it?" asked Dale.

"It's Roderick," said Scherie, opening her eyes again. "It's definitely his power up there."

"You've heard about the fight at Chernobyl?" asked Dale. We all nodded. "A survivor of that fight told me that Roderick took hits from seven shooters, then killed six of them. I figure he's doing the same thing here. He's letting people come up and shoot, then killing them."

"So we go up," I said. "All together, and try to get Scherie close enough to act."

We pressed the button, the elevator opened, and we went in. The blood was sticky on the floor and splattered like abstract art on the walls, but no bodies. In Ukrainian, a pleasant woman's voice spoke in the universal reassuring robot tones of automated service.

"What's she saying?" asked Dale.

"Please touch the biometric lock to confirm your allegiance," I said.

"What the hell does that mean?"

Grace wouldn't meet my eyes. "I think I know," I said. I touched it with my left hand. I felt a dark tingle from my navel through my hand, a bolt of pain like heart disease. The voice said, "Left Hand confirmed. Have a nice day!"

The elevator moved up.

"Nice trick," said Dale.

"I'll explain it later," I said, not knowing whether he'd been in pan-glossic mode for the elevator's last words.

The elevator opened. Like the one who'd gone up before us, we fired. It couldn't hurt. But no one living was there to greet our bullets. We hustled out.

Around the corner, just down the corridor, lay the bodies. They had been butchered—no, ripped apart—and the various parts arranged in piles. A small pyramid of heads looked upon us with flat-eyed stares. Some of the arms and legs still twitched with some little taste of Left-Hand magic that they'd acquired.

Quietly, almost to herself, Scherie had started swearing again.

Beyond the bodies, in a darkened part of the corridor, was the distinctive glow of a smartphone screen, resting against something, upright and above the ground. *The phone.*

"It appears," said Grace, still scanning the hall for hostiles, "that these are the remains of the top craftsmen and women of Ukraine."

"Not all of them," said Dale. He would be thinking of Roman.

"No," agreed a male voice in English. "Not all."

Into the hallway stepped the robed and masked figure of the Red Death. We fired right into him, and he laughed at us as pieces of his robe were blown away.

"Hold your fire!" Dale shouted. I didn't know why the heck he wanted that, but he was the expert, so I stopped firing. "You," said Dale to the Red Death. "If you want a fight, take off your damned mask."

"But these are my party clothes," said the Red Death.

"We've been fooled by this party trick before."

"Very well, but you won't recognize me." He reached up and, with hands in incongruous black rubber gloves, pulled off the mask. Underneath was the face of a golden-haired Slavic angel.

Grace said, "He matches intel."

Scherie said, "Fuck it, I know his power. *Get out, dead man!*"

"Fire!" I said.

But Roderick was moving faster than anything I'd seen. He grabbed Dale's rifle out of his hands and clubbed him aside with it. Then he went for Grace. Even as she rapidly fired the flesh-ripping needles through him, his gloved hand struck out like a cobra for her throat.

"*Thou shalt not!*" The voice came from me. It was not a prayer.

Roderick's hand opened, trembling in interrupted rage, and Grace fell back onto the floor. Through gritted teeth, he asked, "What was that you said?"

But Scherie was already there, gripping his extended arm. "*Roderick, you sisterfucking parasite from a dollar-store hell, get out!*"

An explosion of craft, and the flash of a black-lit Left-Hand spirit. And Roderick, the greatest evil of the age, fell to the ground.

I was on him, hacking him apart with my sword.

"He's gone," said Scherie.

"Yes, but you know *(hack)* these Left-Hand bodies *(hack)* keep going *(hack, hack)*."

Grace got up, touching her throat as if it had been contaminated. Dale was more energetically rubbing his clubbed shoulder.

Before anyone else could ask the inevitable question about Roderick's fate, I said, "That was far too easy."

Dale said, "Speak for yourself." But his face had a grim resignation.

"Another second, and I wouldn't be speaking at all," said Grace. But she too wasn't rejoicing at this sudden victory.

"Scherie?" I asked, as I threw the limbs and head as far away as I could from each other.

"I felt him leave, but it was more like driving out a possessor."

"Shit," said Dale, hand to his forehead. "It's the natural extension of the Left-Hand path."

"What is?" I asked.

Just then, from the far end of the corridor where the phone sat, something groaned.

We went forward slowly, checking for conventional and craft booby traps, gingerly stepping over the body parts and pools of blood. As we approached the phone, the view became clearer. The phone was strapped to a groaning body that sat slumped in a leather office chair, its face fallen forward and hidden.

The body was a twisted thing. Like an insect, it had six quivering black limbs, but these were too thin to have ever supported the weight of the torso, which was still all too human. Black chitinous wings extended to the sides, humming with vibration.

"Who . . . who are you?" asked Dale. But I think he knew. The man-thing raised his head, and Scherie gasped, for it was Roman's bearded face. His eyes were bloody sockets.

When he spoke, his voice was very weak, but he seemed like the old Roman, unchanged with his Slavic cowboy accent.

"Dale, ol' pardner, is that you? Howdy, and congratulations. Like the cavalry, yes? But too late this time. I tried to run from my failure and failed at that."

His eyeless sockets turned toward me. "Forgive me, Father Endicott, for I have worn the black hat. But I paid for it, yes? He blinds me to mock my ancestors, but not before he shows me my new hands and feet. I think—no, I'm sure—he leaves me living just long enough to say 'howdy' to you. I am message."

"You tried to stop him," I said.

"I drew, but he drew faster. He'll always draw faster."

"Why didn't you wait for me?" Scherie cried.

"Scherie baby, alone, you can drive him from body to body like a cow along the trail, but remember, he'll always find another."

As if this confirmed something for him, Dale asked, "Where is he now?"

"Ah, you knew this one here was, how you say, the fake McCoy. He looks more like you now. He said you should have stayed at home."

Dale nodded as if that were an answer. I asked, "What else can we do to make you more comfortable?" A nice euphemism for what we'd have to do.

"Ask not what you can do for me, but what I can do for you. I have a weapon against him. In last bit of sneaky, I swallow evidence. It is some little needle of his brain. If you can remove his spirit from body, you can bind him to needle. If you can, ha, remove needle from me, you will make me, as you say, more comfortable, and give you box to catch him in." He waved an insect arm. "But wait . . . there's a woman at his house. Lara. Please see to her."

"Where is his house?"

He recited some coordinates. "I knew numbers in case need to blow him up. You'll find house at Babi Yar Park."

"Of course," said Dale, with real anger. He seemed as disturbed by this address as anything that had happened today.

"Now, everything is clear, yes?"

I brought out my .45. "Are you ready?"

He sighed. "If anyone ever asks, tell them I was very sorry." His insect arm sketched a rough sign of the cross. "Now, please."

"Lord, into your hands I commend his spirit." With that prayer, I shot Roman once in the head.

"I can do the rest," said Dale, pulling out a knife.

"Thank you, but no," I said. I didn't want to burden any of my friends with this. Quickly and coldly, I cut open Roman's stomach with my sword and retrieved the plastic needle.

Afterward, we looked at the sheet of paper that had been pinned to Roman's body above the phone, marked in odd letters.

"That's Greek," Scherie said.

"It says, 'to the fairest,'" said Grace. Like the old myth of Troy, Roderick had left this phone as some kind of apple of discord, dangling some promise of life extension to the first to make the call. Not trusting any of our options for destroying it, we left it there.

FIFTEEN

A re we done here?" I asked. Besides the obvious reasons for haste, some other urgency was tugging like a frightened angel.

"We should get downstairs," said Dale. "They'll have the Left-Hand labs in the lowest basement floors."

"Why?" We needed to get to Roderick's house, and I could guess what we'd find in this building's basement. Besides the human simulacra, we'd see the means with which Roderick had transformed Roman.

"Roderick has switched bodies," said Dale. "We only have a rough idea of what he looks like now."

"Do you think he'll try to hide?" I asked.

"From us?" Dale shook his head. "I doubt it. But we may not find him anyway, and other people need to have a clear idea of who they're looking for." Before, Dale's ability to empathize with Roderick and the Left Hand would have appalled me, but now I was grateful someone could guess the monster's moves.

We went back toward the elevator. Before we could press the call button, all the lights went out, and the emergency LED strips came on. "Shit," said Dale. "They've finally cut off the power."

"That means they're coming in," said Scherie.

"We can try the other stairwell," said Grace. "The craft traps may have departed with Roderick, or we can try to disarm them."

But they hadn't cut off all the power. We heard the distinct hum of elevators moving.

"Sounds like Roderick's elevator traps and tests are cleared," said Dale.

"They'll have the stairwell covered too," I said.

"Let's hide out for a while," suggested Scherie.

Before we could discuss it, the world went fish-eyed. "Thanks, Grace," I said.

"Wait," said Dale, as the elevator hum moved closer. "You're Roderick. You're a Morton. You've killed everyone you could, but you've left the building with some of your worst enemies alive inside. As a bonus, more people are coming into the building. What would you do?"

"Try to bury us like Abram nearly buried him," I said, and the urgency tugged at me in agreement. This building, like H-ring or most any craft facility, would almost certainly be pre-equipped for self-destruction.

"OK, listen up," I said. "This is an order, Mortons. You're to run down the intact stairwell. Grace, please go with them and assist with stealth and any remaining traps." I couldn't order Grace, but I hoped she'd agree with my plan.

"What are you going to do?" asked Grace.

"I'm going to clear the way out for you by taking command of the security force." *And save the Ukrainians.*

Grace nodded, but Dale said, "We need to talk," worried about either my sanity or the source of such power.

"Not now, Major. Go."

As they hustled off for the stairway, I cleaned and sheathed my sword, then stood at command ready. Both elevators slid open simultaneously, revealing a mélange of Internal Troops and Militia. More guns were pointed at me individually than ever before in my life, and the bastards weren't exactly observing trigger discipline.

Here goes nothing. "Attention!" I said. The Ukrainians stiffened upward from their combat crouches. The natural panglossic seemed to be working along with my amplified power of command, but some of their eyes were drifting to the signs of recent violence. The elevators tried to close. "Someone hold the dang doors."

"Yessir," they chorused, as one of them complied.

"There is an immediate bomb threat," I said. "We're evacuating, and I'm coming with you."

I stepped into the already-crowded elevator like I owned it. "Press lobby. That's goes for you in the other elevator too." I hoped they obeyed. I felt like I was just giving orders naturally now. Someone's pack kept our door from closing. "Ditch that pack, son." Another man helped him remove it and threw it out of the elevator. The door closed.

"You there with the headgear," I said. "Call downstairs and let them know they need to evacuate the building. I've sent some survivors down the stairwell. Give them cover as they exit."

"Yessir."

Like all elevators, this one took forever. Whatever surprise Roderick had in store could happen any second. Without anything more to order, a voice in my head was giving me suggestions. *Take over this country. You can't do worse than the current government. Then, reassemble the Eastern Bloc, only this time, make it God-fearing under the Covenant. Then . . .*

God help me, no.

We were approaching the bottom, so I finally had something else to think about. "When the elevator opens, you run for the exits. Use all available doors."

I pressed myself against the elevator wall. The door opened. "Go!" They ran for the exits, where other security forces were waiting for them. I followed at a trot, last in line. Despite having reached the lobby first, the Ukrainians from the neighboring elevator were moving slower, which had been fine to stagger the evacuation, but it was time to tighten things up. "Run, you lazy assholes." They ran, passing me.

The Mortons and Grace appeared. They looked at the running Ukrainians, stunned. But I was still in command mode. "Get the hell out of here!"

They ran, and I joined them. Outside, the Internal Troops and Militia police were waiting. All of them looked spooked, and some of them looked ready to arrest me, but I didn't give them a chance. "The building is coming down. Everyone needs to get way the hell back, now."

Each man and woman in the security forces faced outward again. The Mortons and Grace made for the direction of Scherie's SUV. Just as the security line was starting to put some pressure on the remaining crowd, I felt the rumble in the ground below me and heard the explosion above me.

Instead of following my friends, I ran straight out, then hit the ground when I felt the building begin to pancake down into collapse.

Glass and debris shrapnelled out at me. I tried to skew the ballistics, but there were too many pieces all at once. A few painful scratches and jabs later, I got up and coughed on the dust. Great, probably the usual mix of asbestos and other poisons. Behind me stood a tall pile of rubble prickly with steel, and otherwise it was as if the building had never existed.

Before I could even check my injuries, the security forces were standing around me, at attention. Their eyes watered and they coughed at the dust, but no one raised a handkerchief or cloth to their face. They focused absolutely on me. So easy to use them.

If I didn't let go now, I never would. "I will report your bravery to the president." Some of the troopers looked dubious at this, until I added, "Whether the president wants to hear it or not. Officers, take command of your units. Please see to the crowd, commence rescue efforts, and assist with first aid."

Like infatuated high schoolers with homework, the troopers reluctantly turned their puppy-dog gazes away from me and toward the tasks I'd given them. The terrifying realization sunk in: they would have followed me to the end of the world. With the strange insistent pressure of their regard finally off me, I walked away, filled with dread of a future of such temptations.

Outside the building, snow fell as thunder rumbled, and Ivan Molfarov of both the Baba Yagas and the *Oikumene* watched the series of unfortunate events. Earlier, he had delivered an SUV to the American woman and then had tracked her to Independence Square. Seeing her meet her comrades, Ivan had given his report to the *Oikumene* through a Delphic object that he had borrowed from the Museum of Western and Oriental Art. The Pythia had given him orders: forget about Lieutenant Rezvani and watch Major Endicott. If that American shows signs of abusing the transnational power or misusing Left-Hand magics, kill him.

Ivan was reflecting on how happy he was to have avoided the self-immolation of the Baba Yagas, though he might miss one or two of them, when the Internal Troops and Militia finally assaulted the building. Perhaps this would shorten his watch for the Americans. Then the Ukrainian forces were streaming out, and it appeared they were under Endicott's command. The Left-Hand glow radiated from him.

If Endicott gave one more craft-impelled order, just one, Ivan would have to kill him on the spot rather than wait for a better opportunity. Otherwise, his power would continue to grow, an exponential explosion of authority over more people, lands. But the American managed to slink away before compelling further obedience.

Damn, thought Ivan. *Now more tracking.* Maybe Endicott would do him a favor and leave the country, so some other *Oikumene* member would be stuck shooting him.

I reached the poet's house and the SUV. My friends seemed happy to see me, and Grace embraced me right in front of them. That was maybe the least difficult thing I had to explain to the Mortons.

"Let's go," I said. "We need to get to Roderick's house."

"He may not be there," said Dale. "What Roman told us about stay-ing home sounded oracular, but in some other direction."

"Right, maybe it's just one of his sick games—another murderous goose chase. But we have to eliminate the obvious, and maybe he had to leave sooner than he thought. Either way, we need to see his house."

"I'm driving," said Scherie, as Grace was moving toward the driv-er's door.

"Shotgun," said Dale. "This thing have GPS?"

But of course it did. Before anyone could check their notes, Grace reeled off the coordinates. "Eidetic memory," she said. One more thing about her that would both intimidate me and turn me on.

Grace and I sat in the backseat. She picked the glass out from me, and I thought about what I had done. I had commanded Roderick without invoking or even thinking about God, putting my own will first. That I had done it from incipient love and seeming necessity in no way excused my lapse. *Lord, please forgive me. I have committed the sin of Moses, and even aspiring to that guy's sins is grievous pride.*

As if she could read my thoughts, Grace said, "Thank you, Michael, for saving my life."

"Just one of my gifts." *Lord, please keep me from blushing and say-ing "aw, shucks."*

I looked out the window at the weather and the very dark clouds. "Feeling moody, Morton?"

Dale turned away from the GPS to face me and, seeming suspicious of the punch line, nodded.

"Me too," I said.

"Don't look it," he said, giving me a once-over inspection and, as usual, making light of things. "You lose weight?" Then, he gave me a soldier's stare, eye to eye, all humor gone. "Are you OK? You've tapped into something serious, and not all of it is good."

Grace raised a hand, but I interrupted. "Got gut shot in the Chun-nel. Somebody here thought I was worth saving. She used some alchemical injection we confiscated from one of Roderick's special friends."

Dale nodded. "Yeah, I'd know that touch of black light in your aura anywhere. Hearing any interesting suggestions in your head about—just as an example—killing us all?"

"Yes on interesting suggestions, but the worst of them may not be Left-Hand."

"Oh?" said Dale.

"I've been able to tap the local spiritual power wherever I go, but when I do, my brain wants to play Caesar and take over the world."

"So that's how you stopped Roderick's meat puppet," said Scherie as she took a right turn. "And that's how you ordered those Ukrainians around."

"Yeah," I said. "But it doesn't want to stop there."

An awkward silence followed. Then, with subject-changing desperation, Scherie said, "So, you took the Chunnel train?"

"No, we bicycled through the service tube," said Grace.

"No shit?" said Dale.

"You wouldn't have liked it," I said.

"Damn straight," said Dale, shuddering.

"The Morton taphephobia?" asked Grace.

"How do you know about that?" asked Dale, with an indignant glance at me.

"Everyone knows about that," said Grace. An underground and underwater tunnel wouldn't go well with the Morton fear of live burial.

Scherie made a turn into the woods of Babi Yar Park, and everyone was quiet again. The GPS showed us approaching the coordinates Roman had given us, but I couldn't see a house. "I see the way," said Grace, and then I saw it too—a narrow, gravel-paved way through the bare trees.

Dale asked, "Break into any traps lately?"

"Stop here," I said. Scherie stopped. "Scherie, when I give the word, you'll turn onto that gravel and drive as close to Roderick's house as you can. When we stop, we exit the vehicle and hit Roderick's door. I'm point this time. Mortons, you're on cover, traps, and corners. Grace, make sure no one's on our tail. Understood?"

"Yessir," said the Mortons. "Yes," said Grace.

"Good. Scherie, go." We turned into the driveway for Roderick's house. A flurry of overgrown branches whipped against the windshield, and in seconds we stopped at the driveway's end in front of a closed garage and ten yards from the front door. "Move out!" I said.

Ivan tracked the Americans to Babi Yar, and he knew where they must be heading. A bad sign. He stopped his car well away from the residence of the abomination, then popped its trunk and removed his rifle. For the Americans, their moving in stealth made it difficult for them to notice him, even amidst the bare trees and brush of the parkland.

The SUV was in front of the abomination's house. No sign of conflict—they had gone in willingly and unopposed. From everything Ivan had seen, the Pythia's wishes were clear. If Endicott emerged from that evil house unscathed, Ivan would kill him.

We went for the door double time. It was hanging open, as obvious a mockery as anything yet that Roderick had done. Still, we didn't break discipline. We entered and progressively cleared the floor: living room, kitchen, and, through the open way between the bookcases, the bedroom. Scherie took point on the last. "Some clothes here, some knives, some nasty-looking goop. A laptop computer near the bed—seems to be fried. Some weird décor to check out on a second pass. But I don't see a woman."

That was fine with me. After seeing Roman, I hadn't been looking forward to witnessing what had happened to the woman he had asked us to retrieve.

With the floor cleared, Grace shut the front door, then crossed the room to check the view out back. "We've got spiritual company."

I went back to look while Dale and Scherie continued to cover the floor. A ragtag line of smiling and waving ghosts stood outside in the woods. Some of them might have followed us, or followed me, from the Baba Yagas' building. Maybe they'd be helpful, so I would wait to dismiss them. Only a handful of these spirits resembled the dead of the Second World War that might have resided at Babi Yar: the hundred thousand that the Nazis had killed here.

On a hunch, I sent Grace to cover the front of the house again and called Dale to the window. I told him what I wasn't seeing, and he breathed out with relief. "Good. That's all I see too. Most of them must have moved on, leaving just a bad feeling. I thought he might be doing something serious here."

"What?"

"Something I saw in Japan," said Dale, "at Yasukuni. I'll explain it later."

The thought of any Morton, even Dale, going anywhere near that decaying doomsday machine disturbed me, but I stuck to the business at hand. We checked the small finished attic and the unfinished basement. We found some computer equipment in the living room and kitchen, but as with the laptop in the bedroom, electrical kill switches had been pushed on each hard drive and interesting chip array. The place smelled of lemon and hospital antiseptics, as if biological messes had to be frequently cleaned, but nothing invited further investigation, and no glow of Left-Hand craft anywhere.

"Whatever Uncle Roderick was up to, it must have been either online or in the Baba Yagas' basement," said Dale.

"You're forgetting something," said Scherie. "Roman's friend, Lara.

I wonder how many other guests Roderick had here? Let's take one more look at the bedroom. He has a table in there that . . ."

As if in reply, from the bedroom, a creak of hinges and a thud. Anything or anyone Roderick left for us couldn't be good. "Mortons, stay on cover," I said. "Grace, you're with me."

Before we could react, a woman in a sepulchral dress stood between the bookcases. She was tall, pale, and thin—Roderick's type. Her eyes took in our weapons, pointed at and beyond her. Then, with unearthly calm and hyperprecision, she spoke. "*Dobrý den*. I am Lara. How are you?"

Behind her, the "table" that Scherie had seen was open, revealing itself to be a coffin. Grace was appalled. "Did he put you in there?"

"Who?" asked Lara.

"Roderick Morton."

"No," said Lara. "I just wanted to see what it was like." She was staring past us now. "Are you Mortons? I have messages for Mortons." Ignoring our guns, she walked past us toward Dale and Scherie.

"Hold up," I said, belatedly. Lara stopped, but perhaps it was only because she had gotten to where she wanted to be.

"Where is he?" asked Dale.

"Roderick?"

"Yes!" shouted Dale.

Lara closed her eyes. "He said he does not stay because, like you, he hates the 'storm the fortress' part."

Dale and Scherie glanced at each other with real concern. "How could he fucking know that?" said Scherie.

"Also," continued Lara, "he said, ask them, do you know that you lose yet?"

"Lose how?" I asked.

"He said you have sinned against him, but you are in the wrong fucking country, and besides, he'll kill you all."

Grace tutted. "He knows I'm with you. That's old Kit Marlowe's words he's butchering."

"He also said we should have stayed at home," said Dale. "When he's not lying, he has the farseer's taste for riddles and inside jokes. He was being literal."

I finally got it. "God help us. He's gone back to America. But where, and why?"

Lara interrupted me, eyes staring at a blank spot of wall. "Someone here. She says she is not whore; she is Ukrainian. You must go, but please, tell her to go first."

Scherie turned in the direction Lara was pointing. I saw nothing, but Scherie said, "Oh. Please, leave this awful place. *Go!*"

A small flash of craft, and Scherie's head and shoulders slumped. Lara focused her flat affect on her. "She is gone. I go with you."

"Yes," agreed Scherie. "You're coming with us." She raised her eyes and looked around at her husband, me, and Grace to see if we'd contradict her.

I wasn't going to be the one to say no. Scherie must have seen something that made her trust this woman's allegiance against the Left Hand. But the woman was certainly creepy, and I hoped we could soon drop her off someplace safe.

We hustled outside to the SUV. Trailing us, Lara blinked her eyes in the daylight, puzzled as an owl. "What is Ivan doing here?"

A moving blind spot in the trees. "Down." I instinctively moved to cover Grace. A rifle flash, and my world burst into light and pain.

Then, like mercy, darkness.

PART VI

LOOK HOMEWARD, KILLER ANGELS

America is not a young land.
—William S. Burroughs

With the instant reflexes of emotion and training, Grace responded to the rifle shot by dropping to Michael's side and getting to work. She felt for a pulse, and finding none, she straddled Michael and put her hands to his chest. Needing direct words, she spoke in English. "*Pump. Pump.*" She worried about the continuing threat from the sniper, but only because it might interfere with this necessary, heart-shattering task.

As if in answer, Dale said, "Help him. I'll cover you."

Like a nemesis at an assassination, Lara pointed toward the brush and trees. "Ivan is there. You come out, Ivan. These people are nice."

Scherie went to her knees beside Grace. With a finger's touch, Scherie stopped the bleeding, but the bullet had blown out part of Michael's skull. His right eye was destroyed, just part of the mess that had slashed out with the bullet. Even this craft newcomer could see that it was hopeless. Healers didn't replace eyes, or brains. The best American healers had tried to save Lincoln and Kennedy, but no one could save the victim of such a brain-damaging head shot.

"*Pump. Pump.*" Grace kept the heart going. But each beat of Michael's heart required renewed craft. This could only go on so long, and what for?

An exorcist like Scherie could see a soul's departure. With brutal gentleness, she asked, "Isn't it time to stop?"

Grace looked at her. "Not yet."

"When?"

"You want to help your husband? Then go." *Pump.* "But I'm not leaving Michael, not yet." *Pump.* "I think we're supposed to keep saving each other's lives for at least a few minutes longer." *Pump.*

Scherie quietly stood up and left Grace alone with Michael.

Grace added physical pushes to her tiring craft. The Left-Hand power from the injection moved under her hands like serpents desperately seeking some life to extend, and finding none. Would he become a meat puppet for Roderick? No, she'd see to that. For the first time in many years, Grace's eyes blurred not from artifice, but sorrow.

Good-bye, Michael. So much for the feeling that maybe this was a merciful universe, and that all those years of spiritual service to the Crown had some reward besides more service. Good-bye.

Pump, goddamn you!

Good-bye—but not just yet.

I was floating free in a dark void. Then in the distance, a small bright dot. I drifted toward it, or it came toward me, and the dot grew into a tunnel of light. Well, it was a bit clichéd and non-biblical besides, but that didn't make it untrue. As I had tried to do my whole life, I moved toward the light and God's grace.

There, waiting for me in the luminescence, was the figure of a familiar young woman, dressed this time in the frumpy officewear of 1990s Washington, D.C. "Mom!" Like a small, lost boy, I ran toward her, arms wide, and hugged her. She felt warm and alive, not like any ghost. Surely this was a sign that this was her true soul and not an earthly echo.

"Mikey," she said. "I'm so glad you're here."

Here it was, the culmination of my earthly life. "Will you take me to Heaven?" I asked.

"Not yet. We have to talk first."

Oh God, please, this couldn't be. "No! I am not having a near-death experience! It's New Age hippie nonsense, and I can't even be sure it's really happening. I'm either dead or I'm not. Either way, let's get going."

"Call it what you like, Mikey, but right now you're stuck in between. I'm so sorry."

A near-death experience was bad, but upsetting my mom was worse. I took a deep breath of the aether. "OK," I said. "Let's talk. I'm not positive, but I think I was shot in the head."

"Yes. My poor baby."

"Mortally wounded."

"Yes. You're clinically dead. Anyone else would simply be deceased."

"Then what's the holdup?"

"Too much synergy. Your new power, your recent Left-Hand alterations, and your Endicott stubbornness have combined to hold the final death at bay. If you will it, you can go back."

I thought about my friends, and the things I still needed to do for my country and the world. I thought about Grace. Yes, as I saw my Christian duty and my heart's desire, I should go back. But when the path of duty had been clear, my mother hadn't been the type for long discussions. "OK, Mom, what's the catch?"

"Sweetie, you've been badly hurt. You've lost an eye."

Oh. That was unexpectedly hard, and even in my disembodied state, I wondered what Grace would think.

"And," my mother continued, "that may be just the first of many hurts, not all of them physical."

Not all of them physical. Those words brought a mental itch into full view. "Mom, if I come back after a fatal head wound, that's like the Antichrist of Revelation."

Mom's hands went to her hips in indignation. "Michael Gabriel Endicott, are you calling me the mother of the Beast?"

"No, ma'am."

"I didn't think so. So don't make me a liar. I suspect that for some reason, God's plan may require that an Endicott be humbled."

"God's plan seems to have a lot of that lately—not that I'm complaining."

Seeing my discouragement, my mother gave me another hug. "You may become something else, but knowing about it in advance won't do you any good. But I should tell you, though I have not read the Book of Life, I see that your soul is ready, and Heaven now is a pretty sure thing. Given your current path, it may not be so certain for you later, despite the many sufferings you'll endure. So, what are you going to do?"

That was easy, like a trick question in Sunday school. I smiled and, seeing that I got it, Mom smiled back, full of love and pride in her good son.

"Lord," I said. "Thy will be done."

In a flash of God's light, the world went dark again.

I came to consciousness with the worst headache in the history of the world, unless someone else had ever recovered from a mortal blow to the skull. Hoping to find something else to think about, I opened my eye. Eye, singular. My view of the world was like I was staring through a monocular. So that much of my embarrassing near-death experience was true.

My view was also fuzzy, but what I saw was perfect. Grace was kneeling over me and looking up at the sky. Without warning, her hands pressed hard against my chest.

"Ugh!" I said.

In one quick motion, Grace stood up and pulled her flechette pistol on me. Her face had blanched. "His eye is open!"

"I look that bad?" I asked.

Dale came running. "Tell me his sins," said Grace.

Filled with shock and some dismay, Dale's eyes glanced at me, then rolled up toward the sky. "Oh, it's Mike in there all right. I'd know that huge capital *P* for Pride with any Endicott. Though there appear to be some new little letters . . ."

"Thanks, Morton, I know what they are." The mocking bastard sounded a little choked up. I sat up, and the world went wobbly.

"Whoa, take it easy," said Dale, and Grace was at my side again, trying to lower me down. Dale pointed to his own eye. "There are snaky things here; they're still knitting your head back together."

"I'm OK," I said, pressing against Grace's hands to stay up. I could feel the movement in my flesh where my missing eye had been. I looked around, and saw some splatter which appeared to include some bits of skull and brain—mine. "Messy," said Lara, and she bent down and touched some of it with her right index fingernail. A bit of tissue and her fingernail dissolved, and Lara nodded in seeming satisfaction. Weird. I briefly wondered if my personality would be changed due to this brain damage. Then I decided that my life had been changing so fast that it might be hard to tell.

"Where's the shooter?" I asked.

Scherie appeared. "You're back! Alive!"

Maybe, but my patience was DOA. "Lieutenant, where is the shooter?"

"We've got him in the car, sir," said Scherie. "He helped me when I first got here, in Kiev, and set me up with the car and weapons, but he must have tracked us. He's *Oikumene*. I think they want you dead."

"His sins look very Nuremberg," said Dale, with contempt.

"OK, let's get away from this mess," I said.

"You're in no shape," said Grace

"I'm in fine shape," I said. "I have it on the best authority."

"God?" asked Grace.

"My mom," I quipped.

"You saw your mother?" she asked. But I'd run out of words for the moment, so, tentatively at first, with Grace under my arm for support, I walked to the car.

Ivan lay in the back of the SUV, hogtied. He glared at me with two baleful, healthy eyes. This earnest-looking young man had just tried to kill me, and had succeeded for a few minutes. I was spitting furious at this *Oikumene*, though I couldn't show it. I wouldn't kill a captive without reason, but for some reason I didn't even want to kill him. I just wanted to shake some sense into the idiot.

Instead, Grace opened the car door and helped me tumble down into the backseat. I was tired and still a little regretful of my miraculous return to this world. Grace sat next to me and the Mortons sat in the front. Scherie started the car, and I finally dared to look at myself in the SUV's rearview mirror. Scherie's healing, the Left-Hand serum, and my own new power had fleshed, seared, and scarred over my right eye socket and nearby skull, but it was a horror to look at. I touched a finger to the damage, and felt the still-tacky blood and the slight groove that remained running from the socket to my temple. Sad that it had to occur now, when I had just met Grace, but that was the way these things happened. An attractive woman like her wouldn't want a monster hanging around.

I buried my heart deep; if I had life and time enough later, I'd bring it out then. Even a monster had certain standards, so I would have to get my face properly cleaned and covered. First, business. I checked the rear compartment to find Ivan still staring up at me. I smiled and said, "The adults need to talk now, boy. *Ivan, in God's name, take a nap.*"

Ivan's annoying eyes instantly shut and his breathing slowed. "Where are we going?" I asked.

"The airport," said Dale. "We need to get back to the States."

"A commercial flight won't be fast enough," I said. "Roderick knew we were coming. He's ahead of us by hours. We'll need something supersonic to keep up. That means military."

"I could steal something," said Grace.

"I could call in another Russian favor," said Dale.

"I bet Ivan has a sympathetic object for communication with Delphi," said Scherie. "I could shake down the *Oikumene*, threaten them for some transport, though we couldn't trust it."

Too much time. Unless a supersonic jet large enough for all of us was ready to go, any plan to get it would still take too much time.

"Just a second," I said. God, my head hurt, but I had to think. "Dale, you've been cryptic long enough. What's Roderick going to do in America, and what's it got to do with that damned Yasukuni dooms-day machine?"

"It's something my father was working on," said Dale. "Before he died, he was asking questions at the Yasukuni Shrine. He asked the dead where magic comes from."

"A child's question," said Grace, "and a very dangerous one."

"They told me the usual stuff," said Dale, "plus one other thing that I'd never heard before: magic can come from dead worlds, where nothing remains except for things like that Yasukuni monstrosity on a global scale. I think Roderick wants to open a door to one of those dead worlds and tap into that tremendous power. I think he wants to be a Left-Hand god incarnate."

"Why America?"

"My best guess?" said Dale. "There's one place where the Left Hand tried for decades to crack into what they called another dimension, a realm of one of their gods. They didn't have many dead to work with on this end, but they were very powerful, very evil dead. I think Roderick is going back to the House of Morton."

"OK," I said. Mortons were always obsessed about the House, but that wasn't the immediate problem. "Tell me what I'm missing. Roderick arranged our recent misfortunes to draw us out, to perhaps kill us but definitely delay us, until we were on the other side of the world from his real plan—to get into your empty House."

"That's about it," said Dale.

"Can't be," I said. "Because it wasn't just Roderick. Couldn't have been. Attucks personally gave me an assignment for which, as Grace has gently pointed out, I was particularly ill-suited. Dale, coincidentally C-CRT lets you go off and investigate your father's past in a country that's halfway around the world. Scherie, the one person Roderick might actually fear, is left dangling out in Istanbul. Istanbul! Grace, I don't know if MI13 was in on this, but does anyone think that Langley or PRECOG completely missed something on this scale? No fricken way. Our own people were involved in this, and I want to know why."

Just then, Scherie's phone in the glove compartment blasted full volume. "Roderick?" I asked. Before we could find out, the radio began to speak to us.

For the first time as a fully embodied being, Roderick was flying. As a Morton weatherman, he had manipulated the air to elevate himself for a few seconds and had even glided for a short distance, but this was true flight, thirty thousand feet up in a jet. Though his mostly disembodied self had been on a plane for his journey to Kiev from America, he hadn't been in any condition to enjoy the view. It was exciting, though he felt a queasiness that no amount of craft seemed to quite remove. Ah, the joys of the technological sublime. Every mundane yokel who could afford the ticket was given this god's-eye view, little knowing that a true god didn't see the world like this at all.

He was somewhat distracted by the task of operating the meat puppet he'd left in Kiev via long distance. It was doing a very good job of killing Ukrainian craftsmen. He wondered how long that lesser vessel would last.

Roderick deplaned at London Heathrow with his two carry-ons, which included a small but very important briefcase containing a yellow sheaf of wheat he had reaped himself from a Ukrainian field. The case also held a glass tube, some filled paintballs, and other seemingly innocuous materials for godhood and destruction. Regarding the wheat, Roderick wasn't much for whole grains, but he wasn't one of the hungry. The Heathrow stop was convenient, as he had a fellow traveler to meet for the next leg to America.

Roderick recognized his flight companion in the airline's exclusive lounge. The fixer was as lean and pale as a male Madeline, but only average height. But of course, this dubious servant would not recognize Roderick, as Roderick no longer looked the heroic Slav. He had put on another body that used more Morton phenotype with its Morton DNA. This seemed natural, as he was going home. However, he did not resemble his original nineteenth-century form, when he had sacrificed every physical attribute in a pursuit of his goal. Nor had he kept the weak chin and other unattractive recessive traits (from this distance in time, he could finally acknowledge that Left-Hand inbreeding had been a bad idea). Now he wore the appearance of a healthy Morton. Though he had despised Joshua Morton more than any other being, living or dead, he found that he didn't mind a slight physical resemblance.

Roderick approached his hired servant, who went by the name of Mr. Cushlee but whose real family name was Renfield. Every Family might have a Left Hand, but some Families like the Renfields had nothing *but* Left Hand. In orthodox circles, the Renfields couldn't ever use their own name, not since that Stoker bastard had advertised it to the world for what it was.

Cushlee was sitting in a lonely corner of the lounge in one of its many broad leather chairs. Roderick took the chair next to him, separated by a shaded reading lamp. Roderick and Cushlee had arranged some nonsense about recognition signals, but Roderick wasn't in a patient mood. "You might have killed at least one of them for me."

"Well, a fine day to you, sir. Next time, give me some rules of engagement that make bloody sense and perhaps I will."

The man smiled, seemingly proud of his horrible teeth. Roderick pursed his lips in surprise, though he should have expected this tone. Despite the slavish reputation they got from Stoker, the Renfields dealt

sharply with their powerful clients—payment in advance, and no re-
funds ever. Still, Roderick had a reputation of his own to uphold. "You
know what I could do to you, even here, and yet you speak to me that
way?"

"If you think my death will get you a refund, forget it."

Roderick considered carrying out his threat against Cushlee for failing to kill Endicott and Marlow and for this lack of respect. But Cushlee had otherwise carried out Roderick's orders exactly, and someone
who could follow precise instructions was surprisingly hard to find
and absolutely necessary for Roderick's plan.

Decisions, decisions. As if putting a thumb to the scales, Cushlee
said, "I've brought you something extra," and nodded over toward the
viewing window at what appeared to be an extremely old man wearing dark glasses, a hat, and a scarf, as if attempting to show as little
bare flesh as possible. A cane rested against his neighboring seat.

"My plans are at their most sensitive stage, and you bring me
that?" Roderick said. But that old man had been the one they called
the Don. Roderick should not have cared, but he couldn't help being
pleased.

Cushlee shrugged. "There's been a bleeding war going on in MI13
since Marlow sent that bloody confession. He's been hiding from the
orthos and trailing me like a whining puppy, saying he'd speak to you
or report us all to the Crown."

Better and better. "Very well," said Roderick. "Let's get this over
with."

Cushlee stood up slowly. "Still healing from that Endicott's pig-
sticker."

"I understand completely," said Roderick. They walked over to the
seated, motionless figure. A fragile orchid decorated the table next
to him. Beyond the viewing window, flights departed.

"Thank you for meeting with me," said the Don, in a voice like the
faint scurryings of rats. "I have served your interests well. I could serve
them still."

"Oh, you are indeed priceless," said Roderick. He frankly stared at the remains of the Don, admiring his work. Even during his captivity, Roderick had used the same coded signals that had eventually freed him to begin spreading the Left-Hand knowledge to a chosen few. That long campaign had led to this: the total corruption in body and soul of the last scion of the House of Dee.

Up close and using craft, Roderick could see how much of the Don had been hollowed out with the loss of his alchemical serum. Plastic-like integuments varying from translucent to transparent covered some, but not all, of the remaining natural bones and muscle and the unnatural connective webs that strained to hold the remnant together. The brain that this academic spy had been so proud of was also dissolving away. A cutaway of his skull would show the same hollow pockets as the surface flesh, where neural tissue had dried and gone to dust. If Rezvani were here, would she be able to expel Dee's spirit as a thing already dead?

Even in this state, the man wasn't begging. Roderick was delighted. It was costing this man so much to preserve this insignificant scrap of dignity.

As if he thought he should exchange this broken gift, Cushlee turned to Roderick, "Sir, would you like me to handle this?"

Alive enough to this threat, the Don said, "I have taken certain precautions." Yes, he had. But he had used the phone and computers, even though he of all people should have known better.

"So have I," said Roderick. "*Please be still.*"

A Dee should have been able to resist this command, but much of this hollowed man belonged more to Roderick than to its nominal owner. Only Dee's eyes, still his own, desperately tracked Roderick's movements, pleading for succor. But without another word, Roderick and Cushlee returned to their former sitting area. Then, in a faint whisper that no one but Cushlee could have heard, Roderick said, "*Please go away.*"

Like a raptured Jedi knight, the form of the old man crumbled, leaving only a pile of clothes. Well, clothes, and some nasty fleshy bits for the investigators to sort out.

Roderick strode away with Cushlee even as two lounge attendants approached the Don's chair and reacted to his disappearance. "Oh, dear," said Roderick. "Another strange incident for the craft militant to explain." Besides that, this death would make those dependent on his craft all the more desperate to please him. But he and Cushlee had a plane to catch.

SEVENTEEN

On the SUV's radio, Eddy Edwards was playing DJ just for us. "I can't do this for long. Someone please pick up your phone."

I nodded at Scherie, who answered the phone she had left in the glove compartment and put it on speaker mode. "Talk to us, Eddy," I said.

"My farseers tell me it's at least eighty percent that you've figured out that your scattering away from home was not an accident and not just due to Roderick's manipulation."

"Ah, hell, Eddy, I thought you cared," said Dale, with a malice I hadn't heard from him since my first visit to his House.

"By the way, Roderick's listening," said Scherie, adding "you far-fucking idiot" under her breath.

"We're seventy percent certain," said Eddy, "that Roderick needed Ukrainian technical support for his global eavesdropping capability, and we're absolutely certain that if that's not true, we lose anyway."

He let that sink in, then continued as we were approaching a traffic circle. "We have a plane waiting for you at the airport—not Boryspil, but the other one, Zhuliany, so turn to the right now!"

"Do it," I said. Instead of going three-quarters of the way around the circle and onto the bridge over the Dnieper River, Scherie made the right turn toward the other, smaller international airport.

"Call this number for further instructions," continued Eddy. He reeled off some digits. "All will be explained. But please understand that it was done for the good of the country and to save at least some of your lives."

Some of your lives. He hadn't seen that we'd all make it, more or less. Or maybe our losses were still to come.

"We'll be there," I said. Eddy's plane fit our plans, but I wasn't any happier about this news than the Mortons. If he hadn't rescued us from the Pentagon, Eddy would be on an old-fashioned Family vengeance list.

After the call, Grace asked, "Who was that?"

"Langley," I said.

Grace gestured back at Ivan. "What do we do with him?"

"Can you keep him out of sight?" I asked.

Instead of speaking Latin, she turned and covered Ivan with the beige carpet-like cover that had hidden the weapons. "It's been a long day," she said.

In response to some unsaid plan or desire regarding Ivan's fate, Scherie said, "He won't follow us. They'll get someone else from wherever we go."

That seemed right, and besides, I had another use for the chicken-shit asshole.

While Dale reprogrammed the GPS, I called the number Eddy had given us and got more specific directions to the FBO area of the airport. Scherie drove up to a security fence gate, which opened for us without question, and then we proceeded right onto the tarmac and waited as our jet taxied up. Langley had thrown money and clout around to smooth our way. Eddy had already filed our flight plan and had amended the passenger manifest.

I turned toward the back and spoke in panglossic. "*Wake up, Ivan.*" His form squirmed under the cover. "We're going to leave you here for your people to retrieve. My recollection is that the *Oikumene* is led by someone called the Pythia. Tell her I understand her concern, but that I have things under control. Tell her that if she tries to take preemptive action again, I'll make the *Oikumene* destroy itself."

Lara said, "Say hello for me too. Say I can kill him, but it is not yet necessary. Have a nice day."

Our plane had arrived, and my friends gave me a hand out of the car, though it wasn't so necessary now. Some power continued to rush my healing along, and every second I felt a little more functional. I asked Lara, "What you said to Ivan, was that true?"

"Yes, it is not yet necessary to kill you."

"But you can?"

"Probably." She held up her shortened index finger. "Nail melted with your brains on road. I was weapon against Roderick. If I touch, he and I both melt like wicked witch. Do little Left-Hand things keep you alive too?"

I looked at Scherie, whose eyes were wide at this exchange. But I didn't answer. God was keeping me alive, but I wasn't sure about his immediate method for doing so.

"Does not matter," continued Lara. "I do not like touching. Touch me not, Endicott."

Fine with me. But that left another question. "Why didn't Roderick kill you?"

"I think I am weapon when dead too," said Lara. "He said he will leave Ukraine. He asked me not to touch him again. I said yes, I will not touch him again, never."

"He believed you?" asked Scherie, incredulous.

Lara looked at Scherie like she was the one not making sense. "He left Ukraine," she said. "I do not like touching."

Instead of trying to sort out this strangeness, I appraised our ride home. I was unfamiliar with this jet's design, but Dale whistled at it.

"We still won't catch Roderick," I noted.

"No, but he might not get the lead he expects. This is a new supersonic for private individuals and businesses, and Langley too, it seems. Max airspeed of Mach 1.5. Shit, it's a shame, but I bet we can't go supersonic until we're over the Atlantic. Even with its dampening design, the sonic booms would be way too public a disturbance."

The Mortons and Lara packed the weapons we'd used or might want into cases to bring with us, ignoring Ivan as they did so. Grace helped me up to the plane, though I was feeling steadier. As we entered the cabin, a young woman greeted us with a salute. "I'm your copilot and crew for this flight. Please take your seats immediately and we'll get underway." She didn't bother with a rank or cryptonym or service—we had no need to know—but even with my one blurry eye, I could tell her flat accent and corn-fed farm-girl looks resembled those of the Gale Family line, notorious for their countercraft assassinations and fine-tuned weather control.

The Gale returned my examination of her face by betraying a mild surprise. "Major, I didn't expect to see you. After takeoff, you'll find medical supplies in that overhead cabinet next to the galley."

Ignoring the copilot's instruction, Grace went immediately for the cabinet. Failing to hide her annoyance, the Gale said, "We weren't expecting her either."

"She's a commander with MI13," I said. "We all vouch for her."

By then, Grace had already returned to the seat next to mine with supplies, and the Mortons and Lara had entered and were storing our weapons in the overhead compartments. The Gale turned toward Lara, her voice betraying a slight distaste. "Her we had some inkling of."

"I can vouch for her," said Scherie, trust apparently unrattled by Lara's danger to me.

"I vouch for you all," said Lara.

The Gale closed the cabin door, and the plane was immediately taxiing for takeoff. Grace rummaged through the medical supplies, then stopped, as if she had struck gold in a toy box. She pulled out a small, black, silk object. "My view's still a little fuzzy," I said. "What is it?"

"An eye patch," she said, sounding solemn.

The patch's presence was suspicious, as if the possibility of my injury had been foreseen along with the probability of my death. "I'm fine," I said.

"You will be," she said. "Please let me do my job." She cleaned me up and applied some bandages. Then she put the patch over my bandaged socket. She studied me a moment. "That will do nicely."

The plane rose above the gray residue of clouds into bright sunlight. The pilot was good; the flight preternaturally smooth. The copilot sat back with us, popping a dangerous number of Nicorettes, empty tabs on a table, eyes staring outward into the spiritual beyond. The Gales weren't Morton caliber, but she could at least keep watch on the air currents and let Dale relax with the rest of us.

We perused the cabin. The fully stocked galley was the size of a small poolside bar but with a granite surface. Some of the seats were arranged around a table, and there was a couch running along one of the cabin walls. Everything gave off a sense of clean comfort lacking in a normal airplane. The cabin air even smelled fresh and pleasant and free of whatever plagues afflicted the airlines.

Scherie said, "Finally, the James Bond treatment. Why don't we get this more often?" Dale opened his mouth to explain, but Scherie cut him off. "I know."

I knew too. The Families all have money, but my family couldn't have afforded anything like this, and those Families that could would regard it as too flashy or decadent. That Langley was footing this bill just showed how desperate things were.

At the rear of the cabin but still well before the tail was a door in a wood-finished partition. I thought maybe it led to someplace to wash my hands and face or a larger conference table where we could plan our next move. But when I opened the door, a dim light revealed a queen-sized bed.

"Huh, a plane with a bedroom," I said.

The others came over to see. "You've been through a lot," said Scherie. "Maybe you should lie down for a bit."

"I'm feeling fine, really," I said.

"Which means you're delusional," said Grace. "I'll take care of him."

Dale's face went oddly bland. "Yes, you do that."

"Hey!" I said, as Grace gave me a shove into the room, then shut the cabin door behind us with emphasis. It wasn't a thick door, but the noise of the plane seemed to drown out any world outside this little space.

As good a time as any to have the necessary conversation. I wouldn't be Grace's charity case even for another instant. "It's very kind of you to offer to take care of me, but really, I'm fine." My voice lost its steadiness. This was more difficult than I'd thought, but I plowed on. "Don't worry about what we discussed before. I won't let it be awkward; we have a job to do. This sort of thing happens in combat, and it's best to just move on, so . . ."

With her preternatural swiftness, Grace seized my head in her hands and brought her lips against mine. I surrendered to the kiss for some eternity until she stopped and whispered into my ear. "You are my pirate. I thought I had lost you, and by God and you as my witnesses, I'm not going to lose you again, come Roderick, the Left-Hand gods, and Hell itself. And if you try to run from me, whatever power you think you have, I can and will kill you. Do you understand, Major?"

She was telling the absolute, honest-to-God truth.

"I do," I said.

Very romantic, but actually, I was a little unclear on the details. Was this what they called a craft marriage? But I wasn't going to die saying no to love, so I would assume we were married in some fashion to mitigate any sin. I didn't expect that she'd be able to prove me wrong before we all perished.

She tilted her head and raised her eyebrows at me. "Do you need further orders, Major? Something from Henry V or Nelson?"

"No, ma'am." No, my dark lady, my English rose.

What happened next was very private and personal. I'd often heard that first times could be awkward at best, and that practice made perfect. But when I'd been a boy performing my daily spiritual exercises, my maternal grandfather had winked at me and said that all that prayer and meditation would come in handy some day. To the delight of all concerned, it did.

As for Grace, her name was what she did, and how she did it.

During an in-between time, Grace told a story. Apparently, her ancestors had a thing for one-eyed men. In the 1800s, Jane Howe, a weatherperson and spiritual instructor of great ability, had married her boss, Edward Rochester Marlow, despite the damage that his insane Left-Hand first wife had done to his face. Fortunately, this marriage also redirected Jane from a colonial assignment in India in which the entire craft contingent was killed.

"That's nice," I murmured, playing dumb.

"She acquired a nickname from her manipulation of the weather," said Grace, patience weakening.

"Hmm. Jane Storm?" I ventured.

Grace huffed with exasperation. "You have no idea who I'm talking about, do you?"

I tried to keep up the stupid American act, but I couldn't control my laughter. "I get it, I get it!" I said, as she hit me with the thin pillow. "It's very romantic. But is there a book your family isn't in? You're worse than the Mortons."

Even after meeting Dale and Scherie, that Family name could still give Grace pause. "You Yanks live too much Poe."

"And what craft-nosey classics do you prefer, besides the ones the Marlows are in?"

"Dickens," she said. "Every bloody word of Dickens."

"Me too," I said, but something about that choice made my heart ache. Dickens had all of those selfless women doing good, which was a better life model than Poe's consumptives and metempsychotics, but not by much. To repeat myself, I knew the difference between self-sacrifice and pointless self-immolation. My hand drifted to my missing eye.

"Oh, no you don't," said Grace, taking my hand, placing it on the curve of her bare waist. "I'm happy you've read my favorites, but don't hyperanalyze my bookshelf."

Thus ended the spoken interlude. Above the Atlantic, we broke the sound barrier.

When we emerged from the bedroom, relaxed but not very rested or even sated, I noticed that everything in the plane seemed sharper and more colorful, like going from fuzzy analog to high-def. It seemed I'd regained full depth perception, which made no optical sense. In fact, I was seeing better than I had before. That made no sense at all, whatever healing power Grace might have recently wielded. A minor miracle, though I didn't think Saint Paul had ever gone to this sort of Damascus: zero to the mile-high club in one flight. *Lord, if this is a sign of your continued love for this sinner, thank you.*

Dale kept his eyes fixed firmly on a tablet, though the corner of his mouth was twitching. Lara gazed at the staring copilot, fascinated by the Gale's quiet stillness.

Scherie, however, was staring at me. "Is something else wrong?" I asked.

"It's nothing."

"Nothing?"

"You're glowing. I mean, your eye is glowing a bit in craftsight," she said.

"Right," I said. "I'm seeing better too."

"That's great!"

"But something's still wrong," I said.

"Well, you might have to be careful about Middle Eastern assignments from now on. I'm not very religious, but it's just that, with your one eye all crafty like that, you resemble the *Dajjal*."

"The what?" I asked.

"He's the equivalent of the Antichrist in Islam," she said.

Great, so it wasn't just my fellow Christians who would be getting prophetic dread from me.

Dale looked up from his tablet. "Antichrist, feh. I think he looks like Odin. Good and pagan."

Grace studied my face as if it were somehow new to her. "I think he looks like a pirate. A complete rogue."

Laughter was about to explode from Dale. "A pirate?"

Scherie gave me another look-over. "She's got a point."

"Both are wanderers," said Lara, breaking her silence.

Pagan or pirate jokes, I didn't mind. Because if one man in the world today deserved the title of Antichrist, it certainly wasn't me. The man we were hunting might deserve it, but God alone knew for certain.

Then, the cabin light seemed to shift, and a wave of uncertainty passed through me, like entering the Sanctuary. I was immersed in tremendous power, familiar, yet also strange and alien. Like the power everywhere we'd gone, this spiritual fount was ready to my hand.

The copilot spoke. "We've just entered American airspace. Welcome home."

"You shall wander far," said Lara.

On American soil, Roderick breathed in the air, then dabbed his lips with a handkerchief. "So much life!" Before his flight had left from London, he had disposed of his Kiev-tailored suit in favor of more comfortable street clothing that doubled as combat gear, but he'd kept the handkerchief. He missed his mask and robes, but in these end times he had come to see that costume as mere pretense—he wanted to be the Red Death incarnate.

A nondescript, used Honda Civic was waiting for him. Rather than rent or lease a car, he had purchased one outright. He could have gotten another top-tier sports car like the Bugatti he'd left in Kiev; for the time left until his apotheosis, Roderick had more cash than he knew what to do with. But where he was going, craft alone wouldn't hide anything for long, so he bought a car that went counter to his profile.

Roderick placed his small briefcase in the trunk. Passing through customs, he had not declared the wheat as agricultural produce. For this evening in central Providence, he held the sky clear of cloud— he wanted the stars themselves to witness the path of his ascension. All of human history, all the failed prior attempts, had led to his moment.

He parked a few blocks away from the House of Morton, outside the perimeter of his enemies' attention, and walked the rest of the way in the brisk evening air. As his only physical weapon, he carried concealed in his jacket a kitchen knife, which seemed appropriately domestic. After several lifetimes of captivity and subsequent exile,

Roderick was finally going to confront the House that had betrayed him.

From a distance, before he sensed anything else of it, he felt House's hatred for him, seemingly undiminished with time—if anything, stronger, as it had no reason to hide the depth of its feeling from him anymore. *As if it were the wronged one.* Two centuries before, Joshua Morton and Abram Endicott had entered House with its connivance and had found Roderick in his trance attempting his greatest magic. Abram had quartered Roderick and then hacked him to bits, leaving only the head intact. Even decapitated, Roderick had felt every blow.

It bothered him that Joshua and Abram's descendants had been so successful in getting to Ukraine and in disposing of his former body. He had predicted a high probability of suffering and death for them and those they cared about, but his farsight hadn't been as clear with them as it was with nearly everyone else. He had a theory about that blind spot, and he'd taken some further precautions, but for now Dale, Scherie, and Endicott didn't matter, as they were hours behind him. Roderick would take his time with House, the only true home he had ever known. It wouldn't be a party unless his guests showed, and rushing things wouldn't help.

He strode up the steps of the tiered garden. In the reconstruction, a new gate had been built, but Roderick said, "*Please open,*" and, lock and hinges squealing in protest, it did. This was his first time at the old House in the flesh since Abram Endicott had taken Roderick's still-living head away. Roderick stood for a moment in the courtyard, running his mundane and preternatural senses over everything—the hibernating bats, the garden going to rest for winter, the breeze through the dead leaves, the cold breath of House's silent hate through the crack in the wall.

Finally, hearing no greeting or curse, Roderick addressed the door of his former abode of seven gables. "Did you think I'd never return? That you wouldn't have to pay for your betrayal?"

Go away, tyrant. Kill you this time.

"Tell me why you did it, House. I only asked you for a few more hours of resistance. So much grief could have been avoided."

No wait. Root and stone despise you.

Roderick sighed. "My dear, foolish House. There are few truly sentient buildings in the world. Did you think to wonder why? Jonathan made you, but you owe your awareness to me and the Left Hand. For you, sentience was dialectic."

Thank you and fuck off.

"That, House, was inexcusably rude," said Roderick. "One question before I destroy your door and much else besides. I was the rightful owner, descendant of Jonathan. How did you defy me, House?"

"We'll answer you." A black-lit shadow fell across the door, whirling like a slow tornado into a human shape. Madeline stood before him, a spiritual provocation, dressed in male hunting clothes of the nineteenth century, clothes that Roderick had worn when he was master here. Madeline smiled at him, feral but relaxed, without the crazed passions that he had loved. "Brother," she said, "your blind spots are antediluvian. In the crisis of whom to obey, you assumed House was as patriarchal as you. If anything, House is a *she*."

"Greetings, sister. I am pleased to see you here. But your little sophistries cover nothing of your treachery."

"You should be going," she said, "to and fro in the earth, walking up and down in it. Anywhere but here."

"But here I am," he said. "And you've been wandering far more than I, despite your supposed confinement to the lower chambers. What's your game, sister?"

"We've reached a modus vivendi with House in response to your threat."

"Which is?"

"You intend to use House as you planned in our first lives. We will oppose you. But there is another way."

Oh, there were many other ways. But first, he'd try Rezvani's trick, just to break the ice. "*Please depart this world forever.*"

Madeline winced with pain, or at least annoyance, then stretched her hand out toward him. "*Come with us!*" she cried, and a black-lit darkness reached for his heart.

Roderick dug in his psychic heels, and his spirit remained grounded, but the effort left him breathing hard. "Perhaps we should just chat some more."

"Oh, let's!" she said.

Roderick knew his alienist lore about encountering death. First denial and anger, now bargaining. "Beloved, I'm here to offer you life. I can give you a new body based on Morton DNA. You can return to your birthright: immortality."

She laughed in his face. "If we didn't know you, we'd call that kind. But we know you absolutely, so your gift is eternal perdition. Even if you could undo Rezvani's expulsion, and we don't think you can, even if I, Madeline, could leave our consolidated form, I would never accept such a gift from *you*. So here's our offer: drop dead."

"That's not much of an offer."

"We're very serious. You would become a hero-ancestor, like us. Oh, you wouldn't stay here, of course; you'd have to find another Morton shrine to haunt. But you'd enjoy the afterlife of an ancestor-deity. We've received our descendants' honor and fear, and now we've been giving them sharp-edged advice. I like them. We will still kill them in the fullness of time, but then we'll all be together again. My death after so long a life made for a different spirit, much more powerful and capable of continued change. It will be this way for you as well."

No, this idyllic patter wouldn't do; she must focus on him and him alone. The others were getting closer, and he needed to finish all business with his sister. "Maddie," he declared, "you are no true deity or anything else. You're a shadow creature, a two-dimensional version of a four-dimensional being."

"Do we seem so limited to you?" Red lightning flashed through her black-lit aura.

Time for the final moves in a dance with death; time to give her the really bad news and keep her from interfering with his true plan. He had her complete attention; her wave function had collapsed to this place and time. Before acting, he couldn't resist another taunt. "The living can do things you cannot. The living can bleed."

With the speed of a Western desperado, Roderick drew his knife and cut his perfect hand. Blood dripped. Madeline yelled with rage and the dark power ripped again at Roderick's aura, but Roderick was already speaking the necessary words: "*I bind you again to the lower chambers, and I bar the House from loosing you. I respectfully request this as the senior and rightful lord of the House of Morton and give great praise and thanks to the dark powers that make all our works possible.*"

As Roderick spoke, Madeline's form dissolved again into a dark cyclonic cloud and, with a moan of horror, vanished into the earth. Roderick relished the moment, for he'd had nothing like it since his first life. "You're back in your box," he said, "and you'll stay there until you're a good girl."

In answer, a sound of a choked-off breath or a cut-off sob. Then, deep from the foundations of the House, Madeline spoke like the Earth itself. "You taught me never to give an enemy the courtesy of my intentions, but know this, Roderick Morton: amass what power you may, I shall see your life end, and there shall be no afterlife in this world for you."

One chilling threat deserved another, so Roderick said, "I'll be back for you later, beloved," and turned away from the House to face his oncoming guests. The candles were lit, the balloons were up, and it was finally time for everyone to jump out and say "surprise."

Attucks led his small force down the leaf-strewn street toward the House of Morton. He and four others represented the best that each branch of the craft service had to offer. A Gale weatherman from

WENA-CON, a black-ops Marion from SCOF, a Van Winkle from PRECOG, a Johnson from enhanced combat (ENCOM), and Attucks himself from C-CRT. Along with their specialty talents, each was also fully combat ready, and they had worked out a synergistic attack plan that stood some chance against Roderick. Perhaps his wife, Kat, should have represented PRECOG, but he hadn't changed his mind on her joining this mission. And of course, the Mortons and Endicott weren't here—that was half of what this mission, this attempt to draw Roderick into open battle, was about. In Langley's farsight, Roderick only came alone to the House when the Mortons and Endicott had no probability of being here as well.

Other soldiers of lesser craft would remain in position outside the House, weapons at ready, in order to either mop up the victory or report the defeat.

Despite their desire to join immediately in the attack, Attucks had also kept the three craft civilians, Queen, Longhouse, and Alchemist, in reserve, hidden and undisclosed to his craft regulars. Eddy's reports had indicated that an attack of just regulars would fail, but Attucks didn't think the mere presence of the three civvies would make a difference. The force of those three had to be brought to bear at the right time.

At the head of his four regulars, Attucks arrived at the foot of the steps that led up to the courtyard. Before signaling the charge, he briefly prayed that after so much time and sacrifice, Roderick would be there as predicted.

Roderick stood his ground as the five rushed up the garden stairs and through the gate, spells blazing. He was a Left-Hand object per se, and therefore beyond any protection of the laws against summary execution. From behind him, he felt cold hands reach into him for his spirit. The so-called orthodox Morton dead and Rezvani's

Persian ancestors had belatedly joined the fray. Dale's father, Will, and grandfather Ben were leading this charge. Roderick resented that they hadn't come forward to defend Madeline, though perhaps that had been a question of tactics as much as preference.

Using the House's own wards despite its hostility, he saw that other combatants waited in position outside, perhaps to slow him if he tried to run. Had these insects seen what he had done at Chernobyl? But they had worked out an interesting combat dynamic. The PRECOG woman was constantly calling out probabilities of Roderick's next moves, the black-ops witch was trying to usurp his body's Left-Hand nanites, the weatherman was defending his team from losing their air supply, and the enhanced combat colossus was working with Attucks to land blows physical and magical. They were not trying to use firearms on him—perhaps they were uncertain of their further precautions against his power of command.

This would have been fascinating if his godhood didn't await. Seeing that no one else was entering the combat, Roderick drew upon the power in this ground—this was still his home—and conceived a spell to freeze their bodies, to freeze their very blood, when the PRECOG woman said, "Now!" and she and the ENCOM soldier drew two concealed pistols.

With sure instinct, Roderick changed his command, "*Not Attucks!*"

The PRECOG and ENCOM fired their guns, and the black-ops witch and the weatherman fell dead to the ground. The look on Attucks's face at this betrayal by his trusted comrades was almost worth the inconvenience. Roderick had guessed some treason within H-ring was planned, but he'd assumed that black ops would've been in the cabal and that the treason would've been more helpful to him in its execution. In any scenario, he could easily imagine what the orthodox would do; it was the would-be Left Handers who continually surprised him.

He addressed his putative allies. "Did I request your help? Your presence? You could have turned as my worm within H-ring for years."

Also, the bastards had made him command without politeness. He would have made them use their unsecured weapons against themselves, but he had other plans for them and for their former commander.

"Attucks," said Roderick, "my cousin Joshua admired your family. He said your line was truly the greatest. Despite that, my plans do not include your death today." Or at least they didn't now. He wanted this incipient craft civil war to continue; therefore, all of those here needed to survive. "*So please depart.*"

To Roderick's wonder, Attucks did not move. Brow sweating, teeth clenched, he said, "The Attuckses obey no enemy."

Roderick had forgotten that detail. Sloppy. Then, in further evidence of his negligence, three other craftspeople came through the gate. From his visions in H-ring, he recognized them as survivors of the purge that he'd inspired in Abram and Madeline. These odds would completely ruin his civil war diversion.

The New Orleans woman was a marvel of multicultural imagination in her spells, and the San Franciscan was shooting darts at him that would have melted his body if his flesh had been normal. As the Michigander attempted to close physically, he was calling down on him some very old craft, which, if Roderick hadn't had the Morton lore, would have been very dangerous.

So it was the Michigander who had to go. Fortunately for Roderick's plans, the newcomers had made a crucial mistake, and they all focused on him instead of the easier targets of the PRECOG and the ENCOM.

As if to point his accusing finger of craft, Roderick delivered a one-two combination of punches at the Michigander. "By coming here, you've broken our covenant," he said. "*Heart, please explode.*" Roderick leapt into the air and delivered a flying kick into the man's chest, then spun away, and not even bothering to check on his success, strode toward the gate, repelling everything thrown at him. He had left the already flagging Attucks, the New Orleans woman, and the

San Franciscan against the traitors from PRECOG and ENCOM. Close enough odds to last awhile.

As a farewell, Roderick commanded friend and foe alike: *"Please do not follow. I'm done here, for now."* Then, at the courtyard gate, he paused. He should dispose of Dale Morton's grandfather and father, lest they interfere again. *"Ben and Will Morton, please depart this world forever!"* But he did not sense their presence before his spell nor their disappearance after it. The cowards may have already left. No great loss.

As the craftspeople turned on each other behind him, Roderick left his old home and its dust behind him. When he returned, it would be in radiant glory. *Please do not disappoint me, Mr. Cushlee.*

While Roderick moved through starry Providence, Mr. Cushlee the Renfield moved through the cold rain of D.C., his legs considerably improved, thank you much. He was a complete cipher of intent as the strategic defense beams passed through him. He repeated a benign-sounding mantra: he was in town to play a game of paintball. He worked a different stealth than the usual invisibility. His was a profound mundaneness, out-boring the dulling craft of the capital.

Still, if someone had been watching, they would have seen each beam passing through him reveal something hidden in Mr. Cushlee's features: squamous or skeletal, bestial or mechanical, but never something warm and empathetically human. But no one was watching Mr. Cushlee. Roderick was providing a great distraction. All of Langley's Peepshow and Pentagon's PRECOG focused to the north. They must be desperately afraid.

Mr. Cushlee dressed in a suit and tie and a long trench coat that wasn't nearly warm or dry enough against the weather. (He wouldn't complain about the rain, though; in fact, it was right on schedule.)

At home, he might play the mature chav, with East End accent and tracksuit and bling, but that was to distract people from looking further into his affairs. In this city, he spoke in that stage American that made him sound West-by-Midwest.

He crossed Memorial Bridge and passed through some of the many Arlington ghosts, trying to hide his amusement that there were so many that death had undone. Death would undo many more if Roderick had his way, but Mr. Cushlee didn't worry that his employer would destroy the world and the Renfields with it. Renfields never worried about the *reductio ad absurdum* of their employers' plans. Nothing ever worked 100 percent, even when a Renfield was in charge.

He snuck through the gate and onto the grounds of Arlington National Cemetery with ease, and he strolled toward its center. There, on the eastern side of the Memorial Amphitheater, was his objective: the Tomb of the Unknowns.

He made his stealthy way toward the hedges to the south and west of the Tomb. The ceremonial guard paced his rounds of twenty-one steps and twenty-one-second pauses, but he did not spot Mr. Cushlee. The Renfield could just make out parts of the inscription on the Tomb's west face: "HERE RESTS IN HONORED GLORY AN AMERICAN SOLDIER KNOWN BUT TO GOD." His angle of fire would be sharp, but given his objective, that would be fine.

The guard had turned and was now pacing solemnly away from Mr. Cushlee's position. Slowly, like a tree unbending in a fading wind, Mr. Cushlee took out his gun, raised himself just above the hedge, and fired. A succession of paintballs splattered against the Tomb's west panel, sounding little different than the splash of the hard rain that was now falling. The balls were filled with one of Roderick's special recipes. The nanocraft liquid had a sort of insect hive intelligence, and it swarmed toward the carved letters.

His job complete, the Renfield walked away. He would keep moving until he was home again. Since the cock-up of the Romanian job, the Renfields never hung around for the culmination of their masters' schemes. Succeed or fail, the grandest schemes would always cause plenty of damage to nearby friend and foe alike.

Not that it was his business, but the Renfield had a rough idea of what would happen next. The letters on the Tomb would become a series of interlocking circular indentations, illegible, and without meaning or power. The rain and the guard's ritualized movement meant that by the time he observed the smoke and smell it would be far too late.

To the mundanes, it would seem such a pointless bit of trivial destruction. They'd just recarve the letters. But they didn't know the protection this memorial had provided. When war had begun to generate anonymous young corpses at an industrial rate, the risk had increased that some composite spirit like the Left-Hand dead of the House of Morton would form and grow. The Tomb's blanket remembrance was a ward to keep a spontaneous Yasukuni from happening. It was an excess of caution—such ghostly death machines seldom happened spontaneously, and that any living American would want to create such a thing deliberately seemed ridiculous. As a result of Mr. Cushlee removing this forgotten linchpin of occult protection, Roderick would be able to summon the spirits of all the unknown dead of America's wars, including the many Civil War unknowns memorialized elsewhere.

By the time Mr. Cushlee reached Memorial Bridge again, the rain had completely stopped, right on schedule. *Nice one, Roderick.* As if the last trump had blown, the thousands of spirits of Arlington's unknowns rose up into the clearing night sky.

NINETEEN

In all the rush of takeoff, we hadn't actually heard any itinerary. Now, finally in U.S. airspace, I belatedly asked, "Are we going directly to Providence, or are we landing someplace else first?" But this got no response from the Gale except for some New Age–sounding crap about how knowledge of our destination would make us easier to track.

"I'd like to see the double-blind study of that," said Dale.

"Amen," said I.

But soon, we felt the plane descend, and a little before touchdown, Scherie looked out the window and said, "Yep, it's home."

"Not for me," said Grace, eyes searching. "I don't even have good spiritual sight here. Odd."

"Are you using stealth?" I asked. "You're not showing up in spirit-sight as a practitioner." She shook her head. This lack of spiritual power in America wasn't a good sign for our future happiness.

When the plane stopped taxiing, the Gale practically pounded down the door, desperate to exit and light a cigarette despite her Nicorette binge.

Cool air entered the plane. Winter was here.

"So we go to the House," I said.

"Like Joshua and Abram," said Dale. Then, perhaps remembering the long-term results of that siege, he added, "but not exactly."

We gathered our carry-ons and choice armaments and hustled off the plane. I had my sword, the needle-like sample of Roderick's neural tissue, my .45, and not much else. The Gale was looking about the tarmac, pacing, nicotine buzzed and restless. "There's supposed to be a couple of H-ring folks here. Tough ones, and guns, lots of guns."

"Doesn't matter. We'll make do with what we've got."

"Hold on a second," said the Gale, raising up a hand. She stopped pacing and picked up her phone, which at that very moment started buzzing. A car motor dopplered closer; a black van swooped toward our landing area. "It's my boss," said the Gale. "I'm out of here." With a race-walk step, she followed the colored line leading to the terminal.

The van squealed to a stop. A cold wind blew, cutting deep. Alone, Eddy emerged, black trench coat flapping tightly in the wind. Either he'd foreseen that greeting us solo might keep things from escalating past harsh language, or he just didn't care anymore. He stood relaxed, open to any blow we chose to give.

"Well?" said Dale. "This had better be good."

Eddy nodded with the deliberation of someone who was otherwise very still. "You were all sacrificed to save the world."

"Oh," said Dale. Eddy's blunt math deflated him.

But not Scherie. "You could have fucking told us. Or don't you think we've fucking proven ourselves under fire?"

"No," said Eddy. "You couldn't know. You had to be scattered around the globe as if by accident in order to bait Roderick to return early, before he gathered his full potential power. Then, those who survived long enough had to trigger events in Ukraine that would further motivate Roderick to depart Kiev prematurely, when we'd be ready for him."

The long explanation meant something was wrong; I had a hunch what it was. "All very clever," I said. "So where's Roderick now? Is he at the Mortons' House?"

The farsighted Eddy paused, brought up short by my simple intuition. "He's gone. He came, he saw, he conquered, he left."

"Where to now?" asked Scherie.

"Conquered?" said Dale, anger renewed. "Ah, hell, if we don't know where we're going, we're going to the House. It's only fifteen minutes away even if we drive like mundanes, and we ain't going to do that."

"Agreed," I said. "Everybody in the van."

Eddy didn't object; he just held his hands open in the pose of a man too deeply in debt to ever call things even again. This was how they slowly went mad over there in the Peepshow.

I called over to the pilot, who had finally ventured outside. "Keep the plane here, refueled and ready for takeoff." Eddy nodded his confirmation at the man, and the pilot replied, "Yes, sir."

The van was blasting heat inside, which felt fine after the tarmac. Scherie drove with Eddy in shotgun, who continued to brief us about the fight at the House and the apparent treason within H-ring. Dale and Lara sat in the back. To my right in the middle seats, Grace was mumbling Latin, but nothing spiritual seemed to be happening. Eddy had brought a change of clothes for everyone in haute camo style, très guerilla chic. With very little self-consciousness, everyone but Scherie changed into them; my French suit hadn't fared well through recent events. While I changed, I had questions. "OK, Eddy, you say that Roderick showed up at the House, beat up the good guys, and left. That doesn't make much sense."

"He also bound his sister to the House."

"Revenge?" I asked.

"Maybe," said Eddy. "But he took crucial time to do it. Since he left the House, we've seen nothing. This is as predicted. We follow someone like Roderick not directly, but through how he affects others. In earlier farsight, all Roderick timelines vanished after his homecoming. We thought that made the Morton House the crucial point. But we were wrong. I was wrong."

"Dale," I said, "if he didn't do what you thought, what could he have wanted at the House?"

"Not sure," said Dale. "But he might have done something else with the Left-Hand dead besides bind them. I'd like to talk to my dad and grandpa."

As we zoomed at unsafe speed down 95, the van got abruptly colder, and Dale's father, Will, and grandfather Ben appeared in the far back, crouching over Dale and Lara's seat. Ghosts and the living all yelped in surprise and sudden discomfort. We were all crowded together, even with a van. Had Eddy even anticipated these dead passengers? I didn't bother asking; Langley seldom showed its hand.

"We were looking for you," said Ben.

I had seen so many spirits in my travels that it no longer seemed odd that these Morton ghosts were visible to me. Dale asked his dead relations questions, but meanwhile, Eddy was listening to his Peepshow earpiece. He spoke to us as information came in: "Something has happened at Arlington Cemetery. Vandalism at the Tomb of the Unknowns. No clear details yet."

Dale broke off his conversation. The eyes of this brave man had a real fear in them. "The Tomb of the Unknowns? That sounds like something Roderick could use."

"I'll find out more." My father had been buried at Arlington after he'd sacrificed himself to save me during the H-ring fiasco; he was now one of the spirit guards for the Cemetery and the Pentagon. I concentrated. I pressed against Grace to make a little room for another ghost to my left. "*Dad, please come here.*" As if someone had opened a window, the van grew colder, and my father was crowded in with the rest of us. He appeared as if he'd just arrived from a battle in some desert, though even in photos I'd never seen his First Gulf War service.

"What is it, Major?" he said, gruffly. "As you may have heard, I'm very busy right now."

A summoning was still a little embarrassing for both of us, but I'd sort family matters later. "Please give us a report on Arlington, sir."

My father described the vandalism of the Tomb of the Unknowns. "We didn't see the intruder before or after. Some strange stealth seems to protect him from living and dead observation."

Grace chimed in. "That sounds like a Renfield."

"Who are you, ma'am?" asked my father.

I had other business to report that might only add to the awkwardness. "Dad," I said, "this is my girlfriend, Grace Marlow."

Grace briefly raised her eyebrows at "girlfriend," though whether because I presumed too much or too little was still a little unclear to me. But she didn't question the word.

My father's mouth formed an O, then he sat a little taller and, smiling as if with living warmth, placed a hand over his chest in a traditional spiritual greeting. "Very pleased to meet you. Sorry it's during a council of war—I'll enjoy getting to know you better, but it'll have to wait." Fixing me again with his commanding stare, he took the time to say, "You'll be squaring this situation with God, H-ring, and MI13, right, Michael?"

"Yessir." Though I had no idea how.

"Outstanding."

And that was all he had to say about that. God, I missed my dad sometimes. But back to the real business. "Then what happened?" I asked. The perp's ID as a Renfield or whoever could wait a moment.

"The unknown dead rose," said my father, "so damned many, and those just in Arlington. Perhaps they could have once identified themselves to other dead like me, but they were all past that. They still manifested in their uniform colors, but they were blurred, tattered spirits, some almost shapeless. They rose high into the sky. Those of us on patrol called to them, but it was as if they couldn't hear us. I fired warning shots. I . . . I may have hit one."

Ectoplasmic blasts against the fallen didn't concern me right now. "Sir, how many?"

"At least four thousand spirits from the Civil War left Arlington, but I think others rose too—the forgotten. For a moment, I felt . . ." *No*, I wanted to insist, *you're never forgotten*, but my father just shook his head and said, "Never mind. The Arlington number doesn't matter. The problem has spread. At all the Civil War battlefields, all those sections of numbers without names, the unknown ghosts have left."

"Where did they go?"

"If I knew that, I'd be there. They rose, then disappeared in a flash. We can't see them anymore. They've gone somewhere hidden, like H-ring."

We were pulling up to the front of the House of Morton, for once hypervisible and radiating more hate than I'd ever felt from it. I might be House's friend, but what about my father? "Dad . . ."

"For now, I'll stay in the van," he said.

As we walked up the House's steps, the Rezvani ghosts were drifting along with us. Scherie spoke to them soothingly in Farsi. House was roaring and crying, and I had to remind myself that we were friends now.

In the courtyard, we were greeted by Captain Kat Hutchinson, who looked like a younger version of our Colonel Hutch with darker hair. It still choked me up to see a Hutchinson. We'd all seen one another last at Hutch's funeral, and there were no names hidden among us. One difference between Kat and Hutch was that Kat had none of the colonel's power of reassurance; in fact, she tended to cause the opposite reaction. She looked exhausted, and spitting mad.

Eddy noted dryly, "You're here without orders."

"Goddamn it, Eddy, and goddamn Calvin too for trying to keep me out of this. When is he going to learn? Just because I pretend not to know things doesn't mean I don't see them, that I don't care. I'm in PRECOG!"

I had some sympathy with her anger at Attucks, but time to rein things in. "Captain Hutchinson," I said. "I could use a report."

"Yessir," said Kat.

Eddy prompted further, "On your own authority, you brought reinforcements?"

Kat nodded. "With the cover of a training exercise, I organized a relief team in Boston and had them at ready, then brought them down after the predicted commencement of combat with Roderick. He left the scene, but the fight with rogue craft elements went on for about one-half hour after his departure. Then Van Winkle farsaw our imminent arrival and told her co-conspirator to run for it. She and the ENCOM traitor fled with the survivors of their outside support. We missed them by just minutes before we marched in. Three were dead here, three others dead in the immediate area. I had medics for the wounded. The unofficial practitioners known as Queen and Alchemist were badly wounded, but they'll survive."

"And General Attucks?" I asked, with concern for her and the whole service.

"The general will be fine," she said. "At least until he's well enough to explain this fucked-up plan to me."

As if to bring her back to focus, Eddy asked her, "Can you see Roderick? Can you see him anywhere?"

She closed her eyes. "No. He's still gone." Her eyes flashed open. "Eddy, I can't see anything past tomorrow."

"Good," he said. "Neither can I."

Kat seemed as surprised at this statement as I was. "Why is that good?" I asked.

"The whole world's timeline might be one big flux," said Eddy, "but that's better than certain doom."

"Still not very good," I said.

"No," agreed Eddy.

Punctuating this discussion, we made room for the cleanup crew. They were here to remove the dead. They'd finished the outside work, and they were just leaving with the two bodies from the courtyard. The House's stealth should have made their job easier, but right now, House was moaning in despair. Below that noise, a familiar voice called to us as if from the bottom of a sealed-off well. "Let us out."

"Madeline?" said Scherie. "Where are you?"

On hearing Madeline's name, Grace shifted into a combat-ready stance.

Madeline, not visible, spoke with a stony control. "Roderick used the old family blood magic. He has chained us tight to the subbasement because he thought we could interfere. We know how. Release us and we can help you."

"We've got a lot going on right now," said Dale. "Give us a moment."

"You don't have a moment. We may already be too late."

Ben Morton said, "Don't listen to her."

Will Morton said, "What? You think she can make things worse?"

Lara approached the House and put her open palm very close to the door. "In Kiev, Roderick talked to you. He has put you in the box again."

"Who are you?" said Madeline, voice finally breaking into rage.

Lara addressed Scherie instead. "Tell her to go to the far shore. Much happier for all."

"But will she help?" Scherie asked.

"Help, but not friend," said Lara.

"Yes," hissed Madeline. "We're not your friend. We're your ancestor, and ancestors call their descendants to death. But not tonight."

"She saved my life," said Scherie simply.

"It's your and Dale's call," I said. Dale had taken this risk before, and the stakes had been smaller. Eddy and Kat remained silent, perhaps disinclined to question a Family's authority on its home ground regardless of the result.

"Scherie," said Dale. "I think we have to defer to someone else. One being gets the final say. Roderick bound these spirits to House forever, but that tie only works when it's knotted at both ends, and Roderick never seems to get that House isn't just a passive thing. I'm not going to make that mistake again." He faced the door. "House, last time I ordered their release. This time, we're asking. Shall we release them?"

A pause, and a vibration through the ground like a small earthquake. Then, the House of Morton spoke, and for the first time I heard the words with my own ears. It spoke like the rocks and stones of the Gospel might have, but its words were damnation. "*Yes,*" House said. "*Release. Kill him.*"

"Scherie," said Dale, "please help me with this." When Joshua had bound the Left-Hand revenants, he'd done so with terrible words and probably years of his own life. Dale's last attempt to unbind them along with the destruction of the House hadn't even fully taken. This would require some serious spiritual work.

Dale produced a jackknife, and Scherie and he each cut the palm of one of their hands. They dribbled the blood onto the courtyard stones, and Dale said, "*Hear us. We are the rightful living family of the House of Morton. We speak for the dead, for Jonathan and Joshua and all the others of our line.*" Dale raised his hand as if beginning the sign of the cross, then brought it down like a butcher's cleaver. "*We break the craft of Roderick, who is of the dead. We declare the time of binding over, and we free the spirits of the condemned. Madeline Ligeia Morton and all the revenants with you, rise and be free.*"

Lightning flashed across a clear winter's sky, and dark fire shot up into the night. Then Dale and Scherie collapsed to the ground, spasming like epileptics in a seizure.

As Grace went to their aid, House's door flew open, and out strode Madeline Ligeia Morton, dressed as a warrior queen from Victorian imaginings, but the black-lit flames where her eyes should have been gave true dread to her appearance. She carried a spear and shield. Like a ruler of the damned, she roared at the Heaven she didn't believe in: "Free forever!"

A stillness followed her ringing words. Then, I heard my father at the courtyard gate. "Again? You've let them out again?"

A voice in my head said, *Try your power of command on her.* I did my best to ignore it, even as Madeline looked down in disgust at Dale and Scherie, still quivering with their eyes rolled back in their heads. "Stop the faux groveling. Only the real sort will do."

She pointed her spear, and real spiritual energy, not ectoplasm, sprung from it into the living Mortons. Their bodies relaxed. Dale blinked up at Madeline and asked the question we all dreaded. "What will you do with your freedom, Auntie?"

Rubbing her hands against her temples, Scherie gave Dale an incredulous smile. "Sweetie, when the world's going to end, killing anyone besides Roderick wouldn't be sporting."

Madeline grinned and spoke through unmoving aristocratic teeth. "That's the Morton spirit!" She nodded at my father's ghost, a man she had fooled, fought, and helped to kill in life. "You say my brother has unleashed the unknown dead. We will search for them, though it may be too late. If we find them, we'll keep them away from Roderick."

I was uncertain that her means of doing this wouldn't be as dire a problem. But then Ben Morton's ghost said, "If you don't mind, Aunt Madeline, we'll go with you."

The ghost of his son Will gaped at him. "You posthumously senile old man!" But Will must have seen something in Ben's eyes, because then he said, "OK, Dad. Better than hunting Roderick with the kids."

I kept my approval to myself. It would be good to have the orthodox Morton dead keeping an eye on Madeline. But where would we the living go to hunt Roderick?

In spiritual matters, like sought like. Madeline would hunt, but she had her own desires, and I wasn't sure how like Roderick she was anymore. I had Left-Hand power in my flesh, but I felt no push or pull in any direction of the compass.

Compass. A compass worked with a needle, and I had the perfect one. "Someone get me some water. In a small bowl. Quickly."

Staggering to his feet, Dale went inside and found a small metal mixing bowl and filled it with water. I brought out the sealed needle of tissue.

"Let me see that," said Eddy, reaching for it.

"*Hands off,*" I said. Eddy's hand jerked back like it had been burned. I quickly added a silent prayer of "*In God's name.*" But the damage had been done. Everyone was looking at me a little nervously, except for Lara, whose skittering eyes locked onto me with renewed interest. Eddy rubbed his retracted hand and said, "That's an interesting power you've got there, Major."

"We'll discuss that later." I placed the needle in the bowl, and despite its seeming density, it floated, as if clean water repelled it. The tissue drifted for a moment, then began to spin like a true compass, settling into a line that pointed southwest or northeast. There wasn't much of America to the northeast of Providence, but plenty to the southwest. Something had already happened at Arlington; perhaps Roderick would be going somewhere nearby.

I snagged the needle from the water. "We'll figure this out on the way to the airport," I said. "Sir," I said to my father, "stay with me for a little longer." I had a feeling we needed some old knowledge for this problem.

In the van, I asked Dale, "If you were going to work serious Left-Hand craft near Washington, D.C., where would you go?"

"I would find the biggest hole nearby," said Dale. "Some kind of mine or any other good wound in the earth."

"Near the capital?" Grace shook her head. "Perhaps not a mine. Perhaps a bunker. We had one in the Cotswolds in the event of nuclear war." I saw her meaning. Some wounds were bloodier than others.

"We have a lot of 'secure locations' down that way," I said. "Which one would Roderick choose? Greenbrier is open to the public. Mount Weather is still active, but he could probably force his way in if he didn't plan on staying too long."

Dale's face fell. "Mount Weather. My dad was near there when they found him, ranting out in the woods, walking toward D.C. It's Mount Weather."

"No," said my father. "Not Mount Weather. Not exactly."

A memory came to me. "Dad, when I was a kid, you packed us up in the middle of the night to go somewhere out in Virginia, and only stopped when you got an all-clear signal."

"Yes," he said. "It was when the Soviet Union was collapsing. Some commie craft diehards were planning something desperate. I brought you with me, against orders. We were going to H-ring's relocation bunker. It's near Mount Weather, and it's deserted. It's the perfect place for him." Some of his living command returned as he fixed me with his eyes. "In God's name, you must hurry."

PART VII

TERRIBLE, SWIFT SWORD

O gentle Faustus, leave this damned art,
This magic, that will charm thy soul to hell.
—Christopher Marlowe

Like something getting chewed by something
huge and tireless and patient.
—David Foster Wallace

CHAPTER

TWENTY

Miles and hours to the southwest of Providence, Roderick sprinted alone through the dark woods between his abandoned car and the craft bunker near Mount Weather. A late autumn cold rain was tapering off, and it didn't touch him anyway. He had driven insanely fast to get here, but his power was sufficient to cover him from law enforcement or craft observation. Now, carrying his small briefcase filled with wheat and other seemingly innocuous objects, Roderick ran, not from anxiety of pursuit but from the sheer joy of arrival. Years of planning and anticipation had come to this.

Perhaps he had not eluded all pursuit. He'd felt some sympathetic craft from the northeast; just a twinge, but it'd been more than he'd expected the opposition to muster. He thought that he'd left nothing behind that allowed such distant tracking magic. No matter—he would not dally.

The paved way to the bunker had been torn up, buried, and overgrown, but he didn't need it. He reached the side of a hill. This was the place. He felt the land's revulsion, for such bunkers represented the opposite of life. Various wards played off his flesh and raised the small hairs on the back of his neck, but the door he wanted remained hidden by craft. The blast door had been left sealed with mundane and magical mechanisms, but neither would keep him out, because as the Chimera machine, Roderick had given a hand to the design.

Still, that had been decades ago, and Roderick's organic memory had unavoidable holes. He felt around, discerned the misdirection magics, then moved the correct way instead. His fingers found a simple keypad, and it became visible. He entered the pass number, which was not the Number of the Beast (despite his usual sense of humor). It was 09 17 1787, the day of his and Madeline's conception. They had been born about ten months later. This piece of timing had been the last careful attention to the details of their lives that their father, Joseph, had given. "I tied your birth to the birth of a nation," he'd said. "I hope you appreciate the power in that."

The armored door became visible; its bolts moved with the grinding noise of decades. Now, the simple password, but one tailored to his craft. "*Please open.*" With a groan, the door swung out. Anyone who had begun their spell with a word other than "please" would have been locked out forever. Anyone who, like an Endicott, compulsively invoked God's name would have set off the traps in the ground below the entrance.

Roderick entered the tunnel. He would have barred the door behind him, but it was laden with too much craft, and he needed a clear channel for the spirits to join him. Besides, the remote contingency of opposition pursuit only added a certain piquancy to the moment and a containable karmic counterweight to his magics.

"*Some light, please.*" Roderick walked down the long tunnel through the paired armored doors of the first airlock, which had been left open, and toward the area of the bunker proper, where the path split three ways. The right-hand path was a service tunnel for the mundane and alchemical machines that would have kept the bunker habitable. To the left another long, craft-hidden, and secured tunnel connected this H-ring bunker to the mundane government bunkers at Mount Weather. That tunnel was supposed to have been collapsed with decommission, but through Roderick's manipulations it had been left intact, just in case he needed the extra room in the mundane facility for his first base of campaign.

The central path passed through an inner airlock threshold, with both doors a smaller variant on the bank-vault style of the outer blast door, though again this passageway had been left open. No radiation screening or sterilization apparatus here—a healer would've managed those issues. Roderick now walked a corridor with irregularly spaced doors on each side. It felt like home. Before bombs and air raids, his people had built bunkers, and this was just another subbasement. He had even intervened to give the bunker the aesthetic style of his old House, despite the risk in an attack of the splintering and cracking of weaker materials: fine-grained hardwood floors, exposed brick in the walls, and white plaster hiding the concrete-and-steel shell that protected the space. The only exposed metal was the brazen-colored alchemical tubing for processing pure air and water, with some hidden outlets for the always necessary body tanks.

Five of the doors led to split-level offices and quarters for the five commanders of the H-ring sections, their immediate staffs, and their chosen best. The sixth door led to rooms covertly reserved for certain figures from the Office of Technical Management—Madeline and Abram's fallout shelter fantasy room. Two doors led to supply areas stocked with plenty of food and water. Roderick felt a little hungry, as his new body still needed conventional food, but he would not eat this disgusting packaged matter.

This bunker was built as a safe place for H-ring to hunker down, preserve American lives (particularly their own), and take vengeance on America's enemies. It would also have been a shelter from those mundane former friends who, in a post-nuclear strike world, would readily kill all craftspeople as witches in a misguided apocalyptic rage. Unlike Greenbrier, civilian discovery hadn't caused its abandonment. Instead, farsight had given the contingency planners the bad news: none of it would matter. Even if farsight anticipated a strike and allowed the craft leadership to beat POTUS to shelter, all would be lost in the aftermath, if not from radiation and nuclear winter, then from the resulting global Yasukuni-style engine composed of billions of dead that would consume any survivors. Best not to waste any more resources on what would only delay the inevitable.

Roderick went through the last door on the left into the main room, which, unlike the more specialized compartments of the larger government bunkers, would have served multiple purposes: a conference room (perhaps even a broadcast room), mess hall, and social area—the mead-hall style of space in which people had gathered to keep out the monsters from Grendel on.

Here, and in nearby Mount Weather and other bunkers, America had made its capital for the end of the world, denying that death alone would have dominion. His fellow Americans had been prepared to sacrifice the whole world for ideology. For one bleak moment, Roderick felt trivial in his schemes next to this viewing stand for a global funeral pyre.

The object in the center of the room brought him back to himself. The long, dark hardwood table for meetings and meals seemed solid enough to support the whole bunker on its legs. Stored against the walls were the table's chairs, five large for the section chiefs and many smaller ones for staff. This dusty table's surface would serve as his altar to bring about the new age.

Their colors faded, spells lay about this main space, passive and waiting. The spells resembled wards, but Roderick would use them to channel and shape the forces he'd summon.

Roderick checked his watch. Had the Renfield succeeded in his task? Roderick thought he should have felt something, like one of those science-fictional tremors in the Force from millions screaming, but he felt nothing. Only one way to know for certain.

Roderick opened his briefcase on the conference table and pulled out the glass tube. *In case of apotheosis, break glass.* He pivoted and, exhaling with tantric force, threw the tube against a blank wall. The glass shattered, spraying its contents. "*Please write this: for the unknown soldiers, all known to me, come.*" The alchemical solution hissed as it etched his words into the wall, a smell of burnt wood and metal. He didn't need to be so literal as the Yasukuni model and list all the dead he intended to bind. From H-ring's center, he had seen them all, and that was enough.

But those unknown American soldiers would only be the tip of the spear, the diamond in the drill bit. They wouldn't suffice to punch the hole that Roderick needed. So he again reached into the case and brought out the small sheaf of wheat grown in the black soil of the Ukraine. In Ukrainian, he combined biblical words with his spell. "*A measure of wheat for a penny, please, and three measures of barley for a penny. You millions, murdered with hunger, all known to me, come.*"

He had misdirected the opposition with his residence at Babi Yar. Yes, he'd been disappointed by the dearth of spirits left from that sub-set of the Holocaust, but he'd suspected that he couldn't get those ghosts, and he needed more than a hundred thousand anyway. So he'd found a greater harvest in Ukraine's famine dead. All those Ukrai-nians that Stalin had killed, all those innocents never properly laid to rest, were now millions of hungry ghosts. His wheat sheaf had left a silver thread from Kiev to here, a clew for them to follow. That was the reason (besides the simple joy of it) that he'd had to destroy the Ukrainian craft service as he exited—they could have blocked this mass summoning of their forgotten dead.

One final ritual action would complete the motive engine for Rod-erick's machine. With one of the shards of the glass tube, Roderick reopened the cut on his palm and dripped blood to the ground. "*I have summoned you all. I bind you to this place. Please come.*"

The summoning and response would take a minute or so; he would use the time to deploy the last three objects in his case. These things would serve in a remote but very enjoyable contingency. They had been extremely difficult to obtain, even for someone like himself who had seen their locations. First was a fragment of marble chipped from a gravestone in Iran. Second, a ragged and singed piece of cloth from a Red Sox jersey found buried in a Middle Eastern tell. Third was a poppet from colonial Salem, preternaturally preserved through the centuries as an heirloom of the Left-Hand Mortons, representing in folksy style a bearded man in Puritan dress.

These talismans were insurance against a daydream. His main

enemies couldn't possibly arrive in time, but he'd thought that about Joshua and Abram, and they had badly surprised him. Some secret craft, some nascent precog or its antithesis, could make certain individuals and their associates difficult to track. His main opposition could, at crucial times, be mere shadows in bright farsight. He would not be taken unprepared again.

Roderick stepped onto the conference table as if it were a royal dais, and as he had all those years before during the siege of the House, he lay down to commence his trance. He held the three talismans close, with the stone in his left hand, the jersey fragment in his right, and the poppet clutched against his chest under his arm like a sleeping child. This summoning would be horrible. Concentrated in this small space, the ghosts would try to rend his spirit from his body and consume it. He gathered his energy for the coming trial. He had no doubt of the outcome. Despite all, this country was still his home ground. Also, he was, first and foremost, a necromancer in the purest sense of the term. He took power from death and the dead, not the other way around.

Roderick waited and tried to avoid distracting thoughts. It was difficult. He felt awe at the greatness of his fate. Of all the humans that had ever lived, he would be the one. He would open just the smallest crack to a world of the dead. Such worlds had a surplus of the quantum-like possibilities that fueled craft, for all their human choices were gone. The dead of such worlds were coalesced entities of raw power, and Roderick could tap that energy too.

The sheer force at his command would be more than this one, niggardly Earth had ever given him or anyone else. As for the Morton specialty, weather, he could summon a ocean-sized hurricane. Combat? His mere words would be life or death across the globe.

With such power, he could bring about the new craft order. Practitioners wouldn't hide anymore. His disturbances of the existing regime weren't just good tactics, but a statement of principle: magic should be known. By his actions today, craft would rule the world, and he, godlike, would rule the craft. Then, the stars would be their destination.

Some culling of the population might be necessary. Roderick knew that some currently living would make a big deal about all the killing, but he'd never cared before, and he wouldn't have to later.

From afar, he felt the opposition—they were definitely drawing beads upon him. It was time. Where were his dead?

On that cue, the soul-shattering force of a thousand dying black-lit suns slammed into the room. Roderick screamed with agony and even horror as the rending pain and pressure grew, but the central quiet point of his mind was in ecstasy. *Welcome, welcome, my lovely dead.*

When we got to the airport, the pilot had deserted his post. "In answer to your question," said Eddy, though nobody had spoken, "yes, he was a little precognitive."

"You guys have a real morale problem in a crisis," said Dale, as I helped him and Scherie out of the van. They were still wobbly from their unbinding of Madeline, though Scherie had managed to slip into her fashionable camo wear. Eddy returned to talking and giving orders on the phone, as he had been ever since leaving the House of Morton, though he'd been driving at combat speeds.

"I can fly it," said Grace.

"You can?" I said, not skeptical so much as in renewed awe.

"I'm good with all forms of transport," said Grace. "I don't need to use any spiritual force for it. It's a natural talent that assists with my license to steal."

We boarded, and Grace took the stick. Almost immediately after takeoff, we went to Mach 1.5, leaving a sonic boom like a scar across the airspace of the Eastern Seaboard. We were giving the mundane establishment a lot of things to explain in a short time. A serious problem, but it was a distant second to the end of the world.

The Mortons had set their seats to full recline for the flight, trying to recharge as quickly as possible. Eddy lowered his voice as he continued to make calls filled with commands and code phrases. Lara sat bolt upright as if in meditation, but her head and eyes lacked the single-point focus and ticked about from thing to thing and person to person as if all were equal.

My father was still along for the ride, but he was flickering—technological speed didn't always mix well with the supernatural. He gave me directions to the craft bunker. "It has spiritual camo, but if Roderick is there, it's probably more exposed. Anyway, your eye is looking like Judgment Day itself as far as revealing hidden things."

My one eye's sight had spiritually sharpened, but I didn't think that was why, despite the flickerings, my dad seemed very near and clear to me. As the Mortons had explained to me, proximity to mortal peril brought ghosts into focus.

My father flickered again, and he said, "I may have to go to ground soon." Partings seemed as awkward as summonings. Out of nowhere, he added, "I wish you'd known your mother better. She would have been pleased to see you like this, in command, moving into the fire."

"Mom's seen me," I said. "You should look for her. In the Chunnel, I saw an echo of the two of you together."

The idea seemed to catch him by surprise. Then he cut out again for a moment. Another Morton lesson: ghosts didn't like agitation. On returning, my father's next words were like a recording of his old self. "I'm not big on failure, son, noble or otherwise. Win. Beat him."

Before I could say good-bye, he was gone.

We landed in Upperville, Virginia, at a private airstrip that the government occasionally borrowed, and all too close to Washington. I felt the energy, the excitement, of possibilities like dominoes all in a row. I could go there, commanding followers on the way. D.C. was the most direct route to hegemony. But no, I was busy, busy with something important.

Could I stay busy and distracted from temptations of conquest for the rest of my life?

This time, I also brought an HK416 rifle off the plane with me. It was for Grace to use, but I didn't want to discuss that with her yet.

Eddy had two classic black government sedans waiting for us, one with someone in the driver seat. "I'm heading back toward Langley," said Eddy. "I'll continue to organize my people for the apocalypse. We're sending what support we can."

"This time, try getting there a little earlier," said Dale.

Eddy ignored this and nodded at Lara. "Should I take her with me?"

"No," said Lara.

Something was wrong in Eddy's tone when he said "support," and was wrong again when he asked about taking Lara away. Then I realized that Langley's plan hadn't really changed. "How long do we have, Eddy?"

Eddy's sad face relaxed, a meta-tell of professional liars. "I don't know . . ."

"Not this time," I said. "Here, I'll help you. Once you persuade the president, you'll have to get a nuke or bunker buster there with a way to deliver it that totally destroys the bunker without desolating a prime chunk of the East Coast, and which also avoids Roderick's power over the air. That probably means a ground force. The only reason you haven't rushed it is you want us inside distracting Roderick while you get things in place. So how long?"

Eddy spoke with deliberate calm. "I'm not going to talk about my plans. If you want to speculate, go ahead, but keep it to yourself. You can do the math as well as I can." He opened his car's rear passenger door and nodded at his driver.

I turned to stop any of my friends from doing harm to this repeat offender, or maybe just to restrain myself, but the Mortons were holding each other close, and Grace was putting an arm around me. Eddy's car drove away.

Echoing, Lara said, "I am good with equations. We go."

At all due speed, we went. Grace drove at somewhere over a hundred miles per hour, reacting to changes in the road with her own mundane skill, as she couldn't enter the stretched time of practitioner combat mode.

"These are our objectives," I said. "We need to destroy Roderick's body or drive his spirit out."

"Sir, last time, it took both," said Scherie.

"Right, and even then, he had a way out. This time, you'll need to direct his spirit to this needle." I thought of our other weapon. "Lara, I can't order you . . ."

"Good," said Lara, with sharper feeling than I'd heard before.

Scherie gave me a confirming nod. OK, assuming Scherie still wanted her along, we'd leave Lara alone for a bit. "I'll order our deployment at the site." I had a tough decision that I didn't want to make, and maybe I wouldn't have to.

We followed my father's directions and reached a side road through the woods near Mount Weather. Grace passed a car parked on the roadside, slowed, and came back around.

Through the woods, I saw a glow like a hint of sunrise and the barest hint of black-lit footprints leading from the parked car into the false dawn. No one else seemed to notice. "This way," I said.

I took the lead this time, Grace immediately behind me. The Mortons followed, and Lara trailed with unhurried robotic precision. Grace and I trotted through the woods, and other than the residue of Roderick's footsteps I saw no hint of spiritual power, much less traps. In a short time I saw a large metal door opened within a rounded alcove in the side of the hill, like the house of a terminator hobbit.

I held up a hand and halted. "Keep back." A stream of ectoplasm smeared against the night sky was funneling down into the open doorway. Ghosts flew by like the windblown damned of Dante's Hell, as if the entryway were a spiritual vacuum and the ghosts were so much carpet dirt. Some of them were as my father had described: faded American soldiers. But others were Eastern European peasants, skeletally thin. As they passed through the wards against mundane and foreign intruders and into the heartbeat-pulsing glow of the entranceway, the ghosts sparked and their clothes changed from the faded blues, butternuts, and peasant earth tones to a tubercular bright red.

I spoke in a low voice, as if it would make any difference. "Scherie, is Roderick here?"

She narrowed her eyes in concentration at the bunker. "Mother-fucker is in there all right, but this craft flow is all one way. He isn't reaching for us." She shut her eyes tight with apparent pain. "So many ghosts."

No sign of Madeline and the Left-Hand Mortons, though. "Grace, are you seeing any of the spiritual activity?" I had ulterior motives for asking this question, motives that were going to make us both un-happy all too soon.

"No, nothing," she said. "Still no spiritual power of any kind."

Lara stared at the spirits, face no longer passive, but twitching. "Thief," she said, then pointed at Scherie. "You. Tell them to go away."

"She's right," I said. "We need a path cleared."

Scherie screwed up her face and began barking out a series of curses so blasphemous that I feared for every soul that heard them. The stream paused. Scherie strode toward the dead, clearing a way into the tun-nel for us. But the ghosts were not fleeing so fast and far as they usu-ally did in her anathemic presence.

"OK, we'd better go in while we can." I turned to Grace. No good way to say this. "But I'm asking you to do something out here."

"What kind of bloody insane, patriarchal shite—"

"There are wards barring the way," I said, "wards particularly at-tuned to the foreign and mundane. Sure, we could fight them, but it'll take too long, and then what? The fight with Roderick could be purely spiritual. So I'm asking you to do something else. Something vital."

Grace didn't say anything, so I continued. "You need to stop any-one else from getting in here or doing anything to this bunker, who-ever they are—Roderick's allies, U.S. spiritual ops, mundane special forces—anyone. We need an hour, no more. You'll need these." I handed her the HK416 and some clips.

"You want me to fight your own government?" she said as she

automatically took the assault weapon and handed the flechette rifle to me. She sounded skeptical, but at least interested.

"Sue me, but I'm a spiritual elitist, and right now, we're the only active force on the map." I spoke rapidly now, trying to convince her, since I couldn't order her. "I don't think Roderick is going to let any number of lower-level practitioners or mundane soldiers deliver a nuke or any other weapon that would actually inconvenience his plans. But that doesn't mean we'll succeed either. If you know we've failed, or if we don't come out in an hour, get away from here if you can, and let whoever likes join the party inside. Get back to England, and try to rally a response there."

"Right-o, but perhaps I shall get my power back, and then . . ."

I shook my head. "There's something else you need to wait for. To battle Roderick, I'm going to call on my full spiritual power. If I survive, I expect I'll be out of control. You'll have to warn that damned *Oikumene* and the whole world. But if you get the shot, you'll need to kill me. I think you're the one person who'll get me to hesitate long enough, and you'll be able to do it."

I went close to her and whispered, "Nothing says 'I love you' quite like killing your amok boyfriend."

She embraced me fiercely with her free arm. "I can think of better ways." She released me. "One hour. Go."

The Mortons and I walked to the doorway. Lara stood still, her eyes ticking this way and that.

"Lara, we're going in," I said.

"Good-bye," she said, and she folded her hand once in a single "wave."

"We need your help to kill Roderick."

Her neck palsied at this statement as if she were malfunctioning. "He is gone from Ukraine. I said I will not touch him again, never. I am not your weapon. I will not die for you."

Not the words to tell someone who was probably going to die for the rest of the world shortly, joined by a couple of his friends. Whatever Scherie had to say for her, I was long ago done with this creepy practitioner. "Why the hell are you here then?"

"I am here for them." She pointed at the Eastern European–looking spirits, caught in between the suction devil of the bunker and the deeply angry sea of Scherie's craft.

Once again, I had no good response for this blank-faced enigma. "Fine, stay." I handed her the flechette rifle, and I called to Grace, "You got this?"

"She won't cause any problems," said Grace, which was a succinct enough threat.

As the Mortons and I passed through the wards into the tunnel, Dale said, "You know, if the world doesn't end, you're going to be in real trouble."

I gave him a grim smile, but for once his paradoxical reassurance only irritated me. Even with such a small chance of success, what I resented most was that the *Oikumene* might be proven right, and that they, or Grace, would have to put me down. And if Grace and I both survived, what the hell were we going to do, with America hostile to her craft, and me an international target? I had faith in God's grace for the world, but, to my shame, I was still wondering about Grace's love for me.

As Roderick lay in corpse-like stillness atop the wooden table, his mind was more active than ever before. Using his own magics and those laid down decades before in this place, he spun the countless spirits like an enormous vat of cotton candy, then tightened them as a spider draws an enveloping web around prey. Roderick's flesh and mind became the crucible in which his dead were forged into a world-piercing spear. He fed off some of their energy to sustain himself and this process. Like the Left-Hand revenants or the Yasukuni machine, the ghosts' identities dissolved and fused as he consumed them and they consumed each other.

They were still trying to take his spirit with them—he felt his astral form being pulled hard, like a bad tooth in his former flesh. This would only get worse when he opened the way to the dead world, but he was well anchored to this body.

Fewer ghosts were now streaming into his spiritual acid bath. Roderick didn't need more spirits, but he hadn't expected the stream to go dry so soon. What had happened?

First things first. His vortex of ectoplasm had congealed and hardened; the ghosts were sufficiently unified and shaped. Roderick began the true great working. Within this dimension, he channeled the force toward a secondary projection/TV wall of the conference room directly opposite the door, but the real blow was going in no speakable direction and against no palpable target.

He mouthed the final words. *"I create this in sympathy with the Dead Worlds. I beseech you, please open the gate."*

With a blur of spinning motion and sparks of ectoplasm and aether, Roderick's death machine sought to puncture the walls of the world. *Drill, ye tarriers, drill.*

Then, unmoving in the center of the bunker's network of wards, Roderick felt vibrations along magical threads of intruders crossing the threshold. Against very long odds, his main opponents were here. He wished he could tell them how profoundly grateful he was. However short their survival, his glorious apotheosis would have witnesses.

TWENTY-TWO

O ur weapons at ready, the Mortons and I entered the tunnel. I took point, and we passed through an open airlock. The overwhelming power of command ran through the ground beneath my feet, as it had everywhere else. Here, it flowed through the red cardiac pulse of Roderick's Left-Hand craft more like a kindred than an antithetical force. It only waited for an invitation. I had no reason to wait, as Roderick could hit us at any time. What words were proper? Was it blasphemous to invoke God for this unholy level of force? But I would not do anything of importance without prayer. *"Lord, I accept this power to serve you. Help me stay on the true path. Amen."*

In an unseemly eager rush, the power ran through me. Hosanna in the highest. I felt like I could order the bunker to collapse on Roderick. So, I gave it a try. *"In Heaven's name, bury Roderick."* A brief vibration, but nothing. Good to know my limitations. Unlike the Chunnel or the train crash, this was not neutral ground for me to easily control, so I'd save my energy for Roderick's presence.

Scherie was mumbling invective punctuated by the word "Roderick." It pushed back on the bloody, evil craft. Dale did the same by maintaining a weather front in miniature around us, and a sickly sort of precipitation, a red rain, ran down it like water down an umbrella.

Dale said, "Scherie, can you force Roderick out?"

Scherie shook her head. "No. It's like before in H-ring, only worse. He's as slippery as a rabid otter. I may need direct contact. Shit, I may need to stick my fingers in his brain."

We reached a branching in the tunnel and continued through an inner airlock, also open, into the bunker proper. The place had the dark Victorian-look of a furnished crypt. Roderick, perhaps with Abram and Madeline, must have stuck his hands into the design of this place. The alchemical tubing offered the rare glint of metal.

We had many doors to choose from, and each could lead to many rooms. "Scherie?" I asked.

Her throat moved like she was trying to swallow down her own bile. She pointed at the last door on the left. "His craft is coming from that direction."

At that very moment, an inhuman scream of eternal rage and hunger came from behind the door, the sound scorching my ears and my very soul. My mind stopped, and I could not give an order. I knew in my bones that the sun would fail and this scream would go on burning, forever damned.

Scherie had covered her eyes with her hands, but she was the first to speak. "Goddamnit, it's like a nuclear flash in there, and it's just growing."

Dale said, "You're the expert, Mike, but that sounded like Hell itself."

"No," I said. "Hell is just." I ran for the door. "Hurry!" Though I feared we were already far too late.

The heavy door was thumping, as if something tremendous were trying to escape it, but it was unlocked, which as ever was a bad sign. I swung it outward with a heave and a crash. A force like a hurricane blew against our very cells, stopping us for a moment, pushing the Mortons' spiritual shields back against us until they hugged our skin like plastic.

On the wall straight in front of us, a small mote, like the micro lens of a camera, was radiating the impossible amount of power, maybe more than all the spiritual energy I'd ever seen in my life. Fortunately, only the overflow was working against us. The rest was flowing into a man's body on the table, perpendicular to the blast. He had changed his appearance, but as Roman had said, he looked more like a Morton now. There before us, Roderick lay in a trance-like state, just as he had when Joshua and Abram had found him in the House of Morton two centuries before.

The instant I recognized Roderick, I shot at him, but despite my helpful prayers my bullets were swept away as soon as they left my .45. My eye, focused on him, could see the smallest of details. He was holding something in each hand, and something doll-like was under his arm. His fingers were shaking. Even entranced, he could work many spells at once. "Forward," I yelled above the storm, "before he focuses everything on us!"

Lord, give me the strength to move. I strode slowly, like a man climbing a steep hill with far-spaced footholds, closer and closer to the table. Though bullets hadn't worked, soon I'd be in sword range, and he had reason to fear that blade.

Another step forward. In Roderick's right hand, two fingers tightened around a piece of cloth, and he mouthed some spell: *Please stop.*

Scherie called out, "Dale!" I didn't even turn around. The only defense we had was a quick offense.

Another stumbling step forward. Jesus, this hurt like hell. In Roderick's left hand, a finger moved ever so slightly over a bit of stone, and he mouthed another spell: *Please come.*

Scherie shouted her obscene dispellation at whatever Roderick had summoned. I slid another foot forward. A guttural sound in some foreign tongue behind me. Then Scherie yelling again, "Dale, no!" She said some horrible words of exorcism. Then the sound of martial blows exchanged, and the heavy door slammed behind me.

I wanted to turn and help, but that would only kill us all. It was almost a relief. For the moment, I wouldn't have to worry about anybody else. This fight was just between me and Roderick. "*Lord, just another step.*" With all the strength in my legs and heart, I pushed forward.

I'd made it. I stood above Roderick's entranced form. Here the repelling force abated, as all the nearby energy rushed into Roderick's solar plexus. I raised my sword, and slashed down at the abomina-tion's throat. "*In Jesus's name, cut.*"

Roderick's right hand slashed up and grabbed the blade. The blade halted. His eyes were like scarlet fire. "Not this time, Puritan." His left hand had discarded the stone and now gripped the arms and legs of a poppet dressed like a Puritan settler of Massachusetts Bay.

I prayed, "*Please, God, cut him.*" But my arms had no more strength, and Roderick was now fully awake.

After Endicott opened the door, Scherie heightened her craft and slogged forward toward that sisterfucker's body. "Fuck, fuck, fuck," she said through clenched teeth. She kept a lockstep pace with Dale. She had crawled blindly through most of that Penta-gon assault. This was better.

Then some craft flashed from Roderick, and Dale stopped moving. "Dale!" she called. Something about his face reminded her of the time she first met him in front of her family's restaurant, when that blood curse had him paralyzed.

No, not that again—surely he was well beyond it now. Careful to not be toppled backward by the craft storm, she moved to shake Dale out of it. She'd always been the solution to this problem before; just give her one moment.

But Roderick wasn't giving moments today. His still form blasted another bolt of craft, and Scherie's own personal hell was upon her in the form of an all-too-familiar ghoul, a white-haired Persian man with a mustache and an otherwise smooth face. This revenant of a former family friend had been the worst of those that had assaulted her young mind and had tried to take her body from her. She refused to remember his name. He floated toward her, leering with the false avuncularity of the pedophile, and Scherie was again a desperate, haunted little girl.

She tried again the craft she had unwittingly used as a girl: "*Motherfucker, get the fuck out of this place and out of my life.*" But the ghoul merely flickered and darted around her, protected by the aegis of Roderick's magic. She continued her obscene mantras. The ghoul circled her, moving in to touch her mind as he used to, and she, a United States officer and one of the most powerful mages on the planet, wanted to curl up and die.

She reached through the memory of childhood violation for more anger and more power to dispel this nightmare once and for all. Too late she realized her error—he had made her childlike again, and like a child, she had thought this was about herself. Instead, the ghost swung around her and slammed into the body of her husband. The ghoul had come for Dale.

Body still rigid, Dale's mouth opened as if to yell, and then he spoke Farsi, not in the guttural of his curse, but in the polished cadences of the ghoul. "At last, you are mine!"

"Dale, no!" She reached out to make contact and expel his possessor. "*Get the fuck out of him, you child-raping liar!*" But the ghoul broke the paralysis of Dale's body and swung his left fist into her shoulder, sending her reeling backward as the otherworldly craft pushed her back out the door. The ghoul pursued her into the corridor. With a slam of a mousetrap, the door to Roderick's room swung shut, and a bolt clacked home.

Scherie dropped her rifle and pistol to the floor, as they weren't the sort of blunt weapons that would be helpful just now. She faced the ghoul in a ready stance. The ghoul laughed at her, leveled his MP5, and pulled the trigger. Nothing happened. "Safety chip?" he said, as if seeing the words for the first time in Dale's brain.

Even as he spoke, Scherie lashed out with a punch, again more for expelling touch than damage, but the ghoul bobbed and weaved, then brought the stock of his rifle around in an attempt to club her. He swung short as Scherie slid back, then dropped his rifle to the ground as well. "Yes, let's touch," he said. "Your man was weaker than you.

Perhaps he could have blocked one of the gateways into his mind—that hick sorcerer's curse or the voice of the Morton abominations—but not both at once. So here I am. And I must insist on my conjugal rights."

Scherie was appalled, but she recognized that she was being played for time. "*Go fuck yourself, you piece of shit.*" She fell into the stretched tempo of combat and hit Dale with a series of one-two punches, and kicks, trying to make contact for long enough for her dispelling invective to work.

At first, Scherie pulled some of her punches to spare Dale's body as she strove to free him. But after only a few exchanges of blows, she saw how the ghoul was avoiding Dale's Native American–derived martial art, with its control of the other person's movement—that style had a prolonged contact with the opponent's body just short of judo. Instead, the ghoul's blows were lightning strikes, with a lot of footwork and ring dancing.

He connected to her face. She responded with a combination punch and kick, but nothing seemed to slow him down. These few blows and their inflicted pain that she was trying damned hard to ignore were enough to prove a point: if this turned into all-out mortal combat, she was screwed. Dale had far more training and experience, and the ghoul seemed to have co-opted much of Dale's muscle memory. If this style of fight went to the finish, she would have to kill Dale or be killed herself.

Even in accelerated mode, time was running short for all of them. Scherie had one last gambit. She stepped back and dropped out of the preternatural speed of combat. With all the love in her heart, she wiped the blood from her face and held out her arms. "I won't kill my husband. Do what you will."

The monster that animated Dale smiled at her with corrupt gentleness, and seemed to savor the windup of his arm for the coup de grâce blow. His fingers twitched with eagerness; he would rip her love-filled heart out. "Less than a woman!" he snarled, and his hand lashed for her chest.

In Allah's name, what an idiot! Scherie was a trained soldier who never would surrender her weapons for any hostage. She spun into the blow, deflected it, and hit the ghoul's descending forehead with a craft-enhanced headbutt. *"Pass out, Dale."*

Dale's eyes rolled into his head and his body crumpled to the floor. The arms and legs still twitched with the ghoul's efforts to animate them, confirming Scherie's strategy of divide and extirpate. She laid her hands on the side of Dale's face as if she intended to passionately kiss him. *"Motherfucking ghoul rapist, go to hell!"*

In a blinding explosion, with all the energy of her earliest naive efforts, she sent the ghoul out of this world. *If there's both a hell and justice, perhaps he is there.* She should have saved more juice, but she didn't want to see that fucker around here no more.

Hands still framing his face, Scherie spoke gently to her husband. *"Dale, wake up."*

Dale's eyes opened, and his hand went up to one of Scherie's. "Shit, my head. Did I do or say something stupid?"

"Yeah," said Scherie. "You owe me a fish sandwich."

"OK," he said, wobbling to his feet.

"In Istanbul."

"That bad?" he asked.

"Let's go save Endicott," she said. *And wait until I get my hands on you, Roderick.*

But when she tried the door, Scherie found that she'd forgotten one thing: the door was barred against them.

Roderick restrained my limbs with a poppet and his craft. Why this poppet gave him power over me, I didn't know, but I was vulnerable to whatever attack Roderick made next. In a desperate counter, I commanded, *"Freeze. In Jesus's name. Freeze. In Jesus's* name." He froze, but I had to repeat the command like a mantra to keep him still. We were trapped in a standoff.

Face caught in a time-lapse series of contortions, Roderick strained and invoked against me. I prayed and leaned into my sword, and where our powers met was a star of bright light, heat, and ozone. My power flowed through me, wanting to drive Roderick before it and make him kneel. Roderick's power seemed to emerge from thin air near the wall and arc into his abdomen like electricity from a hose. Around the edges of this quasar, the energy of the unknowns and Ukrainians still worked like a hollow-pointed conical drill to hold and widen the hemorrhaging wound between the worlds. From my angle, faces of the dead soldiers and peasants would flash into view on the cone's surface, then stretch and melt away into the mass. I wasn't sure whose power was greater now, but I was sure Roderick's was growing.

Mid-prayer, I switched my command to "Break hold." Roderick seemed to have the same idea at the same time, as we were flung apart from each other. As I stumbled backward, Roderick gracefully rolled off the side of the table closer to the energy portal and onto his feet. His hand was barely cut, but smoke was rising from inside of the poppet. Roderick gave the poppet a kiss and said, "Thank you, Tituba," then tossed it aside.

Tituba. Had Grace's ancestor designed the poppet for use against all Endicotts? Morton mind games—I couldn't let him distract me. I held my sword up at ready. Roderick worked his way around the table, but kept his distance from me. The otherworld's wind no longer forced me back, and the howl of the damned was now just a low, almost mechanical growl. The dead world's energy was focusing further on Roderick, following him around like an umbilicus. Within the black-lit aura of his face, the whites of his eyes glowed red and deadly at me.

But Roderick was not the worst thing that I could see. My preternatural eye caught a retinal flash of the world beyond the rift. The

Left-Hand gods had always been a joke in my family; their "indescribable horror that drove men mad" was a testament to weak Morton minds. But now I saw, I felt, the merest hint of such a being, and I wasn't laughing. This beast, assembled from the unnumbered dead of an alternate Earth, strained against the bars between dimensions, hungry and slavering, rabid and insatiable. With his small, domesticated lapdog of a death machine, Roderick was sawing at the damned bars.

Nothing in Family history indicated that Roderick was suicidal, so I tried reason. "You're going to turn this world into one of the dead zones. You'll destroy the Earth and yourself with it."

"There are always other worlds," he said.

All kinds of problems with that idea, but I didn't think he was serious. "You're risking this world for a mirage of power."

Roderick laughed. "Look around you! This is what the powerful do. What those you serve have done and will do, even if I do not. In as many ways as their folly can conceive, they risk the world, and for far less cause than I."

Roderick was giving me time, which confirmed that he must be growing more powerful. I had to stop him and heal the breach between the worlds soon, before that thing got through. I advanced on him with my sword. Roderick coolly drew out a pen-sized tube and flicked it forward. A line of metal as long as my blade sprung out. "I had this made especially for you," he said. "It's diamond hard with a molecular edge. When Abram dismembered me with that kitchen knife of yours, I felt every cut. I shall serve you as he served me."

The Endicott sword was state-of-the-art seventeenth-century tech. Roderick would chop me and my weapon to pieces. But only if my spiritual power failed me first.

Lord Jesus, blunt his edge and protect your servant, amen. Blade met blade, and sparks like a grinder's wheel flew, but my family weapon held against his flying edge. I felt as energized as I had in the Chunnel. In a flash, I knew: this was how it'd always been with those named, terrible swift swords. It had really been the wielder's power, and when the wielder died, Excalibur and Durendal and all the rest just became hunks of metal, unless a new spiritual master found them.

"*In God's name,*" I prayed, "*thou shalt not move!*" Like his meat puppet in Kiev, Roderick hesitated, but only for a fraction of a combat second, too short to take advantage of without some other ploy.

The duel went on, thrust, parry, lock. With each blow, our conflicting powers seemed to precede our weapons like penumbras and clash before matter connected. Energy flowed through my hands into my sword, and flames were flickering from my fingertips. My burning skin smelled like bad barbecue, but Left-Hand nanites kept rebuilding it.

Though snaky lines of healing continually repaired him, Roderick's flesh seemed to be faring far worse. He was burning all over, playing a faster variation on his eternal decay. His head wasn't much better than the oozing thing we had found in H-ring. But his strength and quickness only seemed to increase, demanding more from me.

"Why?" he asked, thrusting in again for a heart or lung. "Why haven't you incinerated yourself yet?"

Hell, he was figuring it out. For the first time in our fight, I feared Roderick more than the thing from the other world. I needed to finish this soon. Where the living heck was Rezvani?

In a stunning gambit, Roderick struck out, barely cutting the skin of my shoulder, but leaving himself badly unbalanced. As if my sword remembered its taste for Roderick's flesh, I gave him a quick and deep stab to his gut for his error.

Face contorted in pain, Roderick pulled out from the blade and skipped out of reach. Then he smiled at me like a mischievous schoolboy caught in a prank. A drop of my blood was on the tip of his strange weapon. He flicked the drop onto a finger, then stuck the finger to his tongue, tasting. His smile broadened. "I've been a fool."

I was already running for the door, yelling, "Scherie! Dale! Now!" Every bit of spiritual lore told me what would happen next. Like would call to like, and I was suffused with Left-Hand craft.

The door was bolted shut. I pounded on it. "*Open, in the name of God!*"

"*My children,*" said Roderick. "*Please hold him still and silent and take his craft for yourselves.*"

The nanites heard their master's call. I was frozen in place. I prayed mutely and desperately for release and for harm to Roderick, but nothing happened.

"*Please drop his weapon,*" said Roderick. My sword fell from my hand and clanged to the ground.

I felt his finger trace my shoulders as he walked around me, admiring his work. "I cannot believe it. You used my serum. Another Endicott has fallen to Left-Hand craft. I did not notice your transgression, not with all the other craft in the room and in you, but now I know. You have my blood in your veins. You are mine."

Once again, he brandished his alchemical-tech blade. "I think I will start with your feet."

TWENTY-THREE

Grace Marlow retreated into the woods at an indirect angle, up-hill and away from an imaginary line that ran through the bunker entrance and back toward the road, as she expected whoever arrived next to at least investigate if not occupy some position close to that line. She set up a sniper's nest in the brush behind a rotting log, though she lacked an appropriate sniper's rifle. She sighted down the hill in the direction of the way back to the road, targeting one tree, then another. Then she panned about and around. They could come from any direction, though the path she'd taken from the road was the easiest.

The ground felt cold and wet, and she could do nothing about that or her visibility. She was a mundane, ordinary. She still had her conventional training, but she'd lost her preternatural edge. This was more than a problem in self-image or combat skills. If incoming forces were misguided friendlies, she would just try to keep them occupied. If they were Left-Hand hostiles, she would want to start killing them immediately. Being able to see their craft would have helped. At least she wouldn't show up as a practitioner in their craftsight, which might skew their tactics.

Below her, through the doorway and down that sloping tunnel, Michael was probably going to die. That beautiful soul would be apart from her for the rest of her life.

The spooky Ukrainian Lara had followed Grace, but instead of hiding she'd gone into the stealth mode that her people did so well. She'd dropped the flechette rifle to the ground, where it became visible just a yard away. Lara herself was close enough that Grace could hear her breathing.

"You might share some of that stealth," said Grace.

"No," said Lara.

"Why?"

"I am busy with problem. How to touch, how not to touch."

Soldiers had been shot for a lesser refusal, but that would just attract attention. "You're making this difficult," was all Grace said. She was trying to prepare her mind for the necessary combination of skill and sacrifice.

"Courage is Grace under pressure," said Lara. A pause. "I see the ghosts hover near and clear. Poor starved ghosts."

Though Grace had been able to see the powerfully manifesting Madeline, she still couldn't see these mundane ghosts. She kept trying to perform some spiritual work that would bring her preternatural talent back. She softly spoke, chanted, and sang words in Latin, English, and even a little Greek. She had traveled the world, and she had never experienced a day without access to the fountain of spiritual power. But she had never been to the United States, only Canada.

Maybe she was somehow antithetical to this country. It had enslaved her ancestors, and they had left it as soon as they were able. Did she have to placate this land in some way? The very thought threatened to enrage her. Or was she supposed to formally marry Michael to be naturalized to this country's craft? A little late for that in a number of ways.

The damp chill inexorably seeped through her clothes and into her bones, turning minutes into hours. Then, human noises from down the path. Whoever and whatever they were, they were making a bloody racket.

Grace whispered, "Are they Left Hand?"

"I am still thinking," said Lara.

Six people emerged into the open. They weren't devoting much attention in her direction; rather, with minimal cover, they set up to meet whatever would come up the path next. No big weaponry either. Grace guessed that these were would-be Left-Hand protectors of Roderick who hoped to profit from life extension.

More very long minutes. Then louder, machine noises from the woods. Grace guessed that an ATV was towing something very large and explosive. These would be the orthodox craft servicepeople with the bomb that Michael had predicted.

Through craft and skill, the Left-Hand defenders had become more difficult to spot. Grace very much wanted to join the orthodox newcomers and warn them about the ambush awaiting them. A straight-up firefight, and then Grace could delay their destruction of the bunker.

But no, Grace had to act sooner and in a way that left her an independent agent for whatever followed. With only a second's deliberation, she fired off a round into the woods and over the head of the newcomers. A chaos of crossfire ensued, including some fire that hit a tree behind her. Both the newcomers in the woods and ambushers on the near ground might have some idea she was up here.

The tree behind Grace exploded, and Grace felt sudden pain. Bloody hell, a dart of wood was sticking up out of her back like a hedgehog spine. A thud next to Grace, then Lara appeared, lying beside her, stealth dropped. A longer and thicker piece of tree shrapnel was sticking out of Lara's upper arm.

"Ouch," said Lara. She pulled the shrapnel out, examined it briefly, and flicked the blood on it toward Grace. "Ah, problem solved." She was nodding emphatically.

Not getting this, Grace reached around and pulled the oversized sliver from her back. Lara asked, "Do you have cloth?"

Just then, Madeline Morton manifested above them. Any other day, and Grace might have been terrified. Instead, as she turned onto her back and started cutting and ripping a piece of her camo blouse for Lara and herself, Grace greeted Madeline with "You haven't proven very useful."

"We've been working here," said Madeline. "Ben and Will headed some of the unknowns off."

"Why did the dead get into the bunker then?"

"Because I didn't foresee the fucking Ukrainians."

"I did," said Lara, as she snagged the whole piece of shirt before Grace could rip it into narrower strips and, instead of bandaging or tying off her arm, dabbed different parts of the fabric in her blood.

Below, Left Hand and orthodox were still firing at each other, but neither side seemed to have further interest in Grace's position. Grace heard the shouts of soldiers calling in more support. Nothing further of interest would happen here before the end.

Grace kept her eyes on the fighting, but she had a question for Madeline. "I need to get my spiritual power back. What rite will work to get this land to accept me?"

"You need your craft?" In a flash, Madeline was in front of her, in her face and obscuring the view, sneering and snarling. "Maybe this land wants you to come crawling back, to beg forgiveness for your ancestors' leaving it just because of a little misunderstanding over human bondage. So get down on your knees, bitch, and crawl."

The rage in Madeline's voice was startling. But Grace Marlow understood the anger, because she'd been thinking that this was exactly what she might have to do, and how much she would hate herself and this land if that were so. It wasn't, and that was what Madeline was telling her, in her own ironical, Left-Handed way.

"Thank you," said Grace.

"Don't thank us," said Madeline, voice not softening at all with the loss of irony. "We'd love to see you and Endicott die, and soon. But Dale and Scherezade are mine, and you are the tool at hand."

"No. I am not your tool," said Grace, and like a fierce libation she jabbed the wooden dart with her blood on it into the ground. In her mind's view, Grace wasn't lying flat behind cover, but standing, as she addressed the forest, and the creeks, and the sky. She would tell them the truth in words very different from what Michael had sung in the Chunnel.

"I am Grace Marlow, descendant of Tituba and of Toby Howe, who were brought to this land against their will and forcibly enslaved. The Howes fought against their oppressors and chose freedom in another land. By grace of God, I am a spiritual practitioner in the service of the Crown of the United Kingdom. I owe you nothing. Yet I have come to aid this country in its time of need. Perhaps I shall stay, and perhaps I shall not, but by God, you shall do me the spiritual courtesy of allowing me my powers and privileges here."

Without waiting for any sign, Grace again spoke to Madeline. "Please distract them."

Madeline disappeared, and instantly reappeared in the woods, putting on her "warrior queen of the damned" show. All eyes, guns, and spells were upon her.

Grace scrambled down the hill to a point above the bunker entrance, then flipped over with a half twist like a vaulting gymnast to a perfect dismount, well in front of the doorway. The long-violated ground rumbled. Lara, trailing, looked down at her blankly. "Pretty," she said.

Grace could see the tantric color primaries of the wards now, within an arm's reach, at best ready to slam the door in her face for her foreignness. She could probably stealth through them. But stealth wasn't her current mood, nor was compromise. She spoke a spell in clear Latin, then added another phrase as a prayer: "*Permitte amor meus januam patefacere.*" *Let my love open the door.*

The hostile wards melted into inviting rainbows. "Very pretty," said Lara, startling Grace from immediately behind her shoulder.

"You're following me in?"

"Yes," said Lara. She picked up a small stone from the ground and wrapped the bloody cloth around it. "Problem?"

But Grace Marlow was already running into the tunnel.

———

Scherie and Dale shot at the door to the main room of the bunker, then pulled and pounded on it, tried to wrench it open, flung spells at it, and swore at it. Nothing. Bits of it blasted away, other parts were hot to the touch, but the door would not open. "It practically begged us . . . to open it before," said Scherie between breaths. "Could Roderick be making us think that it's closed when it's really blasted wide open?"

"Like in *Star Trek*?" asked Dale, also winded with recent efforts. He shook his head. "Roderick has so many more interesting things that he'd make us see if he could. I think he's just put a lot of energy into sustaining that door."

"That's a good sign," said Scherie. "He's still worried about us getting in." She put her hands on the door to the main room of the bunker. "Maybe this will distract him." Envisioning the millions of ghosts that Roderick had violated, she began to stoke the anger for a massive dispellation. "*Goddamned abomination, release them!*" She felt herself on fire.

Dale reached out and grasped her wrist. "Take what I've got too."

The force against the door grew, and she and Dale were completely absorbed in their task. Then, a noise of running echoed down the tunnel. They had neglected their perimeter. Belatedly, they ceased their craft and brought their weapons to bear on the new threat.

"Bloody hell!" said Grace, hands raised. "Hold your fire. I thought you'd hear me from a mile off."

Lara came up behind Grace in a rigid sort of race-walk step. She peered at Scherie, then held out her blood-soaked cloth and stone like a child offering to share a doll. "You bleed. Good."

Grace and Dale didn't try to hide their disgust. But Scherie focused on Lara. "That's your blood?"

"Yes."

"And you want my blood on there too."

"Yes."

Whatever the risks of Lara's blood, Scherie liked the sound of that synergy. She took the cloth and wiped her own cuts with it. Dale grimaced.

"Michael's behind that door?" asked Grace.

"It's barred," said Dale.

"Not against me," said Grace. She ran her hands over it, assessing what it would take. "Say when."

As if Lara were a dangerous bit of farm machinery, she snatched the cloth back from Scherie. Lara faced the door and said, "Inside, when friends give word, I give best shot."

As Scherie and Dale lined up behind Grace and Lara moved to the rear of them all, Scherie remembered the Morton lore on plans. *In craft, sometimes waiting for a plan is a kind of cop-out. Craft is a kind of faith in the necessary.* It was necessary to trust this strange woman once more. "When friends give word," agreed Scherie.

With a gesture and a naked "*please*," Roderick elevated Endicott a few inches off the floor and floated him away from the door. Then, he made the Puritan's arms outstretch wide at his sides. Roderick had enjoyed a mock crucifixion or two in the old days, and here it seemed appropriate enough. Ever since Saint Peter, believers really hated it when this happened.

Roderick laughed, but like Pagliacci, he wasn't really enjoying this moment. He didn't want to admit it to himself, but he knew he was covering for a delay. The power kept coming, and he used as much of it as he liked, but it flowed through him, never accumulating to those divine levels he desired. So, even as he held the room in isolation and considered his dismemberment of an Endicott, Roderick worked meta-magics and ordered his flesh to transform at the cellular level, changing himself into a more perfect vessel. The delay was frustrating, and he was tense when he should be triumphant. He needed an outlet.

Oh, right, he had one right here. With demonic speed, Roderick brought his blade down on Endicott's right foot, slicing half of it clean off, shoe and all.

The pain in his enemy's remaining eye was delightful, and that he couldn't scream was fine. Roderick wanted to see the suffering, but hearing it could be acoustically painful.

Roderick took the half foot and flung it at the energy portal, but it wasn't wide enough for gross matter, so it just exploded into a mist of leather, blood, and meat, which drifted back to form a halo around Roderick. Nice.

The deep red of Roderick's death engine was fading, its spin slowing, and its size shrinking. Roderick couldn't tell whether this was because of attrition or whether Rezvani had killed her husband and was now exerting her exorcist powers from outside the room. It didn't matter—though the gap might eventually close if not maintained, the flow of power was ample for his current purpose.

Endicott's eye had recovered some composure. Time already for the other foot? This might go too quickly, but no other amusements were at hand. Roderick lifted his blade . . .

With the speed of craft combat, the door to the room crashed hingeless down into the corridor and Dale, Scherie, and Endicott's woman raced over it, into the room and running at him.

"*Please stop,*" he said. They froze, looking absurd.

He felt Lara lurking about outside, an object lesson against showing mercy even for the perversity of it. "*Please don't come in here, Lara, until I invite you.*"

"I won't," she said.

"As a new god, I should be careful what I wish for," he said, addressing all his opponents. "As I secretly wished, you are with me to witness my apotheosis. I've been fighting you with both arms and legs tied, but it took all that you are simply to get here. Your end is not in doubt."

W ith my mouth useless, I was screaming inside. Maybe it wasn't the worst physical pain in my life, but it was the worst situation. I was maimed, paralyzed, and desperate.

I could see everything with my eye. Entering, the Mortons had taken point, while Grace had run toward me. Roderick had stepped back, but only to hold all of us in his field of fire. With murmurs of polite craft, he was probing their vulnerabilities, trying to reopen Scherie's physical wounds and Dale's mental ones, considering in what order to torture me and Grace for maximum combined suffering. Unlike me, my friends' spiritual powers weren't ended, only contained, but they would soon fail.

As for Roderick, his flesh was singed, and his head remained like that hideous thing in the heart of Chimera, but his growing, soon limitless strength gave him an infernal majesty in my enhanced sight.

I am not a tactician; Endicotts lack the subtlety. We prefer to put force on the ground and let the math work for us. But I now saw desperate lines of actions forward, lined up like dominoes, if only I could move the first one. My body was a cage.

So, only one thing I could do. It was another Left-Hand abomination—the worst one—and the cost might be my soul. I needed to leave my body and enter another one.

The Don and all those others using the Left-Hand serum wanted to do this, but couldn't. But I had certain advantages. I had left my body before—I had died. I had access to power greater than any man should rightfully have; power that had allowed me to fight otherworldly Roderick to a standstill. But after I left my body, I would have to do other things that were more abominable, risky, and terrifying. Maybe God would spare me. I was here only by his will, and surely not just to lose the Earth. I had to trust in him, even in the face of that beast in the other world.

This act of Left-Hand craft could not require the usual mental or physical actions, or it would not work at the moment of death. It must require only ability and the will. One by one, I let go of my moral, emotional, and instinctual inhibitions. With all my will alone remaining, I leapt out of myself.

I launched into a black-lit glow world, the world of Left-Hand craft. The spirits of the living were bright like stars, but Roderick's was a dark and ever-imploding sun. I had only one place to go.

I set my mind in motion toward Grace. But I did not immediately enter her mind; not even the direst necessity could compel me to that. Instead, at the speed of thought, I spoke to her soul. *Grace, will you let me share some of your brain and body for a while?*

Michael, the world's about to end, and you're standing on ceremony? Get the hell in here.

But I could tell she had appreciated—no, loved—that I had asked her. I went in, not as a possessor, but as a guest lodger.

In a blink, I looked out at the world through her eyes. A thin silver line spun out from Grace to my solar plexus. Grace's body and mind were free of the Left-Hand taint, while I still hoped to wield my original and new spiritual powers. In a series of words and images, Grace briefed me.

I asked, *What is Lara carrying?*

Grace told me. *She's waiting for the word from you. From us.*

God, every word is a prayer now. "Lara, now!"

We added, "*Hit his face*," both to impel it and perhaps throw off Roderick's response. Then we dove for my body as Lara was pitching the cloth through the open doorway into the room.

As we'd hoped, Roderick raised his hands to block Lara's throw. The cloth hit his left palm, and stuck, smoking from contact with Lara's antithetical blood.

We grabbed the needle out of my body's pocket. My soul felt the pull of its carnal home. *Not yet.* "*Scherie, speak!*"

The weapon that was Scherie Rezvani exploded, but this time like a focused charge, all in one direction. In the austere language she reserved for her worst enemies, she said, "*Roderick, you are dead. Go!*"

The blast of Scherie's craft went through her blood in the cloth directly into Roderick's damaged hands. "No," he bellowed. "This is my body. I have never died."

But the truth of Scherie's words manifested in a burning red line of dispellation spreading from the cloth through his hands and slowly up his arms. He was already losing. With all his energy committed to this battle, he lost his hold on the room. Scherie was walking toward Roderick, her own hands outstretched. Adding his power to the fight as he moved forward, Dale yelled an invocation of wind, pushing them both on toward Roderick, and forcing Roderick back toward the table and the gate.

In a burst of black-lit craft, Roderick's spirit fled. His body, still tied to the energy of the other world, exploded into blood, ichor, and pieces of burnt meat and bone that futilely snaked about as they fell to the ground. But I felt the sudden cold of his liberated malice, and I could see his spirit coalescing and condensing as he considered whose body to possess. He might go for Dale or Lara.

We held up the needle high into the air. "*Come here.*"

Like a dog strangling itself on a leash, Roderick's black-lit spirit was pulled sharply into the needle. We dabbed the needle with my blood from my severed foot. "*We bind you to this forever.*"

It didn't take. Maybe Roman had known other lore and could have done it better. Already Roderick's spirit was struggling out in spinning spiral-armed revolutions.

This left a last horrible option. *Any alternative?* I asked Grace.

No, she said.

We shouted "Everyone keep back!" and leapt over the table. We stood as close as we could bear to the gate of the dead. Roderick's dissipated ghost machine was still at work on the hole. I imagined the Earth as one big land, one common home. *For just a few minutes, give me all of your magic.*

From somewhere distant and deep, a mother's voice was speaking reassuring sounds to her infant. The sounds meant *Little one, what do you think I've been trying to do?*

We cocked the needle up like an American football. "*Open wide,*" we said.

From a nearly dimensionless pinprick to a terrifyingly substantial gap, the hole grew. Like children peeking through a serial killer's keyhole, we saw the world of the dead straight on, without my special sight. The sight alone of what was there nearly killed us.

In the gap between heartbeats, we threw the needle through to the other world. "*Stay on the fucking target,*" we said.

Like called to like, dead world to dead man. The needle went through. I thought I could hear Roderick screaming. With a backburst of black-lit power, one of the greatest and most evil spiritual practitioners who had ever lived passed from this life and this world.

But now the hole was growing, inviting the greater threat that mad Roderick had thought to tame. In a rush, I went back to my body, just as, with Roderick's departure, it hit the ground.

The pain of impact on my half foot sent a convulsion through the rest of me. With no dignity, I fell sideways to the floor. I was lightheaded and still losing too much blood. Lord forgive me, but with Roderick gone, the Left-Hand alchemy in my blood was wholly mine to command. I said, "*You are mine.*" Like my pride and my other sins, mine alone. "*Stop the bleeding from my foot.*"

Grace and the Mortons were helping me up. But the thing from the other Earth was at the gate, stretching malefic tendrils of power through, reaching for us. Couldn't my friends see them?

With Roderick gone, Lara entered the room. "Scherie," she said, "send the rest of the dead to me. Now."

"Can you handle them?" asked Scherie.

"Is job like any other," said Lara.

"*Go to Lara. Now!*"

A tornado of ghosts unraveled and then spun into and around Lara's body. Lara collapsed, but the gap and the beast were still there.

"Get out," I said. "All of you. That's an order. I need to shut this gate, and you need to report what happened to H-ring and Langley and stop them from blowing this place up."

"Why, sir?" asked Scherie.

"The rubble will only get in their way—it won't stop what's coming through. Now go!"

Dale nodded. He knew the math. If either he or Scherie stayed, they both would, and that was just stupid. The Mortons left, hauling Lara between them.

But Grace didn't move. "Not this time," she said flatly.

"Not even if I ask really nice?" I said.

"I'll help you over."

I put an arm over her shoulder, and I hobbled over with her to the gate of Hell. Maybe the thing trying to get through wasn't a demon, but it was close enough.

"*In God's name, seal and heal.*" This just seemed to make the ravening thing on the other side angrier. Another tendril of greater power burst into our dimension and seemed to taste the air in front of my face.

Grace and I stood our ground. I tried a more humble prayer, a prayer against the end of the world. "*Lord, please, not yet.*" I reached out to the other presence, the one that seemed to be giving me this dubious power. *Just one more push, Mother Earth.*

The bunker trembled, like an earthquake. I held on to Grace and she held on to me. Were they bombing us? No. The very foundations of the world were shifting.

Ever so slowly, the hole to the world of death irised shut.

CHAPTER
TWENTY-FOUR

As Scherie and Dale dragged her through the exit tunnel, Lara recovered enough to walk on her own. Scherie was moved by the sad, strange beauty in craftsight of Lara, who glowed with all the failed Ukrainian angels dancing on pinhead-sized portions of her body.

"Lara," said Dale, "could you hide us long enough for us to check outside?"

"Yes."

Scherie's view went fish-eyed. Outside the blast door were the remnants of some small-scale chaos and some cold and wet soldiers with guns. In front of the soldiers, an automated ATV towing a large and heavy-looking bit of armament was moving steadily toward the tunnel entrance. Dale yelled ahead, "We're coming out. We're Mortons, and if that means anything to you, please stand down. Oh, and Major Endicott says don't blow up the bunker; it'll only make the Left-Hand god hungry."

Hands raised behind his head, Dale stepped out of the stealth bubble and into much shouting. But before Scherie could follow him, Lara said, "I go away now."

"Where?" said Scherie.

"My new job," said Lara. "Guard duty." For the first time that Scherie had seen, Lara smiled, as if at some secret joke.

"There could be trouble back in Ukraine. You could stay here, claim craft asylum."

"No need," said Lara, smile broadening. "I already have sanctuary."

"Sanctuary?" In one leap, Scherie got it, though she wasn't sure she believed it. Could Lara be the next guardian of Ukraine's equivalent to the Appalachian's Sanctuary for the lost? Up until now, Scherie had trusted her intentions, and Lara had retrieved the spirits of her people, but that didn't mean that Lara was free from mental malfunction. Scherie would have to confirm this fantastical hypothesis.

But before Scherie could question, congratulate, or thank her, Lara was gone. Scherie raised her hands, stepped forward toward Dale, and entered the shouting match.

G race let me lean into her and helped me move on my good leg out of the bunker into the tunnel. With a mock casualness, she asked, "Darling, do you feel like ordering anyone to conquer the world for you?" Meaning, *do I have to kill you?*

"No," I said. The acute fever of my power had departed with Roderick. I only wanted to conquer a hospital bed, and I doubted I could manage that. I also doubted whether the *Oikumene* would believe me.

"You're going to need a prosthesis for that foot," Grace said. "I hope you don't get a boring one that tries to blend in. Something chrome and shiny would be the ticket."

I pulled us to a halt.

"Seriously, Grace. I'm falling apart. You really should . . ."

She kissed me into silence. Then she spoke. "I didn't want to tell you this. I didn't want to tell anyone. But I want you to understand me, so here it is. When your soul transmigrated for a brief stay with mine, it wasn't the first time I'd seen it. I see your soul all the time. Not as something separate—it's part of how you appear to me, in a very, very visceral way. Your soul is why you are so beautiful. And yes, even after all your poor soul has been through and the choices you've made, it and you are still beautiful, only more so. OK, love?"

Being dehydrated and low on blood is sometimes a good thing, as my face was having trouble going red or tearing up. "OK, love."

We walked out into the open, and into the rising sun, clean cold air, and lots of guns pointed in our direction. The Mortons were interrupted in their yelling at some officer. We skirted around the robotic bomb carrier that had stood ready to proceed down the tunnel.

Not bothering to get anyone's permission, Scherie went to work with Grace's assistance on my foot, stopping the residual bleeding, eliminating infection, and stimulating some skin growth. But a healer couldn't regrow so substantial an amount of limb, and whatever the Left-Hand craft and other spiritual power had done for my skull, they didn't seem interested in regenerating my foot.

While the women worked on Endicott, Dale stood back, eye on the perimeter, waiting for some other boot to drop. It came in the form of his father suddenly standing next to him. Dad was out of uniform, in worn blue jeans and leather jacket, which meant some new form of trouble.

"Where have you been?" asked Dale. This latest absence at a critical time was a disturbing return to form.

"I've been helping your grandfather round up the American unknowns before they got chewed up in the bunker. Some from the bunker are still intact, but he can handle those alone."

Dale stared his father directly in the eyes. "Is that all, sir?"

"No," said his father. "I couldn't go near that portal thing."

"You mean you couldn't go near a portal thing *again*," said Dale. "It nearly killed us."

"Yes," said his father, dead eyes lowered. "And that's one of the reasons I need to speak with you now, before you go."

"Now you want to talk? Once again, Dad, I have to ask: why didn't you tell me what Roderick would try to do?"

"Because we didn't know who would try to open a portal, just that someone would."

"We?"

"I'll explain that in a minute. We didn't know it would be the old Left Handers, because we didn't know who had survived, and they had failed to do it before. Roderick and Madeline and the rest had the Left-Hand dead to use, which should've been a perfect engine to breach the wall between the worlds. So why hadn't they acted?"

"From what I saw here," said Dale, "I think Roderick had been trying right before Joshua and Abram got him."

"That's likely," said his father.

"Look," said Dale, "forget about *who*. You certainly knew *how*."

"All too well."

"But you didn't trust me enough to tell me."

"You're my son. I didn't want you to repeat my mistakes."

"Yet here we are," said Dale. "Was it Yasukuni that caused your breakdown?"

"No, it was what I found afterward. I went to an appropriate hole, and I opened a moment's crack between the worlds to see, to see . . ." He shook his head violently. "I thought, with that power, we could use it for good, we could defeat what was coming. The portal slammed back shut, but too late for me. When the Gideons found me, I was in the woods near all these bunkers, screaming at them to shut all the doors."

Dale saw the other, figurative hole in his father's story. "Dad, where did you get the energy to open that portal?"

"I was in the Sanctuary. I brought your mother with me to help."

Stunned silence, then Dale said, "OK, I think that's enough for today. We'll talk again soon, Dad." But before he could ask Scherie to show his father out of this mundane plane, another ghost was standing before him.

It was Sphinx, in her big glasses and boots, smiling with stained teeth and gentle sadness. Only one likely way she could be here at will, unsummoned. She must be a family ghost, and Dale had one likely gap in his family. All those years his supposed mother, his father's wife, hadn't cared much for him, were now explained in this woman's presence.

Sphinx finally spoke. "My dear, dear boy. I'm so sorry."

Dale fought to control his many, explosive emotions. "Sorry doesn't really count for much now, does it? My whole life, and you weren't there."

"I couldn't come close," she said. "That way led to your madness. My way only led to mine. But I cared for you. I saw all of it. Your whole life."

"I nearly killed you!"

"Oh, that! That would have been nothing. But it was better instead to die for you."

"Why? Why all of it?"

"You had to be born, for you and your friends to all come together and save everything. And nobody could know. Because you're my son, the child of an oracle, it means that the living Left Hand have never been able to predict clearly the actions of you and those close to you. Me, they could hardly see at all."

Dale's mouth tried to wrap around a new word. "Mom. Why are you telling me now?"

"Because you very nearly died without knowing," said his father.

"And," said Sphinx, "we don't know when, or if, we'll get the chance to talk like this again."

The two ghosts looked meaningfully at Eddy, who was walking toward the women and Endicott. "Good-bye, Dale," said his father.

"We love you always," said Sphinx, his mother. Then, they were gone.

————

Eddy stood above me, peering down over Grace and Scherie. "Is he fit to travel?"

"To a hospital, yes," said Grace.

"We'll talk about that on the way," said Eddy.

"On the way where?" asked Scherie.

"We'll talk about that too," said Eddy.

Dale joined us, and everyone carried me back to the road. Eddy left his own car and driver behind, and we all got into the car we'd taken from the Upperville airstrip.

In the car, Dale drove again. "No 'thank you'?" he said to Eddy. "Flowers and a card might've been nice."

"Or those big *Star Wars* medals," said Scherie. "I've always wanted one of those."

With no humor or hint of a smile, Eddy replied as if someone had asked a different question. "H-ring has issued orders to bring all of you to the Pentagon for an immediate debriefing."

"He's in no condition," said Grace, indignantly.

"However," Eddy continued, "there's been a slight delay while those orders are received and acknowledged by Langley. Nor have we certified that the op has concluded."

I held up a shaky hand to quiet further questions and snark. "I see. Eddy, what happens after H-ring's debriefing?"

Again, Eddy seemingly answered a different question. "Major Morton, you are correct. I and the nation owe you a debt of thanks. I'd like to offer you the services of the private jet you flew in on, to take you and your friends to the international destination of your choice for a well-deserved leave of action."

"That's . . . very good news," Dale said. "Scherie and I . . ."

"Major Morton!" I nearly passed out with the effort. "We'll discuss our travel plans later." I focused again on Eddy. "Is it the national services fighting their Left Hands, the spiritual disturbances in the mundane world, or simply the terror at what Roderick attempted?"

"Yes," said Eddy. "And some of the tricks you pulled along the way."

They thought I might be the new Roderick. "So at best, we'll be ordered back to barracks, indefinitely."

"At best," said Eddy, looking truly sad now.

That left the *at worst* to Dale. "Ex-22," he said. *Thou shalt not suffer a witch to live.*

"At best," continued Eddy, "you should be somewhere where your future is your decision."

"What about you, Eddy?" I asked.

"I was never here," he said. "You took the plane on your own initiative, for valid service reasons."

"I meant long term," I said.

"Remember the old Peepshow joke you told me, Morton, when we first met? We only like to watch. They still need the watchers, and the watchers of the watchers."

We were already at the plane. A refueling truck was finishing up by its side. Doors were opening, and my friends were readying to help me onboard. "Eddy, thank you," I said.

The sad man finally smiled. "I'm just sorry I don't have an engagement gift for you and the commander."

I gaped stupidly at him, but I was smart enough not to question a Peepshow about the engagement. Instead, I said, "I thought this transnational relationship was impermissible."

"Regs nearly got us all killed," said Dale.

Eddy held up a finger. "There's been at least one exception. A British craft Family and an American Family were allowed to intermarry because farsight showed one of their children, though not likely to inherit either power, might be important to both countries."

"How did it work out?"

"We won World War Two."

"Oh, him. Are you saying . . . ?"

"No," said Eddy. "I most distinctly said nothing of the kind. All I'm saying is that your relationship is now the least of your problems—that is, from the official point of view."

They brought me up into the cabin and straight into the bed. Scherie got medical supplies. Grace bent and kissed me. "Bloody typical. We British always have to take care of you Yanks."

"Ah, that subtle British humor," I said, unclenching my teeth for a moment. The day's damage was asserting itself.

"We've been spiritually dampening the pain," said Grace, "but I'm going to administer a nice strong painkiller now so we can all rest." She paused, as if considering. "Then, I'm going to play some rock music on the stereo."

"Sex and drugs and rock 'n' roll?" I asked.

"Sex later," she said.

"After I've recovered?"

"After the wedding," she said, tapping a syringe and injecting it into my IV.

Call me a Puritan, but I've never been so happy to be denied in my life.

CHAPTER

TWENTY-FIVE

By the rivers of Babylon, there we sat down, yea,
we wept, when we remembered Zion.
—Psalm 137:1 KJV

I have nothing to offer but blood, toil, tears,
and sweat.
—Winston Churchill

We defy augury. There's a special providence in the
fall of a sparrow.
—William Shakespeare

On arrival, Scherie and Dale visited the Yasukuni Shrine, while Grace set me up in a hospital. The Mortons secured the ghost of Dale's great-grandfather Dick, but before Scherie could proceed to dispel and liberate any of the other spirits, Dale's old colleague Kaguya-san arrived on the scene with some well-armed ninjas in salaryman suits and some Shinto priests to restrain the unhappy dead. Dale had prearranged the timing with Kaguya-san, as it accomplished several objectives at once. First, we were now official "guests" of the Government of Japan, so an immediate response to orders to return home wasn't possible.

It also allowed the Japanese craft service time to weigh in on Dale's promise to dismantle the Yasukuni doomsday device. Long discussions ensued, with much sucking of breath and declarations that the plan was "difficult." Risk averse in such matters, perhaps the leadership wouldn't have gone along with the Mortons' plan, but Japanese practitioners were at their best in a crisis, and the news of recent events in the U.S. and around the world made for crisis decision-making. The Japanese craft service agreed to our attempt, with a one-month delay to cement consensus. The shrine accepted all of this more philosophically than one might have thought.

In the meantime, I recuperated and got fitted for a custom-made prosthesis. It was as shiny as Grace or a killer robot could've wanted, and it could set off metal detectors a mile away, but Grace said she'd make sure that any detectors remained silent. "I'll just give you a pat down later," she said. The fit was good, and the remainder of my foot seemed to preternaturally grip the prosthesis, making it more integral than I would have thought possible. "Wear sandals," Grace said. "We'll get it weaponized."

We set up a temporary residence in an eighth-floor apartment in the Moto-Akasaka area. It overlooked the grounds of the Crown Prince's palace, and on a clear day we had a distant view of Mount Fuji. Dale guided us down the narrow streets to amazing sushi places and scary karaoke venues. Dale called me "Saint Michael Silverfoot" and sang faux epics of my past missteps. I was very much afraid his nickname would stick.

Grace and I finalized our marriage plans. We would wed at Yokohama Christ Church—a nice old Anglican building, but I wasn't that concerned about the venue for this particular rite. Though her government said they wanted her back, they didn't press her on the fig leaf of being detained by Japan. For now, by staying close to the Mortons and me, she was where the Crown wanted her.

When I wasn't stumbling and grunting in PT, I watched TV and monitored confidential communications from the States. In the news, hundreds of witnesses to the recent spiritual excesses around the globe had come forward, confused, but not completely discreditable. The Internet was full of science-fiction bullshit about these events, though discussions of possible nanotech and weather control weren't that far off the mark. Serious news services were also reporting rumors of costumeless superheroes or supervillains. These reports were sneering and superior in tone, but it was still a bad sign that governments were letting the media mention anything remotely like us, and worse if someone was encouraging this sort of reporting.

The news from within the spiritual services was bleaker still. As Eddy had warned us, American mundane authority had decided to intervene and calm everything in the spiritual world way the hell down. All American practitioners were ordered back to barracks or into house arrest, and that was better than what was happening in some countries. Despite our recent service to the world, we wouldn't be exceptions. Grace and I had used Left-Hand life extension techniques to heal me. Dale and Scherie had let the Left-Hand dead out from the House of Morton again. Worst of all, I had transferred bodies, if only briefly, and some with farsight probably knew that. I could tell them that, if I survived so long, I would lay down my life at the Biblical three score and ten rather than accept any life extension by Left-Hand means, but I doubted my words would make a difference. In the current view, we had to be at least quarantined from the rest of the world until things were back to normal.

A person could reasonably believe that, with Roderick gone, this period of imposed quiet made sense. But all of this ignored the pervasiveness of the rot in the global services. Sure, most of the traitors who had acted overtly had been rounded up or killed, but if the Don was any indication, many more had covertly crossed the line and were now dependent on the Left-Hand techniques. Full pardons were offered to all who reported their transgressions, but many who had ventured and tasted would want, even need, more. Also, the mundane authorities enforcing the new restrictions were themselves suspect. Bottom line: it was far too late to simply clamp down. A war was coming, and the evil had to be dealt with root and branch.

Perhaps I was biased, as I had a personal stake. My power of command made certain demands on me. Right now, planning and recovery was taking all of my focus, but that wouldn't last. I couldn't wait quietly in confinement. I needed to stay occupied, or my new power might slip my control. But I didn't think I was alone in this. Practitioners were like nuke scientists: they needed to keep busy building things or they'd keep busy blowing them up. Too much leisure was dangerous for all practitioners, not just me and the Left-Hand Mortons.

Grace reported some intel from her UK sources. Ukraine now had a spiritual power vacuum due to the decimation of its leadership, and mundane protests had heated up in Independence Square. The Renfields had taken up the slack in supply of certain goods, selling power-of-command countermeasures and something they claimed was Roderick's alchemical serum. They were also reportedly building new bodies on the Ukrainian model and conducting transference experiments. "So besides their usual fees, that's the coin Roderick paid them in," she said.

Scherie told me that the *Oikumene* had attempted to contact her. They seemed to be the only power out there that knew the war continued. But none of us felt like talking to them yet.

One day, a package arrived from Eddy: a uniform that my father had once worn. Dad wanted to attend the wedding, but needed some help finding his way across the ocean. I hung up the uniform, and said, "Dad, are you there?"

My father manifested in non-military formalwear, a statement of the awkwardness of my current position. But he seemed happy enough to see me.

After a brief exchange of news, I asked him, "Are you sure you're OK with this marriage?" He hadn't been very complimentary of our British cousins in the service while living.

"You mean the international aspect?" he said. "I think you've misunderstood me. Did you think all those times I talked about serving America, I meant a specific piece of real estate? Oh, heck, maybe I did, but I shouldn't have. Even crazy John Endicott knew it wasn't the territory. America is shorthand for an idea for the world. And it's time again for that idea to shine for the whole world, including the place we call the United States."

Finally, a month after arrival, and a few weeks before the wedding, Grace and I and the Mortons walked to our meeting at the Yasukuni Shrine. The very words were chilling: during World War II, Japanese soldiers going off to their deaths would say that they would "meet again at Yasukuni."

It was Christmastime. I was walking on my new foot. Without conscious effort, I had developed a spiritual control over its movements in detail, but I still could not feel anything through it besides phantom limb pain. In another part of Tokyo, the holiday lights covered all the trees along the Omotesando-dori. I liked this country, with all its emotion and restraint, but dear God, it was a long ways from home. Back in the U.S., they were working harder than usual to get enough wreaths at Arlington, as if everyone knew that the remembrance of service was even more important this year.

Kaguya-san, as our group's minder, led the way, and her support ninjas walked our perimeter. Scherie was trying to be hip and unconcerned about this woman who clearly had known Dale well, but her smiles were a little forced.

Dick Morton's ghost manifested to all of us at the shrine's inner gate, or *torii*. Though he was no longer within the direct grasp of the Yasukuni dead, he had agreed to remain in the vicinity as an assurance that Scherie would fulfill Dale's bargain.

He gave me a stiff "Major Endicott." Dale had warned him I'd be there; Mortons of his generation had no reason to care for my family.

"Yes, sir," I said. This ghost was my senior in age if not rank. "My father sends his compliments, and wishes you to know how much he respects your service, both living and now." My father and Dale's remained safely distant for this rite, which only highlighted Dick Morton's strength of spirit.

Dick Morton nodded acknowledgment, which was as much as I could expect, then greeted Grace. "Good day, ma'am. You're a Marlow, aren't you?"

"Yes," she said, surprised.

The stern man smiled. "I knew a Marlow during the war. You've got his eyes. Please give him my regards."

He lost the smile again when he greeted Dale. "We're going to finish this today. Right, boy?"

"Right, sir."

Then something happened to the ghost's face when he looked at Scherie, and he spoke with sudden urgency. "I don't care anymore about this deal, it can wait. I can wait."

Scherie grew confused, and a little frightened. "I don't understand, sir."

"My dear girl, you're with child."

"How can . . . I'm just . . . it's too soon to know."

But in our business, that objection was absurd. Dale whooped and held her tight with no tentativeness about her condition or the solemnity of the shrine. Everyone smiled and laughed, except the poor, deeply concerned ghost, who flickered with agitation.

"I'll be fine, sir," said Scherie. "I feel certain. If anything feels wrong, I'll stop."

Scherie and Dale went in, and I stood just inside the *torii* with Grace, holding myself in reserve. I was the stick to Scherie's carrot, and a backup power source to my friends.

Though the number of Ukrainians that Scherie had dispelled had been vast, Yasukuni was far older, more integrated, and more dangerous to dismantle. Scherie worked for an hour, speaking in panglossic. She had a book of Japanese military units that she used, which to the extent the components of the doomsday device remembered their origins broke the tasks into manageable numbers. The final mass of ghosts was still very large, and that in itself seemed to raise Scherie's anger to a white heat. Eventually, with a sigh and a breeze, the last bit of darkness floated away.

When Scherie had finished, Dick Morton came forward to her. "Send me on too," said Dick. "This echo is done."

"Yes, sir," she said, her voice a hoarse and reedy whisper, her face wet with sweat and tears. "Thank you. *Sir, you are dismissed.*" Dick Morton's ghost was gone.

"Thank you, Rezvani-san." Moved by the healing of this place, Kaguya-san's voice shook, and a tear was going down her cheek. "Thank you all. You will find that this service you have done has made our close surveillance of you . . . difficult. Go, or stay, with our thanks." She bowed deeply to us and to the shrine, then signaled her support crew and walked slowly away.

Where would we go next? Morton and Grace were fully outfitted with international accounts and identities to spare—we would have no difficulties from mundane pursuit, and Dale had said that farsight pursuit might have difficulties as well, if we kept a low profile.

Then, as if the emotions of this past month had just been waiting for this pause, we were all weeping, like the exiles by the waters of Babylon. Where could we go? We were, for now, people without a country, absent without leave from lands that wanted to keep us in cages until they were sure we wouldn't bite. Scherie was pregnant. That child could be very powerful indeed. Where would be safe for it to be born?

In a flash, I had a realization. But first I needed to rally my friends, and myself. I wasn't comfortable talking that way, but I gave it a shot.

"Maybe we can't keep a low profile," I said. "Maybe we're being called to war, or at least I am. I can feel my spiritual draft notice. Our countries, America and Britain, need us. They might not know it, but that just makes their need all the more urgent. Wherever we decide to go, for however long, it won't be permanent. We will return home."

"That's just peachy, but what do we do in the meantime?" asked Dale, my friend who knew when to feed me a straight line.

"In the meantime, we'll fight. We'll fight for those who would still loyally serve, whatever their nation or spiritual ability. We'll fight against the Left Hand, which is more than just any given means, but also an end, and which respects no boundaries. Because understand this." And this was my realization. "I still have my transnational power of command. Unlike the *Oikumene*, I don't believe that it's been left with me as a needless temptation. This new power was given to me for a purpose, and that purpose continues. And you—the preeminent weatherman, the most powerful exorcist, and best all-round covert operative of our generation—have not been brought together by accident. We are together for a purpose, and that purpose continues. Somewhere, other great enemies are rising, and the stakes will again be the whole world."

A moment of silence. "Not bad," said Dale, waggling his hand.

"I'm in," said Scherie, with a clap of her hands.

"Not exactly Henry V, but flattery will get you everywhere, darling," said Grace, kissing my cheek with lips that felt electric.

Eyes dried, still sad but determined, arms draped over one another's shoulders, we marched out of the shrine, ready for whatever the world had in store for us.

We were not alone in our little procession. From over my left shoulder, Madeline Morton and her dead whispered into my ear. "Look behind you. Remember that you are a man. Remember that you will die."

And for that, I thank you, Lord. For these gifts, and these friends, and this Grace, I thank you. Amen.

EPILOGUE

THE KING OF THE DEAD

From too much love of living,
From hope and fear set free,
We thank with brief thanksgiving
Whatever gods may be
That no life lives for ever;
That dead men rise up never;
That even the weariest river
Winds somewhere safe to sea.
—Algernon Swinburne

Marley was dead: to begin with. There is no doubt
whatever about that.
—Charles Dickens

Let be be finale of seem.
The only emperor is the emperor of ice-cream.
—Wallace Stevens

The dead Earth took Roderick. When the needle made contact with the otherworld's air, the bit of brain tissue rotted and died, and Roderick's spirit was freed, but there was no place to go, no living thing that could hold him. Despite appearances, the beast wasn't immediately focused there at the portal to greet him, and he had a moment to contemplate his situation. So his spirit roamed, waiting for the daemon.

It was one of the nuked worlds, like a global Pripyat, perhaps because he'd opened the gate in the bunker. By such artifacts that remained, he dated its end to the early '80s, when the paranoid Andropov had his spies looking for evidence of a NATO first strike. In this reality, the West must have lacked a Russian defector to warn them about the very real though unfounded Soviet fears, so Reagan and Thatcher had continued their rhetoric unabated, and Andropov had pushed the button.

This world's demise hadn't started with a Yasukuni-style death engine, but it would've finished with one. Due to launch failures and chaos, a few would have survived the nukes, but the weight of the dead had snuffed them out.

Finally, smelling Roderick's fresh energy like blood, the beast came for his soul. Without resistance, Roderick allowed himself to be devoured.

Roderick could always find something delightful in the most perverse situation, and his endgame was no exception. Inside the mass, even as its ectoplasmic forces started to digest him with exquisite psychic pain, he saw a parody of heaven. They were all here, in alternate versions, little bits of Mortons and Endicotts and Marlows and Hutchinsons. If there had been a variant of Roderick in this world, he'd long ago been completely absorbed in the spiritual mass.

Then the beast's attention slackened, and with all his subtlety and power, Roderick slowly began to work his will upon the components of the beast. They just needed a little guidance. For once, his sister had been right. This was better. All that fleshy nonsense done with. The altar and images of the House's subbasement were revealed to be timeless prophecies of his second coming and his terrible form. This was godhood.

When Roderick was done consuming the consumer from within, he turned his (their) attention back the way he came. His opponents had tried to shut the door behind him, but they couldn't replace the locks, and now the way was easier.

He'd left behind a world that would, in its panic, undermine its craft defenses. It was a ripe, juicy, tasty world of life energy. His (their) all-devouring mouth watered. *Supper's ready.*

APPENDIX

THE MARLOW FAMILY

Francis Walsingham = Ursula St. Barbe

Christopher Marlowe = Mary Walsingham

Tituba of Salem

Kit Marlowe's descendants
(several generations)

Tituba's descendants
(several generations)

Ayuba S. Diallo = Sophia W. Marlowe

Emily Marlow

Grace Newton = Toby Howe   João de Castro e Sousa = Dido "Belle" Marlow

Emma Howe = Horatio Nelson or
Percy Blakeney

Jane Howe = Edward Rochester Marlow

Helen Marlow   Edward Howe Marlow

Kimball "Kim" Marlow

Charles Marlow

Richard Hannay Marlow

James B. Marlow

Catherine Marlow = Jerry C. Marlow   L. Eric Marlow
(cousin?)

Una P. Marlow

Grace Marlow

THE STORY OF
THE MARLOW FAMILY

Part I. The Descendants of Christopher Marlowe

Francis Walsingham was the spymaster for Elizabeth I, who called him her "Moor" for his dark complexion. Contrary to mundane histories, his second daughter, Mary, did not die in childhood, but instead began occult training, at first under John Dee's tutelage. At the age of seventeen, Mary entered a craft marriage with Christopher Marlowe, who besides being a playwright was a fellow practitioner and agent in Mary's father's service. Mary was pregnant with their son when rogue craftsmen ambushed and killed Christopher in Deptford.

Due to certain craft superstitions of the time, the true name of their son remains unknown, though it is rumored to have been Faust, after the subject of one of his father's plays. As he displayed his father's talents, Mary gave him the Marlowe name. His descendants prospered (to the extent anyone prospers in the craft service). Then, in the eighteenth century, Sophia W. Marlowe entered into a brief craft marriage with a formerly enslaved man from America, Ayuba S. Diallo. Despite the general flexibility of the Marlowes regarding contemporary social norms, Sophia's parents strongly disapproved of this liaison. In response, Sophia dropped the final "e" from her name, and the rest of her line would follow that spelling.

Through various deaths and reconciliations, the Marlowe family property came back into the hands of Sophia's granddaughter, Belle Marlow. Belle married João de Castro e Sousa, a distant relative of the then queen consort, Charlotte.

Belle's son, Edward Rochester Marlow, made an unfortunate first marriage to Bertha Mason, who, unknown to him, was from a family of Left-Hand practitioners in Jamaica. The Masons had some ties to the Left-Hand Mortons and, along with an attack on the British craft establishment, they intended the Marlow family's destruction.

Part II. The American Colonial Ancestors

After the enslaved Tituba escaped from the hanging fest of the Salem witch-hunt, she moved to New York. Her daughter joined the crew of the notorious pirate Calico Jack, and other descendants had similar adventures, but the family line always gravitated back to New York.

With hope for a more rational future, Tituba's descendants took the last name Newton in honor of the great natural philosopher Isaac Newton. During the American War of Independence, Tituba's great-granddaughter, Grace Newton, met and married another survivor of the Endicotts, Toby Howe. Enslaved by Stephen Endicott, Toby heard of the British promise of freedom in return for service. He escaped to British-occupied New York, and in the process discovered his preternatural skills. Toby took the last name Howe in honor of the leading British military family of the counter-revolutionary forces.

The Howes and their young daughter, Emma, accompanied the craftspeople under General Clinton in the execution of his "Southern Strategy." The Howes may have done as much harm as good to the loyalist cause in the South, as they would often attack and sometimes kill slaveholders regardless of their allegiance. Clinton, unaware of this, brought the Howes back to England with him. The Howes found that their craft powers grew in that country. They became friends of many noteworthy persons of the time, including Samuel Johnson. An aging Toby returned to America to fight with the British in the War of 1812, but due to the Napoleonic Wars, British craft forces in the United States were undermanned and could do little against the Mortons when they summoned the hurricane that saved the city of Washington or against the Endicotts when they stunned the Crown's forces at New Orleans.

Emma Howe served the Crown in the Napoleonic Wars, and had brief affairs with Horatio Nelson and Percy Blakeney, leading to some doubts regarding the parentage of her daughter, Jane. Emma died at Waterloo from a desperate, vicious French experiment with Left-Hand disease craft.

At the mercy of negligent relatives and rival Family guardians, the orphaned Jane Howe had a difficult childhood, a study in deprivation versus determination. Eventually, she found a post in the craft service under Edward Marlow. She was proficient at training younger practitioners, and her mastery of weather craft earned her a famous nickname.

Part III. The Descendants of Jane Howe and Edward Marlow

The romance of Jane Howe and Edward Rochester Marlow is one of the greatest in British craft history. Jane helped Edward defeat his first wife and her family, though Edward lost a hand and an eye in the battle. Jane and Edward were married soon afterward. Fortunately, this marriage redirected Jane from a colonial assignment in India in which the entire craft contingent was killed.

Jane's grandson Kim made up for Jane's avoidance of India with his own service there and elsewhere throughout the Empire. He had an ability, partially due to family heritage and partially preternatural, to disguise himself as any race.

Charles Marlow became the Imperial craft enforcer, rooting out the Left Hand in all the corners of the globe, whether within the Empire or not. Most famously, the Crown sent Charles to destroy a Left-Hand practitioner who was hiding in the Congo. The target magus was using the millions of deaths to cover his own killings, experiments, and abominations.

Richard Hannay Marlow played a vital role in England's craft defense during the First World War, both at home and in the Near East. Richard was one of the founders of MI13. Around this time, another branch of the Marlow family returned to America, adding the "e" back to their name. They became known for their preternatural talent as investigators.

During the Second World War, James Marlow was in charge of the craft operations of the Special Operations Executive. After the war, he boldly eliminated a series of colorful practitioners: survivors of the Axis occult orders, Communist mages, and international Left-Hand rogues. Despite his being in the deception business, James's colleagues often said that his word was his bond.

James had two sons, Jerry C. Marlow and L. Eric Marlow. Jerry inherited more of the family's dark complexion, while Eric was unusually fair. They worked for MI13 during the anarchic '60s, when New Age and Evangelical ideals awakened low-level practitioners around the globe and a great deal of mission confusion crept into the craft. Within the mushrooming groups of neo-Left-Hand terrorists, occult mobster impresarios, and revolutionary practitioners too radical for Mao, the brothers Marlow operated undercover, perhaps too well. Jerry married Catherine, a cousin with whom he'd been raised. Grace Marlow was their granddaughter.